P9-DNM-037

PORTRAIT
OF
PERIL

PORTRAIT OF PERIL

A VICTORIAN MYSTERY

Laura Joh Rowland

CROOKED
LANE

NEW YORK

Copyright © 2021 by Laura Joh Rowland

Published in the United States by Crooked Lane Books, an imprint of The Quick Brown Fox & Company LLC.

Crooked Lane Books and its logo are trademarks of The Quick Brown Fox & Company LLC.

Library of Congress Catalog-in-Publication data available upon request.

ISBN (hardcover): 978-1-64385-472-4
ISBN (ebook): 978-1-64385-473-1

Cover design by Melanie Sun

Printed in the United States.

www.crookedlanebooks.com

Crooked Lane Books
34 West 27ᵗʰ St., 10ᵗʰ Floor
New York, NY 10001

First Edition: January 2021

10 9 8 7 6 5 4 3 2 1

To my readers, who have supported and sustained my writing for all these years. Thank you.

PORTRAIT
OF
PERIL

London, October 1890

CHAPTER 1

"If I fall, will you hold me up?" I whisper to Lord Hugh Staunton.

"At your service." He smiles and tucks my hand around his arm.

We're standing inside the door of St. Peter's Church in Bethnal Green. My ears ring with anxiety that drowns out the pealing bells and organ music. As we enter the sanctuary, I'm afraid I'll trip on the hem of my wedding dress, a simple, modest frock in dove-gray silk blushed with pink. I didn't want a white gown; that's for a young, virginal bride, and I'm a thirty-three-year-old woman of considerable experience. My hands are clammy in my white kid gloves. My bouquet of white roses trembles.

"Relax, Sarah," Hugh says. "This is nothing compared to a day on the job."

Hugh and I are crime photographers and reporters for the *Daily World* newspaper, and too many of our assignments have involved confrontations with murderers. I flex my left shoulder, which still aches from the gunshot wound I incurred during the last confrontation. But although I narrowly escaped death, my life afterward returned to some semblance of normalcy. I can't imagine this day as resulting in anything less than a complete upheaval of my existence, a transformation of myself from a spinster into a wife.

Hugh and I start down the aisle. The church is cold and smells of burning candles. Colored light from the stained-glass windows bathes us. I'm already out of step with the organ playing the bridal march. The aisle seems a hundred miles long. As we near the guests who rise from their seats at the front of the church, I'm glad the clerk at the dress shop talked me into buying a veil. Pinned to my coronet of braids, it shields me from close scrutiny. On my left, my few friends turn to watch me and smile. They're vastly outnumbered by the guests on the other side. My betrothed's aunts and uncles, cousins and family friends, none of whom I've ever met, crane their necks. I hear murmurs of "She doesn't look like her pictures in the newspaper." I falter, uncomfortably reminded that I'm notorious on account of the *Daily World*'s coverage of my exploits.

"That's Lord Hugh Staunton," someone whispers. "Gorgeous, isn't he?"

Muted grumbles echo through the church, and now it's Hugh's turn to falter. The guests must have heard about the scandal two years ago, when the vice squadron raided a club for homosexual men and Hugh was among those caught in compromising circumstances.

Someone else whispers, "Why is *he* walking her down the aisle?"

Hugh is my dear friend, who has stood by me through the most perilous times in my life, despite the cost to himself. My one regret about this day is that my father, Benjamin Bain, can't do the honors. He'd been missing for twenty-four years before we reunited last month. The prime suspect in the 1866 murder of a young girl, he's a fugitive from the law. He lives under a false name and avoids the public eye lest he be recognized, reported to the police, and arrested. The punishment for murder is, of course, death by hanging.

Now I spot my future mother- and father-in-law. She's small, slender, and pretty, dressed in blue. He's in his best brown suit, leaning on a cane. Doubt tinges his smile. Her smile doesn't conceal her dislike of me, and the peacock feather in her hat quivers with her antagonism. I experience a sudden urge to turn and run. *What am I getting myself into? Is it too late to back out?* I clench my jaw and direct my gaze straight ahead.

White candles and a bouquet of white roses adorn the altar. In front of it stands the solemn vicar in his black cassock and white surplice. My bridesmaid—my half sister Sally Albert—smiles and dabs her handkerchief at tears that have fallen on her rose-colored frock. My other dear friend, fourteen-year-old Mick O'Reilly, grins behind my camera and tripod, holding the flashlamp. His red hair sticks up in a cowlick, but his freckled face is scrubbed clean, and he hasn't had time to outgrow his new suit. Not every bride is lucky enough to have at her wedding two friends with whom she's faced death and survived, who've proven themselves willing to die for her. And there, with his best man, is my soon-to-be husband, Detective Sergeant Thomas Barrett. He's so handsome in his dark-gray morning coat and striped trousers, black tie, and white waistcoat and shirt, a white gardenia boutonniere on his lapel. He's tamed his unruly dark hair with pomade. As he smiles at me, his crystalline gray eyes brim with love.

Everyone else recedes into a blur. He's the man I fell for the moment I first laid eyes on him, when my attraction seemed doomed to be unrequited. *And now he's mine!* I'm barely conscious of Hugh releasing my hand, Sally taking my bouquet, the organ music stopping, and explosions of white light as Mick takes photographs. As Barrett and I stand side by side, my heart races with such giddy joy that if it weren't for the audience and the solemnity of the occasion, I would jump up and down. This ceremony is no longer an ordeal but a gateway to a new life that I'm eager to begin.

The vicar says, "In the presence of God, Father, Son, and Holy Spirit, we have come together to witness the marriage of Sarah Bain and Thomas Barrett, to share their joy and to celebrate their love." After his speech about the purpose and sanctity of marriage, he says, "If anyone present knows a reason why they should not marry, declare it now or forever hold your peace."

When Barrett's mother doesn't speak up, I sigh with relief.

"Thomas, will you take Sarah to be your wife? Will you love her, comfort her, honor and protect her, and, forsaking all others, be faithful to her as long as you both shall live?"

I'm not used to thinking of, let alone calling, Barrett by his Christian name, but I suppose I'll have to start soon.

"I will," he says.

"Sarah, will you take Thomas to be your husband? Will you love him, comfort him, honor, obey, and protect him, and, forsaking all others, be faithful to him as long as you both shall live?"

"I will." My voice trembles with my lifelong fear of speaking in front of an audience.

After prayers and a Bible reading, Barrett and I face each other; we join hands, and the vicar prompts us through our vows.

"I, Thomas, take you, Sarah, to be my wife, to have and to hold from this day forward; for better, for worse, for richer, for poorer, in sickness and in health, to love and to cherish, till death us do part."

He looks more serious than I've ever seen him, and I'm so moved that I stumble through my vows and hardly attend to what I'm saying. "I, Sarah, take you, Thomas . . . till death us do part."

"Heavenly Father," the vicar says, "let this ring be a symbol of eternal love and faithfulness, to remind Thomas and Sarah of the vow and covenant which they have made."

Barrett tugs on my left glove to bare my finger through the slit designed for that purpose. He slips the plain gold band on my finger. The ring feels strange, but it fits, and it's warm from his hand.

"I hereby proclaim you husband and wife." The vicar joins our hands together. "Those whom God has joined together, let no one put asunder."

Barrett pulls me closer to him. He lifts my veil, his smile turns mischievous, and his eyes gleam with daring. He lowers his face to mine.

Oh my God—he's going to kiss me!

For the groom to kiss the bride at a wedding is an old custom that's now considered undignified. But as our mouths touch, I don't care what anyone thinks. Ignoring the murmurs and giggles and my new mother-in-law's horrified gasp, I melt into my husband. I'm happier than I've ever been in my life.

Screams, shrill with terror, cut through my dazed bliss.

Barrett and I spring apart. His face wears the same alarmed expression that I feel on my own and see on everyone else's. We all turn toward a door near the front of the church. There stands the charwoman in apron and headkerchief, fluttering her hands.

"Murder!" she screams. "Help!"

A hubbub of consternation ripples through the pews. Barrett and I look at each other, dumbfounded. Murder is a staple of our work, but how terrible if indeed it's happened during our wedding.

The vicar says, "Surely you're mistaken, Mrs. Johnson. Why don't you have a cup of tea in the kitchen, and I'll speak with you when I'm finished here." The Reverend Douglas Thornton is in his sixties, tall and wiry of physique. With his stern countenance and old-fashioned side-whiskers, he looks the typical rigid, sanctimonious clergyman. But Barrett has told me that the Reverend Thornton is a kind man and longtime family friend. He was certainly kind to me at our prenuptial meeting. He tried to put me at ease, and he didn't criticize my manner of living, about which Mrs. Barrett must have told him plenty.

"No! I ain't mistaken; I know what I seen. There's been a murder, in the crypt!"

Sir Gerald Mariner rises from his seat in the pews that contain my guests. He's the owner of the *Daily World*—my employer. Tall and stout in his expensive suit, he addresses a group of men on the opposite side of the aisle. "It sounds like a matter for the police. What are you waiting for?"

The men—Barrett's friends from the police force—rush toward the door. Barrett gives me a rueful look. "I'm sorry." He's the ranking officer present, and if there's been a crime, it's his responsibility to handle it.

"It's all right," I say. "Go."

He joins the rush. So do Sir Gerald and two of the tough, silent men who work for him as servants, bodyguards, and only he knows what else. Any other bride might break down in tears to have her wedding interrupted by a murder, but not me. I follow the horde. Working for the newspaper has conditioned me to hasten to crime scenes at any hour of the day or night. Although I have today off, the familiar surge of dread and excitement propels me. Hugh and Mick are already lugging the camera equipment after the crowd, which has grown to include all the male guests.

A hand on my arm restrains me. I turn to see my mother-in-law, who's asked me to call her Mildred but whom I still think of as Mrs. Barrett.

"Sarah, come and sit down." She gestures toward the pews, in which other women are huddled. "What a terrible thing to happen at your wedding. I hope it's not a bad omen." The gleam in her eye belies her words. She must have been hoping until the last minute that the marriage wouldn't happen, and now she probably likes to think it may be of short duration.

I'd rather view a murder scene than listen to her snipe at me as she usually does. Pulling free of her, I say, "I'm sorry; I have to go."

Mrs. Barrett folds her arms, sniffs, and says, "Well!"

From the door through which the horde has vanished, Sally beckons me. "Hurry, Sarah!" A ladies' features reporter for the *Daily World*, she's eager to cover a murder story if there is one. She would prefer it to writing articles about fashion and cookery.

We trail the stampede down a passage I've never seen. I've been in this church only once before, when Barrett and I met with the vicar to arrange the wedding and receive the mandatory prenuptial advice. A wedding usually takes place in the bride's parish, but I haven't belonged to a church or attended a service since 1866, the year my father disappeared, hence my wedding here in Bethnal Green at the Barrett family's church. A narrow flight of stairs leads us to the crypt. I fling back my veil, the better to see. People fill a long cavern, its walls and low arched ceiling made of brick. A few lights burn in glass globes mounted on pipes near the stairs. The smell of gas fumes mingles with the foul cesspool odor that permeates cellars throughout the city. The cavern's distant end is lost in darkness. This end is narrowed by crates, furniture, coal bins, stacked wooden planks, and odds and ends placed against the walls. Arched doorways lead to chambers that are all dark except for the third on the left, from which dim light emanates. People press close to it for a look inside.

Sally pulls a notebook and pencil out of her handbag and asks the charwoman, "What happened?"

Breathless, Mrs. Johnson says, "I came down to fetch some coal, and I saw the light, and when I looked in, there he were!"

Amid exclamations of shock and horror, Barrett's voice issues from within the room: "This is a crime scene. Stand back."

So it is indeed murder. My heart simultaneously sinks and beats faster. Sally and I jostle through the crowd, past the police constables, into a chamber that measures some twenty feet square. Hugh, Mick, Barrett, the vicar, and Sir Gerald are staring at the man sprawled in the center of the floor. The large crimson blotch across the man's white shirt draws my attention, like the bull's-eye on a target, eclipsing all else about him. Sally gasps. Hugh retches and flees the chamber; he has a weak stomach. My heart lurches, my muscles flinch, but I've seen so many corpses—some in far worse condition—that I can look and not faint or be sick.

"He was stabbed." Barrett points to a slit on the upper left side of the man's shirt.

Sir Gerald seems unfazed by the spectacle of death, which he must have seen in all forms during a youth spent on merchant ships that sailed all over the world. "The weapon's missing. The killer must have pulled it out and taken it away."

Mick sets down my camera. "This's like bringin' coals to Newcastle."

Now I see four other large cameras on tripods positioned around the room's perimeter, between carved stone sarcophagi. The church is old enough that the dead are still interred in the crypt. Atop the sarcophagi, open suitcases contain boxes of negative plates and flash powder, spare lenses, and other supplies. *The dead man was a photographer.* A dizzy feeling unbalances me, and the air shimmers like gauze on a windy, moonlit night. It's as if I'm having a vision of my own future demise.

Barrett speaks to the crowd: "Everyone except the police offi-cers, please go back upstairs." Amid mutters of reluctance, I hear the mass exodus from the crypt.

"Sarah, what's that in his hand?" Barrett asks.

It's a black rubber bulb connected to a narrow red rubber hose that snakes across the floor and rises up to one of the cameras. The end of the hose is fastened to a plunger on a metal tube at the base of the lens.

"It's a self-timer device," I say, glad to focus on the surround-ings rather than the body. "You pull the plunger to draw air into the tube. When you squeeze the bulb, it opens a valve in the tube, and the air releases and triggers the shutter."

Comprehension lights Barrett's eyes. "So you don't have to stay right by the camera to take a picture. Clever."

"Yes," I say. "You can take a picture of yourself, from a dis-tance. Which is helpful when it's a group photograph and you want to be in it."

"I never seen such a thing," Mick says. "We don't have one."

"Most photographers don't," I say. "Self-timers are a new experiment. They're not on the market. Those I've seen were one of a kind, made by inventors."

"So he were takin' pictures of himself," Mick says, eyeing a battered wooden chair positioned opposite the camera with the timer. "But why down here?"

The drab room seems to contain nothing that would merit four cameras. My gaze returns to the man, and I notice details that I previously missed. Rather stout, he wears black trousers and scuffed black boots. His mane of thick, wavy silver hair contrasts with his dark eyebrows, moustache, and beard. His features would be handsome if not for the mouth flaccid with death, the film that overlays the expression of shock in his blue eyes.

"Do you know who he is?" Barrett asks the vicar.

"No. I've never seen him before." The Reverend Thornton's sonorous voice has a faint hoarseness that I don't remember. "And I can't imagine how he got into the church. It's kept locked at night. We've had a problem with thieves. It was locked when I arrived this morning, and I noticed nothing amiss." He tugs at his white clerical collar as if it's too tight. He seems deeply shaken by the murder, as if he's struggling to remain calm.

"Does anyone besides you have the key?" Barrett says.

"Quite a few people. And there's a spare one hanging on the wall in the vicarage foyer."

I'm about to ask for names when my gaze snaps back to the body like an iron nail to a magnet and belated recognition jolts me. Memory serves up a man with darker hair, the same moustache and beard, a slimmer figure, and blue eyes that twinkle with his friendly smile.

"Oh God. It's Charles Firth!"

Everyone stares at me. Sally says, "*You* know him?"

"Yes." I'm shaken, and not just because a victim at a murder scene is, once again, someone of my acquaintance. "He owned a photography shop in Whitechapel. He sold me my first camera. I'd already been to a dozen other shops, and the prices were so high I couldn't afford them. He gave me a discount." Grief wells up in me because a man so kind and generous to a stranger has met a violent end. "If not for him, I couldn't have become a photographer."

"Oh, Sarah." Sally hugs me. "I'm so sorry."

"Have you any idea why he was taking photographs in the church?" Barrett says.

"No. I purchased equipment and supplies at his shop until he relocated and we lost touch. I've not seen him in perhaps ten years."

We're all silent, contemplating the mysteries of fate. Then Sir Gerald says, "This could be a good story for the *Daily World*. Miss Albert, write it up."

"Yes, sir." Sally sounds delighted by the assignment, even as she gives me an apologetic glance because of the circumstances. Here is her big opportunity to break into writing about important news, albeit at the expense of publicizing the misfortune that befell my wedding.

The best man, a constable named John Young, says, "Barrett, the fellows and I will report the murder and fetch the police surgeon. You shouldn't have to work today." He and the other policemen depart.

"Sarah, I'll take photos and develop 'em," Mick says. "You two can go."

Barrett and I exchange a glance, reading each other's thoughts: a murder investigation wasn't how we expected to begin our marriage, but he doesn't want to hand off a case that cropped up during his own wedding, and I can't abandon a victim to whom I owe much more than my career. Life's big and small events are connected by fragile threads of happenstance. If not for Charles Firth, I wouldn't be a photographer; I wouldn't have met Barrett and wouldn't have married him today. The least I can do for Charles Firth is that which I've had the honor of doing for other people who have died by violence—deliver his killer to justice.

"Reverend Thornton, can you tell the guests to go on to the wedding breakfast?" Barrett says. "Sarah and I will be there in a moment."

Sir Gerald and Sally leave with the vicar. With everyone gone but Barrett, Mick, and me, the crypt is quiet. As Mick takes photographs, the shutter clicks seem unnaturally loud. The blasts of light and falling sparks fill the room, and the acrid smoke from the flash powder joins the sweet, meaty, iron smell of blood. I was too nervous to eat anything today, and nausea turns my empty stomach. To distract myself from it, I survey the floor and see a thin, scuffed-up coat of dusty grime.

"If the killer left any footprints, they've been trampled over," I say.

"No signs of a struggle," Mick says, inserting a fresh negative plate into my camera.

Barrett crouches by the body, careful not to step in the blood and soil his black patent-leather boots. He gently presses his fingers against Charles Firth's cheek. "I think he died sometime last night. The surgeon will have a better estimate."

I think of the first time I saw Charles Firth, when I went into his shop. He bowed, smiled, and said, "What can I do for you, miss?"

His manner was gallant, flirtatious. I was even shier with strangers than I am now, and I closed up like a wounded clam. I was about to run out the door when an expression of sympathetic understanding came into Firth's eyes. He said, "Look around as much as you like. If you need help, just ask," and withdrew to the back of the shop.

I studied the cameras, relieved to be left alone. Other customers came, and he flirted with the women, joked with the men, and discussed technical aspects of his merchandise. He had a talent for adapting himself to other people's needs, and he'd sensed that I wished to avoid attention. That he also noticed my poverty and my pride became obvious when he saw me linger at a particular camera and said, "That one's damaged. I'll give you thirty percent off."

The damage was merely a few nicks on the case. I couldn't afford to say no, but I was afraid he would demand something from me in exchange. But he didn't. Whenever I returned to his shop, he greeted me with a smile, let me browse to my heart's content, and marked down his prices for me. We never talked about anything except photography; on a personal level, we never got past introductions. Some twenty years older than I, he treated me as a teacher would a pupil. The last time I saw him, he said he was moving his shop to a different location and invited me to come by if I needed anything. I never went. For various reasons, I was afraid that it would make us friends. Now I regret not going.

Barrett is searching Charles Firth's pockets. He removes a leather card case, takes out a card, and reads out two addresses in Islington.

"I recognize the address on Upper Street," I say. "That's his shop."

Mick repositions my camera at a different angle. "At least we know where to start askin' questions."

I examine Mr. Firth's cameras. They're professional grade, high quality but not new, their mahogany box cases scratched, their leather bellows supple from use. I open the cameras one by one and remove the glass negative plates in their protective cases. "I'll develop his photographs. Maybe they'll provide some answers."

Footsteps echo down the passage outside the room. Reverend Thornton enters and says, "I've discovered something important. You'd better come with me."

CHAPTER 2

While Mick finishes taking photographs, Barrett and I go upstairs with the vicar. In the vestry we fetch my leather satchel and our outdoor garments—Barrett his black coat and top hat, I my plain gray coat that covers my wedding dress. I remove my veil and don my gray felt hat.

The parish clerk is waiting inside the door of the empty sanctuary. "Excuse me, Mr. and Mrs. Barrett, you need to sign the parish registry."

I'm startled to be addressed, for the first time, as Mrs. Barrett. My new husband and I look at each other, chagrined because we forgot this last bit of official wedding business. After we sign, Barrett says, "Sarah, you go on to the wedding breakfast. Our guests are waiting. At least one of us needs to be there."

"They can wait a little longer," I say. "I need to find out what's going on."

"Sir Gerald doesn't expect you to cover the story," Barrett says.

"I know. But it's personal, because I knew Charles Firth." Unable to consider him a friend, I suppose I could call him my patron or benefactor.

"Well." A slight frown clouds Barrett's expression. "All right."

It's not rare for us to disagree and for me to do as I choose instead of yielding to his wishes, so I don't understand why he seems more irritated than usual. We accompany the vicar outside. The autumn fog has set in, not to lift entirely until spring. The chill air smells of bitter coal smoke, fumes from the factories, and foul vapor from the River Thames, and it's so misty that I can't see the end of the short road that extends from the front of the church between terraces of brick houses. The same fog concealed Jack the Ripper and helped him evade capture while the police and my friends and I pursued him through the streets of Whitechapel two years ago. Now we have a new murder to solve.

I'm brimful of questions, but the vicar looks sterner than ever, as if he's angry about something. His jaw is tight, his gaze fixed straight ahead while he and Barrett and I walk along St. Peter Street. I glance back at the church. Romanesque in style, St. Peter's is built of flint, stone, and brick, darkened by soot. Over the arched main entrance rises a square tower topped with an octagonal lantern and conical spire. Ravens perch on the eaves like gargoyles. Dark holly bushes crouch against the walls beneath the stained-glass windows. Within the black iron fence that encloses the churchyard, oak trees shed their brown leaves. We turn down a narrow lane and pass a schoolyard where girls are playing ring-around-the-rosy. One is wearing a disconcertingly sinister rabbit mask made of papier-mâché. Halloween is next week, and some children can't wait to show off their costumes. The yard is enclosed on two sides by a brick compound with gables, mullioned Gothic windows set in stone arches, and many chimneys. St. Peter's School occupies the large, three-story section. The smaller, two-story section is the vicarage, into which the Reverend Thornton leads Barrett and me.

The foyer smells of smoke, mildew, and cooked cabbage, a miasma soaked into the scuffed wood of the floor and staircase and the dingy tan-painted plaster walls. The oppressive air is brightened by a toy sailboat in the corner and child-sized red rubber boots on the shoe rack beneath the coats hung on pegs. Gasps, wheezes, and cries issue from the parlor. It sounds like someone being strangled. Barrett and I exchange glances of alarm.

The Reverend Thornton strides in ahead of us. The vicar's wife, Mrs. Thornton, hovers near a thin young man seated on a divan. His mouth is wide open one hand pressed to his concave chest as he struggles for breath, his white clerical collar loosened around his jerking Adam's apple. His short brown hair recedes far back on the high, round dome of his scalp. When he sees the vicar, his eyes bulge with fright behind his gold-rimmed spectacles. His body spasms as he gasps.

"This is Clyde Nugent, my curate," the vicar says in a frosty tone. "When he heard about the murder, he became a bit distraught."

The ailing Mr. Nugent is obviously the cause of the vicar's anger. Mrs. Thornton says to him, "It's all right, dear. Just try to relax."

Her voice is calm, soothing; during her years as a vicar's wife, she must have tended to many distraught parishioners. Square and robust of figure, she has thin gray hair wound into a coil at the back of her head, with a short fringe in front. Her face is lined but rosy and healthy. A white apron covers the brown poplin frock she wore to my wedding. I like her because she's been pleasant to me and hasn't nagged me to attend her husband's services.

She offers a cup of tea to Mr. Nugent. "Drink this."

His hands shake so badly that she steadies them as he gulps the tea. He swallows, breathes easier, and lies back against the sofa. "Thank you."

The vicar introduces Barrett and me and invites us to sit on the divan opposite the one occupied by Mr. Nugent. Our divan is upholstered in rose-patterned chintz, his in frayed brown horsehair. The whole room is furnished with mismatched items. Ornate modern chairs and tables clash with spindly antiques; the carpet is threadbare, the damask curtains faded. This is a poor parish that can't afford luxuries for its vicarage, and the Thorntons either lack private resources or care little for material goods. The place is clean and comfortable enough, but cheerless.

"I'm sorry," Mr. Nugent says. "I get these attacks when I'm upset."

The Reverend Thornton responds with a notably impatient lack of sympathy. "Detective Sergeant Barrett is investigating the murder. Tell him what you told me."

Mr. Nugent cringes. "It was I who allowed Mr. Firth into the church last night. I lent him my key."

That's one question answered. Barrett asks another: "Did you kill him?" He sounds as if he doesn't believe it. I don't either.

Mr. Nugent's eyes goggle. "No! But it's my fault he was killed!" he wails. "I never should have let him in."

"You're right." Disgust twists the vicar's mouth. "I've warned you about thieves, and you gave a stranger the run of the church. Thank God none of our parishioners were injured."

"Douglas, I'm sure Clyde didn't mean any harm," Mrs. Thornton says with mild reproach.

The vicar frowns and paces the floor, hands clenched behind his back. I think that a murder in his church after the rules were broken is legitimate reason for him to be angry. Barrett asks the curate, "How did you know Mr. Firth?"

"He came to a service two Sundays ago. Afterward, he introduced himself to me and asked if he could spend a night in the church."

I picture Mr. Firth sitting in a pew, eyeing the vicar and the curate. With his talent for reading people, he would have known which man to ask for such a dubious favor.

"Why did he want to spend the night in the church?" Barrett says.

"He said he was a spirit photographer and had heard that St. Peter's is haunted. He wanted to take pictures of the ghosts."

This revelation disturbs me, although not because spirit photography is unusual. Even in our modern era, belief in the supernatural is widespread. Spiritualism is all the rage, and mediums, fortune-tellers, and all manner of other practitioners abound. Many folks think that although ghosts may be invisible to the eye, the camera can capture their images. Ghost photographs sell for high prices. But I am a skeptic who has never seen a ghost or heard convincing evidence that they exist. And I have reason to know that some spiritualists invent otherworldly manifestations to trick the gullible public. I'm appalled to learn that Mr. Firth was involved in a business that is rife with fraud.

"All right, so the church has ghosts and Mr. Firth wanted their pictures." Barrett sounds as if he's skeptical too but suspending judgment in the interest of getting the whole story from Mr. Nugent. "That was all it took for you to give him the key and say, 'Have at it'?"

Even as Mr. Nugent flinches, he rallies to his own defense. "It may sound stupid to you, but St. Peter's really is haunted—by the ghosts of people who died in 1832."

Reverend Thornton stops pacing. "Nonsense! St. Peter's wasn't even built until 1840, which you well know."

Shrinking from the vicar's disapproval, Mr. Nugent explains to Barrett and me. "In 1832, there was a cholera epidemic in London. More than three thousand people died. There were so many bodies that needed to be buried quickly that the cemeteries couldn't accommodate them all. They were buried together in pits. One of the cholera pits was on the future grounds of St. Peter's. Ever since then, many people have sighted the ghosts of the dead, wandering in the church."

"You're an educated man," the vicar says. "You should know better than to believe that humbug!"

"But I've seen the ghosts myself!" Mr. Nugent's eyes blaze with sincerity. "A few months ago, I went to the church late at night to fetch a book I'd left there. I heard footsteps in the crypt, and when I went down to see who it was, I saw . . ." Recollected terror hushes his voice. "There were two of them—a dark man and a pale woman. The man was carrying the woman, like so." He extends his arms, and I picture a limp, ethereal white form cradled in them. "It must have been the ghost of a resurrectionist with a corpse he'd stolen from the pit."

Resurrectionists were grave robbers who sold corpses to hospitals and medical schools for dissection. I shudder despite my scorn for the curate's tale.

A muffled cry turns everyone's attention toward the doorway. There stand a boy and girl—the Thorntons' grandchildren. The vicar introduced me to them the day Barrett and I met with him and explained that he and his wife are raising Daniel and Lucie because their parents are dead. They're twins, and they're twelve years old, but they don't look it. Lucie is small, delicate, childish, and dark. Her hand is clamped over her mouth, and her black eyes are round with fright. Daniel is blond, rosy, and big for his age—almost a man. He puts his arm around Lucie and glowers at us, as if we're a threat and he's her protector.

Mrs. Thornton hurries to them. "Daniel. Lucie. What are you doing here?"

"We wanted to know what's going on." Daniel's voice cracks—it's changing already—but his face is still soft and boyish. He casts a wary glance at Barrett and me.

"You're supposed to be upstairs doing your lessons." Flustered, Mrs. Thornton explains to us, "They don't go to school. They have a tutor and study at home." She turns on Mr. Nugent. "See what you've done—you've frightened Lucie with your talk of ghosts. Come, children." She hustles them out of the room.

It seems peculiar that they study at home when the church school is right next door. They seem an odd pair.

Reverend Thornton takes up the conversation where it left off. "The bodies of the cholera victims were wrapped in cloth soaked with tar, then covered in lime, so they would be too decomposed for dissection," he tells Mr. Nugent. "A resurrectionist wouldn't have stolen from a cholera pit. That's just one reason you didn't see what you thought you saw."

"I did see it!" Mr. Nugent says. "And corpses covered with tar were known to show up in the dissecting rooms."

I wince at the thought of blackened, decomposed flesh.

"Another reason is that the crypt was dark," the vicar says. "It was probably a trick of the shadows and your imagination."

Mr. Nugent juts out his trembling chin. "I know what I saw. You can't change my mind."

"Your mental state makes me wonder whether you belong here."

Dismay flares in Mr. Nugent's eyes. "Do you mean to terminate my curacy?"

"It may come to that. Perhaps you would be better suited to a different profession."

Although I don't believe Mr. Nugent, I think the vicar is being too harsh on him. I feel sorry for Nugent because his convictions could cost him his career in the Church.

Barrett hastens to smooth troubled waters. "The murder has been a shock to all of us. Let's not make big decisions right now." He speaks with the calm authority he's learned during eleven years on the police force.

The vicar frowns but nods. Mr. Nugent's concave chest swells and deflates with a sigh of tentative relief.

"I've a few more questions," Barrett says to Mr. Nugent. "Who else knew that Charles Firth was in the church last night?"

"Nobody, as far as I know." Mr. Nugent casts a guilty look at the vicar.

"You should have told me," the vicar says between clenched teeth.

"I knew you wouldn't approve. But I was hoping Mr. Firth would get photographs of the ghosts. I wanted proof to show everyone that what I'd seen was real."

"Mr. Firth might have told someone," I say.

"He might have let the killer in," Barrett says.

"The killer could be someone among his relatives, friends, or acquaintances." Once again, I wish I'd known Mr. Firth better, so that I might have their names.

"But the church door was locked this morning. Mr. Firth couldn't have let the killer out and locked the door, because he was dead," Barrett says.

Mr. Nugent says timidly, "If the killer was a ghost, it wouldn't have needed to be let out, or in."

As I picture a translucent wraith walking through the church wall, I begin to understand how people come to believe in ghosts. The imagination is powerful. I shake my head. The ghost angle is an unwelcome complication that could make the case harder to solve. A public uproar, false tips, and controversy could muddy the waters in which Barrett and I must fish for suspects.

Reverend Thornton bends a warning look on Nugent. "The killer must have taken the key and locked the door when he departed. I'd better have the locks changed."

"Did you or Mrs. Thornton see or hear anything unusual last night?" I say.

"No. We were asleep."

"What about Lucie and Daniel?" Barrett says.

"They were asleep too."

But I know from personal experience that children aren't always asleep when they're supposed to be, and they see and hear more than adults realize. "Perhaps we could talk to them?"

"They would be of no help, and children shouldn't be interrogated about a murder. Daniel and Lucie are particularly sensitive children, and Lucie is already very upset, as you saw." The vicar then says to Barrett, "Isn't it high time for you and your new bride to attend your wedding breakfast?"

CHAPTER 3

Our wedding breakfast is in the church hall, located a block from St. Peter's. As Barrett and I walk there, he draws my arm through his. I glance around to see if anyone is watching this display of intimacy—and then remember that it doesn't matter anymore. When we were single, I was embarrassed to flaunt our relationship and think people were speculating about the nature of it; now, it's completely aboveboard. We smile at each other, and I feel as though we're radiating light, outshining everyone around us, and I'm secure after a lifetime of insecurity. *Those whom God has joined together, let no one put asunder.*

When we enter the church hall, I experience a sudden stage fright. All the guests are waiting, and I'm the center of attention again. Cheers and applause greet Barrett and me.

Barrett's father hurries up to us. "Did you solve the murder?" A retired police constable, he loves to talk shop and enjoys living vicariously through his son.

"Not yet," Barrett says.

Mr. Barrett and his police cronies hasten to offer their theory that the killer is a member of one or another East End gang. Mrs. Barrett interrupts, "Please, dear, none of your morbid police chatter now. It's time to eat."

She herds everyone to tables that she's decorated with white linen cloths, ribbons, and roses. When I told her I wanted a simple celebration, she said, "Don't be silly. A girl wants things special on her day, and since you haven't a mother to help you, leave everything to me." Now I'm thankful, because the decorations are lovely, and I hope they mean she's trying to overcome her dislike of me. Barrett and I sit at the main table with his parents, Sir Gerald, and Sally. It's not a company designed for easy conversation. I have little in common with Mr. and Mrs. Barrett, and her disapproval makes me tense and quiet. And although I like Sir Gerald and I'm thankful to him for my job and the generous salary he pays Hugh, Mick, and me, his presence is equally inhibiting. I'm glad to have Sally for moral support, but she's shy with Sir Gerald and the Barretts, none of whom she knows well.

Sir Gerald stands and raises his glass. "A toast to the new Mr. and Mrs. Barrett. May they live a long, prosperous, and happy life together."

Amid cheers, we drink champagne that Sir Gerald has provided. The liquor calms me. I take a deep breath for the first time all day, and the horror of Charles Firth's murder recedes a little. My mother-in-law is positively giddy about having Sir Gerald at her son's nuptials. I'm surprised he's stayed this long, for he must have important business to attend to, but of course even England's wealthiest, most powerful men need to eat.

When he tastes the first course, creamed rice soup with vegetables, he says, "Delicious."

Mrs. Barrett preens. "Thank you; I made it myself. The menu is based on Princess Beatrice's wedding breakfast." She laughs gaily. "I'm a big admirer of the royal family."

She overruled my suggestion of sandwiches, cake, and tea. I tried to explain that Barrett and I needed to save money to furnish our new home, but she said he was her only child and this would be her only chance to organize a wedding, so we let her have her way and paid the bills. She economized by doing the cooking herself, with the help of her sisters and nieces. They must have been up all night. As we progress through lamb cutlets with mushrooms and beef filet wrapped in bacon, I'm glad everyone seems to be enjoying it. The whole day has an air of unreality. The conversation around me goes in one ear and out the other . . .

Until Mrs. Barrett says to Sir Gerald, "Will you be very sorry when Sarah leaves the *Daily World?*"

"I wasn't aware that she's leaving," Sir Gerald says.

They both turn to me. "I'm not," I say.

"You mean you're going to *keep working* now that you're married?" Mrs. Barrett speaks as if I'd announced my intention to become a circus performer.

"Yes." It's obvious she assumed I would stop and that Barrett hasn't told her otherwise. When I catch his eye, his sheepish expression says he wanted to avoid her reaction.

Mrs. Barrett demands of him, "And you're letting her?"

"Sarah and I both think it's a good idea." Barrett's tone is apologetic. "We could use the money."

"Money is good reason," Sir Gerald says.

My biggest reasons for keeping my job are more personal. Given my history, I'm loath to give up my financial independence and rely on a man for support as other married women do. That's a sensitive subject I've not discussed with Barrett. Now it occurs to me that perhaps he would rather I quit my job. It's certainly caused him enough trouble in the past.

"And you're going to photograph more dead bodies and chase more murderers?" Mrs. Barrett says to me, lowering her angry voice so that guests at other tables won't hear.

Her husband is busily eating, not wanting to get drawn into the argument. I don't want to fight with my mother-in-law on my wedding day, but I'm not about to back down. "Yes, I am."

"That's not only improper but dangerous. Look how many times you've almost been killed!"

She knows about my exploits, at least the details that have been published. She doesn't know that I have an affinity for danger, a quirk in my otherwise sedate nature. Although danger scares me, it also excites me and makes me feel alive. A dangerous person or situation is like a sleeping wolf that I feel an irresistible urge to poke and wake up.

"Sarah has solved crimes and delivered criminals to justice," pipes up Sally, my loyal admirer. "She's a heroine."

"You're just as bad as she is," Mrs. Barrett says. "Working for the newspaper, following in her footsteps! You'll be lucky to get a husband."

Sally flushes and looks at her plate. She's twenty-three, and she's said she would like to marry, but she hasn't any suitors. Before she recently began working for the *Daily World*, she was a maid in a wealthy family's house, and her prospects were limited. She's achieved her dream of becoming a writer, but marriage still isn't in the picture.

"Don't you talk to my sister that way," I say to Mrs. Barrett. Sally is dearer to me than she would be if we'd grown up together instead of learning of each other's existence less than two years ago. I couldn't love her more if we shared a mother as well as a father. The common factor in our pasts has formed a unique bond between us.

Mrs. Barrett ignores my sharp retort and Sally's discomfort. "When you find out how much work it is to take care of your husband and your home, you'll be glad to quit your job."

"Since we don't have a home yet, my job won't get in the way of my domestic responsibilities," I say.

Mrs. Barrett's jaw drops. "What do you mean, you don't have a home yet?"

I frown at Barrett. Here's another thing he neglected to tell his mother. As he winces, she says to him in an accusing tone, "I thought you'd rented a flat. I thought you'd moved in already and Sarah would be joining you there today."

Barrett's shoulders hunch up to his ears. "I didn't actually *say* that. I let you think so because I didn't want you to worry. I'm still living in the police barracks."

"We haven't been able to find a flat," I say. I want one close to Hugh and Mick, and decent flats in Whitechapel are hard to come by.

Mrs. Barrett gasps. "Do you mean that until you find one, you're going to keep on living with *those males*?"

That's how she refers to my friends. She hates that Mick is a former street urchin with a history of petty crime and Hugh a homosexual. She thought it disgraceful enough that her son's fiancée lived with two single men of such bad character; now she's even more scandalized that her daughter-in-law will do so.

"They're my family," I say, vexed by her conventionality, defensive on my friends' behalf as well as my own. After my father disappeared, I had no friends until I met Hugh and Mick more than twenty years later. They're as dear to me as Sally and my father, who are my only blood kin. "If you would get to know them, you would learn what good men they are."

"But what will people think?" Mrs. Barrett wails.

"I don't care what they think." Beneath my demure facade, I have a temper, and I'm on the verge of losing it and telling her that I don't care what *she* thinks.

Barrett clears his throat. "Sarah, why don't you and I visit with our guests?"

"Good idea," Sir Gerald says. With more kindly tact than I thought he had, he says to Mrs. Barrett, "What did you think of Princess Beatrice's wedding gown?"

Thankful to escape, I accompany Barrett to other tables, and he introduces me to people whose names I immediately forget. Then I discover that his mother has seated Mick beside my friend Catherine Price, a beautiful young, blond actress. Mick is in love with Catherine, but she considers him an enemy.

"There's a good show at the Alhambra," Mick says to her. "How 'bout I take you tomorrow night?"

Catherine sniffs. "I've already seen it." She's angry because last winter he ruined her romance with a wealthy swain.

"Aw, for cripes' sake!" Mick says. "You're lucky you found out that guy was no good. Ain't you ever gonna forgive me?"

Her blue eyes fix him with an icy glare. "Not in a million years." She sees Barrett and me, smiles brightly, and says, "Con-gratulations!"

We chat with her and the other guests while Mick broods. I feel bad because his problems with Catherine were a direct result of investigating a murder with me. At the next table, Hugh is arguing with one of Mr. Barrett's police cronies.

"If I'd had my way, I would've arrested you and thrown you in the nick along with the other degenerates," says the crony, an older man with a squashed face like a bulldog's. "But no—the boss said to let you go because you're a lord."

My heart plummets. This man must have been on the vice squadron the night of the raid. Whenever the subject comes up, Hugh usually shrivels into mortified silence. Sometimes he manages to turn detractors into friends—such is the power of his charm. Normally a most courteous and kind person, he wouldn't dream of quarreling at my wedding breakfast, but lately his demeanor has changed. He's devastated by his recent breakup with Sir Gerald's son Tristan Mariner, a former priest who fled to Switzerland. His usually sleek blond hair is mussed, his green eyes bleary, and his reddened complexion tells me that he's been drowning his sorrows in too much champagne.

"If I'd had *my* way," Hugh says, "you would have caught Jack the Ripper. But no—you coppers are good for nothing except persecuting people who've never caused you any harm and scratching your behinds."

I want to clap my hand over Hugh's mouth. The Ripper is a sensitive subject with the police, whose failure to catch the notorious killer made them the butt of public scorn. Hugh, Barrett, Mick, and I are among the few people who know why the Ripper has never been caught. It's a deep, dark secret that, if revealed, could send us to the gallows.

His adversary grabs Hugh by the lapels. "You take that back!"

"Or what?" Hugh shoves the man away and laughs. "You'll cry uncle while I tan your hide on behalf of all us degenerates?"

An appalled hush descends on the room. I'm less upset about Hugh's making a scene than worried about him. His troubles, like Mick's, stem from our work, and nevertheless, both my friends have stuck with it—and with me. That's no small act of friendship and loyalty. I would excuse almost any misbehavior from Hugh and Mick. As I start toward Hugh, intending to escort him from the room, the thin, gray-haired man seated beside him rises, takes him by the arm, and says, "Let's go home." It's Fitzmorris, officially Hugh's valet, unofficially our housekeeper, manager, cook, and accountant.

As Fitzmorris leads Hugh out of the room, Mrs. Barrett glares after them, then forces a smile and announces, "It's time to cut the cake."

Pretending nothing happened, everyone gathers around the huge cake decorated with white frosting scrolls and flowers. Mick takes photographs as Barrett and I cut into it with a silver knife.

A man barges into the hall. Big and thickset, in his forties, he's dressed in an old tweed jacket that strains across his paunch. His curly, graying brown hair and beard are longer and shaggier than when I last saw him a few weeks ago. He's John Porter, once a police constable and Barrett's assistant. His ruddy face wears an ugly smile.

Barrett frowns at him. "You weren't invited."

"I just stopped by to pay my respects to the blushing bride." Porter's smile turns contemptuous as he beholds me. "I wouldn't wish the likes of you on anybody except him. Bet he ends up hoping 'death do you part' happens sooner rather than later."

Porter was fired from the police force and blames Barrett and me, although it was his own fault, the result of a scheme to sabotage our last investigation. My temper, already vexed by my mother-in-law, flares at Porter. That he would try to spoil my wedding day!

"It's not us you should hate," I tell him. "Inspector Reid put you up to the scheme." Reid is Barrett's superior, another person with a grudge against us. "When it went awry, he let you take the punishment."

Barrett stares Porter down and speaks in a quiet, ominous voice. "Get out."

As everyone watches in fearful yet eager suspense, my heart pounds, sending currents of dread and excitement through me. I tighten my fingers around the cake knife. When a fight starts, I don't sit on the sidelines; I pitch in.

Sir Gerald's two bodyguards advance on Porter. Their heft and menacing expressions brook no defiance. Even as Porter backs away, he jabs his finger at Barrett and me. "I'm going to make you both pay. Just see if I don't."

He stalks out, leaving an awkward silence in his wake. Everyone consumes cake and coffee; nobody mentions him; but the festivities are over.

"Your carriage is here," Sally says to me.

Guests gather outside to see Barrett and me into the carriage we hired to take us to the hotel where we'll spend our wedding night. We didn't have time to plan a honeymoon.

Amid the farewells, Mrs. Barrett squeezes my hand hard, kisses my cheek, and whispers, "You'll think about what I said, won't you, dear?"

Inside the carriage, riding away from the church, Barrett and I slump back against the seat, exhausted. "Porter will make more trouble," I say.

Barrett pats my hand. "If the worst he can think of is to crash our wedding breakfast, I don't think we need to worry."

Instead of letting the driver take us to the hotel, I tell him to stop at the train station. I have an important rendezvous. Barrett says, "I'll come with you."

"That's not a good idea." Seeing displeasure cloud his expression again, I remind him, "You know why."

"All right." He kisses me, helps me out of the carriage, and says, "I'll see you tonight."

CHAPTER 4

I take the train across the River Thames to Battersea and emerge from the station into a fog that's much thicker and colder than in the East End. Battersea is on the bank of the river, engulfed by its moist breath and steam from the waterfront factories. The perpetual darkness of winter starts early here, and although it's just past one o'clock in the afternoon, it looks as if twilight is descending. A horse-drawn omnibus materializes out of the smoke and fog, and I jump backward just in time to avoid being run over. Dodging porters with handcarts and men in sandwich boards, I make my way to the rank of cabs for hire.

A brief ride takes me to a public house named the Gladstone Arms. Signs on the front advertise Watney ales and rooms to let. I stroll up and down the busy thoroughfare, pretending to browse the shop windows. The grocer's is stocked with barrels of apples for bobbing at Halloween parties and roasting on sticks over bonfires. I dawdle until I'm sure I don't see anyone I know and nobody seems to recognize me. Then I dart along the alley to the back door of the Gladstone Arms. I slip in and tiptoe up the back stairs. On the second floor, I find closed doors along a dim passage. I knock on the door numbered 3. There's no answer. I knock again and again while panic tightens my chest. Then I hear heavy footsteps on the stairs, I turn, and there stands my father, Benjamin Bain, a stocky man with white whiskers.

"Sarah." His smile crinkles eyes narrowed from a lifetime of peering through a camera viewfinder. "I'm sorry—have you been waiting long? I went to the kitchen for some hot water." He holds up a teakettle.

My body goes limp with relief. "No, I just arrived."

One day when I was ten, he didn't come home. He was just gone, without warning. My mother told me he'd been killed in a riot during a workers' protest demonstration he'd organized. Two years ago I learned that he was still alive. Last month, after a harrowing search, I found him. Our reunion was a dream come true. Now I realize how afraid I am of losing him again.

He sees my thoughts on my face, his expression turns rueful, and he hugs me. "It's all right. I'm here."

He smells the same as I remember from childhood—clean, with a bitter tang of the photographic chemicals that have permanently discolored his hands. It recalls his gentleness and patience while he was teaching me photography, opening my eyes to the beauty and secrets of the visual world. As I embrace him, he feels solid, real. The memory of his love was a steadying force in my life after he disappeared. The knowledge that somebody had once cherished me helped me bear the many years when nobody did, until Hugh and Mick became my friends. When I let go of my father, I fight the impulse to hold on so he can't vanish into thin air.

We go into his room, small and plainly furnished but clean. His suitcase stands at the foot of the bed, and a little table is set for tea, with cakes on a plate and a white rose in a glass.

"I'm sorry I couldn't be at your wedding," he says. "I wanted us to have a little celebration together."

"How nice. Thank you." I cherish his thoughtfulness because it's proof of his love for me, which I crave even though I know he didn't abandon me voluntarily. For more than twenty years I was haunted by my childhood belief that his disappearance was somehow my fault, but it's been mere months since I learned the real circumstances.

The day before fourteen-year-old Ellen Casey was found dead at a road construction site, my father had photographed her in his studio at our home. The police later identified him as the last person to see her alive and decided he was guilty. When he disappeared, they assumed he'd run away to avoid arrest, conviction, and hanging. What really happened, according to him, is far different. He'd been in his darkroom in the basement when he heard Ellen screaming. He rushed upstairs to find her half-naked and strangled to death in the kitchen with my mother and her adult son, Lucas Zehnpfennig.

Lucas was the illegitimate child my mother had by a man whose identity I don't know, before she married my father. I wasn't aware of his relation to me until recently.

My father discovered that Lucas had raped Ellen and that my mother had killed her to stop her screaming. In the panic of the moment, he struck a terrible bargain with them: he would help them cover up the murder if Lucas agreed to leave England with him for good. He thought he could keep an eye on Lucas and protect other girls, including me, from harm.

He was wrong.

My mother consented, but Lucas went on to do more evil, and in her rage at losing the son she loved above all else, she wove a poisonous web of lies whose effects still cause me pain. I can't confront her, because she died in 1875. And I'm not the only one who suffers.

Sally hurries into the room, breathless and radiant. "Sarah. Father." She hugs and kisses him, as reluctant to let go as I was.

Eight years after my father left my mother and me, he came back to England and eventually remarried. Sally is his daughter by his second wife. Later, he disappeared on his second family too. Sally and I share a history of abandonment, of wondering why he left us, unjustly blaming ourselves, and praying for him to come back. She's the only person of my acquaintance who also knows how it feels to reunite with a long-lost parent. On the ruins of the past, my sister and my father and I have built a new family, precious and fragile.

As we all take tea, Sally and I tell him about my wedding. He smiles sadly as we name the guests. He's met none of them—not even Barrett, Hugh, and Mick, who are aware that I see him and know the basic facts of his history but nothing else. The fewer the people who know his whereabouts, the safer the secret. Sally and I meet him in obscure places far from the East End where he might be recognized. And there's another reason I haven't introduced him to his new son-in-law. Barrett is a policeman, and I can't let him know the whereabouts of a fugitive. It would be a breach of duty for him not to turn my father in. I trust Barrett with my life, but I hesitate to trust him with my father's. I know it's unfair to Barrett, as he has no secrets from me.

"Mick took photographs," Sally says. "Sarah will show you later." By tacit agreement we don't mention the murder, lest it spoil our precious time together.

"That reminds me." My father goes to his suitcase, removes a cardboard folder, and hands it to me. "A wedding present."

The folder contains an enlarged photograph of Sally and me. He took it a few weeks ago on the beach in Brighton, where he lives and works as a photographer, taking pictures of tourists. It's the day I reunited Sally with him. The fact that we're sisters is obvious; we're both slender and fair, with angular faces. Sally, younger and prettier than I, beams at the camera while the ocean breeze whips tendrils of our ash-blond hair around our faces. My smile is tempered by my fear that it's only a matter of time before Benjamin Bain is arrested and punished for the crimes my mother and Lucas committed.

"Thank you." I kiss my father's rough cheek. "I just wish you were in it." I think of Charles Firth's self-timer.

My father sighs. "Ah, well."

It's dangerous for him to appear in photographs, and for his daughters to possess photographs of him. They would be proof that he's alive and we know where he is—evidence that we're shielding a fugitive, that we're accomplices after the fact of Ellen Casey's murder. This portrait of Sally and me reminds me of spirit photographs I've seen. Our father seems more present in it than the ghosts that the charlatans claim to have captured with their cameras.

"When are you leaving?" Sally asks him.

"Tomorrow."

The more time he spends in London, the more opportunity there is for old acquaintances to sight him and report him to the police. The next time he comes, he'll stay in different lodgings; never the same place twice. We won't know when or where until he notifies us via unsigned letters posted from a distant neighborhood.

Sally's eyes shine with tears. "I can't bear seeing you only once in a while." Because of our jobs, Sally and I have little time to visit him in Brighton, four hours away by train.

He clasps our hands. "Nor I you." His voice trembles.

"We can't go on like this!" Sally says. "There's so much of each other's lives that we're missing, so much from the past that's still unfinished."

I know she's thinking of her mother, who hasn't seen Benjamin Bain in the eleven years since he deserted her, prefers not to believe he's alive, and doesn't know we're in touch with him. With my own mother gone, I don't have that extra complication, but I feel a heaviness, as if drops of liquid iron in my blood have solidified. The time for reckoning with the past is here.

I say to my father, "We have to clear your name."

His expression says that some of the sins attached to his name can never be cleared. But Sally brightens and exclaims, "Yes! Then you won't have to hide anymore."

"But how?" my father asks me. "Your mother is dead. So is Lucas. Even if they'd ever wanted to confess and exonerate me, they can't now."

This is the man who when I was a child seemed so strong and capable, the man I counted on to protect me. Now it's up to me to protect him from the law.

"We have to prove that my mother and Lucas are guilty," I say, and Sally nods.

Trepidation clouds my father's eyes. "If you succeed, will people have to know that your mother was a murderess?"

"I don't think it can be kept a secret." Owing to my own notoriety, the story of Ellen Casey's rape and murder and my father the fugitive suspect has been splashed all over the newspapers. The press would have a field day with the news that my mother and her illegitimate son were the actual culprits.

"Sarah, I can't do that to your mother."

"Why not? It can't hurt her."

"I don't want her reputation ruined."

Vexed by his scruples, I say, "She ruined *your* reputation by letting you take the blame for the murder."

"Because of her, you've spent twenty-four years as a fugitive," Sally reminds him.

He bows his head. "I loved her. That's why I never told the police what she and Lucas did. I still love her."

My animosity toward her verges on hatred. "How can you?" My mother was cold and unloving toward me. Only recently did I discover that it wasn't my fault; it was because Lucas was her firstborn, her favorite, and no other child could compensate her for his absence.

"She was my wife." My father's gaze pleads for understanding. "She was your mother."

"A wife and mother shouldn't have done to her husband and daughter what she did." Because of her lies, and her wish to protect herself and Lucas, my father was unjustly accused and I lost him for all those years.

Sally, indignant on my behalf, says, "She doesn't deserve your protection." Her own situation with regard to my mother is more complicated. If my father hadn't become a fugitive, he wouldn't have met and married Sally's mother and Sally wouldn't have been born.

"She was a sad, broken woman," my father says. "She needed me. I needed to be needed." He says to Sally, "I don't know if Sarah has told you this, but I was an orphan. My parents died when I was a baby. I grew up in a children's home. No one there had any use for me. I was just a burden on charity. When I left, I worked at odd jobs. One was at a photographer's studio. The man was kind enough to give me a camera."

My skin prickles as though in a cold breeze. His experience echoes my own with Charles Firth.

"I traveled around the country, taking photographs. I stopped in different towns to work when I needed money. That's how I met Mary. She worked at the hotel where I was staying. She'd had Lucas when she was fourteen. He'd been adopted by her married sister. Mary was an outcast, a burden on her family, without friends. She was almost as alone as I was. It seemed as if we were kindred spirits." My father smiles, remembering his happiness. "When I married her, I promised to protect her. I always have." His manner turns defiant. "How can I stop now?"

His loyalty to my mother humbles me despite my ill will toward her. Only a few hours ago, Barrett and I promised to protect each other. The gravity of the marriage vows strikes me harder now than ever. Will we abide by the vows as literally as my father has? But I can't let his misguided loyalty stand in my way.

"Sally and I have no obligation to protect my mother," I say. "Our concern is for you. We won't let you sacrifice your life for her." Exonerating him isn't my only objective. I crave revenge on my mother; I want her to pay, albeit posthumously, for what she did to him and me. But he doesn't need to know that.

"Father, we're going ahead with or without your permission." Sally sits up straight, as if armored for battle. I smile at her, thankful that I needn't shoulder the whole, challenging responsibility for his exoneration by myself.

"But even if I told the police what she and Lucas did, they would think I was lying to save myself," my father says.

That's a big problem I can't deny. "We'll treat this as if it's any murder investigation. We'll gather information and look for evidence."

"How can we?" Despite her faith in me, Sally notes the weaknesses of my plan. "The murder happened twenty-four years ago. What evidence could be left?"

"The witness." I look to my father. "Meaning, you. We need you to tell us everything that happened the day of Ellen's murder."

Now Sally sparkles with inspiration. "Father, I'll interview you. I'll write down all the details, no matter how small. You might remember something important."

He frowns as he nods. I can tell that he feels as if he's betraying his wife. I love him because he's not a vindictive man who would hurry to punish her for her sins when given the opportunity to benefit himself. I love him all the more because he's cooperating with my plan because of his love for Sally and me.

"What will you do, Sarah?" Sally says.

I dread the task I've been avoiding. Beneath my anger toward my mother, some vestige of a child's love and loyalty remains. "I'm going to investigate my mother's life. Maybe some evidence against her will turn up."

CHAPTER 5

I leave Sally with our father. She's eager to begin interviewing him, and he's agreed to stay in London until they're finished. I take the train to Victoria station and transfer to the underground train, heading home to change my clothes. I can't traipse around town, hunting secrets from my mother's past, in my bridal dress. But I stop at Blackfriars station and walk to Fleet Street, thinking I should see if Mick has developed the photographs from the crime scene.

These are excuses. My real reason is that I'm afraid of what my hunt will reveal. Maybe I'll discover that my mother isn't the only parent who lied to me.

Maybe my father did too.

When I found him, I learned that he, by his own admission, is capable of murder. Maybe the blood on his hands includes Ellen Casey's. I'm forced to acknowledge the other reason I can't introduce him to Barrett. It's because Barrett, with his policeman's instincts, might think my father is guilty and feel duty bound to arrest him. I can't let that happen unless I find out, heaven forbid, that it's true.

On Fleet Street, the headquarters of the *Daily World* dominates the other tall buildings where rival newspapers have their offices. Its huge size, Greek columns, Moorish arched windows, and Baroque turrets still impress me even after I've worked there for more than a year. It rises up among the smoke and steam from printing presses, impervious to the traffic of wagons, omnibuses, and pedestrians. Above the giant clock on the corner, the Mariner insignia—a marble sculpture of a ship—honors Sir Gerald's past as a shipping magnate.

Inside, on the ground floor, the giant presses and Linotype machines clatter. The whole building vibrates, and I taste the fumes of chemical ink, hot metal, and engine oil. It seems extraordinary that I was married this morning and I'm now at work as usual. Despite the troubles my work has gotten me into, I like it much better than I would a life of nothing but domestic chores. Barrett's mother wouldn't understand.

On the second floor are the photography and engraving studios. I find Mick in one of the darkrooms, with negative plates in the rack and wet prints hanging from pegs clipped to a string above the work top.

"I haven't developed the crime scene photos yet," he says. "I did the pictures of your wedding first. The society editor wants 'em for tomorrow's paper."

I hate the idea of my wedding splashed across the society page, and not only because I need my privacy. Publicity about me could lead to more coverage of Ellen Casey's murder and more calls for information regarding my father's whereabouts.

Mick points to the prints. "I think they turned out pretty good."

"Yes, splendid." He's done a good job with composition, focus, and lighting, but I wince because my face so clearly reveals my emotions. I feel as exposed as if I were naked. And Mick didn't neglect to get a shot of Barrett and me kissing.

"Don't give the editor that one," I say.

Mick grins and nods.

"Let's develop the crime scene photos." I set down my satchel, which contains, amid the necessities I carry around, my father's photograph of Sally and me. It's another that will never appear in the paper.

"Ain't you got other things to do on your weddin' day?" Mick says.

"I'm not meeting Barrett until later."

We pour fresh chemical solutions into trays, set out the four flat cases that contain the negative plates from Charles Firth's cameras, and turn off the gaslights. Accustomed to working in complete darkness, by touch, we open the cases one by one, remove the plates, and immerse them in the solutions. The darkness makes it easier to talk about personal matters.

"I'm sorry about Catherine," I say.

Mick pauses before he says, "Yeah, well."

"I'll give her a talking-to next time I see her."

He sighs. "Don't bother. Come to think, I'm glad she gave me the air. Showed me it's high time I gave up."

I'm sorry that I'm happily in love while he's not. "There'll be someone else for you."

"Right." Mick doesn't sound convinced.

With the negative plates safely in the fixer solution, we put the lights on and study the results. The dark and bright values are reversed, but we can see that three images are of the empty crypt.

"If there were any ghosts, he didn't get 'em," Mick says.

The fourth shows Charles Firth. It's very light—underexposed—and out of focus, as if he moved while the shutter snapped. I shiver, knowing it's the last photograph of him alive.

"He musta taken his own picture by mistake while he was setting up," Mick says.

"It doesn't look like there are clues in these. But let's print them just to make sure we don't miss anything."

Working in the red light of the safe lamp, we enlarge and make duplicate prints of the four photographs. In those of the empty crypt, the rough texture of the brick walls and the carved ornamentation on the stone sarcophagi are visible; they're long exposures. When we behold the photograph of Charles Firth, Mick says, "Whoa!"

Sometimes a print is so different from the negative, it's as though photography is a magician's act. The reversal of the values is a black cloak, and the secrets behind the cloak are revealed when the printing process restores the values to normal. This print is still out of focus and too dark, but it reveals subtle details that we missed in the negative. Charles Firth stands with his body tilted and arms out to his sides, as if he's stumbled off-balance. The air hose on the self-timer device is a fuzzy line connecting his right hand to the camera outside the frame. A pale figure, blurred by motion, assaults him. It's vaguely human in shape, only its head distinguishable from its amorphous body. Firth's face is blurred too, but I can see that his eyes are wide, his mouth open as if in a scream of shock and pain.

"Is that a ghost?" Mick says, his voice hushed with awe.

My skepticism provokes me to immediate resistance. "Of course not." A ghost in the photograph would lend more credence to the theory that a supernatural force is responsible for the crime. The waters are getting muddier, the logical process of identifying suspects and motives more complicated. But the photograph is an astonishing and not entirely unwelcome new clue. "But it looks as if Charles Firth took a photograph of his own murder."

★   ★   ★

Sir Gerald's office is located on the top floor of the building. Although it's past six o'clock, Mick and I aren't surprised to find him there; he often works late. In addition to the newspaper, he runs the banking empire that earned him his second fortune. His first fortune came from his shipping fleet. He now owns several newspapers around the kingdom, and he's building himself a news empire. It's the rags-to-riches story of a cabin boy from Liverpool.

Now, the helmsman of all his businesses, he sits in his leather chair, reading glasses perched on his nose, studying documents by the light of a lamp suspended over his massive wooden desk. The telescope on the windowsill points toward a view of the city's rooftops as they vanish in the fog. Business isn't the only thing that keeps him at his desk long after dark. Hugh tells me that Sir Gerald is devastated because his son Tristan fled to Switzerland. After Tristan quit the priesthood, Sir Gerald had put him to work at the bank, intending for him to learn the ropes at all the Mariner businesses and prepare to take charge after his father's retirement. Tristan's departure has dashed Sir Gerald's dearest hopes as well as broken Hugh's heart. Sir Gerald doesn't want to go home and face his loss.

Now, as Mick and I hover outside his door, Sir Gerald says, "Come in."

His face betrays none of his suffering. I see him note that Hugh is absent, but he doesn't inquire after him. Hugh also tells me that Sir Gerald blames him for "corrupting" Tristan; Sir Gerald wrongly thinks Tristan didn't become a homosexual until he met Hugh. Sir Gerald bears a grudge against Hugh for dashing his other hope— that Tristan would marry a woman and sire the next heir to the Mariner business empire. I want to ask Sir Gerald if he's heard from Tristan; I've seen Hugh search the post every day for a letter that never comes. But Sir Gerald rarely welcomes personal discussions.

"What've you got?" Having seen the photograph in my hands, he cuts right to the chase.

I lay the photograph on his desk. Sir Gerald's eyebrows rise. His finger jabs at the pale shape. "Are you telling me that this is a ghost stabbing Charles Firth?"

"I think it's a person wearing white," I say.

"People have heard that the church is haunted," Mick says. "The killer coulda dressed up as a ghost, for a disguise."

Chin in hand, studying the photograph, Sir Gerald says, "Now that the Sleeping Beauty case is wrapped up, we need another big story."

The Sleeping Beauty case involved a woman found unconscious by the river, her face slashed. Barrett, my friends, and I identified her and her would-be killer. The ache in my shoulder reminds me of the consequences.

"I'll run it on the front page tomorrow," Sir Gerald says, "with the headline 'Murder by a Ghost?' "

He means to publish the story ahead of whatever facts the investigation turns up. I hesitate to challenge him; he's not only powerful but dangerous. I know of at least one instance where he killed, with his own hands, someone who ran afoul of him. Still, I feel obligated to speak up, and I think that the experiences we have in common—and the secrets we share—give me the right.

"But there's no proof that it's true," I say.

Sir Gerald responds with a sly smile; he's unpredictable, and sometimes, rather than taking umbrage when people stand up to him, he likes it. "When has that ever stopped a newspaper from publishing a story?"

Mick nods; we all know that newspaper articles are often as much fiction as fact. But I have to say, "A story that says there's a murderous ghost at large could bring in false tips."

"It could also bring in genuine leads," Sir Gerald points out. "At any rate, that's why I'll put the question mark in the head-line—so that if it turns out the killer's an ordinary human, I won't be laughed out of town for publishing nonsense."

I note the word *if* in his statement. "So you think it *could* be a ghost?" I'm surprised that a worldly, practical man like him could entertain the possibility.

"I'm not ruling it out." Sir Gerald narrows his eyes at me. "You're obviously a disbeliever, Mrs. Barrett."

It's his first acknowledgment that he attended my wedding today. For the first time I wonder what effect my marriage will have on my job. I'm beginning to feel pulled in different directions—between Sir Gerald, who expects me to photograph crime scenes at all hours of the day and night, and Barrett's mother, who expects a conventional daughter-in-law. Intimidated by Sir Gerald's critical tone, I'm also compelled to poke the wolf.

"I think ghosts are imaginary."

Sir Gerald shrugs, taking no offense. "You've a right to your opinion."

I recall once hearing him say, "I didn't get where I am by listening only to people who agree with me." I respect him for that, along with his strength and ruthlessness, which I also fear.

"But in my travels around the world, I've seen a man killed by a witch's curse, and I've seen the dead come back to life. So although I've never seen ghosts, I'm willing to consider the possibility that they're real. You should keep an open mind."

His words are a reminder that although he takes dissenting opinions into account, he brooks no opposition when he thinks he's right. He hands me the photograph. "Tell the engravers to have this ready for the morning paper. Oh, and I'm taking you and Mick and Lord Hugh off crime scene duty so you can investigate the murder."

It's a mixed blessing. My friends and I will have time to hunt Charles Firth's killer, but Sir Gerald also didn't get where he is by keeping people on his payroll who don't deliver results. Moreover, he's invested a fortune in his growing newspaper empire and staked his reputation on it. Sometimes I feel sorry for this rich, powerful man upon whom my livelihood depends. Fortune and reputation are all he has left now that he's lost his son, his stake in the future.

"Keep me posted," Sir Gerald says. "I want to be the first to know if there's anything to the ghost angle."

Chapter 6

Mick unlocks the door to our studio, in a row of eighteenth-century shop buildings on Whitechapel high street, and I smile with pride at the sign, painted in gold letters over the display window: S. Bain Photographer & Co.

By day, this is the respectable part of Whitechapel. Now, at night, when the shops are closed, the traffic diminished, and most of the buildings dark, it embodies Whitechapel's reputation as the hunting ground of Jack the Ripper. Beneath the gas lamps whose yellow glow diffuses in the cold fog, streetwalkers from the nearby slums wander into the Angel, White Hart, and Red Lion public houses. They come out accompanied by men. The couples duck into alleys for amorous congress. Drunken laughter punctuates the rumble of trains, and the fetid stench from the slaughterhouses drifts through the smoke and chemical fumes. But this is home, and the knowledge that I'll be leaving soon brings tears to my eyes.

Inside the studio, Mick puts the photography equipment away. The tears blur my view of the room that he and Hugh helped me furnish. With its Turkey carpet, crystal gas chandelier, and carved furniture, it could be an elegant parlor if not for the cameras on tripods, the rolled backdrops on a stand, and the gallery of my photographs on the wall near the door to the darkroom. After I move, I can return to use the studio and visit my friends, but it won't be the same.

"I'm goin' back to Bethnal Green to look for witnesses," Mick says.

"Don't you have school at the Working Lads Institute?" I say.

His formal education has been sporadic since he began living on the streets at age eight. It consisted of stints at an orphanage, from which he repeatedly ran away, and at a local school. He hates sitting still in class, being treated like a child. My attempts to persuade him that he needed an education went nowhere until after his quarrel with Catherine. Then he decided that an education would help him become a man of means, compete with her other suitors, and win her hand. Now he attends the Working Lads Institute, which provides classes that employed youths can fit into their spare time. It aims to draw the boys away from the evils of the streets and qualify them for better jobs.

"I'm takin' the night off," Mick says.

We go upstairs, and he opens the drawer in the table in the parlor. There lie four identical pistols—one each for Mick, Hugh, Barrett, and me. Barrett keeps his here because police don't carry guns and he hasn't a secure place to store his at the barracks. Mick removes his, loads it, and tucks it in his pocket. The gunshot wound in my shoulder suddenly aches.

"Education is still important." I'm afraid he'll quit school now that he's given up on Catherine.

"One night off ain't gonna make a difference." He stalks out, closing the door so hard that the bell jangles.

I sigh and tell myself that I should stop trying to act as a parent to Mick, who's an adult by circumstance if not age, but I care about him, and I know he wants to rise within the ranks of Sir Gerald's employ, and for that he needs an education. I also don't like him roaming the city armed with a gun, spoiling for trouble.

I go upstairs, wondering if things will look different now that I'm married. But there's the chaise longue that I rarely get to enjoy because Mick and Hugh monopolize it, the fireplace that warms us while we drink our cocoa on winter nights, and the other furnishings that we've acquired mostly from junk shops. No matter that I'm eager to establish a home with my husband, how can I bear to leave?

Fitzmorris comes out of the kitchen, dishcloth in hand. He and I share the chores. Mick pitches in, but Hugh is useless at domestic tasks, and soon Fitzmorris will have to shoulder the major burden alone. His family has served Hugh's for generations. Fitzmorris's parents died when he was a child, and after the Stauntons gave him and his siblings a home, education, and affection, he repaid them with devotion to Hugh, whom he loves as a younger brother. His devotion extends to Mick and me. He's a bachelor with no children, and the three of us are his family. I'll miss him, but I can count on him to look after Mick and Hugh when I'm gone.

"Where is Hugh?" I say.

Fitzmorris points upward. "Sleeping it off."

I haven't the heart to criticize Hugh for his overindulgence. I never liked or trusted Tristan—I thought him rigid and standoffish—but he was Hugh's beloved, the only relationship that had been serious enough to last for more than a few encounters. And I can't deny that Tristan had sacrificed much for love of Hugh. He'd given up the Church and attempted a new, disliked career in Sir Gerald's business empire so that he and Hugh could be together. Eventually Tristan crumbled under the pressure from social disapproval and his own conscience. That the relationship was doomed from the start doesn't mean its end is any less painful for Hugh.

"Barrett stopped by and left you a note." Fitzmorris gestures at the dining room table.

I read the note: *Broke the news to C. F.'s wife. Went to the morgue at St. George's for the autopsy. Meet me at the hotel. B.* I smile. It's my husband's first letter to me. How romantic.

I go to my small, cramped room on the top floor. Its attic ceiling slants low; it's cold in the winter, hot in the summer, and noisy from the traffic on the street; but it's dear to me. After my father disappeared, I lived with my coldhearted mother in a series of cheap, comfortless lodgings. Then came boarding school, her death, and living on my own. This is, since the age of ten, my first real home, where I'm loved.

When I take off my wedding dress, I find a brown acid spot on the skirt, from the photographic chemicals. I sponge the spot with water, hang up the dress, and put on a dark-blue wool frock. Instead of traveling to the hotel by myself, I decide to meet Barrett at the morgue. I go downstairs and hesitate in the parlor, torn between the need for protection and reluctance to bring my gun. St. George's Church is less than half a mile away, but even though the Ripper no longer stalks the streets, Whitechapel is dangerous by night, especially for a woman alone. My wounded shoulder twinges. I leave the gun in the drawer.

Outside, I hail a cab that conveys me to St. George's. The ornate Baroque church, surrounded by dark tenements, looks as inviting as a mausoleum. In the flickering light from the streetlamps, trees cast spooky shadows on its white stone walls. The fog is so thick that I can't see the boundaries of the churchyard, and I don't know where the morgue is. Starting down a path, I hear footsteps but can't tell if someone is following me or they're echoes of my own. Foliage drips water on me, cold moisture veils my face, and I shiver. Then I see a weird glow in the distance. I pass old gravestones tilted at odd angles. It's said that the veil between the realms of the living and the dead is thinnest at Halloween, but it's not Halloween yet, and I don't believe there are ghosts in this cemetery or anyplace else. The glow emanates from the windows and open door of a small brick building amid high shrubs that seem intended to hide it from view.

"Barrett?" I call.

He appears in the doorway, much to my relief. "Sarah? What are you doing here?"

"I came to meet you. Is the autopsy finished?"

"No. It's just about to start."

I peer into the morgue and see a blanket-covered figure lying on a table while a man in a gray smock removes instruments from a cabinet and arranges them on the work top. I think of the time I visited a morgue and photographed the dissected corpse of Annie Chapman, the Ripper's third victim.

"You came alone?" Barrett looks around for Hugh and Mick, my usual companions in nighttime expeditions. "That was dangerous."

I feel a little hurt because he's not pleased to see me. "I made it all right."

"I told you to meet me at the hotel. Or didn't you get my note?"

"Yes, but I thought that if I came here, we could go together."

"You can go now. I'll walk you to the train station."

"Since I'm here, I may as well watch the autopsy." I don't really want to, but his peremptory manner rouses my stubborn streak.

Barrett frowns. "You can't. It's against procedure."

"Remember Sir Gerald's deal with the police."

Sir Gerald and the top police brass agreed that his reporters would have access to investigations, and the *Daily World* would give the police good publicity and help them solve cases by encouraging readers with information to come forward.

"Never mind Sir Gerald's deal." Barrett draws me farther from the morgue and lowers his voice. "Didn't you promise to obey me?"

I pause, confused, before I recall our wedding vows. I laugh because I think he's making a joke. "Well, I didn't mean it so literally."

He's not laughing. "Why not?"

"Surely you don't think you can order me around, and I should do whatever you say, just because we're married now?"

I've seen his father order his mother around, and many other husbands doing the same with their wives, but although Barrett has often disapproved of my actions, he's always respected my independence. I thought he found it attractive and indeed liked having a woman who was adventurous instead of domestic, wayward instead of meek. We stare at each other, stunned by the realization that marriage has already changed things between us.

I take a step toward the morgue. He puts out his hand to stop me. We both freeze.

Barrett drops his hand. "You can watch."

"No, I'll go." I feel the same simultaneous reluctance to give in and eagerness to please as I hear in his voice. We both perceive that something bigger than winning this argument is at stake.

The morgue is no place to hash it out. We walk to the door, and he stands aside so I can enter first. Confronted with the doctor, his grisly array of sharp tools, and the shrouded corpse, my heart starts to pound. The discolored white plaster walls and the stone floor exude smells of absorbed decay that the cold air from the open door and windows doesn't alleviate. I begin to wish I had obeyed Barrett.

Barrett introduces me to the doctor—George Phillips, the police surgeon. In his fifties, with muttonchop whiskers and wearing a high-collared white shirt and black stock tie under his smock, he looks as if he stepped out of a portrait from the previous century. Barrett explains that I'm his wife and a reporter for the *Daily World*, with official permission to observe the autopsy.

Dr. Phillips smiles, and benevolent lines crease his face. "Well, this is a first for me—a lovely lady to watch me at work. But are you certain you want to, Mrs. Barrett? Postmortem examinations are not for the faint of heart."

"I'm certain."

My heart didn't fail me when I saw Annie Chapman with all her organs removed, but I've never watched the actual cutting and eviscerating. As Barrett and I join Dr. Phillips at the table, we look at each other. He doesn't seem squeamish; he's watched autopsies before. We share wan smiles, and I can tell that he's thinking what I'm thinking: how bizarre to find ourselves standing together at an autopsy table as we did at the altar this morning. It feels right, even though I imagine it would seem wrong to other people.

Dr. Phillips dons rubber gloves and peels the blanket off the body. Charles Firth looks shrunken, his skin gray; death has extinguished his personality, reduced him to a mass of decaying flesh. I breathe shallowly but still catch a sweet, rotten whiff of the dried blood on his clothes. When Dr. Phillips unbuttons and opens the white shirt, it sticks to the skin underneath.

"I don't think we need an internal examination." Dr. Phillips studies the narrow cut between Charles Firth's upper ribs. "The cause of death is obvious. You're in luck." His wry smile at me says he knows I dreaded watching the cutting.

It's not only the cutting that would have distressed me; it's also the posthumous violation of a man I knew and liked, to whom I owe my good fortune.

"The crime scene was the first I've ever seen at which the victim was killed during a photographic session," Dr. Phillips says. "What was he trying to photograph?"

"Ghosts," Barrett and I say in unison.

Dr. Phillips raises his bushy white eyebrows at us. Barrett explains about the supposedly haunted church.

"A murdered ghost hunter; how peculiar," Dr. Phillips says. "I must confess, I think photographs of that sort are an abominable hoax."

Although I hate to challenge his skepticism and my own, I say, "I developed his photographs. Look at this one." I take a duplicate print out of my satchel.

Barrett and Dr. Phillips purse their lips as they scrutinize the pale figure assaulting Charles Firth.

"I think it's a person," Barrett says.

"I agree," Dr. Phillips says. "The blurriness makes it appear to be a ghost."

But they don't sound entirely confident. I say, "The *Daily World* is going to publish this photograph tomorrow, with the headline 'Murder by a Ghost?' "

"Get ready for trouble," Barrett says. "Remember the panic during the Ripper murders? People were seeing him on every street corner and going mad with fear."

"I attended the Elizabeth Stride murder scene and performed the autopsy." Memory clouds Dr. Phillips's expression.

I was the first to discover her body. That's one of my secrets related to the Ripper case. "Heaven help us if people start thinking they see ghosts."

"It behooves us to prove that this is not a case of supernatural crime," Dr. Phillips says. "I can tell you that aside from the circumstances, this murder was a simple stabbing. The weapon was a sharp blade approximately half an inch wide. Nothing the least otherworldly about that."

"Many people already think the Ripper is a ghost because he committed six murders and escaped without being seen." Even if I were to tell them his identity, they would probably disbelieve me and cling to their superstition.

"Is there any way to rule out a ghost?" Barrett says.

"Let us take a closer look." Dr. Phillips examines Charles Firth's stiff hands. "No wounds. He didn't try to defend himself. He must have been taken by surprise." Walking slowly around the table, Dr. Phillips examines the clothed body from head to toe. He pauses to touch a gloved finger to the sleeves and lapels of the black jacket.

"Have you found something?" Barrett says.

The bright lights in the morgue reveal what the darkness in the crypt concealed—traces of a pale, greenish substance, a dried slime. Dr. Phillips leans close to the slime on Firth's jacket, sniffs, makes a face, and draws back.

"It has a strange odor. Foul, but with an aromatic tinge."

"What is it?" Barrett says.

"It could be mucus or vomit. Although I've never encountered any with that odor." The doctor probes Mr. Firth's nostrils and open mouth with a cotton-tipped stick. "Hmm, none in there. It doesn't seem to be his."

"I didn't notice any at the scene," Barrett says. "Did you, Sarah?"

"No. But if it didn't come from Mr. Firth, then where did it come from, and how did it get on his clothes?"

"I'd better have another look around the crypt later," Barrett says.

Dr. Phillips uses scissors to cut slimy patches from Mr. Firth's clothes and puts the bits of fabric in a small glass jar. "I'll send these to a chemist for testing."

An unwelcome thought occurs to me. "Could it be . . . No, it's impossible."

"Impossible to be what?" Barrett says.

The thought is like a feather stuck in my lung, and I have to cough it out. "Ectoplasm."

"Ah—the supernatural substance with which ghosts supposedly take physical form," Dr. Phillips says. "It makes them visible to humans and allows them to do things they can't when they're mere disembodied energy."

"I heard about a séance where ectoplasm came out of the medium's mouth." Barrett speaks hesitantly, as if afraid to sound foolish. "It took the shape of a devil with wings and flew around the room howling."

I muffle an unladylike snort of disgust.

"Most certainly a hoax," Dr. Phillips says.

I think of the hoax that was once played on me. Soon after my mother told me my father was dead, I took the money she gave me to buy groceries and spent it on a medium. The fat old woman lit candles, burned incense, moaned, and went into a trance. As her body trembled and her eyelids fluttered, she said that my father was in heaven, he sent me his love, and he promised me that we would be together again someday. That the prediction came true and we actually have reunited doesn't make up for the fact that she couldn't have received a message from his spirit because he wasn't dead. She tricked a bereaved child. Now I hate to add more credence to the mistaken idea that a ghost killed Charles Firth.

"Do we have to tell anyone about this?" I point at the glass jar of samples. It repels me as though it contains a genie that will whip London into a panic. I picture Barrett and me so busy chasing nonexistent ghosts that we haven't time to catch the real, mortal killer.

"I'll have to mention it in my autopsy report," Dr. Phillips says.

"Can we keep it quiet until the test results come in?" Barrett says.

"A wise idea," Dr. Phillips says.

"I won't tell Sir Gerald yet," I add.

"If he finds out later that you withheld information, he'll be angry," Barrett says.

Sir Gerald might fire me, which would please Barrett's mother. "But if I tell him, his next headline will say, 'Ectoplasm Found on Murdered Spirit Photographer.' "

"All the more reason to solve the case fast," Barrett says.

* * *

The Savoy Hotel towers nine stories high above the Strand. The wind from the river ripples the flags on its roof, and its domed turrets dissolve in the fog. Its glazed white brick walls and the lights in its countless windows shimmer, mirage-like, amid the dark city.

The cab lets Barrett and me off in the courtyard. The tinkling of the fountain in the center greets us. We've traveled three miles from morgue to palace, from the lowest depth to which humankind can sink to the heights of its worldly aspiration.

"We should have gone someplace cheaper," I say, afraid the hotel is too fine for our budget and the likes of me.

"My bride deserves the best." Barrett's smile says he's willing to put aside our differences so that we can enjoy our wedding night. He tells the uniformed doorman that we've booked a room for the night.

The doorman ushers us into the hotel, bows, and says, "Enjoy your stay, sir and madam."

I'm impressed because Barrett seems as confident as if he's at home. But of course he's a policeman, accustomed to barging in wherever he chooses, whether he's welcome or not.

In the lobby, our footsteps echo from the black-and-white marble floor throughout a vast space decorated with potted palms and fresh flower arrangements. Square white pillars that look to be twenty feet high, crowned with gilded capitals, support a white coffered ceiling from which hangs a giant crystal chandelier. A clock somewhere chimes ten times. At this late hour, few other guests are coming or going.

The suave clerk at the desk says, "Ah, yes, Mr. and Mrs. Barrett. Your room is waiting, and the baggage you sent has arrived safely. I see that you reserved a table for dinner. I'm sorry to say the restaurant is closed."

"That's all right," I say. The visit to the morgue has taken away my appetite.

The clerk signals a bellhop, who escorts us to the lift. I've ridden in the one Sir Gerald installed at the *Daily World* building, but this is larger, with wood paneling, a mirror, carpet, and an upholstered settee. We glide up to the seventh floor and proceed down a wide, hushed corridor. When the bellhop opens the door to our room, the sweet scent of flowers welcomes us. He reaches inside and flicks a switch on the wall, illuminating the room.

"The Savoy has electricity and central heating," he says.

The room is the warmest, coziest place I've been all day. My feet sink into thick, plush carpet. The canopied bed has a gold satin duvet, and tapestries and gold-framed landscape paintings decorate the walls. A bouquet of fresh gardenias and roses graces the mantel. The bellhop shows us a bathroom with porcelain fixtures and marble walls and floor, fit for a Roman emperor.

"There's hot and cold running water twenty-four hours a day." He steps over to the window, which is festooned with gold-and-white brocade curtains. "You'll have a fine view from your balcony in the morning."

Barrett and I exchange delighted smiles; we can't believe this luxury is ours, even for just one night. Now I'm glad he splurged.

"If you need anything, feel free to use the speaking tube." The bellhop demonstrates how to operate the round metal mouthpiece on the wall, then wishes us good-night and departs.

On the rare occasions when we have complete privacy, we usually plunge into immediate, frantic lovemaking. But tonight, a discomfort left over from the argument we had at the morgue inhibits us, as does the novelty of the situation. Barrett flicks the switches, chuckling as he turns the electric lights on and off. I turn on the tap in the bathroom sink; the water is steaming hot. Barrett skims the menu, talks into the speaking tube, and orders food. At last we turn to each other. He raises his eyebrow, and I blush as desire flares between us. We realize that there's no hurry to finish making love before we're interrupted, and our wedding night calls for a little more ceremony than usual.

"I'll get ready," I say.

In the armoire, I find my empty suitcase and my things neatly unpacked. I carry my nightgown and toiletries into the bathroom, run water in the tub, throw in pink bath salts from a jar on the shelf, and undress. Then I lie in the hot, rose-scented suds and revel in the most luxurious soak I've ever had. I contemplate the gold ring on my finger. This has been one of the strangest days in my life, and that's saying a lot. When I climb out of the tub, I dry myself on a fluffy white towel, then put on my new nightgown. It's daringly sleeveless, white satin trimmed with lace. I unbraid my hair and brush the long waves. Then I go out to the bedroom.

"Thomas?" I say, feeling shy as I call him by his Christian name for the first time.

He's drawn back the duvet, and he's lying on the bed in his shirt, trousers, and socks, fast asleep.

He looks so peaceful that I don't want to disturb him. I turn off the lights and lie down beside him, thinking I'll just rest a while, and then I'll wake him up, and . . .

Drowsiness closes my eyes, and I'm asleep before I finish the thought.

CHAPTER 7

"What time is it?" Barrett exclaims, bolting upright in bed. I open my eyes to faint daylight and look out the window. Lights twinkle through the fog, from buildings and streetlamps by the river.

Barrett glances at the clock and groans. "Six thirty! Why didn't you wake me?"

"I fell asleep too."

We begin to laugh, vexed but amused because we wasted the night. Because both of us are due at work soon we hurriedly wash, dress, and pack. As we're leaving, I see a covered tray in the hall—the food Barrett ordered last night. Whoever delivered it must have knocked but failed to rouse us.

Downstairs, when we check out, the clerk says, "Did you enjoy your stay?"

"Very much, thank you," Barrett says with a wry smile.

On the street, newsboys cry, "Man murdered by a ghost! Read all about it!" I buy a copy of the *Daily World*, whose front-page article has Sally's byline and ends with a request for anyone with information about the murder to report it to the police. As we walk to the underground train station, I show Barrett our wedding photograph on the second page.

"We'll never look that sweet again," he says.

In the train, we're mashed up against other passengers as we cling to the straps. We part ways at my studio, after he carries my baggage upstairs, and he says, "I'll drop by tonight."

Mick and Fitzmorris are at the breakfast table, eggs and toast on their plates. "Lord Hugh went out last night and hasn't come home," Fitzmorris says.

"Oh, no."

When Hugh is troubled, he roams the city, drinking too much. I fear that he'll fall prey to cutpurses, or engage in intimate relations with shady characters, or be attacked by people who hate men of his kind. Worse, Tristan's desertion could propel him into the same black depression that came upon him when he was exposed as a homosexual and disowned by his family. Back then, he tried to commit suicide and was rescued. If he tries again . . . I read the same unspeakable thought in Mick's and Fitzmorris's eyes. After all the times Hugh made bad jokes that brightened dark moments, all the times his optimism rallied us during crises, we can't bear to lose him.

The sounds of the bell on the front door jangling and footsteps on the stairs provoke sighs of relief from us. Hugh trudges into the dining room, his coat buttoned the wrong way, his eyes bleary, reeking of liquor. He collapses into a chair.

"Don't all look at me as if I'm something the cat dragged in."

"You all right?" Mick asks.

"Never better." Hugh smiles with a falsely jaunty air.

"Would you like some breakfast?" Fitzmorris says.

Hugh grimaces. "Ugh. I've got a bit of a hangover."

"I'll bring your usual remedy." Fitzmorris passes me a full plate and goes to the kitchen.

I eat, hungry now that the immediate crisis has passed. "Why don't you go to bed?" I say to Hugh.

"At nine in the morning? Haven't we a murder to investigate?"

"Sarah and I can do it," Mick says.

"I mustn't slack off while I'm on Sir Gerald's payroll," Hugh says. "He's probably eager for an excuse to give me the boot. I think the victim's home is a good place to start detecting. Did you find out where he lived?"

"Yes." I memorized the addresses on the card Barrett found in his pocket.

Fitzmorris returns and hands Hugh a cup that contains tomato juice, Worcestershire sauce, vinegar, salt, pepper, and a raw egg. Hugh says, "Thank you," gulps it, gags, and pants. "Ah, that's better. I'll be ready in a jiff."

He bounds up the stairs, and I hear him trip at the top. Soon he comes back neatly groomed, scented with bay rum shaving lotion, looking almost his usual, handsome self. But his impeccably tailored clothes are baggy; he's lost weight. He's chewing a peppermint to freshen his breath, and his smile can't hide the dark shadows under his eyes.

As he and Mick and I walk to the station, he says, "Sarah, I'm sorry I made a scene at your wedding breakfast."

"It's all right." I know how much effort it's costing him to act like his normal, cheerful self, to be the trouper who doesn't let his friends down. I don't want to scold him and make him feel worse than he does.

"No, it isn't. I shouldn't get in fights."

"The other guy started it," Mick says.

"Well, I took the bait," Hugh says. "Sarah, please convey my apologies to Barrett and his family. Next time I'll control myself."

Mick and I fill him in on what we've learned about the murder. Once we're on the train, two young ladies make eyes at Hugh and giggle, and he strikes up a conversation with them. He's not interested in women, but he flirts with them to disguise his true inclination, and I know he's doing it now to prevent Mick and me from talking to him about his troubles. At St. Pancras station, he runs ahead of us to hire a cab, and during the ride he chatters about whether we should move to this pleasant northern district, away from the crowds, stench, and crime in the East End.

In Lonsdale Square, elegant Gothic-style townhouses with steep, pointed gables, mullioned windows, and arched front doors surround a garden. Men are raking the fallen leaves on the grass, children laughing as they jump in the piles. The fresh, earthy smell reminds me of autumn days in the country with my father, taking photographs, when I was young. Two police constables stroll

along, guarding the residents against buskers, beggars, streetwalkers, and cutpurses.

"Spirit photography must be a lucrative business," Hugh says.

"Yeah, we should give it a try," Mick says. "How about it, Sarah?"

"No, thank you."

At the address I remember from the card, I lift the brass knocker, rap on the door, and get no answer.

"I saw the curtain move. Somebody's in there," Mick says.

I knock harder. The door flies open, and a woman dressed in black says in a loud, ragged voice, "Don't you know that when people ignore you, it means they don't want to see you? Are you stupid?"

She's tall, her back slouched as if to minimize her height. A crocheted black snood covers her hair; only the gray-streaked brown fringe is visible. With steel-rimmed spectacles perched on a beaky nose, plus a jutting chin, her face is severe rather than pretty. She looks to be in her forties, her sallow complexion marred by age spots. Her frock is made of heavy black crape, its high collar adorned with a jet brooch in the shape of a woman's hand holding a rose. She's in mourning.

"Mrs. Firth?" She's not how I expected Charles Firth's wife to look, but I didn't know him well enough to predict his taste in women.

"Yes?" Suspicion narrows her deep-set gray eyes, which are red and swollen from weeping. "Who are you?"

I introduce myself and my friends. "We're reporters for the *Daily World*—"

"You're vultures who feed on people's misfortunes. Go away!"

As Mrs. Firth tries to push the door shut, Mick and Hugh hold it open. I say, "I was a customer of your husband's. His murder was discovered during my wedding."

She blinks as if startled, then silently lets us enter the house. The foyer is dim, the air hazy with smoke that smells of sweet, tarry incense. A staircase ascends to the darker second floor. Paintings hang on the walls. The two nearest me show men falling from a tower struck by lightning and a warrior driving a chariot. They're images from tarot cards. I can't picture Mr. Firth here. He seemed an open, cheerful man, and this place is so closed up and gloomy.

"Is anyone else here?" Hugh says.

"No," Mrs. Firth says. "I need to be alone. So that Charles can come home."

Her words imply that she doesn't know he's dead, although her grief and her mourning garb say otherwise. I remember Barrett's note. "Didn't Detective Sergeant Barrett tell you . . . ?"

"Oh. The policeman. Yes," Mrs. Firth says. "I meant so that Charles's spirit can come."

So she believes in ghosts, and she thinks her husband will appear to her. I pity her for her foolishness.

"Spirits won't come if the atmosphere is unsympathetic." Mrs. Firth looks closely at my friends and me. "Are you sympathetic to the spirits?"

We all nod, aware that if we say no, she'll tell us to leave. She leads us down the passage to a room furnished as a library, with bookshelves that cover the walls. The black velvet curtains are closed, and the only light comes from a candle in a silver holder atop a heavy round wooden table. Beside the candle, incense sticks burn in a green ceramic jar. The smoke is so dense that my friends and I cough. Mrs. Firth sits in one chair at the table, motions us to seat ourselves, and folds her hands.

I picture her keeping vigil like that ever since she learned her husband was dead, patiently waiting for his ghost to appear. "Did your husband believe in the supernatural?" I ask.

"Oh, yes." Mrs. Firth pauses. "Well, not when we first met. But while we were courting, I talked to him about the things I've seen and introduced him to my friends in the spiritualist community, and he eventually came to believe."

I wonder if he adapted his personality to hers, just as he adapted it to those of his customers. Was it the kind of compromise that many married couples have to make? I glance around the room. On the shelves, in front of the books, are figurines, crystals, animal skulls, strings of beads, feathers, bells, and demonic masks. Either Charles Firth was a believer or didn't mind living with the trappings of his wife's superstition.

"The policeman said there were negative plates in Charles's cameras at the church. He mentioned the wedding." Mrs. Firth fixes her hopeful, eager gaze on me. "You must be his wife. He said you were going to develop the negatives. Have you? Was there anything on them?"

So that's why she let us in—to find out if her husband photographed any ghosts. I reach in my satchel, take out the print of Charles Firth, and warn her, "I'm afraid this may be disturbing to you." Then I lay the print on the table.

Mrs. Firth gasps as she touches her fingertip to the pale, blurred figure assailing her husband. She looks up, her eyes shining with elation. "He captured the image of a spirit!" Then sorrow crumples her face. "A spirit that killed him."

My friends and I don't try to contradict her; I doubt she would listen. I say, "Did you know that your husband was planning to spend the night in the church?"

"Oh, yes. I had heard that St. Peter's is haunted, and I told Charles it would be a good place for spirit photography. If I hadn't sent him there, he would still be alive." She covers her face with her hands and quakes with sobs. Her hands are large, the joints knobby, with a ring on each finger. The plain gold wedding band looks out of place amid others set with chunky garnets, turquoises, and opals. "It's my fault he's dead!"

Perhaps it's her fault in a different way than she means. When a married person is murdered, the spouse is a logical suspect. Mick slips out of the room, presumably to search the house for clues. As Mrs. Firth mops her face with a black-bordered white handkerchief, Hugh asks, "Where were you the night before last?"

She doesn't seem to notice that Mick is gone. "I already told the policeman I was at home by myself. He didn't say so, but I know he suspects I killed Charles." She utters a woebegone laugh. "Of course I didn't. And here's proof." She touches the "ghost" in the photograph.

But she hasn't an alibi. "How long were you married?" I say.

"Eleven years."

"Have you any children?" I'm seeking other people who might have information germane to his murder, and even youngsters might. I remember the vicar's grandchildren, whom I suspect know more than they've been allowed to tell.

"No."

"Was your marriage happy?" Hugh says.

Mrs. Firth plays with her rings. "Yes." She tugs the wedding band over her knuckle, then pushes it back into place. "We had our troubles, but yes."

Glancing toward the bookshelves, Hugh wiggles his eyebrows at me. I look over there and see a knife lying in front of some books. It appears to be an antique, with a carved ivory handle. I notice other knives on other shelves, a veritable collection. I wonder if Mrs. Firth cleaned the murder weapon and hid it in plain sight.

"Do you know of anyone who might have wanted your husband dead?" I say.

"No. He was well liked." Then she bursts out, "Why are you bothering me with these questions? My husband was murdered by a spirit."

I struggle to be tactful. "We're helping the police investigate the murder. We need to explore all the possibilities and determine precisely what happened in the crypt last night."

"I'll ask my husband. He was there. He saw everything."

I remember the fake medium from my childhood, and anger rises like a wall in me. "Do you propose to conduct a séance?"

"Unfortunately, I haven't the gift for summoning the spirits. I can only wait for them to come to me of their own volition. They speak to me through automatic writing." Mrs. Firth goes to a desk, fetches a sheet of white letter paper and a pen, and brings them to the table. She sits down, takes up the pen, and rests the nib on the paper. "If the spirits are willing, they take control of my hand and write messages."

While I struggle to conceal my revulsion, Hugh says, "Does it really work?"

"Oh, yes. There's a famous example. When Mr. Charles Dickens, the author, died in 1870, he left his last novel unfinished. Only the first six installments were published. His spirit was troubled because he'd left his readers desperate to know how the story ended. He channeled the conclusion through an American named Thomas Power James. Mr. James was an uneducated man, barely literate. He couldn't have written it, let alone imitated Mr. Dickens's style."

"Remarkable." Hugh widens his eyes, as if he's impressed, but there's a flat note to his voice.

My opinion can't be uttered in polite company. Mr. James must have engineered a hoax somehow. I think that if Charles Firth didn't believe in the supernatural, he should have tried to dissuade his wife from believing. Some compromises are too big to make, even for love.

"Now, please, be very quiet." Mrs. Firth breathes deeply, swaying from side to side and back and forth, as if her body is a net trying to catch her husband's spirit as it swims in the ether. "Charles, are you there?" she says in a hushed voice. "It is I, Leonora."

The incense smoke stings my eyes, infiltrates my lungs. I begin to feel light-headed, and I hear whispery sounds. Hugh looks queasy, as if he's experiencing the same phenomena. It can't be spirits; probably something in the incense causes hallucinations.

Mrs. Firth's hand jerks. The pen zigzags across the paper, as if controlled by an invisible puppeteer, then draws a crooked heart. A smile trembles on her lips, and tears leak from her eyes. "He's here. He says he loves me."

I'm torn between anger and pity. She draws wavy lines that spiral around the page into the center, where they form two blobs. My eyes water from the smoke, blurring my vision. The pen scribbles letters of the alphabet in seemingly random groups and positions. Mrs. Firth shudders and whimpers while jagged marks cover the blobs. Her arm stiffens, and her hand flings the pen across the room. She slumps over, hands pressed against the table. She gasps and blinks, mouth agape, like a woman who was drowning in the ocean and has been flung ashore by a wave.

Hugh gets to his feet. "I say, Mrs. Firth, are you all right?"

I open the curtains and the window, letting in light and fresh air. Mrs. Firth grabs the paper, crying, "Look! Charles drew his murder. That's the spirit that killed him!" She points at one of the blobs. "I told you so!"

If I strain my imagination, it and the other blob have vaguely human shapes, but I think Mrs. Firth, either intentionally or subconsciously, copied the photograph that's still lying on the table.

She touches the jagged marks. "The ghost is stabbing Charles with mystical energy. And see these words." Her finger moves around the page, tapping the scribbled letters. "*Thief, hide, gold, steal.* The ghost was once a thief who buried his loot where the church now stands. He thought Charles was trying to steal it. Now we know what happened!"

Scorn vies with my pity. The whole alphabet is there; she could spell out any words she liked and interpret them in countless ways. The "message" is as false a clue as I expected.

Mrs. Firth spells out more words. " 'Good-bye until we meet again.' " She looks up, her eyes luminous. "Charles will be coming back."

"*Rubbish!*" Hugh slams his hands down on the table.

Mrs. Firth and I both jump. Hugh shouts at Mrs. Firth, "This is nothing but your wishful thinking disguised as spirit communication." His face is so dark and twisted with rage that I'm alarmed; I've never seen him like that. As Mrs. Firth protests, he snatches the paper from her. "You poor, stupid, deluded fool. He's never coming back."

"Hugh!" It occurs to me that Mrs. Firth isn't the only one who's lost somebody and Hugh isn't really talking about her husband.

"Give me that!" Mrs. Firth screams.

She grabs the paper, and it rips. Hugh crumples the part he holds in his hands and throws it on the floor. Mrs. Firth drops to her knees, picks it up, and holds both parts to her bosom. Hugh stands huffing like a cornered bull, opening and closing his fists, his eyes wild with rage and grief. I lay a soothing hand on his arm, but he violently shakes me off.

CHAPTER 8

When my friends and I don't immediately answer the door, it opens. A man carrying a wicker picnic basket steps into the foyer and removes his black silk top hat. He says in a cultured voice, "I'm here to give my condolences to Mrs. Firth."

His dark, expensive coat and trousers drape loosely on his tall, thin, willowy frame. He's like a fashion illustration for a smart haberdashery, only too old, looking to be in his fifties. His blond hair is turning silver, and the skin on his long, bony face sags. His pleasant smile reveals large, yellowish teeth. "The name's Richard Trevelyan." He extends his hand for me to shake.

Caught by surprise, I shake his hand and introduce myself. After Hugh and Mick follow suit, I say, "Did you know Mr. Firth?"

"Yes, we were close friends. I'm also the publisher of his books."

"Richard!" Mrs. Firth hurries into the foyer.

Mr. Trevelyan sets down the picnic basket and takes her hands in his, which have long, manicured fingernails. "I came as soon as I heard. My dear Leonora, I am so sorry."

Mrs. Firth turns her tear-stained face to my friends and me. "I thought you'd left."

I don't want to go yet; Mr. Trevelyan might have useful information. I frown at Hugh, irritated at his rudeness as well as sorry for his pain.

"Mrs. Firth, I apologize for my terrible behavior," Hugh says. "I don't know what got into me. There's no excuse." He bows his head. "I beg your forgiveness."

Mick, alerted by Mrs. Firth's scream, rushes into the room. He takes one look at Hugh and says, "Sarah, let's get him out of here."

As we pull Hugh to the foyer, he sags between us, his strength drained, the wildness on his face yielding to misery. His drinking, his staying out all night, and his scuffle at my wedding breakfast were but preludes to this episode, and I fear that worse is yet to come.

A loud knocking at the door startles us all.

Mrs. Firth eyes Hugh as if she doesn't know whether to trust his latest abrupt change in mood. Mr. Trevelyan, obviously puzzled because he doesn't know what transpired between them, says, "Why don't we all sit down for a nice chat." He holds up the picnic basket. "It's near lunchtime, and I had my cook pack some provisions. Leonora, dear, I wanted to make sure you keep up your strength. There's enough for everyone."

"That's very kind of you, Richard." Mrs. Firth addresses my friends and me. "Please do stay." We murmur our thanks, and I feel guilty because we're imposing on her during her bereavement. She says quietly to Hugh, "I forgive you. Often, the people who most need to believe in the abiding power of the human spirit are the most vehement disbelievers."

The dining room is dark and gloomy, the table cluttered with books and papers. While Mrs. Firth moves them to the sideboard, Mr. Trevelyan opens the drapes. Outside the window is a back garden enclosed by ivy-covered walls. There, weedy-looking plants, perhaps herbs, grow in ceramic pots. Mr. Trevelyan unpacks the picnic basket, setting out bottles of milk and cider and unwrapping roast beef sandwiches, cheese, pickles, fish pies, and iced cakes. Mrs. Firth rummages in the cabinets for plates, glasses, and silverware. When we're seated, Mick devours his food, taking care to chew with his mouth closed and wipe it on his napkin instead of his sleeve. I'm hungry, but I swallow guilt with each bite.

Mr. Trevelyan cuts his sandwich in small pieces with a knife and fork, as if he were dining at a banquet. "How do you know Charles?" he asks my friends and me. After I explain that I was once a customer of Mr. Firth and his murder was discovered during my wedding, he says, "How extraordinary! The cosmic forces must have brought you back together."

"Miss Bain and her friends are photographers and reporters with the *Daily World*," Mrs. Firth says. "They're working with the police to investigate Charles's murder."

"I see." Mr. Trevelyan's tone says he's mystified as to how that state of affairs came about, but before he can ask, Hugh speaks.

"Are you a believer too?" Hugh has eaten nothing, but he refills his glass with the hard cider. His polite tone has a derisive edge, and I kick him under the table.

"I am indeed." Mr. Trevelyan sounds proud.

Hugh ignores me. "You actually think that communication with the dead is possible?"

"I do. And I'm in excellent company." Mr. Trevelyan reaches in his pocket and brings out a pamphlet, which he spreads on the table in front of Hugh and me. The title, in ornate lettering, reads *The Society for Psychical Studies*. "I belong to this society. So do many of the kingdom's most prominent, respected individuals."

Mrs. Firth eats mechanically, as if she doesn't taste the food. "Look at the member list on the back page. You'll see the names of scientists, scholars, and members of Parliament."

"There's a meeting tomorrow, at noon at the Kew Observatory," Mr. Trevelyan says to Hugh. "It would be a good opportunity to educate yourself."

Hugh thumps his glass down on the table. "Sir, are you calling me ignorant?"

Taken aback, Mr. Trevelyan says, "Not at all. I'm just saying that before you scoff at spiritualism, you should learn the facts."

"*Facts*?" Hugh snorts. "Everything about spiritualism is half-baked mumbo jumbo." I kick him again, and he says between gritted teeth, "Sarah, stop kicking me." He pushes back his chair. "I've had enough of this." His voice breaks, and he stalks out of the room.

It's the first time he's walked out on an investigation, a bad sign. As the front door slams, Mr. Trevelyan looks bewildered and Mrs. Firth relieved to see the last of Hugh. Mick starts to rise, glances at me, and hesitates; he can't decide whether to go after Hugh and leave me alone with two potential murder suspects or stay. He sits back down.

Mr. Trevelyan breaks the awkward silence. "Perhaps you would like to have this." He hands me the pamphlet.

I thank him. The list could point me to other people who knew Charles Firth. "You said that you're Mr. Firth's publisher.

What kinds of books did he write?" I'm less interested in the books than in determining the nature of the relationship between the men.

"They're collections of his photographs, with his descriptions." He fetches a book that Mrs. Firth moved to the sideboard. "Here's the latest."

The book is about an inch thick, expensively bound in purplish-brown leather and embossed with stylized blossoms. Stamped in gold letters is the title: The Spirit Photography of Charles Firth, Volume 3. I open it at random to a photograph printed on smooth, heavy paper, of a young woman in black mourning garb. She stands beside an open coffin in which a bearded man lies beneath a white shroud covered with a bouquet of lilies. In the upper background hovers a translucent image of the same man's face, gazing down at the woman. The heading on the opposite page reads Mrs. Antonia Wall and the spirit of her late husband Joseph, Kensington, 1889. The text contains information about the subjects as well as the camera, lens, lighting, exposure, and developing process that Charles Firth used. I flip through pages and view portraits of other people with the ghosts of their dead loved ones. They contain none of the theatrical effects that provoked my scorn for others I've seen—no halos above the ghosts, no famous people among them. They look disconcertingly real.

"Not only did Charles capture the spirits with his camera, but these photographs are beautifully composed and technically excellent," Mr. Trevelyan says. "He was an artist."

I nod, forced to agree. I can admire Charles Firth even as I deplore that he was one among many frauds, and my desire for justice for him doesn't diminish. I put great stock in the fact that he did me a good turn despite how he treated other people.

"His books are very popular," Mr. Trevelyan adds.

Mrs. Firth has slipped out of the room, and now she returns with the photograph I brought. "Charles took this just before he died."

"Good Lord." Mr. Trevelyan gapes. His astonishment changes to delight. "Leonora, we should publish special-edition prints of this. It will become a collector's item—the most sought-after spirit photograph ever!"

I wonder if Mr. Trevelyan really believes in ghosts or just recognizes that they're good for business. He stands to gain financially from the murder—perhaps he was the "ghost" in the photograph, disguised in a white sheet. But how could he have known that Mr. Firth would trigger the self-timer on the camera? And with Mr. Firth dead, there will be no more spirit photographs from him, no more books to sell. Why kill the goose that laid golden eggs? Nonetheless, Richard Trevelyan is still a better suspect than an imaginary ghost.

Mrs. Firth's eyes cloud behind her spectacles. "I don't like the idea of profiting from Charles's death."

"Nor do I, but Charles would have wanted us to secure his position among the greatest spirit photographers. We'll donate a portion of the proceeds to the Society for Psychical Studies."

"Very well," Mrs. Firth says with a weary shrug. "I'll leave it to you, Richard."

"Can I borrow the negative?" Mr. Trevelyan asks me.

"I'm afraid not." I abhor the idea of wealthy collectors bidding for a photograph of a murder in progress, and the thought that it will be used to perpetuate belief in ghosts is equally repellent. "It's evidence in a police investigation."

"I don't see why there needs to be an investigation," Mrs. Firth says. "We already know who killed Charles. He told us." She reaches in her pocket, brings out the torn page of automatic writing, and shows it to Mr. Trevelyan. "It was the ghost of a thief. He thought Charles was trying to steal the gold he'd buried under the church."

Mr. Trevelyan strokes his jaw as he contemplates the scribbles and random letters. "Extraordinary."

Because he sounds less than convinced, I ask him, "Have you a different idea about who killed Mr. Firth? Did he have any enemies?"

"Um." He glances at Mrs. Firth, obviously reluctant to contradict her.

"If you know who done it, better speak up," Mick says, "or else he'll get away with it while a ghost takes the blame."

Mrs. Firth glowers. She seems stubbornly certain that her husband's killer is a ghost, but perhaps she wants a ghost to take the blame because she's guilty herself.

"Leonora, we have to rule out the possibility that the killer is human," Mr. Trevelyan says. "There's a Miss Jean Ritchie. She's started a club that debunks spiritualists. It's called the Ladies' Society for Rational Thought. She's gone all out to make an example of Charles and destroy him. Perhaps she took things a step too far."

At last we're getting somewhere instead of chasing ghosts.

Mrs. Firth drops into a chair. "I know nothing of this woman! Why didn't Charles tell me about her?"

Mr. Trevelyan puts his hand over hers. "He didn't want to worry you."

"Then *you* should have told me!" She pulls her hand away.

"Yes, of course. I apologize."

Mrs. Firth slumps over the table, buries her head under her arms. "What else didn't he tell me?"

Mr. Trevelyan puts his manicured fingers to his lips; if he knows, he's not going to reveal it, at least not while Mick and I are present. I want to ask him about his relations with Charles Firth, but I can't bring myself to do it now, in front of the grieving widow who's just discovered what may be the first of her late husband's secrets.

Instead, I say, "Where can I find Miss Ritchie?"

"Her club holds meetings at the A.B.C. tea shop in Oxford Circus every Saturday at noon," Mr. Trevelyan says. "There should be one today."

"Where can I reach you if I have further questions?"

He hands me his card and smiles. "It was a pleasure meeting you, Mrs. Barrett, Mr. O'Reilly. I'm as anxious to get to the bottom of this terrible crime as you are. Should you require my assistance, don't hesitate to ask."

Mick and I rise, and I say, "Mrs. Firth, please accept our condolences, and thank you for speaking with us. If I might trouble you for one last thing?"

She raises her tear-streaked, miserable face.

"I'd like to see your husband's studio."

"I can't bear to go there. I'll give you the key, and when you're finished, bring it back and drop it in the mail slot."

★ ★ ★

Outside the house, Mick and I look around Lonsdale Square. We hoped Hugh would be waiting for us, but he's nowhere in view.

"Should I go look for him?" Mick says.

I sigh. "No. If he doesn't want to be found, he won't be." We've gathered that he wanders in obscure corners of the vast city, like a moving needle in a haystack. The times when Mick tried to follow him, he rode trains to major stations and lost himself in the crowds. "Let's just hope he doesn't get in trouble."

We walk to the high street. Although the traffic and crowds rival those of Whitechapel, it's many notches up on the social scale. The building whose sign reads CHARLES FIRTH, PHOTOGRAPHER is one in a block of buildings with glittering display windows and white classical architraves, cornices, and parapets.

"His previous studio was a bit of a hole-in-the-wall," I say, unlocking the door with the key Mrs. Firth lent us. I suppose his spirit photographs paid the higher rent on this place.

On the ground floor is a tidy shop filled with merchandise I would love to own. I touch the expensive cameras and study the lenses and accessories in glass cases. Everything is of the latest design. I'm uncomfortably aware that my own equipment will soon be obsolete.

"Let's help ourselves," Mick says, not entirely joking.

In the gallery of framed photographs on the wall, most are country landscapes, scenes of London, and portraits of well-dressed, attractive ladies and gentlemen. I study the few spirit photographs, all taken in a cemetery, apparently using long exposures at night. Translucent white wraiths hover in the deep shadows around mausoleums and stone angels. A little girl with ringlets, dressed in a pinafore and pantaloons, carries a pug dog. A man wearing the white powdered wig and knee breeches of the eighteenth century bows. The most striking is a woman with long, bedraggled blond hair, pristinely beautiful features, and eyes so pale they're almost white. Dressed in a diaphanous white sheet wrapped around her slim body, arms and legs bare, she looks like an animated corpse escaped from a morgue. The images are so powerful that I can imagine myself in the cemetery, encountering the spirits of the dead. For a moment my skepticism is as insubstantial as the corpse-woman's sheet.

"What kinda evidence are we lookin' for?" Mick says.

"Letters, documents, photographs—your guess is as good as mine."

Mick climbs the stairs, and I follow him. Mr. Firth's studio occupies the whole, large second floor. Huge windows and sky-lights have curtains for adjusting the amount of outdoor light that enters. Three expensive cameras stand on tripods beside flash-lamps. Backdrops hang on rollers on one wall, and built-in cabi-nets cover another. Furniture, statuary, and live potted plants serve as props. The darkroom is twice as big as ours, equipped with run-ning water and two new enlargers.

"The lucky stiff," Mick says.

"He couldn't take it with him." Even as I remember his kind-ness to me, I detest the means by which he must have earned his luxurious studio. I walk to a cabinet and rummage through the costumes hung inside.

"Looks like just a bunch o' clothes," Mick says.

"Maybe not just clothes. Maybe proof that he faked his spirit photographs."

"Proof, like white sheets for dressin' people up as ghosts?"

"Or old-fashioned costumes to make them look like people from the past." I hold up a ball gown that's twenty years out of style.

Mick opens another cabinet. "White sheets in here. And look at all these wigs."

The wigs are of every hair color, in both men's and women's styles, modern as well as antiquated. We also find wooden manne-quins, stage makeup, and extremely realistic wax masks of adults, children, and infants. Because I don't believe in ghosts and was anticipating evidence that Mr. Firth faked his spirit photographs, it shouldn't bother me—but it does. He sinks even lower in my estimation. But my desire to find his killer increases. If my investigation exposes his fraud to the world, I'll have repaid his kindness by destroying his posthumous reputation. The least I can do is deliver his killer to justice.

"Well, this is plenty of proof that he were a crook," Mick says, "but it don't explain what happened in the church."

"I'll search the darkroom. You take the office." As Mick bounds down the stairs, I pray I won't find anything else that blackens Mr. Firth's character.

In the darkroom, I locate metal boxes that contain exposed negative plates. I take out plates and hold them up to the light. They're all portraits, of people seated or standing, alone or in groups, sometimes with corpses in coffins. Postmortem photography is a common practice; I've done it myself. There aren't any spirit images on the plates. Also absent are images of Charles Firth. Some photographers prefer not to be on the other side of the camera. I am one. Photographs of myself, such as in my wedding pictures, make me feel too exposed. Perhaps Charles Firth had his own reasons.

I go downstairs and find Mick in the office, pawing through the drawers in the desk. He says, "Nothin' here but bills and other business stuff. You find somethin'?"

"Yes and no. There aren't any ghost images among Mr. Firth's negatives. So I can't prove he superimposed them on his photographs of live people."

"How would he do that?"

"By putting one plate on top of the other in the enlarger and printing them both on the same sheet of paper. Or by hiding a plate with a ghost image in the camera, then making a double exposure by using it for a photograph of his client. He must have kept his ghost negatives hidden someplace, or destroyed them after he finished using them." That possibility disturbs me because it suggests that Mr. Firth knew full well what he was doing and took pains to cover it up.

"Just because he had a shady side don't mean he wasn't a good guy," Mick says. "He was nice to you. That's important."

I smile, grateful for Mick's attempt to comfort me. But I can't help thinking that people are killed more often because of the bad things they've done than because of the good things, and I suspect that was true of Charles Firth. "Maybe the photographs he sold and published weren't the only examples of his fraud." I broach another troubling idea. "Maybe the photograph he took in the crypt was a fake too."

Surprise lifts Mick's eyebrows. "How could he have faked it? There were only one negative plate in that camera, and we developed it and printed it ourselves. He couldn't've put in the ghost—or whatever it was."

"He could have staged the photograph with an accomplice."

"Oh, you mean an accomplice dressed up like a ghost."

"But it still could be a photograph of his murder." I remember the terror on Charles Firth's face. I don't think it was simulated. His only portrait that I've seen was taken at a moment when he felt himself in extreme peril.

"And the killer's the accomplice. Yeah, that makes more sense than a ghost who thought Firth was stealin' his loot."

"We need to find out if someone went to the church with him that night." I glance at the clock; it's almost noon. "But first we should pay a visit to the Ladies' Society for Rational Thought."

CHAPTER 9

The Aerated Bread Company produces cheap, wholesome bread by pumping gas into the dough instead of using yeast to make it rise. I ate many a loaf during the years I was starting my photography business, living in near poverty. A.B.C. also operates tearooms throughout the kingdom, places where women can dine inexpensively and without a male escort. The branch in busy Oxford Circus evokes memories of trudging around London, taking pictures that I hoped to sell but rarely did. On cold winter nights, exhausted and discouraged, I would gaze hungrily at the fancy cakes in the window, then go inside and order a poached egg on toast and a cup of coffee. The A.B.C. kept me from starving.

If we don't solve this case and we lose our jobs, my friends and I can avail ourselves of cheap meals at the A.B.C.

Now the window contains Halloween fruitcakes with prizes inside. When I enter the tearoom with Mick, the decor is familiar—walls covered with floral paper, the glass lamps on the chandelier shaped like poppies. Waitresses in black frocks and white aprons carry laden trays to customers who are mostly female; the few men seem out of place. Perfume mingles with the odors of coffee and sugary pastries. I call to a waitress, raising my voice above the din of shrill voices and clinking china and silverware.

"Excuse me, where is the meeting of the Ladies' Society for Rational Thought?" I ask.

She points up the stairs. Mick and I ascend them to a darkened private room, where people occupy rows of chairs. We stand at the back of the room. At the front, a black curtain covers the wall behind four women seated at a table covered with a black cloth. A candle burning in the center casts weak, flickering light on their faces.

"If this lot thinks ghosts are fake, then why're they havin' a séance?" Mick whispers.

"Shh!" hisses someone in the audience.

A woman at the table speaks in a sonorous, melodic voice: "Oh, spirits, come to us." Loud rapping sounds interrupt the quiet. The audience gasps. The woman exclaims, "They're here!"

I can't see where the rapping came from or who caused it, and I'm unnerved in spite of myself. Now I hear weird, screechy music, as if from angry cats singing. The audience shifts uneasily. As I search the darkness for the source of the music, the woman—supposedly the medium—groans and sways. The table slowly rises from the floor. Murmurs sweep through the audience. Up and up the table rises; then it suddenly crashes down. Everyone jumps, including Mick and me. I know there's no ghost, but my nerves would be calmer if I knew how the trick was done.

Leaning forward, the medium begins to cough. Her mouth disgorges a pale, filmy material. The audience recoils amid cries of "Ectoplasm!"

As I think of the slime on Charles Firth's clothes, the material floats up out of the medium's mouth, above her head, billowing like an unfurled, translucent flag. Chairs scrape the floor as people stand, the better to see. A dark, hazy face shimmers in the ecto-plasm. A woman blurts, "A ghost!"

The audience grows noisier with fright. Mick and I gape at each other, our skepticism a scant defense against the supernatural onslaught. The music combines with eerie laughter and gibberish. Mick exclaims, "Look—up there!"

A pale, glowing green hand flies about, swooping down on the audience. People scream and duck. When I fling up my arms to protect my face, the hand grazes my wrist with a cold, damp touch. It soars to the front of the room and vanishes. Another green, glowing object rises from behind the people seated at the table.

It's a head—bald as an egg, with dark voids for eyes and mouth. It howls, laughs, and gibbers. A frantic scuffling erupts, and chairs tumble as the shrieking audience rushes toward the stairs, carrying Mick and me along.

"Wait," the medium calls. "There's nothing to be afraid of. Lights, please!"

The window curtains fly open, and daylight floods the room, revealing two women holding the cords. The medium stands and says to the fleeing audience, "Come back, and we'll show you how the séance was done."

She's tall and willowy, her thick auburn hair twisted in a casual knot, her voice warm and husky. Her imperious upper-class manner halts the crowd, which comprises perhaps fifty women, mostly young, who look to be shop clerks in cheap but stylish clothes and factory workers in humbler, rougher garb. They quiet down and nervously resume their seats.

"Ladies, come out," the medium calls.

The curtains behind her part to expose three women dressed in black. One wears a tight cap that's apparently made of rubber and covers her hair. The cap, and her whole face except for her eyes and mouth, are painted pale green. The second holds a violin under her chin and saws at the strings with a bow to produce the screechy music. The third wears a black veil and holds a contraption that resembles a fishing rod. From the end, attached to a string, dangles a green false hand.

"These are our ghosts," the medium says. "Allow me to introduce Emily Hammond, Ruth Lee, and Diana Kelly."

The audience bursts into relieved laughter. The medium says, "The ethereal glow is due to phosphorus paint. For the other tricks, I made the rapping sounds with my feet." She indicates the women at the table. The two on either side of her are holding hands with each other. "At some séances, the medium joins the hands of the clients seated beside her. They think they're holding her hands, but not so." She raises and wiggles her hands, which wear black gloves. "My hands were free to levitate the table, and to stuff this in my mouth and wave it over my head." She holds up the ectoplasm. "It's just a photograph printed on silk gauze. At some séances, they use flour-and-water paste or chewed-up newspaper." Dropping the gauze on the table, she says, "So that's the medium's bag of dirty tricks. Now you know better than to be fooled."

The audience cheers and applauds. Mick and I join in. I'm glad someone is taking the time to educate potential victims of fraud, and it was a good show.

"Please spread the word and invite your friends and relations to our next meeting," the medium says. "And please stay for refreshments."

Women queue up at a table that holds platters of food and urns of tea and coffee. Mick and I join the queue. The medium glides over to us, smiles, and says, "Hello! You're new here, aren't you?" She's pretty despite a face that's too long and a complexion that's all freckles. Her eyes are a rare amber hue, her lips like dark-pink rose petals, and she exudes vitality. "I'm Jean Ritchie, president of the Ladies' Society for Rational Thought."

I'd expected Jean Ritchie to be older, mannish, and unattractive, like some Temperance Society women. I introduce Mick and myself, and when I tell her that we're from the *Daily World*, she says, "Splendid! I've been sending our pamphlets to the newspapers, hoping for some publicity. Is that how you heard about us?"

"No, it was from Richard Trevelyan," I say.

Jean makes a sour face. "That foppish buffoon! Did he tell you that we're evil bitches who are out to crush people's hearts? Did he send you here to twist our knickers and smear mud on us in your newspaper?"

I blink at her language, which is at odds with her accent and gentlewomanly appearance, but I have to smile. Hers isn't a completely inaccurate description of Mr. Trevelyan. "Not exactly." And though she's a murder suspect, I can't help liking her for her outspokenness. "We're investigating the murder of Charles Firth. Have you heard about it?"

"I couldn't not have heard. The story is all over town."

Women gather around to listen while they sip their tea and nibble scones, meat pies, and currant buns. The "ghosts" stand close to Jean. Diana Kelly has taken off her rubber skullcap, and the fair hair pinned atop her head contrasts vividly with the green face paint.

"When we asked if he had any enemies, Mr. Trevelyan mentioned you," I tell Jean.

"Well." Jean sounds amused. "I suppose the shoe fits."

We've reached the refreshment table, and Mick loads up his plate. "So why'd you hate Mr. Firth?"

"Men of his kind prey on vulnerable people, mostly women. They're like leeches who bleed their victims dry." Jean's three accomplices murmur in agreement. "I've made it my business to pour salt on the rich, bloated leeches, so they'll shrivel up and die before they can take advantage of anyone else."

She speaks with such vehemence that I can't believe her business is merely a noble act of charity. "Did they prey on you?"

"Not me personally, but someone very dear to me." Jean takes a deep breath, as if fortifying herself to relive a painful episode. "My mother was the heiress to a railroad fortune. She and my father liked to travel abroad, so I was raised by my nanny. Her name was Hilda. I loved her as if she were my mother. She stayed with me until I was twelve, when my parents sent me to school in France. I saw Hilda only when I came back to England during holidays. After I finished school, when I came back for good, I found her living in a slum in Shoreditch. She was seriously ill. She confessed that my parents had given her a generous sum when she left their employ, but she'd paid it all to a medium who called herself Countess Tatiana. The woman purported to be reincarnated from a Russian noblewoman, and she received messages from Hilda's dead brother. Hogwash!"

Jean fairly spits the last word. "By that time, my parents had died, and I'd inherited their fortune. I moved Hilda into my house and paid doctors to treat her. But it was too late." Jean's amber eyes shine with tears. "Hilda's friends came to her funeral, and I learned that some of them had been cheated too. I realized there must be scores of charlatans and innocent victims. So I established the Society. It was something good I could do with my inheritance."

I respect her for her wish to do good rather than fritter away the money on parties, dresses, and gold-digging men, but her sense of justice is flawed. "It wasn't Charles Firth who cheated your nanny."

"Yeah," Mick says, "so why not go after the real crook?"

"She flew the coop," Jean says regretfully. "If I'd been able to get my hands on her, I'd have made her sorry, believe me. But after I established the Society, I met plenty of Charles Firth's victims. Some are here today." She extends her hand to Emily, Ruth, and Diana. "Tell everyone what Charles Firth did to you."

"He charged me ten pounds for a picture of me with the ghost of my late husband." Diana Kelly has an Irish lilt to her voice and pretty features under the ghoulish face paint. "The ghost looked just like my husband did in the only picture I had of him. I kept the picture in my hope chest. When I looked for it there, it was gone. Mr. ████ must have stolen it. I asked Mr. Firth to give me my money back, but he wouldn't. He said the ghost in his photograph was real and I must have misplaced my husband's picture." Diana scowls; she looks like an angry green goblin. "That was money I needed after I lost my job as a maid at the hotel. Don't ask me what I had to do to feed my children until I found another. And now I haven't any picture of my husband except the fake ghost one. The bastard!"

"Amen." Ruth Lee, dark of hair, complexion, and eyes, holds up her violin and bow. "I play the fiddle round town; that's how I earn my livin'. He saw me playin' in a pub and struck up a conversation. When I told him my mum and dad are dead, he said he could take pictures of their ghosts. I gave him all the money I'd saved up. Well, he couldn't've used Mum and Dad's pictures from when they was alive—there ain't none. The ghosts didn't look like them. He used other folks as models."

I remember the costumes and masks at his studio. I can't imagine why such a kind man turned to such a cruel trade.

Ruth adds, "I had to pawn my fiddle, and I'm not ashamed to say where I got the money to get it back. I picked pockets."

Emily Hammond flings back her black veil, revealing a thin, lined face. She's over forty, her hair salt and pepper, her large gray eyes brimming with pain and fury. "I was once a member of the SPS—the Society for Psychical Studies. I joined because I wanted to contact the spirit of a man I'd been secretly in love with when I was young." She lowers her gaze, and her sallow complexion blushes pink. "His name was Gordon. I was his children's governess. Many years later, I heard that he'd died in a boating accident. Charles Firth's wife, Leonora, befriended me. She contacted him through automatic writing. Such wonderful messages! He said he'd been secretly in love with me too." Emily smiles with joyous nostalgia. "But the messages weren't enough. I wanted to see him. Leonora suggested that I hire her husband to take photographs of me with Gordon's ghost. So I did. And he was just as I'd remembered, only more handsome." She sighs, lifts her eyes skyward, and clasps her heart.

I think she must have described her beloved to Leonora Firth, who passed the information to Mr. Firth, who found a look model for the ghost he inserted into his photographs of Emily.

"But then . . ." Emily flushes with rage. "I found out that Gordon is still alive! It was his *brother* who'd been killed in the accident. He couldn't have sent me messages, and he couldn't be the ghost in the photographs." She sniffles and wipes her eyes.

I remember how overjoyed I was to learn that my father wasn't dead. In a bizarre reversal of my situation, Emily was devastated to learn the same about her beloved. I'm having trouble maintaining my good opinion of Mr. Firth, whose kindness to me doesn't negate his cruelty to these women.

"I told Leonora and Charles that they were despicable frauds," Emily says. "I canceled my membership in the SPS and joined the Ladies' Society for Rational Thought."

"And I'm glad to have you," Jean says. "The more of us there are, the better the chances we have of putting the charlatans out of business for good."

The women gathered around us applaud. The idea of a crusade against Charles Firth troubles me, no matter that his actions justified it. "Well, Mr. Firth is certainly out of business for good," I say. "Do we have you to thank for that?"

The wide-eyed, openmouthed shock on the faces of Jean and her ghosts seems a second too late and quite overacted. Jean says, "If you mean, did we kill him, the very idea is bloody ridiculous!"

"If you're all innocent, then you won't mind tellin' us where you were the night before last," Mick says.

"I was at home with my invalid mother," Emily says.

"I spoke at a women's club in Yorkshire that afternoon," Jean says. "Diana came with me. We stayed for dinner and took the night train back to London."

"I played my fiddle at a party that lasted until about three in the morning," Ruth says. "A bunch of us passed out on the floor and didn't wake up till noon."

Mick and I exchange glances, noting that all these alibis leave room for doubt. The "ghost" in Charles Firth's photograph could be a woman, and who better than one that's adept at pretending to be a ghost?

"We're not gangsters who settle disputes with a knife," Jean says. "We prefer civil methods. I've been helping Ruth, Diana, and Emily bring a lawsuit against Charles Firth. I hired a solicitor to advise them and represent them in court. They were suing for a refund of their money plus compensation for their mental suffering. We thought we had a good chance of winning, and the publicity would have helped our campaign against hoaxers." Jean finishes on a rueful note. "We can't wring money out of a dead man. He was worth more to us alive."

I suppose Jean has a good point, but Mick says, "He didn't take the money with him. I reckon he left it to his wife. You could sue her for it."

Emily, Ruth, and Diana laugh in derision. "We can hardly proceed with the lawsuit now," Jean says. "Imagine the three of them testifying against him and demanding money from his widow after he's been viciously murdered. The court's sympathy would be all for him. They'd be sure to lose, and the bad publicity would undermine our mission."

I think she's cleverly turned the circumstances to her advantage. I also think something is off about this conversation, but Jean speaks again before I have time to figure out what it is. "Charles Firth's murder has only fed the public's belief in the supernatural. At the train station this morning, all the conversation I heard was about sightings of ghosts. Even if we had killed him, we wouldn't have made it look like a ghost did it and faked that photograph that's in the *Daily World*."

Even as I admire her wits, I say, "Making it look like he was murdered by a ghost would have been a good way to cover up that you did it."

"We would rather he were still alive and we could make an example of him," Jean says.

"Besides, how would we have known that he was going to be in the church?" Emily demands.

"There are other people who probably did know," Jean says. "And we're not the only ones at odds with Charles Firth. If you're so keen to know who killed him, you should look at his own coterie—the Society for Psychical Studies. You'll find he had plenty of enemies there."

★　★　★

As we walk through the crowds in Oxford Circus toward the train station, Mick says, "Did you notice that they never said they didn't kill him?"

"I only noticed something was off," I say. "Thank you for putting your finger on it."

"They didn't actually say they didn't know Firth would be in the church, either."

I feel compelled to contradict that, because I like Jean and sympathize with her friends. "I don't see how they could have known. I hardly think he'd have told them his plans." We now have four new suspects, but I don't want any of them to be guilty. They've all suffered from the kind of fraud I despise, and in their own way, they're as committed to justice as I am.

"Yeah, well, if I was innocent, I would say it straight out."

"So would I," I have to admit.

"Maybe they thought they could fool us by doing hocus-pocus with words, like with the green paint and the fake hand. Well, I ain't buyin' it. I think one of 'em done it and the others were in on it."

If I want justice for Charles Firth, I can't refuse to consider the possibility that Mick is right, and I also can't let people who tried to ruin my former patron get away with his murder.

"I'm gonna start checkin' their alibis," Mick says. Before we left the women, we obtained their addresses, the location of the pub where Rose had played the fiddle, and the name of the station where Jean and Diana had arrived on the train from Yorkshire.

"Fine, but we shouldn't ignore other leads," I say. "I think it's worth attending the meeting of the Society for Psychical Studies tomorrow."

CHAPTER 10

While Mick checks alibis, I take the train to Battersea. I want to be with my father as much as possible, to make up for our lost twenty-four years, and if Sally's interview has produced any clues, maybe I won't need to excavate the painful territory of my mother's past.

At the Gladstone Arms, when I knock on the door of his room, Sally answers, to my surprise. "What are you doing here?" I ask.

"Working on my interview with Father. Last night, I had to leave before we could finish." Sally grimaces in annoyance. "You know Mrs. Webb expects me home by ten o'clock."

She lives in a lodging house for young ladies, run by the strict Mrs. Webb. Any lodger who drinks, stays out late, or indulges in other unseemly behavior will find herself locked out and her baggage on the stoop.

When I enter the room, our father stands up from the table and smiles. "Sarah. I'm so happy you came back." Sally beams, glad to have us all together again.

I see a reason to appreciate Mrs. Webb's curfew: I'm afraid of Sally spending too much time with our father. Unlike me, she's convinced of his innocence, and she believes his every word is true. My doubt is like an invisible sliver in my finger, the skin sore because I keep picking at it. He seems the kind, gentle, trustworthy man I remember from my childhood, and I love him, but he contrived to cover up Ellen Casey's murder, and how can we be sure he's not deceiving us? The closer our relationship with him grows, the worse it will be for Sally if it turns out that he's neither honest nor innocent.

"Aren't you supposed to be at the *Daily World*?" I ask her.

"I told the editor I wasn't feeling well and left early."

I look askance at her because she's risking her job.

"It's all right—I've finished my next three ladies' feature stories." She smiles proudly. "The editor says I'm his best writer."

She won't be for long if she plays hooky too often. I fill her in on the latest developments in the murder investigation. Taking notes, she says, "This will make a marvelous story! I'll get another byline. Do you think Sir Gerald will promote me to news reporter?"

"Maybe." What I'm thinking is that now Sally's career hinges on the success of the investigation.

"I didn't think I would see you today," our father says.

"I came to find out how the interview is going," I say.

He gestures toward the table at Sally's notebook, the pages covered with her handwriting. "We've gone over the day Ellen died. But I'm not sure it's of any use."

I wonder if he's told Sally everything.

Sally hands me the notebook. "Read it, Sarah. Maybe you'll spot a clue."

With considerable trepidation, I read. The account of how my father discovered what Lucas and my mother had done contains disturbing details he left out when he told me the facts. It describes the aftermath of the rape—the raw scratches on Lucas's face where Ellen had clawed him while trying to fight him off; the blood oozing from between her legs as she lay dead on the kitchen floor; the expression on my mother's face, horror-stricken yet satisfied.

It's hard to say which disturbs me more—these details, or what isn't in Sally's transcript.

During my previous inquiries, I discovered that my father had photographed Ellen undressed, in seductive poses. He doesn't know that I know. I can't believe he's forgotten, and I think he deliberately neglected to tell Sally. Our relationship with him is seeming all the riskier. I skim the section that describes the bargain he offered my mother, the objections from her and Lucas, and their eventual assent. It hurts so much to see in writing that she was willing to deprive me of my father in order to protect herself and Lucas. I'm still fervently thankful that I found my father, and I should give him the benefit of the doubt . . . for now. The transcript ends at the point where my father and Lucas carried Ellen's body to the cellar and hid it in a trunk. The last sentence catches my attention.

I look up, preparing to tell Sally and my father, seated across the table from me. The room is dim, and my father's dark jacket recedes into the shadows. With his pale face and white hair and whiskers, he looks like a ghostly, disembodied head hovering beside Sally, the effect startlingly similar to Charles Firth's spirit photographs. Indeed, my father has haunted me as if he *were* a ghost. His absence has shaped my life. He's the reason I stopped going to church: the parishioners shunned my mother and me because, I recently discovered, they thought he'd killed Ellen and we were guilty by association. He's also the reason I've made few friends and I took so long to commit to marrying Barrett: I have an ingrained distrust of other people, and I've always feared that any man I love will abandon me. I hope my distrust of my father is based only on old history and old habits.

I read aloud the last sentence of the transcript, in which my father is quoted as saying, "I told Lucas to come back at midnight and help me dispose of Ellen's body. He went home to his lodgings at Forty-Nine Great Sutton Street, near the Cannon Brewery where he worked." I say, "I didn't know Lucas's address until I read this."

I met Lucas only once, soon before my father disappeared. At the time I knew nothing about him. He was in our house one moment, fondling me on his lap, and gone the next, after my father ordered him to get out. Not until recently did Sally and I learn that Lucas was the one thing our father's two disappearances had in common.

"We could go to the house and see if anyone there remembers Lucas," I say.

"Yes, let's!" Sally makes a visible effort to tamp down her excitement, not wanting to get her hopes up too much. "Of course, it's been a long time. Everybody who knew Lucas could be gone now."

"The house may not even be there anymore." Our father sounds defeated by years of believing that he'll always be wanted for Ellen's murder, a fugitive his whole life.

"This clue is all we have right now." I don't tell them the other reason I'm eager to investigate and find evidence that will help us pin Ellen's murder on Lucas. I'm hesitant to incriminate my mother in order to exonerate my father if there's any chance she's not guilty. My mother, in spite of every wrong she's done, shouldn't be blamed, even posthumously, for a murder she didn't commit. That would an injustice to both her and Ellen Casey, and injustice is a sharp-edged stone, hard to swallow.

★　★　★

Sally and I emerge from the underground train station in Clerkenwell, where my family lived before my father disappeared. In the paved expanse known as the Green, in the center of the district, people materializing out of the gray murk bear a jarring resemblance to those I remember from my childhood—the blacksmith, the magistrate, the seamstress. I almost expect to see my mother, my father, and red-haired Ellen Casey come walking toward me, looking the same as they did in 1866. Leonora Firth isn't the only one trying to communicate with the dead. Sally and I are on the trail of a ghost, Lucas Zehnpfennig, hoping he'll lead us to the evidence we need.

Great Sutton Street is near the Smithfield meat market. Fog conceals the vast building where butchers sell beef, pork, lamb, and poultry, but the air reeks of blood and decay. In the gutters, fetid water runs amid feathers and bone shards. Great Sutton contains rows of old, narrow, terraced stone houses that front directly on the cobblestone lane, similar to the place where I grew up. Old women sit on crates outside their doorways, watching toddlers play. A younger woman chases after a little boy riding a hobbyhorse.

Sally points to the house labeled 49. "It's still here!" She runs up to the door and knocks. I follow slowly, not ready to face whatever is on the other side. A woman answers. An old-fashioned lace cap covers her gray hair, and her brown wool frock fits awkwardly over her dowager's hump. Before Sally can introduce us and explain why we're here, the woman gapes at me, clutching her throat.

"*Mary Bain*?" She looks as if she's seen a ghost.

My mother was Mary Bain. I resemble her, and this stranger apparently knew her. The woman looks at Sally, who resembles me, and her sagging jowls drop at the sight of two ghosts. I hurry to say, "I'm not Mary; I'm her daughter, Sarah. This is my sister, Sally."

"What is your name?" Sally says.

"Emma Kirby. Mrs." The woman speaks in a breathless rush, as though we've punched the words out of her. She starts to close the door.

I hold it open. "A man named Lucas Zehnpfennig used to live here. Did you know him?"

She casts a wild glance beyond me toward the street, pushes harder on the door, and cries, "Begone!" as if we're evil spirits come early for Halloween.

"If you don't want us to come in, we can talk out here," Sally says loudly, for the benefit of eavesdropping neighbors. "What can you tell us about Lucas?"

Mrs. Kirby reluctantly stands aside so that we can enter the house. The parlor gives me the nightmarish sensation that I've walked into my childhood home. It has the same entrenched odor of cooked cabbage, onions, and roasted meat, the same narrow, cramped dimensions, with only one possible configuration for the furniture. I can imagine myself ten years old again, my mother in the kitchen and my father downstairs in his darkroom. Mrs. Kirby sinks into the armchair; Sally and I perch on the divan. Although the floral patterns of the upholstery and wallpaper aren't the same as in my family's parlor, they're of the same vintage, with worn places on the cushions and peeled-off areas on the walls.

"How did you meet Lucas?" I say, forcing myself back to the present.

Mrs. Kirby talks over me in a loud, angry voice. "Don't speak that name here." In a quieter tone, she says, "After my husband died, I rented out the attic. *He* was my lodger."

Foreboding makes me hesitate before I ask, "What did he do that was so bad?"

"I shouldn't have taken him in. I'd never had a man lodger before." Mrs. Kirby's manner turns fretful. "But he was clean, with nice manners. And I thought she was too young for that sort of trouble."

"Who was too young?" Sally says.

"My daughter Annie. She was twelve."

Sally and I look at each other in dismay. From our previous inquiries, we know that Lucas violated at least two girls besides Ellen Casey, and it sounds as if Annie was another victim.

"I didn't think *he* was that sort," Mrs. Kirby says. "After all, he had a lady friend who was a lot older than him."

I'm surprised, because I've never heard that Lucas had a relationship with a mature woman. "Who was she?"

"Why, it was Mary Bain." Mrs. Kirby pauses to stare at me, as if newly disconcerted by my resemblance to my mother. Contempt twists her features. "And her a married woman."

"But they couldn't have been—"

"Oh, they were, mark my word. If you'd seen her hanging around here, kissing his cheeks and stroking his hair and putting her arms around him when she thought nobody was looking, it would've been obvious to you too."

It's clear that Mrs. Kirby doesn't know Mary and Lucas were mother and son. My mother would have kept the nature of their relationship a secret; she wouldn't have wanted people to know she'd had an illegitimate child. A revolting thought makes my skin crawl. Did she love Lucas so much that, when he grew up, she developed romantic feelings for him? I suddenly remember that often, when I came home from school, she wasn't there. She must have been with Lucas. Were they indeed lovers?

I glance at Sally, whose puzzled expression says she doesn't know what to make of Mrs. Kirby's story. She's not inclined to think the dirty, ugly worst of people.

Mrs. Kirby says, "He sure had me fooled. He must have had Mary fooled too. How could any woman stand to be with him, knowing what he was?"

My previous inquiries confirmed that my mother had known, long before he raped Ellen Casey. Were her own desires so perverted that she didn't mind his? I burn with more anger and hatred toward her than ever.

"Can we speak with your daughter?" Sally says. "Does she live here?"

Tears run down the creases in Mrs. Kirby's cheeks. "Annie's been gone these twenty-four years."

As we murmur our condolences, I regret compelling Mrs. Kirby to talk about such painful matters.

The woman's eyes spark with anger. "After he left, I found out that Annie was with child. She broke down and said he'd sneaked into her room at night."

I envision the layout of the house, the same as that of my family's, and Lucas creeping down the attic stairs to the tiny second-floor bedroom that belonged to Annie while her mother was asleep across the hall.

"She died having the baby," Mrs. Kirby says, her voice ragged and bitter.

My stomach sickens with horror at the news of another sin Lucas committed, another that led to a death. Sally squeezes my arm, and I see eager anticipation in her eyes. Here we have a witness who knows that Lucas did to her daughter what we know he did to Ellen Casey, who can help us pin the blame for Ellen's rape and murder on him. Maybe the journey to exonerating our father is near its end.

"Do you remember the murder of a girl named Ellen Casey in 1866?" I say.

Mrs. Kirby works her mouth. "How could I forget? When she went missing, the coppers were all over looking for her. Then she was found lying on the dirt at the roadworks on Gough Street.

Everybody said that photographer interfered with her and killed her. Benjamin Bain." She peers at me, as if trying to fit together the pieces of an old puzzle. "Mary's husband. Your father?"

"Yes," I say, "but he didn't kill Ellen. Lucas did."

"Shush—don't say that name!" Suddenly belligerent, Mrs. Kirby says, "It was a long time ago. Why're you raking up the past?"

"We want to clear our father's name," Sally says.

"You think *he* did it, don't you?" I say.

Mrs. Kirby's tongue probes a broken, rotted tooth.

"You know what he did to your daughter," I say. "You think he did the same thing to Ellen and then killed her to keep her from telling." I shamelessly lay my mother's crime at Lucas's door.

"The coppers think it was Benjamin Bain. It's not my place to think any different."

I'm about to lose my temper, but then Sally jumps up and looms over Mrs. Kirby. Her gentle face flushed, her normally mild eyes ablaze, she says, "You kept quiet, and Lucas Zehnpfennig got away with murder. It's time for you to tell the truth!"

Mrs. Kirby shrinks from Sally's anger, from the sound of the hated name. She bows her head, surrendering to our pressure and her own need to tell. She whispers, "I don't just think he did it. I know."

My thankfulness for a wish granted is so strong that I would fall to my knees if I weren't sitting down. Sally, openmouthed with excitement, lowers herself into her seat beside me.

"It was the day he moved out," Mrs. Kirby says. "He was upstairs packing his things. Mary was with him. I heard them arguing."

That must have been shortly after my father convinced Lucas to leave England with him and go to America.

"Mary begged him not to go. He said that was the deal, and if he didn't, her husband would tell the police what they'd done to Ellen. Mary was crying and wailing. He tried to calm her down."

"What else did they say?" I ask anxiously.

"She said they should run away together. But he said they couldn't, because that would be like telling the world they'd done it, and if they were caught, they would get the rope."

Although I already know that my mother didn't love me as much as she loved Lucas, and although I previously learned that she had planned to go to him in America as soon as I was grown, it crushes me to hear that she would have left me when I was only ten. "Did they say anything more about Ellen?" I ask.

"Not that I know of. I stopped listening because I heard them kissing." Mrs. Kirby grimaces in disgust. "I was glad to get that man out of the house."

Sally looks aghast; she now understands that the relationship between my mother and Lucas was likely incestuous. "They were terrible people! They deserved to be hanged. Our father doesn't." She beckons to Mrs. Kirby. "Come with us and tell the police."

"No!" Mrs. Kirby flings up her hands as if warding off the horsemen of the apocalypse.

My wish to exonerate my father undermines my sympathy for this woman who's suffered as much from Lucas's deeds as Sally and I have. "Why not?"

Mrs. Kirby shuffles to the window and points outside. "Look." Joining her, Sally and I see the young mother and little boy playing and laughing. "That's my granddaughter." Affection tinged with pain softens Mrs. Kirby's voice. "Her name's Martha. She looks just like her mum. She's married to the postman—such a nice young fellow. That's Henry, their son."

Sally and I gape. The mother and son are Lucas's descendants! My search for our father and the truth about Ellen Casey's murder has already turned up Sally and Lucas, two relatives I didn't know I had. Now, here are two more—my niece and grandnephew.

"I raised Martha," Mrs. Kirby says. "When she was little and asked me where her father was, I told her his name and said he'd died, just like her mother. I couldn't tell her what really happened, could I?" She turns to Sally and me, shame and distress branded on her face. "If I talk to the police, everything will come out. What'll that do to her and the boy? Please, have a heart and go away. Please don't tell anybody what I've told you, and please don't come back."

CHAPTER 11

After being trapped in an underground train that stalled in the tunnel for more than an hour, I arrive in Whitechapel at five o'clock. Through the window of the Angel public house, I see a whirling flame. A game of apple and candle is in progress. A stick suspended from the ceiling spins horizontally with a lit candle at one end and an apple at the other. Men are laughing as they jump and snatch at the apple with their teeth. I look away, hoping there won't be many burned faces before the Halloween season ends.

At home, I find Barrett at the kitchen table, drinking tea while Fitzmorris cooks supper. Barrett smiles and says, "I dropped by to see my wife."

"I'm glad to see my husband." Indeed, my spirits rise like the bubbles in the champagne we drank at our wedding breakfast.

Fitzmorris stirs diced leftover roast beef with onions and chopped potatoes in a hot frying pan. "Mick went to spend the night outside St. Peter's Church, watching for ghosts. As for Hugh—" Fitzmorris points at the ceiling to indicate that Hugh is upstairs, sleeping off another overindulgence in liquor.

My family is all accounted for, if not all well. My tense nerves relax. I wash my hands and put on my apron, and while I slice bread, I tell Barrett the results of today's inquiries. After I describe the meeting of the Ladies' Society for Rational Thought, he says, "Diana Kelly? Hmm, that name rings a bell, but I can't place it. Maybe it'll come to me later. At any rate, I'm glad you managed to dig up some suspects. I haven't gotten around to it. The case isn't a high priority at the station."

"Oh? Why not?"

"A member of the Clerkenwell Boys gang was found beaten to death early this morning. Word on the street says the Somers Town Boys did it. There'll be an all-out war unless we catch the killer and quiet things down. Whereas Charles Firth's murder seems like an isolated incident, not a threat to the public."

"The idea that a murderous ghost is at large could cause mass panic."

"Maybe. We're already getting tips about ghost sightings in and around St. Peter's. Folks are saying the murder is the first in a series and calling the killer 'The Ghost.' "

My fear is becoming reality. Barrett says, "But we aren't forming a special squadron or putting extra patrols in the East End the way we did for the Ripper. Inspector Reid is waiting to see how this case develops before he decides whether to make it a big issue."

"Is Reid still overloading you with cases in the hope that you'll quit or die of exhaustion?"

"No. His superiors have been watching him pretty closely since the hangman murder investigation." Last January, Reid's mishandling of that investigation got him in hot water. "They noticed that he'd been giving me extra assignments while other fellows were twiddling their thumbs. They put an end to that." Barrett laughs without humor. "I'm sure he's got something else in store for me."

"Such as what?" I remember the scene that ex-constable Porter caused at our wedding breakfast. Reid is smarter, with more resources on tap, and therefore more dangerous.

"No idea, but I've got eyes and ears on him. I'll find out." Barrett has many friends on the police force. "In the meantime, it'll help if you check the suspects' alibis."

"Mick has already started. And we may find more suspects soon." As we eat the beef hash with bread, cheese, and stewed fruit, I tell Barrett about tomorrow's meeting of the Society for

Psychical Studies. Then I describe my visit to Lucas Zehnpfennig's former landlady.

"Good progress on both fronts," Barrett says. "What are you going to do?"

"Mrs. Kirby's story is evidence that my mother and Lucas killed Ellen Casey, but I can't let you report it. It would ruin her granddaughter and great-grandson's lives."

The mere assumption of my father's guilt made outcasts of my mother and me. The same could happen to Lucas's descendants if their neighbors hear that Lucas was guilty of the murder.

"Your father's life is at stake," Barrett reminds me.

"Yes, but Mrs. Kirby didn't actually hear Lucas and my mother confess."

"Well, I suppose Inspector Reid would say there's not enough evidence to drop the charge against your father."

"I'll have to find another way to exonerate him." I'm sorry that pinning the crime on Lucas wouldn't be as harmless as I anticipated.

"When the truth comes out, the publicity could still ruin those people's lives."

"Maybe the whole truth won't have to come out. I won't need to reveal that Lucas violated Ellen if I can show evidence that my mother killed her." Fate has circled me around to the task I've dreaded—investigating my mother's past and proving she's a murderess. She was, in spite of everything, my mother, and while I hate her now, I loved her when I was a child.

When dinner is over, Barrett says, "I should go." He's been careful not to wear out his welcome with the other members of my household. We look longingly at each other.

"If you don't mind my making a suggestion," Fitzmorris says, "you could spend the night here."

Barrett looks surprised, then says, "I guess I could, if you don't mind. Now that we're married, it wouldn't be improper."

My body stirs with anticipation at the thought of our making love tonight. My cheeks warm because we'll be under the same roof as my friends and they'll know.

"Oh, we don't mind," Fitzmorris says. "We've talked about how nice it would be if you moved in with us. 'One big, happy family,' as Hugh said."

If I can overcome my embarrassment, Barrett living here would be the perfect solution until we find a flat.

The doorbell's tinkling interrupts us. "I wonder who that is," I say. I know it can't be a summons to a crime scene, as Sir Gerald has temporarily relieved us of those duties.

"I'll get it." Barrett goes downstairs and returns with his mother.

I'm astonished; Mrs. Barrett has never darkened my door. She's dressed up in her fur-collared best coat and her hat with the peacock feather. Her face wears the nervy expression of a soldier scouting enemy territory. Barrett looks dumb struck.

Fitzmorris breaks the uncomfortable silence. "Mrs. Barrett, how do you do? I'm Fitzmorris—Lord Hugh's valet. We met at the wedding."

He offers her his hand to shake. She looks at it as though it's contaminated; he's one of the "males" with whom she doesn't think her daughter-in-law should reside. She bows to him, says, "How nice to see you again," and flashes a bright, artificial smile at me. "Hello, Sarah dear. So this is your home." She looks around with avid curiosity.

She must have expected gaudy decor such as one imagines in a house of ill repute, because when she sees how ordinary my surroundings are, her face falls. The meal I just ate sits like lead in my stomach as I brace myself for another spat.

"May I take your coat?" I say.

"That's not necessary. I won't be staying long." Though still smiling, Mrs. Barrett speaks in a tight voice, as if she's trying not to breathe my bad air.

Barrett recovers his voice. "Please sit down, Mother."

"Thank you." She perches on the edge of a chair, and when I offer her food and drink, she says, "I've already eaten."

Fitzmorris says, "It was nice to see you again, Mrs. Barrett." Then he excuses himself and goes upstairs.

Barrett and I seat ourselves, sharing an uneasy glance.

"Sarah, I can tell you're wondering why in the world I'm here," Mrs. Barrett says. "Thomas, I'm glad you're here too, so I can tell both of you at once: I have the perfect solution to the problem of where you're going to live." She pauses, smiling, like a magician about to pull a flower out of his sleeve.

"You've found a flat for us?" Barrett sounds hopeful but cautious.

Mrs. Barrett laughs as if he's said something silly. "No, no. You can move in with your father and me."

I choke down a gulp.

"Uh, I don't think that would work," Barrett says.

Mrs. Barrett flicks a sharp glance at me, but she keeps smiling. "Why not? I'll fix up your old bedroom, and you and Sarah can live there, as cozy as two bugs in a rug."

"Bugs in a rug," Barrett echoes, clearly as appalled as I am.

I scramble for a reason that's more pleasant than the truth, which is that I couldn't endure her scrutiny, her disapproval, and her carping on a daily basis. I can't tell her we wouldn't have enough privacy for lovemaking; the very thought makes me blush.

"It's nice of you to offer, but you would be too crowded with us there," I say.

"Nonsense." Her voice is merry, brittle. "We would be one big, happy family."

I shudder at her use of the phrase. "I'm sure we'll find our own flat soon."

"We won't charge you rent. You can save your money."

"That wouldn't be fair to you and Dad," Barrett says.

I can see him weakening; he loves his parents and has difficulty saying no to his mother. "My job entails getting called to photograph crime scenes," I say. I haven't discussed practicalities with the *Daily World* crime editor, but I suppose that after I leave this house, I'll get the calls and fetch Mick and Hugh. That's another reason I want a flat close to them, aside from wishing to have their companionship, look after them, and keep them out of trouble.

"You wouldn't want strangers knocking on your door at all hours of the day or night."

Mrs. Barrett narrows her eyes. "I'm glad you mentioned your job. We need to talk about that."

My back goes up, and I put my foot down. "I'm not quitting."

Barrett's eyes widen in alarm at my open defiance. I feel sorry for him, caught in the middle of my conflict with his mother.

"Sarah, I understand your problem," Mrs. Barrett says in a gentle, condescending tone. "Thomas tells me that you lost your father when you were very young, and your mother had to go to work. She couldn't teach you about marriage and a woman's proper place. Of course you grew up with the wrong ideas."

I turn on Barrett. "*You told her that?*"

Even while he cringes from my accusing tone, he says, "Well, not exactly. But she's my mother. She wanted to know about the woman I was going to marry."

I feel as if he's stripped off my clothes in front of her. "You don't know anything about me," I snap at Mrs. Barrett. "You're the one with the wrong ideas." But I'm shaken to think that maybe she's not so wrong. Indeed, my childhood has affected my view of marriage.

"Sarah." Her smile hardens with her effort to control her own temper. "I can help you. When you move into my house, I'll teach you how to cook and clean, and look after your husband, and everything else you need to learn to be a good wife."

My mother shaped her life and mine around protecting Lucas. Now Mrs. Barrett is attempting to mold me into her notion of the perfect daughter-in-law. Anger launches me up from my seat. "I'm not moving into your house. Leave me alone!"

Barrett and his mother rise too. His expression is sheer panic, hers dark with fury.

Hugh ambles into the room, rubbing his eyes and yawning. He's unshaven and barefoot, clad only in loose pajama bottoms that hang low on his hips. "I say, did I miss dinner?"

Mrs. Barrett sucks in a loud gasp, horrified to see the famous sodomite in the half-naked flesh.

"Oh, it's Mrs. Barrett." Hugh smiles and hitches up his pants. "Good evening."

Clutching the back of her chair as though she's about to faint, she turns to me. "Does he always walk around *unclothed*?"

"Not always." I'm too furious to be polite.

"Are you and he . . . *intimate*?"

Barrett cringes as though he wishes a hole would open up in the floor and swallow him. Before I can retort, Hugh speaks in his frostiest, most aristocratic manner, his defense against this uninvited guest who beholds him with such revulsion in his own home. "My dear lady, there has never been anything improper between Sarah and me. We once went swimming together in a sewer, but we were both fully dressed."

That happened during one of our investigations; we almost drowned. So did Barrett. He evidently hasn't told his mother, who says, "Now you're mocking me," and glares through tears at Hugh and me. "You're both terrible, disgusting, cruel monsters!"

Hugh looks down his nose at her. "And you, Madam, have no right to insult us under our own roof. You have the manners of a fishwife."

Mrs. Barrett breaks down sobbing with rage and humiliation. Barrett says, "Come on Mother, I'll take you home."

As he leads her away, she calls over her shoulder to me, "I wish he'd married Jane instead of you!"

My knees give out, and I crumple into my chair. Hugh sits beside me. "God, I'm sorry, Sarah. I shouldn't have said that."

I'm wondering who Jane is, and my anger at Mrs. Barrett spills over onto Hugh. "No, you shouldn't have. Things were bad enough, and you made them worse."

"I said I was sorry." Hugh's contrition has a sharp edge. "Can you forgive me?"

"I suppose so. I've had to forgive you for so many things recently; what's one more?"

"Well, if you want to be that way, then I rescind my apology," Hugh snaps.

We're taking out our emotions on each other. I don't want to strain our relationship, but his behavior is hurting him more than anyone else. "Forget Tristan Mariner. Pull yourself together, or you're going to lose your friends as well as your job."

Hugh stares at me, shocked that I would address him in a manner so devoid of compassion. There's a brokenness in his gaze, like a shattered window through which I can see the deep, black despair in his soul. Then he carefully pushes back his chair, stands, and says with cold dignity, "Thank you for your advice, Sarah. If Barrett leaves you—and God knows, his mother is probably urging him to give you the gate right now—I'll repeat it back to you." Then he trudges upstairs.

Ashamed because I've hurt my best friend, I call, "Hugh, I'm sorry."

It's too late; he doesn't respond. I cover my face with my hands for a moment; then I wash the dishes. When I'm finished, Barrett hasn't returned, so I go up to my room and prepare for bed. An hour later, at nine o'clock, still no Barrett. I pace the floor in my dressing gown. Then comes his knocking on the front door— three raps, a pause, then two more. My heart leaps. I hear Fitzmorris go down to let him in. When he comes up, he hesitates at my threshold.

"Sarah." He looks tired, his expression filled with chagrin. He's carrying a valise, which must mean he's spending the night as we planned. "Can I come in?"

I sigh with relief; his mother hasn't convinced him to give me the gate. "Of course." But when he steps into my room, I have to say, "I don't appreciate your telling your mother about my personal family business."

"I didn't know you would mind so much. I'm sorry. I won't do it again."

He looks so ashamed and regretful that I nod, letting him off the hook. But the next words out of my mouth are, "Who is Jane?"

"Um." Barrett holds his valise in front of him like a shield. "Jane Lambert. She's a girl I used to see."

"*See*? What does that mean?" I realize he must have known other women before we met, but he's never mentioned any.

"We were, well, unofficially engaged. I've known Jane since we were children. Our families are old friends. It was sort of understood that someday we'd marry."

Even if the engagement wasn't official, theirs was a long, apparently serious relationship. A needle of jealousy stabs me, and I cross my arms over my chest.

"But I never proposed to Jane," Barrett says. "And I broke things off a long time ago."

"Exactly how long ago?"

He pauses. "In March of last year."

"You were still seeing her while you were courting me!"

"Not after things got serious between you and me," Barrett hurries to say. "Then I told Jane about you, and it was over."

How wrong I was to think that Barrett had no secrets from me. More wounded and jealous than ever, I say, "When you and I . . . Did you and she . . . ?"

He drops his gaze, a clear admission that he had carnal relations with her and didn't stop after he started having them with me. I never asked him if there was anyone else, and neither of us promised to be faithful until we exchanged our marriage vows, but it's agonizing to learn that while I never had any other lover, he had Jane. Maybe he was with her on the very same days he was with me!

"Was she at the wedding?" I demand.

"Our families are old friends; I told you."

I try to recall meeting her, but the faces of his guests are a blur. This woman who'd experienced intimate pleasures with my husband watched me marry him! Perhaps she scorned me because I was innocently oblivious to their past.

"When was the last time you saw her, other than at the wedding?"

He still won't look at me. "A few days ago."

"A few days ago?" I shout.

He sighs. "I went to my parents' house. She lives down the street with her parents. She happened to be outside when I passed by."

"That's a likely story." I'm afraid to ask what else happened. "Is she still unwed?"

"Yes, but what does it matter?" Now Barrett sounds exasperated; he meets my eyes. "I'm not interested in her. She's not interested in me."

I've never been in this situation before, and I'm at a loss for how to handle it. All I can do is follow a script that seems bred in the blood, created by a feminine possessiveness I didn't know I had in me. "Are you going to see her again?"

"Not if I can help it." Barrett sets down his valise and puts his arms around me. "I'm sorry I didn't tell you about Jane. I should have."

"What else aren't you telling me?"

"Nothing!"

I stand rigidly silent in his embrace, awash in hurt and confusion.

"Sarah, you're the one I married." His tone is urgent, passionate. "I love you, and only you."

I want to believe him, but my old, ingrained habit of distrust grips me. My father and my mother both hid devastating secrets from me. What others might my husband have besides his former fiancée?

"Am I still spending the night?" he asks cautiously.

No, I never want to see you again; you can go back to Jane.

Please don't leave me!

The opposite impulses steady me, as does the realization that we're married until death do us part. "Of course," I say.

But we're uneasy with each other, and in bed I lie facing away from him as he undresses and washes. He climbs under the covers, and now I'm hot with lust for him. It's high time for our delayed wedding night, but an internal battle between desire and anger inhibits me. I want to make passionate love to him and show him that he's better off with me than Jane. I want to punish him for the fact that he ever knew a woman before he met me.

I lie motionless, nursing my ill will.

CHAPTER 12

I wake to the sound of church bells. It's Sunday, barely light outside. When I turn over in bed, I bump into a heavy, inert form.
I've forgotten that Barrett spent the night. The memory of our
quarrel slaps me wide awake, and the anxious tone of Fitzmorris's
and Mick's voices downstairs tells me something's wrong. I climb
over Barrett, who stirs groggily to life, put on my dressing gown
and slippers, and run down to the second floor.

Mick and Fitzmorris, clad in their nightclothes, stand at the
open door of Hugh's room. "He's gone," Mick says.

"He must have sneaked out while we were asleep," Fitzmorris
says.

Looking into his room, all I see is the evidence of his troubled
state of mind. His expensive clothes are strewn on the bed, chair,
and floor. Empty glasses and bottles litter the table, and the air
smells of stale liquor and perspiration.

"I should've stayed home with him last night instead of lookin'
for ghosts at the church," Mick says. "By the way, I didn't see
none."

"I was here, and I didn't hear him leave." Fitzmorris sounds
angry at himself.

"No, it's my fault," I say. "We quarreled last night. That's why
he left."

Barrett comes downstairs, fully dressed, smoothing his rumpled hair. When I tell him that Hugh is gone, he says, "Hugh's a
grown man. What he does is his own responsibility."

Knowing that Barrett is right doesn't make us feel any better. Breakfast is a quiet, gloomy meal. When Barrett finishes eating, he says to me, "I'd better get over to the station. I'll see you tonight," and he leaves.

I try to put Jane and his mother out of my mind. "The meeting of the Society for Psychical Studies is at noon," I say to Mick. "I've things to do first, so I'll meet you there."

★   ★   ★

After my father disappeared, my mother and I lived in six different lodging houses from the time we left Clerkenwell in 1866 until her death nine years later. They're scattered around London, near the factories where she worked. She moved from one job to the next whenever we relocated.

Our first lodging, in Tottenham, is only about seven miles north of Clerkenwell, but when she took me there, it felt like the end of the earth. Now, alighting from the train at Seven Sisters Road station, I remember waiting on the platform with our few possessions while she hired a cab. The landscape looks much the same as then. In the distance, above the terraced houses, the funnel-shaped chimneys at the tile kilns belch smoke into the foggy air. I remember wishing I could wave a magic wand and send us home to our old, normal life with my father. That same loneliness steals like a cold, desolate sickness into my heart as I walk along the high street. The fog coalesces into raindrops, and I'm glad to open my umbrella to block my view of the shops we once frequented. Reluctance slows my steps down Eastbourne Road. My body stiffens, as though the sight of the house where we occupied a cramped, sparely furnished room will be a physical blow.

The house has been torn down, the whole terrace replaced by a five-story tenement building. My relief is so great that I'm not disappointed when I go inside, knock on doors, and discover that the residents who answer never knew my mother. I head toward the button factory where we both worked before she sent me away to boarding school. This was the route we walked Monday through Saturday, before dawn and after dusk. On a road that backs onto the yard outside the tile kilns, the factory still stands. I halt by the wall that fronts the two-story building. Time has eroded the bricks, stained them with soot. It's closed for the Sabbath, but I imagine the steam from the roaring boilers, the loud buzz of sanders, and the punch-punch of the stamping machines. I picture my child-hood self at a table with twenty other girls, sorting, inspecting, and packaging buttons, breathing the dust from ground animal bones, hooves, and horns. I rub my fingertips together, remembering the cuts from sharp edges on defective buttons. That job strengthened my determination to become a photographer and never do menial, mind-numbing work again.

There's no one to ask for information about my mother, but I'm suddenly struck by the memory, forgotten until now, of why we left the factory.

When I first began working there, the other girls tried to befriend me, but my mother had warned me not to talk to them. They thought my silence rude, and they started bullying me. They mixed up my buttons, called me bad names, pestered me with questions about myself, and blocked my way to the privy so that I wet myself. Then one day my mother stormed up to the table, shoved the ringleader's face into a tray of buttons, and held her down while she screamed. The foreman pulled my mother away, then fired us both. I was happy to leave, and it was one of the rare occasions where my mother had done something nice for me— she usually endured troubles with a stiff upper lip and expected me to follow suit. But now I realize that her assault on the bully wasn't in my defense. She did it to make the girls leave me alone so that I wouldn't be forced to give up information about my family and they wouldn't discover our connection to Benjamin Bain, the fugitive rapist and murderer.

An hour later, on the train, I gaze out the window at the view of London's western suburbs while I think over what happened at the factory. I myself am the witness I've been seeking—the per-son who knew my mother, who observed her tendency toward violence. I picture her holding down Ellen Casey while Lucas watches. But my memory won't hold water with the police. I'm the daughter of Benjamin Bain, and who could blame them for thinking I've invented a memory to support my claim that he's innocent?

That I came away empty-handed isn't the only thing that troubles me about my experience in Tottenham. A vague notion pokes at me, as if from someone stealing up to me on a dark street and nudging my ribs with his elbow, and I can't see who he is or understand why he wants my attention.

After exiting the train at Richmond, I cross the vast park in which the Kew Observatory is located. I've never been here before, and I feel as much a stranger in alien territory now as I did every time my mother and I moved. The park seems deserted, as if everyone in the world has vanished. Mist obscures the tops of trees from which most of the leaves have fallen, sodden grass drenches my shoes, and the breeze from the river chills me. The observatory comes into view, a grand structure built in the Italianate style of the previous century. With its white stucco walls and white balustrades that surround the domed cupola on the flat roof, it resembles a wedding cake. Lights shine through the mullioned windows. I climb the steps to the main floor, and when I enter, I find myself in a cold, drafty, octagonal room. Grecian columns support an upper gallery, and a crystal chandelier hangs over the people sitting in rows of chairs that face a man behind a podium. As I walk toward the assembly, my shoes clatter on the marble floor, and people turn to see the noisy, unwelcome arrival.

"Hey. Sarah!" Mick whispers, beckoning me from a middle row.

My relief is all out of proportion to the occasion. He's a friend among strangers, my family, and a reminder that I'm not alone anymore. I gratefully slip into the empty seat beside Mick. He's brought photography equipment—the small, lightweight camera, tripod, and case of supplies—and placed it on the chair on his other side. I look around. On the walls, glass-fronted cases contain shelves of books and scientific instruments—antique clocks, telescopes, thermometers, sextants, and others I can't identify. The people are conservatively well-dressed ladies and gentlemen, not a magician or fortune-teller visible among them. Everything seems illuminated by the broad daylight of reason.

The man at the podium speaks in a resonant, upper-class voice. "Welcome to the meeting of the Society for Psychical Studies. I'm Dr. Everard Lodge, president. I'm a professor at University College and a research physicist here at the observatory." Tall and spare, in his fifties, he has short gray hair and the bony, ascetic features of medieval statues of saints. He wears a physician's white coat over his white shirt and dark tie. "On today's agenda is our field expedition scheduled for Tuesday, October twenty-eighth. Anjali, would you please distribute the programs?"

A small, slim girl moves along the rows, handing out brochures. She's about fourteen years old, dressed in a severe dark-blue frock with a white collar and cuffs, like a governess. Her piquant face is the color of coffee with a little cream, and she looks Indian. Her manner is demure, her gaze modestly downcast, her shiny black hair neat in a long braid that hangs down her back. When she reaches our row, she smiles at Mick and me. Her white teeth flash; her black, lustrous eyes gleam with lively curiosity before she lowers them and moves on. Mick cranes his neck to watch her. I look at the brochure; it's titled "Spirit Detection Expedition, Clerkenwell House of Detention."

I remember that jail from my childhood. My teachers used it to threaten the class into obedience, saying that if we misbehaved, we would end up there.

"The jail was demolished recently," Dr. Lodge says, "but its underground structure is still intact. I encourage all of you to attend our expedition. Many spirits have been sighted at the jail. This is our chance to document their presence, and I'm happy to announce that my new magnetometer is ready for a field test."

Amid a smattering of applause, men wheel in two carts. On one, wires coil around a pack of large glass disks arranged side by side on their edges and attached to brass levers, gears, and a rubber-handled crank. Black cables connect this contraption to another on the second cart—a long, horizontal brass pipe with a square wooden box built around the middle, mounted on a circular brass plate. A glass tube and a thermometer jut perpendicularly from the box's lid. Metal screws and gears are fixed to one end of the pipe; from the other protrudes a thinner brass tube like a rifle barrel. More cables attach the device to a drum wrapped in paper that's marked with a grid. The magnetometer looks like some newfangled, dangerous weapon.

Anjali seems unafraid, standing beside Dr. Lodge while he says, "I need a volunteer from the audience."

Mick raises his hand. Before I can warn him that he doesn't know what he's getting into, Dr. Lodge points to him. "What's your name?"

"Mick O'Reilly. Sir."

"Come up, Mr. O'Reilly."

Mick rises, tugs his lapels, and grins, an incorrigible daredevil. He strides up to the front of the room to stand by Anjali. It's obvious that she's caught his fancy.

"Anjali, please start the generator," Dr. Lodge says.

She turns the crank attached to the glass disks. They spin, sparks crackle from the wires, and the paper-wrapped drum slowly revolves. A pen attached to the drum draws a straight horizontal line on the gridded paper. Dr. Lodge hands a small object to Mick. "Hold this magnet there." He points to the end of the barrel. As Mick complies, Dr. Lodge adjusts the screws on the brass tube. The pen scribbles black spikes. Dr. Lodge tells Mick to walk around with the magnet. He swivels the tube, and the pen leaps when Mick is closer to the barrel, drops down when he's farther away. The audience claps; apparently, the test is successful.

"How is this thingumajig gonna help you find ghosts?" Mick says, then looks embarrassed, speaking with his Cockney accent in front of an upper-class crowd.

"Spirits give off magnetic fields," Dr. Lodge says. "If a spirit is present, the magnetometer can measure exactly where and how powerful it is, and provide a written record." He points to the scribbles on the paper. "The expedition is our opportunity to demonstrate the magnetometer. It should be a groundbreaking event in the history of spiritualism." He speaks with the fervor of a saint making a prophecy.

I think of the Reverend Thornton. How odd that a man of the church, steeped in mystical religious tradition, doesn't believe in ghosts, while this man of science claims he can measure them as if they were a pound of sugar. While he launches into a long, technical discourse about magnetism, the construction and operation of his device, and past research, I think that his theories are horse manure cloaked in science, but when he's finished, the other people applaud enthusiastically. They crowd around the magnetometer and admire it as if it were a sacred relic and pepper him with questions. Mick is enjoying his role as assistant, exchanging smiles with Anjali. I, the only one still seated, am left to wonder how to broach the subject of Charles Firth's murder.

Dr. Lodge adjourns the meeting, says, "Luncheon will be served in the dining room," and walks over to me. "Would you please sign the attendance book? If you would like to join our society, write down your address, and I'll mail you an application blank, Miss . . ."

In an irritable mood, I say, "Sarah Bain—I mean, Mrs. Barrett." I forgot that I'm married. "No thank you. My friend Mr. O'Reilly and I are photographers and investigators for the *Daily World*."

Dr. Lodge takes a moment to consider the information as seriously as if it were a scientific test result. "I hope your story will cover the scientific aspects of our work and not lump us in with the lunatic fringe of the spiritualist community just to sell papers."

I bristle at his implication that I'm more interested in creating a sensation than in the truth, but I mind my manners because I need information from him. I gather that there are factions within the spiritualist community and that not all is harmonious between them. "I'll do my best. May I photograph the magnetometer?"

"Of course."

As the crowd departs for lunch, Anjali remains, watching Mick and me set up the camera. I insert a negative plate and say to

Dr. Lodge, "We're investigating the murder of Charles Firth. Did you know him?"

Another moment passes before Dr. Lodge replies. It seems to be his habit, not a sign that he's alarmed by the direction in which I've steered the conversation. "He was a member of the Society." His somber, thoughtful expression doesn't change, but I hear displeasure in his tone.

"A member who wasn't in good standing?" I suggest.

This time Dr. Lodge's hesitation lasts a little longer. Mick is loading powder into the flashlamp, explaining to Anjali, "This is magnesium and potassium chlorate. It makes light for the picture." She listens raptly.

"Charles Firth was a bit at odds with the Society," Dr. Lodge says.

I think he doesn't want to speak ill of a murdered man but also doesn't like to compromise his integrity by lying. "At odds in what way?"

"The Society takes a scientific approach to supernatural phenomena. We investigate serious matters, such as what happens to the human soul at the moment the physical body dies, and we document instances of encounters with spirits. But Mr. Firth was worse than the lunatic fringe I mentioned—those amateur ghost chasers whose antics are fit for the penny dreadful theater. He was one of the many profiteers who take advantage of the gullible public. He gave spiritualism a bad name and damaged the Society's reputation."

I'd thought Dr. Lodge a cold fish, but the tight skin across his cheekbones reddens; his ire toward Charles Firth has heated his blood. I dislike that Charles Firth profited by duping his customers, but I also dislike the sanctimonious Dr. Lodge. "I'd have thought you would believe that ghost photographs are real."

"I believe that some are."

Mick continues to demonstrate how the camera works. "You turn this crank to adjust the focus. When you snap the shutter, the flashlamp goes off, and the negative plate inside the camera gets exposed, and just like magic, you got a photograph."

"How do you see what you're taking a picture of?" Anjali says. Her voice is high and sweet, her English crisp, unaccented, and upper class.

"You look through the viewfinder," Mick says. Although he's near Anjali's age, he seems mature by comparison, because of experiences that made him grow up too soon. "It's easier to see when it's dark, so you get under this black cloth. Come on, I'll show you." They duck under the drape that hangs from the back of the camera. I hear whispers and giggles, and then Mick says, "Sarah, could you and the doc stand over there?" His hand motions us closer to the magnetometer.

We move. Mick holds up the flashlamp. The powder ignites in a loud white blast; sparks fly. Anjali squeals with delight. Blinking at the dark afterimage of the flash, I say to Dr. Lodge, "If you think some photographs are fake, doesn't that call the authenticity of all of them into question? If any are genuine, why not Charles Firth's as well?"

"I think it highly suspicious that Mr. Firth managed to photograph enough ghosts to fill three entire books."

"So it's the number of his photographs that made you doubt their authenticity."

"Other spirit investigators have been lucky to photograph a few ghosts in their lifetimes. Whereas Mr. Firth did it for every single one of his many clients." Disgust curls Dr. Lodge's thin lips.

I'm aware that I'm defending what I consider indefensible, but Charles Firth was once my benefactor, and my antagonism toward Dr. Lodge increases. "I must say, I have my doubts that your contraption can really detect ghosts. All you have to do is hide a magnet somewhere near it, and it will give a positive reading."

Flashes explode as Mick takes more photographs. Dr. Lodge seems unoffended by my insinuation that he's as much a fraud as he thinks Charles Firth was. "I can understand your doubts. At one time, I myself was a nonbeliever. I thought spiritualists were the enemies of science in the war between superstition and reason. Then I met the woman who became my wife." His tone warms with the same ardor that gripped him when he spoke of his magnetometer. "She had a psychic gift. When she touched people or objects or went to places, she could read them as if they were books. She obtained information that she couldn't have known. Sometimes it pertained to events in the future."

I think of gypsy fortune-tellers at carnivals. "Surely that's not possible."

"Anjali inherited her mother's talent. Let's see if she can change your mind." Dr. Lodge calls, "Anjali, come here."

Anjali and Mick emerge from under the black drape. They're all smiles; his face is pink, her eyes bright.

I'm surprised to learn that Dr. Lodge and the girl are related. "She's your daughter?"

"Yes."

Mick winces, embarrassed that he's been flirting with Anjali in front of her father.

"Mother died when I was very young." Anjali's manner is frank, untroubled.

"I'd like you to demonstrate your talent for Mrs. Barrett," Dr. Lodge says.

I instinctively back away. Much as I scoff at mind reading, I can't deny my fear that this girl could expose my secrets.

Anjali says to Mick, "Give me your hand."

Mick glances at Dr. Lodge, then at me. When we nod, he lets Anjali clasp his hand. His blush deepens. I feel a surge of anger as I recall the medium I once consulted. These people are about to work the same trickery on my friend. But I stifle my protests. Let Anjali "read" some nonsense and prove that her "gift" is imaginary at best and deception at worst.

I expect her to fake a trance, with theatrical moans, convulsions, and eye rolling, but her manner is calm, alert. She says, "Deirdre."

Mick jerks as if she's given him an electric shock.

"She's been gone a long time, but you think of her every day," Anjali says.

As Mick stares at Anjali, the blush drains from his cheeks and dismay fills his eyes.

"You wonder where she is and what she's doing and if she ever thinks of you."

He pulls his hand free, tucks it in his pocket as though it's an object of shame, and stalks out the door.

Anjali turns her woebegone face to Dr. Lodge and me. "I didn't mean to upset him. I'm sorry."

She hurries after Mick, leaving me dumbfounded. I move to the window and see her chasing Mick across the lawn.

Dr. Lodge joins me. "Anjali's readings often have that effect. She tends to open the book to the page one most wants to keep private."

I watch Mick slow his steps, then halt and face Anjali. She catches up with him, gesturing as she talks. The mist partially conceals them, and I can't see their faces. "She could have made a lucky guess. An Irish boy like Mick is bound to know somebody called Deirdre."

Dr. Lodge responds with the superior smile that a member of an elite religious order would give an unenlightened outsider. "You seemed reluctant for her to read you. Why, if you're so certain she's a fraud?"

I avert my gaze from his shrewd perception. "You shouldn't put a child up to such stunts." I like Anjali, and I dislike her father for exploiting her to further his cause.

"She would do it with or without my permission. It's her calling, as science is mine—or photography is yours."

Indignant that he would equate my photography with his and his daughter's pursuits, I say, "Aren't you concerned about what will become of her? Chances are, someday she'll say the wrong thing to the wrong person."

"I'm very concerned. That's one reason for my animosity toward Charles Firth and his kind. Their antics cast doubt on people like Anjali, who have a genuine gift. Those who don't know her think she's just another money-grubbing hoaxer." Dr. Lodge adds, "Anjali and I never charge for her readings. I've taught her that her gift is to be shared with the world for free."

I suppose that puts them a step above Charles Firth and his kind. I also see that Dr. Lodge had a personal as well as a philosophical reason to hate Mr. Firth.

"The Society's board of directors was about to expel Mr. Firth," Dr. Lodge says. "We'd planned to take the formal vote today."

"His murder saved you the trouble. Did you kill him?"

Dr. Lodge laughs, a rusty sound, as if mirth doesn't come naturally to him. "Of course not. I prefer institutional means of censoring those whose behavior I find reprehensible. Besides, I didn't know he was going to be in that church."

I wonder if two excuses are enough to count as suspiciously too many. "Then where were you during the murder?"

"At home, with Anjali."

I glance out the window. Anjali and Mick have moved farther from the observatory; they're barely visible in the fog. She would probably lie for her father; heaven knows I've lied for mine. But I find myself reluctant to suspect Dr. Lodge or see him charged with Charles Firth's murder. Regardless of whether Anjali is a genuine psychic, I don't want her put in my position as the child of an accused criminal. I think of Mrs. Kirby and her granddaughter and great-grandson. Investigating this case as well as exonerating my father would be much easier if I had nothing in common with and no sympathy for the people involved.

"If you really want to find Charles Firth's killer," Dr. Lodge says, "you should look among his detractors. Such as the Ladies' Society for Rational Thought. That band of harpies was out for his blood."

"I have. The president, Jean Ritchie, told me to look among his colleagues."

Dr. Lodge puckers his mouth as if he's tasted something sour. "Jean Ritchie has too much nerve. I wouldn't put murder past her."

"Who else do you think could have killed Charles Firth? Did he have any other enemies?"

Dr. Lodge shakes his head, then pauses and holds up his finger, like a saint about to communicate a vision he's just had. His hands are sturdy, calloused, and marked with old scars, perhaps from cutting metal to build his magnetometer. "There was a woman. She came to a meeting at our club in the city. To be precise, she loitered in the street until we were finished. When Charles came out, she accosted him. I saw them quarreling."

I'm distrustful yet intrigued. "Who was she?"

"I don't know. I'd never seen her before, and Charles didn't introduce her."

"What did they say?"

"I couldn't hear. When they saw me, they moved down the street."

"Can you describe her?"

"Young, with blond hair, dressed in black." When prompted for more details, Dr. Lodge says, "It was dark and foggy. I didn't get a good look."

I wonder if Dr. Lodge has invented a mysterious blonde to divert suspicion from himself. "May I speak with the other members of your society?"

He spreads his arms in the manner of a priest welcoming the heathen into his fold. "Of course. We've nothing to hide."

CHAPTER 13

During my talk with the members of the Society for Psychical Studies, I discovered that roughly half think Charles Firth was murdered by a ghost. The others think the murderer is human, and they eagerly proposed suspects, some of whom are rival spirit photographers. But Jean Ritchie is the hands-down favorite—either she put one of her "harpies" up to killing Mr. Firth, or she did it herself.

When I left the observatory, Mick and Anjali came walking together across the lawn toward me. Their expressions solemn, they didn't speak to or look at each other until they parted. She said, "I live in Bloomsbury, number forty-eight Burton Crescent." Mick said, "Right."

Now, on the train, he keeps quiet, and I stifle the urge to ask questions. It's not until we're in Bethnal Green, carrying the photography equipment along St. Peter Street toward the church, that he breaks his silence.

"Deirdre's my ma."

I'm surprised, and not only because Anjali hit so close to home when she "read" him. He's never told me his mother's name. All he's said is that when he was eight, she ran away with a man. He pretends he doesn't care, but her abandonment must have hurt him as much as my father's abandonment did me.

I don't know what to say, except, "I'm sorry."

"Yeah, well. I do think about her, but it's water under the bridge."

I'm not the only one who's been haunted by the ghost of an absent parent, but I've found mine, while Mick is obviously still missing—and yearning for—his.

"What did you and Anjali talk about?" I want to know what's going on between them. She seems a nice girl, but her father is a suspect in the murder, and I'm far from comfortable with her "gift."

Mick stops and points. "Blimey, will you look at that?" A noisy crowd of men, women, and children outside the church has given him an opportunity to change the subject. I think it's safe to assume that the case has turned personal for Mick as well as me.

In the church's entryway stands the Reverend Thornton, his face stern as he says, "This is a house of worship. If you're here for any other purpose, go home."

Grumbles and protest erupt from the crowd.

"We want to see where the murder happened."

"Was it really a ghost that done it?"

The newspaper stories have brought out the curiosity seekers.

"The Rev ain't gonna let us in either," Mick says. "We'll have to sneak in."

We hurry around the church through a side gate to the yard. Beneath the skeletal oak trees, we follow a leaf-strewn gravel path around evergreen shrubs. A raven picks at a bloody bone. I think of the cholera pit, and I shiver.

Mick tries the side door. "It's locked, but no problem."

He applies his picklocks, and we carry our equipment into a passage. The church seems deserted; the only sounds are the creaks old buildings make. A doorway I've never seen before leads to stone steps that descend into blackness. Recalling things that have happened to us in other dark underground places, I don't want to go there. Mick gropes his way down the stairs, and I hear a gas jet hiss and a match strike. Light flares from a sconce on the wall at the bottom. I carry the equipment down to the crypt while Mick lights other jets along a passage that seems wider than the one outside the crime scene because there's no junk stacked along the walls.

"Anjali's pa's ghost meter would come in handy," Mick says.

I'm disturbed to see that he's half-serious—Anjali has shaken his skepticism as well as mine. We explore chambers with ledges where coffins once sat. The dead have been removed from many London churches and transferred to cemeteries. It's hard to see much inside the chambers because they lack gas pipes for lights. I can't tell if the scuff marks in the dust are signs of recent activity. We come upon a chamber that still holds wooden coffins that look decades old, the wood rotted, the nails rusted. Mick opens them, and I hold my breath so as not to inhale human remains, but they're empty.

"I'll try some photos here," Mick says. "Maybe it's haunted by the ghosts of the people who used to be in the coffins."

"I'll have another look at the crime scene."

While he mounts the camera on the tripod, I make my way along the passage, turn a corner, and enter the familiar area outside the chamber where Charles Firth's body was discovered. Amid the junk are boxes of candles and matches. I light a candle and examine the chamber, averting my eyes from the bloodstain still on the floor. There's no trace of the greenish slime that I don't want to believe is ectoplasm. Charles Firth must have come in contact with it somewhere else. I inspect other chambers, to no avail. In one, between the coffin shelves, I notice a doorway, and I lean through it into darkness. The smell of earth and cesspools is stronger and fouler here. The light from my candle penetrates only a few feet beyond the threshold. The walls of this space are roughly carved from the earth, and brick pillars rise from the dirt floor to a low ceiling with exposed rafters. It looks as if construction on the crypt wasn't finished after the church was built.

If any ghosts inhabit the church, this is where they'll be.

Goaded to overcome my superstitious fear, I inch forward, candle extended. A cold draft elongates the flame. I'm not reassured to know that the cavern has an opening to the surface. It feels as though it's breathing. I hear skittering noises—from rats or cockroaches—and a distant, muffled explosion as Mick takes a photograph. Then, from deeper in the darkness, comes a whimper.

My heart vaults into my throat. I freeze in my tracks. "Who's there?" My voice trembles.

After a long silence comes an eerie moan that sounds replete with sorrow and despair.

Someone's in here with me.

As I turn to flee, a movement catches my eye—a dark shape, briefly silhouetted in the light from the passage before it merges with the shadows. It's between me and the exit, and if it's not a ghost, it could be the person who killed Charles Firth—perhaps one of the suspects I've met, perhaps someone unknown. I back deeper into the cavern. Something soft and airy grazes my face. I stifle a shriek, telling myself it's only a cobweb. The shape, vaguely human now, advances on me, staying in the dim outer radius of the light cast by my candle. The weak, guttering flame now seems too bright, marking my location, rendering me a clearly visible target. Whatever the creature is, it makes no noise, as if it's shod in velvet or floating above the ground. My back bumps into a pillar, jarring a gasp from me. As I step around it, the draft blows out my candle. Blinded, I stumble over something on the floor. I drop the candle, fall forward, and land on what feels like a pile of lumber. As I struggle to push myself upright, the rough boards scrape my hands. Then I hear, from somewhere behind me, another whimper.

I'm caught between two presences that my intuition says are dangerous. Choosing to brave the one I've glimpsed rather than the one I haven't, I race toward the lighted door, toward all that's ordinary and sane. Just before I reach it, the hulking figure of a man dressed in dark clothes steps in front of me. I skid to a stop before I run smack into him. His fair hair catches the light from the passage, a gold nimbus crowning his head. Now I discern his soft, boyish features. He's not a man; he's Reverend Thornton's twelve-year-old grandson.

"Daniel!" The word escapes me in a burst of relief.

He responds with a strange, satisfied smile. "I scared you."

My relief turns to anger. "You shouldn't sneak up on people. What are you doing here?"

He tilts his head, solemnly pondering my question as if it's more complicated than it seems. "You're looking for ghosts, aren't you?"

I grasp at the skepticism that the last few minutes have undermined. "There's no such thing as ghosts."

An explosion from the flashlamp reverberates through the crypt. Daniel says, "Then what's the red-haired boy trying to take pictures of?"

"We're investigating the murder," I say, resenting this interrogation by a child who's made a fool of me. "You shouldn't be here."

"Neither should you," he says with a hint of sassiness. "Grandfather says the crypt is off-limits to everyone except the police."

"But you seem to have the run of it." Here is my chance to get in the questions the vicar prevented me from asking two days ago. "Were you in the church that night?"

A long moment elapses while Daniel ponders again. Is his mind slow, or is he trying to fabricate a good lie? "There are ghosts here, whether you think so or not. Sometimes I see them out of the corner of my eye. I think they're scared of people. But someday, if I sit still enough for long enough, maybe they'll know I don't mean them any harm. Maybe they'll let me look at them." He watches me closely to observe my reaction. "Do you think they will?"

I put on an expression intended to convey an adult's patience with a child's fancifulness. "I think you'll be disappointed." But his matter-of-fact recital was scarier than the curate's tale about the ghosts of a resurrectionist and a cholera victim, and Daniel is a disturbingly odd boy.

He peers into the far, pitch-dark reaches of the cavern. "This must be where they come into the church. There must be an underground tunnel from—" He pauses, then whispers, "*H-E-L-L.*" He must have been scolded for uttering bad words.

I'm not sure I believe in hell, let alone secret portals leading to it, but his suggestion gives me an idea. "Is there an entrance to the church in here?"

Daniel studies me as if I'm an insect stuck on a pin. "You want to know if that's how somebody got in and killed the photographer."

I think he's mentally quicker than he acts, and he's taxing my patience. "Is there an entrance or not?"

He regards me with condescending pity. "It wasn't a person. It didn't need a door to get in." Before I can demand that he answer my questions, he puts his finger to his lips and says, "Shh!" He tenses; his widened eyes search the darkness.

A soft, high-pitched wail makes my heart jump. I forgot that there is another creature in the cavern with me. The wail repeats, louder. I want to bolt out the door, but I don't want to seem a coward.

Daniel's pale eyes shine. "It's coming closer," he whispers.

"It must be a dog that got trapped in the church." My voice trembles with lack of conviction.

The wail peters into growling, indeed like an animal's. My mind conjures up a picture of a werewolf, its human face overgrown with fur, its teeth elongated into fangs.

"Not a dog," Daniel whispers. "A demon."

A slithering noise, like a beast dragging itself across the floor as it wakes from centuries of slumber, accompanies another wail. Under my skirts, something clutches my ankle. I scream. Bony fingers claw my skin. This is no inanimate wax hand on a rod. I kick and yell, lifting my skirts to see what's underneath. The grip on my ankle releases. Daniel bursts into laughter that rises to shrill, maniacal hoots. His twin sister Lucie is kneeling by me, all dimples, disheveled black hair, and merry eyes. She giggles and covers her mouth with hands dirty from crawling on the floor.

Mick rushes into the room. "Sarah! What's wrong?"

I double over and clasp my chest, too breathless to speak for a moment. Mick stares, puzzled, at the children. Their mirth subsides into proud smiles.

"I'm all right." Gasping, weakened by relief, I say to Lucie, "You scared me half to death!" Furious at her trick and my own stupidity, I tell Mick what she and Daniel did.

Mick, who's played many a trick himself, scowls with his effort to avoid laughing. "You naughty brats oughta be spanked."

Lucie's smile fades as she rises to her feet, and she seems so innocent that I can't stay angry at her. Daniel hangs his head, chastened. Although I can see how comical my reaction must have looked to them, I'm annoyed, but I say, "Never mind, there's no harm done." Both twins seem not quite right in the head; they probably didn't know any better.

Mick voices the idea that's occurred to me. "Have you been playin' tricks on other people?" he asks the twins. "Were *you* the ghosts they seen?"

Lucie shrinks from his accusing tone. Daniel puts his arm around her, glowering at us. His fist clenches as though ready to do battle in his sister's defense. "It wasn't us," he says.

Again I think of the curate's description of a resurrectionist with a female corpse, and I picture Daniel carrying Lucie through the church at night while she whimpers and moans. "This is serious," I say to them. "A man's been murdered here. If you've been pretending to be ghosts, it's time to admit it."

"Yeah, so that we're not chasin' false clues while the real killer is out there," Mick says.

"The ghosts are real," Daniel protests, and Lucie nods.

I don't trust them. "Were you in the church that night?"

They solemnly shake their heads, their mouths closed tight. I'm almost certain they're lying, but before I can challenge them, the Reverend Thornton hurries into the chamber.

"How did you get in?" he demands of Mick and me. He turns to the twins. "And what are you doing here?" His face is dark with displeasure as he orders, "Everyone, out!" He marches the twins out to the passage; Mick and I follow. "Daniel and Lucie, what have I told you?"

The twins stand like soldiers at attention, their arms stiff at their sides. Daniel recites, "That part of the crypt isn't safe. We're not allowed to play there."

"Correct." The vicar explains to Mick and me, "The ceiling is unstable. You could have been hurt by falling rocks." He says to the twins, "Go home. You'll be punished later."

They shuffle away. I call, "Wait." As they pause, I say to Reverend Thornton, "I think they were in the church the night of the murder. I need to know if they heard or saw anything."

"You're mistaken." He motions for the children to leave, and they obey. "I already told you they were at home, asleep."

"Do you watch 'em every minute?" Mick says.

"I'm a light sleeper. So is Mrs. Thornton. If they'd left their beds, one or both of us would have heard."

Now I'm more certain than ever that whether or not the children are the "ghosts" rumored to haunt the church, they know something. "There's a killer at large. If he thinks the children are witnesses to the crime, they could be in danger."

"I'm fully capable of protecting my grandchildren, thank you."

"It's important that you cooperate with the investigation, so that the killer can be caught," I say.

"Of course we will cooperate with your husband's investigation, in the unlikely circumstance that we can be of any help. But we're under no obligation to cooperate with the press, Mrs. Barrett." The vicar has put me in my place as the mere wife of a policemen rather than a professional detective in my own right. "And I would appreciate it if you do not publish stories about my grandchildren in your newspaper." He extends his hand toward the stairs. "I'll see you and Mr. O'Reilly out now. If I find you here again, I will call the police."

CHAPTER 14

Mick and I find ourselves on the front steps of St. Peter's with our equipment, like unwanted guests evicted from a hotel. We cross the street to escape the reporters, photographers, and gawkers still gathered outside the church.

"What's the Rev trying to hide by keeping the kids away from us?" Mick says.

I don't want to think the worst. "Maybe nothing. They seem fragile, and he's their guardian."

"Could they have done it?" Mick sounds as reluctant as I am to believe they're killers.

"I don't see why they would have wanted to kill Charles Firth. There's no evidence that they even knew him."

"They're weird, though."

I can't help wondering if Charles Firth was a victim of some game played by Daniel and Lucie.

"Daniel's big and strong enough to stab someone," Mick points out. "He could be the ghost in the picture."

I remember the strength of Lucie's grip on my ankle. The poor orphaned children are two more people, in addition to Dr. Lodge and Anjali, who I hope aren't guilty. And I can't say I really want the culprit to be Jean Ritchie or her friends. It behooves me to find other suspects.

"Let's look for clues outside the church," I say.

We retrace our steps to the gate by which we previously entered the churchyard, then walk along the narrow strip of grass between the church and the iron fence that separates it from the sidewalk. Sharp leaves on the holly bushes planted by the walls snag my skirts. We stop at the front of the building, where the main entrance with the tower atop it juts from the wall. The corner is landscaped with evergreen shrubs and a tree.

"Suppose the killer knew Charles Firth was coming to the church and lay in wait for him," I say. "He wouldn't have wanted to be seen."

"This's a good place to watch the front door," Mick says. "Maybe he left something."

We peer under the shrubs, which are tall and dense enough to conceal a person. Mick says, "Hey, there's a shoe."

A man's left boot, dark brown around the bottom, lighter brown on top with black buttons, lies on its side among dead leaves. The leather is grimy, the sole caked with mud. When Mick grabs the boot, it kicks at him. We exclaim and jump backward. There's a foot inside the boot, and a leg clad in dirty gray-and-black-striped trousers attached to the foot. The shrubs rustle as the man under them pushes the boughs apart and sits up.

"Who's there?" he mutters in a rough Cockney voice. His thin body is padded with layers of clothes, the outermost a threadbare gray overcoat and tattered blue scarf. Dirty knees show through holes in his trousers, and his right shoe is a scuffed black lace-up. A bowler hat and scraggly gray whiskers conceal most of his face except for his bloodshot eyes.

I introduce Mick and myself and explain that we're newspaper reporters. "May we talk to you?"

"About what?" The man is obviously a vagrant of the kind that live in London's alleys and casual wards. Dried saliva crusts the corners of his mouth. He's lying on a filthy gray blanket amid empty wine bottles and bundles of his possessions. He exudes the odors of liquor and stale urine.

"The murder in the church on Thursday night," I say. "Were you here then?"

"Yeah. So what?"

Perhaps we have a witness at last. Mick says, "Did you see anything?"

"Could be. What's it worth to you?" The vagrant holds out a hand clad in a knitted red glove with the fingertips worn through to reveal the grime under his nails.

This won't be the first time I've paid for information. I open my satchel and remove a shilling that I drop in the vagrant's palm.

"Ta." His grin shows gaps between rotted teeth, and he pockets the shilling.

"What is your name, sir?" I say.

"Andrew Coburn."

"What happened that night, Mr. Coburn?"

"Well . . ." He's taking his time, enjoying the attention. "I woke up when I heard someone at the door. I got up to look, and I seen a bloke go in the church."

"What did he look like?" Mick says.

"My eyes ain't too good. All I could tell was he had a lot of trunks and whatnot."

Charles Firth, with his photography equipment. "Then what?" I say.

"I went back to sleep, until someone else went in."

It could have been the killer. I feel a shiver of anticipation. "Who was it?"

"Uh . . . I don't know," Mr. Coburn says, suddenly nervous.

"You're lyin'," Mick says. "Who was it?"

"If he knew I ratted on him . . . I don't want no trouble."

"We won't tell anyone," I say, although I may have to go back on my word.

Mr. Coburn vacillates, then holds out his hand. I give him another shilling. He glances around, as if the person he's afraid of might hear, then whispers, "It were Nat Quayle."

The name hasn't come up during the investigation, and it's unfamiliar to me. "Who is Nat Quayle?"

"He lives at Bethnal Green Workhouse. Promise he won't find out I set you on him?" Mr. Coburn's reddened eyes beseech me. "He ain't somebody you want to run afoul of."

After thanking Mr. Coburn for the information, Mick and I leave the church. We see, halfway down the block, reporters clustered around two constables and a gray-haired, moustached man in an overcoat and derby. It's Inspector Reid, my enemy since we first met two years ago during the Ripper investigation.

Mick tugs my arm. "Sarah, let's get out of here."

I freeze as if I'm on the railroad tracks while a train thunders toward me and I can't decide which way to jump. I crave a confrontation with Reid, even though it could land us in jail.

"Have you any suspects in the murder?" the reporters ask Reid. "Do you think the killer is a ghost?"

"It's early days, fellows. I can't comment at this time."

He must be involving himself in the Charles Firth murder because the publicity has turned it into a high-profile case. He's sniffing around the scene for clues that could help him solve it and boost his reputation, at Barrett's expense. My hatred for Reid is a poisonous yet intoxicating brew. As I drink in the sight of him, I remember the secret I'm hiding, never far from my thoughts, a permanent canker on my soul. I have nightmares about the gallows at Newgate Prison, a noose around my neck, and the trapdoor opening in the platform under my feet. The nightmare will become reality should Reid learn my secret.

Reid turns his gaze in my direction. "Excuse me," he says to the reporters. He and his constables stride around the corner. He doesn't beckon me; he knows I'll follow him, and I do. He's up to something, and my curiosity and my attraction to danger won't let me retreat.

"You're askin' for it," Mick says, but he comes with me.

We catch up with Reid by the schoolyard. He's standing alone, his constables waiting down the block. He's thinner than when I last saw him a few months ago, as if anger is consuming him from the inside. The ends of his moustache are wet; I assume he's been chewing on it.

"Good afternoon, Miss Bain and Mr. O'Reilly. Or rather, Mrs. Barrett." His tone is pleasant; he adds none of his usual sarcastic, insulting remarks. "Congratulations, by the way."

Mick and I exchange glances, alert for trouble. "Good afternoon, Inspector Reid," I say, controlling my urge to poke the wolf. "Thank you."

"I'm sorry your wedding was spoiled by a dead body." Reid's sympathy sounds so genuine that I would believe it was if not for our history. "This must be a first for the *Daily World*—a new bride investigating a murder. Any clues yet?"

As if he thinks I'm going to give him tips! "You'll have to ask my husband. He's the officer in charge of the police investigation."

Reid scowls briefly; he doesn't like the reminder that Barrett was promoted to detective against his wishes. There's also the matter of the Ripper case. He, more than all the other London police, takes personally their failure to catch the Ripper. He blames Barrett, my friends, and me for said failure, as well as other troubles, and he's determined to get the better of us somehow, someday, preferably in the dirtiest way possible.

"Suppose we make a deal," Reid says. "You tell me everything you've learned about Charles Firth's murder, and I'll tell you everything I've learned during my search for Benjamin Bain."

The direction the conversation has taken is like a kick behind my knees when I've braced myself for a punch in the stomach. My heart begins to race, my mind to scramble. *What has he learned?* Fortunately, I've had much experience keeping a calm, straight face. "No, thank you. I'm not interested."

"Oh, come now," Reid says with a jolly chuckle. "I know you've been searching high and low for your father."

Dismayed by the possibility that he's traced my father by spying on me, I see no choice but to flat-out lie. "You're mistaken."

Reid's smile says he doesn't believe me. "Haven't gotten anywhere, have you? Not even with the help of your sister? Sally Albert, the *Daily World*'s fledgling writer?"

He's showing off his knowledge of my family, reminding me that he discovered Sally's existence by having me followed. I'd led his henchmen straight to the house where Sally used to live and work. Since then, I've been more careful, but maybe in vain.

"Looks like two heads aren't enough. Don't you want some more help?" Reid taps his finger against his head and raises his eyebrows expectantly.

Does he know I've found my father? I desperately hope he's just fishing and thinks that if he pesters me, I'll let a clue slip. Catching a fugitive murder suspect who's been on the run for twenty-four years would be a feather in his cap, and he knows that sending Benjamin Bain to the gallows would be the ultimate blow to me.

"If you were as good a detective as you think you are, you'd have found my father already, and we wouldn't be having this conversation," I say.

Reid's muddy brown eyes burn as if hot, molten lava roils behind them. The jovial crinkles around them are like cracks spreading in the earth as the pressure mounts toward an eruption. "Benjamin Bain must be pretty long in the tooth by now. You wouldn't want him to kick the bucket before you can have your happy reunion. If we compare our notes, maybe we can flush him out."

Inside, I'm shaking with anger. If Reid knows where my father is, then he's needlessly tormenting me; if not, he's trying to trick me into helping him solve Charles Firth's murder and betray Barrett. "You can take your notes and—"

"It's time to go, Sarah," interrupts Mick. He pulls me down the street.

After we've gone several blocks, we stop, and I look around to make sure that Reid and his constables are nowhere in sight. "I have to warn my father."

"Sarah, no." Mick grabs my shoulders to halt my rush toward the train station. "That's just what Reid wants. I bet he's got his flunkies watching you, and they'll follow you straight to your dad."

I sigh and nod. Mick is right, and I'm grateful to lean on his judgment when my own is impaired.

"Reid's bluffing," Mick says. "Best thing you can do for your dad is act like you don't know where he is and just go about your business. So let's find that Nat Quayle bloke."

CHAPTER 15

Located half a mile from St. Peter's, the Bethnal Green Work-house is a shelter and place of employment for the able-bodied poor, who receive bed and board in exchange for their labor. Occupying several acres, the large compound of dingy brick build-ings seems cloaked in its own desolate atmosphere of smoke from its many chimneys, steam from its boilers, and the sewage stench from Regent's Canal at the end of the street. A reporter from the *Daily World* recently disguised himself as a pauper, went to live among the fifteen hundred inmates, and wrote lurid articles about his experiences. I'm interested to see whether the conditions there are as bad as he claimed.

Inside the gate, the porter's lodge stands before the long, three-story main block. Mick and I join the small crowd of people queued up at the lodge. They're mostly men and a few women with children in tow. Their clothes are ragged, and the smell of their unwashed bod-ies is so strong that I want to cover my nose with my handkerchief. At the lodge entrance, a man wearing an overcoat and a bowler hat greets them. He's of middle age, accompanied by two younger men dressed in identical gray jackets and trousers, striped cotton shirts, and cloth caps—the workhouse inmates' uniform. They watch while the older man—apparently the porter—takes names, writes them in a ledger, and directs people to another building or rejects them. The rejected include a drunken woman and a crippled man on crutches. When Mick and I reach the front of the queue, I introduce us and tell the porter we've come to see Nat Quayle.

"No visitors allowed."

One of the inmates steps forward. "I'll take you to him."

Mick and I look at each other, thinking it strange that inmates can overrule the official gatekeeper. In a feeble effort to assert his authority, he says, "Leave your belongings here."

I'm reluctant to abandon our photography equipment to the care of the porter, but this may be our best chance to solve the murder. The inmate escorts Mick and me into the main building. In a wide passage, the din of many voices hits me at the same time as the smell—body odor, stale food, and mildew overlaid with bleach fumes that sting my eyes. Cold air wafting from iron grates in the stone floor and the moldy plaster ceiling brings insufficient relief. Open doors reveal large rooms whose windows are too high to see out of. In one, inmates are eating a meal at long tables while a chaplain at a podium reads aloud from a Bible. In another, they're unraveling piles of rope with their fingers and an iron spike. This tedious work is known as picking oakum—dismantling old, frayed rope into fibers that can be reused. All these inmates are female, dressed in aprons over blue-and-white-striped dresses. A few women wait in line outside a chamber that must, judging from the strong odor of urine, be the latrine. The conditions are as harsh as described in the articles, surely intended to discourage anyone but the truly destitute to come here and live on the government dole.

Often in my life when my purse was empty, I feared ending up in a workhouse myself.

As our escort leads us down the passage, other men in workhouse uniforms fall into step behind us. I don't see anyone who looks official. The inmates seem to have taken command here, which would explain why the porter allowed them to override his order.

Mick perceives something wrong at the same moment I do. "Sarah, let's go."

We turn toward the exit, but the men block our way. Mick grabs my hand, and we run in the opposite direction, around a corner, with a shouting mob in pursuit. We burst through a door, into a yard where men are pounding sledgehammers against boulders, breaking them into smaller rocks. The air is filled with suffocating dust, and I cough. Our pursuers are gaining on us, and their intentions can't be good. Mick and I run in blind, frantic search of escape. The men fan out to surround us. Buildings enclose the yard; an archway beckons. We rush through it to another yard surrounded by more buildings. The door to one stands open. Mere steps ahead of our pursuers, we rush in.

The room is as hot as summer, loud with clattering machinery. Amid clouds of caustic steam, women operate washing machines and mangles. We skid on spilled water on the stone floor.

Mick yells as someone grabs him. Releasing my hand, he says, "Run, Sarah!"

Male inmates hurl themselves on him, and he goes down. I pick up a mop and beat at them while he fights them. "Help!" I call to the women.

They stare, openmouthed and immobile. Men wrest the mop from my hands, and as they seize me and lift me off the floor, I scream and flail. I gouge my fingernails into their hands; I kick their faces. But there are too many men, they're too strong, and I can't break free. Even as I sob helplessly, I'm more afraid for Mick than for myself.

A male voice, rough and angry, authoritative, says, "Let her go!" The mob beneath me roils, and I'm dropped to the floor, where I crash onto my hands and knees.

Mick hovers anxiously over me. "Sarah, are you all right?"

"Yes." I sob with relief because it seems we're safe now. I'm trembling because I could have been raped and we both could have been killed. Mick is soaking wet; his clothes drip water on me as he helps me to my feet. I ask, "What happened to you?"

"They tried to drown me in a washtub. Lucky thing he came along." Mick points at our rescuer.

The man, dressed in a gray smock, black trousers, and work boots, isn't very tall, but his shoulders and chest are heavily muscled. A ring of keys dangles from his waist. Clean-shaven, with short blond hair beneath his cap, he has a square jaw and thick lips.

His expression isn't kindly, but I'm so glad to see someone official that I could kiss him. His sharp blue eyes, set in puffy lids, glare at the other men.

"What the hell do you think you're doing?"

A stout brute with a piggish face says, "We was just havin' a little fun." His companions stand around like disobedient, guilty schoolboys.

"You don't have fun unless I say you can." My rescuer shoves the man toward the door and says to all the inmates, "Get back to work." They slink off, and he says to me, "Your mouth's bleeding."

I taste the blood on my lip where I must have bitten it during the attack.

"That's a nasty burn." He points at the red, blistered skin on Mick's wrist.

"Yeah, well, that's what happens when some rotter throws lye on you," Mick says.

I see that he shares my distrust of our rescuer. The man, in his twenties, seems young to have so much authority over the inmates, and his interaction with them sounded inappropriate in some way. But he saved our lives, and I'm grateful.

"I'll take you to the infirmary, get you fixed up," he says.

He leads us out of the laundry. The women keep working as if nothing has happened. In the yard, I say, "Thank you, Mr. . . . ."

"Quayle."

Mick and I look at each other, startled. "You're Nat Quayle?" I say.

"Yeah." He ushers us through the door of a wing attached to the main building. It's a miniature hospital, with separate wards for men and women on opposite sides of the corridor. I see inmates lying in bed, under piled blankets to keep warm. The air smells of medicines and disinfectant. I wonder what diseases they have—cholera, tuberculosis, typhoid?

Nat Quayle unlocks a door and motions us into an examining room. "Do I know you?"

"No," I say.

While I try to compose myself, Mick introduces us as reporters and tells Quayle, "We came here to talk to you about the murder at St. Pete's church."

Quayle's expression is flat and opaque as he absorbs the information. "Sit there." He points to the examining table, then washes his hands at the basin. He apparently intends to treat our injuries himself.

"You a doctor?" Mick says.

"A nurse." Quayle rummages in a cupboard and brings out gauze bandages, cotton balls, a bottle of alcohol, and medicine vials.

He doesn't look like the nurses I've seen, all women in white aprons and caps. I collect my wits enough to ask, "Where did you train?"

"Here. I started out working in the boiler house. The doctor tried me out in here after another nurse left. I didn't faint at the sight of blood. Been here ever since."

I belatedly notice that the shirt under his smock is blue-and-white-striped cotton: he's an inmate. Mick says, "The bosses put you in charge?"

Quayle's eyes glint with amusement. "Not exactly."

I suppose that in the absence of enough officials to govern the workhouse, the inmates take matters upon themselves, and that Quayle, like a street gang leader, has risen to the top of the heap by dint of his forceful personality.

"Let's see that burn," Quayle says.

He cleans Mick's wrist with a cotton ball dipped in alcohol. Mick grits his teeth. I watch Quayle apply salve to the burn and bandage it. He seems to know what he's doing. When he turns to me, I let him pull down my lip to examine the wound. Up close, in bright light, his face is a patchwork of old scars, as if he's been cut apart and sewn back together. He smells of soap, and his manner is professional, but I'm wary. Apparently, he rules the inmates, including those who led Mick and me into the trap.

"It's just a little cut," he says. "This'll dull the pain and prevent festering." He doses my lip with medicine from a dropper.

My lip goes numb. Mick asks Quayle, "Did you know we was coming and those blokes was gonna attack us?"

"If I had, I would've stopped them before it happened." His expression remains inscrutable as he puts away the medicine. "What's the murder at St. Pete's got to do with me?"

"You were seen goin' in the church that night," Mick says.

Quayle's eyes flash briefly with emotion—surprise, alarm, anger? "Who says?"

I don't want to name the witness lest Quayle retaliate against him. "Someone who happened to be outside the church."

"Oh, you must mean Andy Coburn." Quayle smirks at my surprise. "He dosses down in the bushes by the front door. You believed him?"

"He seemed quite certain," I say.

"It weren't me. His brain's pickled by drink. He wouldn't recognize his own mum."

I remember Mr. Coburn's liquor bottles and inebriated state, but I'm not ready to believe Quayle. Mick says, "Why would he finger you?"

"When I was a lad, I robbed people sleeping in the streets." Quayle speaks without shame or regret, as if he's talking about merely a job to earn pocket money. Perhaps his childhood was similar to Mick's and he did whatever was necessary to survive. "Old Andy was one of them. He ratted on me to the coppers. Sent me to jail. He'll do me dirty again if he can."

"Then where was you?" Mick says.

"Here. In the women's ward. Deliverin' a baby."

"Can anyone vouch for you?" I say.

"The baby's too young, but his ma were there," Quayle says. "And the night nurses."

"We'll need to talk to them." But judging from what I've seen, everyone in the workhouse would lie for fear of Quayle.

"Somebody else besides 'Old Andy' might've seen you at the church," Mick says. "If you had an innocent reason for bein' there, you'd best come clean now, before the coppers get onto you."

"I never go near St. Pete's after dark. It's haunted."

At first I think he's making a joke, so I'm surprised by the fear in his eyes.

"Don't tell me you're scared o' ghosts," Mick jeers.

"You would be too if you'd seen what I seen. One night last year, I'm passing by St. Pete's, and I hear wailing in the church-yard. I look around, and there's a woman standing by a tombstone. She's all white—her hair, her dress, her skin. She reaches out her arms, like she wants to pull me into the grave." Quayle shudders. "I got out of there, fast as I could."

Maybe the power of suggestion is strong enough to play tricks on the mind of a tough, practical man like Quayle. But I think he's clever enough to invent the most original alibi I've ever heard—a ghost story.

"Were you acquainted with Charles Firth?" I say.

"No. I never heard of him until after he were murdered."

"That so?" Mick says. "If there's a connection between you and him, we're gonna find out."

"There ain't none," Quayle says, impatient now. "And if I wanted to kill somebody, I'd do it someplace else other than St. Pete's."

★　★　★

Mick and I retrieve our equipment from the workhouse por-ter's lodge. The porter won't look at us, which suggests that he suspects, but doesn't want to know, that the inmates did some-thing bad to us. Mick and I travel home by omnibus, in open-air seats on its roof. The evening fog descends around us, a swirling, wind-blown murk of soot, cold moisture, and chemical fumes. The streetlamps and shop windows are bright, blurry streaks, and I can't see beyond the driver atop the cab in front of us. A din of voices is all I can perceive of the people on the sidewalks. When the omnibus stops, Mick and I haul our equipment down the staircase and join the crowds trudging along the Whitechapel high street. Outside our house, I see Barrett, in uniform, striding toward us.

We halt ten steps from each other. I'm glad he came back, and after what I've gone through, the sight of him is a relief, but the anger and hurt from last night rekindle in me. The shadow of Jane looms between us, like a spell his mother cast to drive us apart.

"Hullo, Barrett," Mick says. He unlocks the door, carries in the photography equipment, and runs upstairs.

"Can I come in?" Barrett says.

"Please do." My manner is stiff, formal.

In the studio, I take my time closing and locking the door and lighting the gas lamp. Barrett sets his helmet on the table, and we stand in silence, neither wanting to speak first. The room is cold, the air permeated with our apprehension.

"I stopped by my mother's today," Barrett says.

"Oh." On top of everything that's happened today, I'm ill equipped to cope with more trouble from Mrs. Barrett.

"She said to tell you she's sorry if she upset you."

There's something not quite right about that apology, but I still hope we can settle our differences. "Tell her I said thank you."

"I will." Barrett brightens, encouraged by this progress toward harmony between his mother and his wife. "She wants us to come for dinner Wednesday."

Perish the thought, but even a hint that I don't want to go will hurt Barrett's feelings. "All right. How nice."

Barrett puts his arms around me, cautiously, as though I'm a cat that might scratch him. I lean into him, his presence a comfort after my ordeal. Pent-up, unfulfilled desire swells in me, and his kiss is like a lit match thrown on smoldering embers. Then his mouth presses against the cut inside my lip. A hiss of pain escapes me as I flinch.

Barrett immediately releases me. "I'm sorry."

He must think I spurned him because of last night, and I hurry to explain, "No, it's just this." I pull my lip down to show him the cut.

His eyebrows rise; it must look worse than it feels. "How did that happen?"

Here's another problem to stir into our pot of troubles, and there's no way to sugarcoat it. I tell him about the witness Mick and I found outside St. Peter's, the ambush at the workhouse, and our close call.

Barrett huffs and stomps around the room, his fists clenched as if he wants to beat up the men responsible. I can't help feeling a certain feminine satisfaction; his anger is proof that he cares about me. "How could you and Mick go in there by yourselves?" he demands. "Everybody knows it's dangerous inside workhouses."

A needle of annoyance pierces my satisfaction. "So you're blaming *us*?"

"Of course not. I'm just saying you need to be more careful. My God, you could have been killed!"

I involuntarily clasp the tender gunshot wound on my shoulder. "I wasn't seriously harmed." But I remember those cruel men, and my terror and helplessness.

Barrett rakes his hands through his hair. "I hate it when you just shrug off things like that, as if they were all in a day's work."

I'm hurt because he doesn't understand my feelings; I somehow think he should, even though I haven't explained them to him, and I could wish for a little sympathy. "It was a good day's work. Mick and I turned up some new suspects." I describe Dr. Lodge, Anjali, and the Society for Psychical Studies. After mentioning their upcoming ghost-hunting expedition, I describe our encounters with Daniel and Lucie Thornton, the vicar, and Nat Quayle.

Barrett nods, reluctantly impressed. "So maybe you're a few steps closer to solving the murder. But I don't see what reason Nat Quayle could have had for wanting Charles Firth dead."

"Neither do I," I have to admit.

"And the investigation isn't worth your life."

"I never said it was!" We've had so many arguments since the wedding, and I'm suddenly frightened. Shouldn't marriage unite us rather than pit us against each other? What's wrong with us?

"Well, you act as if it is. You're so reckless." Barrett holds his head. "I don't know how much more I can take."

I can't deny the justice of his words, but I'm the same person I've always been, and my being attacked in the line of duty isn't rare, so why does he mind more now? "I'll be more careful next time."

"You always say so, but you never are. You could have asked me to go to the workhouse with you, but you didn't. I promised to protect you, but how can I, if you won't let me?"

Our arguments these days always seem to circle back to our wedding vows. In my desperation, I try to joke him back into good humor. "If you had gone with me, we both might have been killed and we wouldn't be having this conversation."

Barrett glowers. "What else happened today?"

I hesitate.

"Sarah . . ." His warning tone reminds me that my keeping secrets from him is another sore point.

If I don't tell him, he'll hear it from someone else, and there will be hell to pay. I sigh, then describe my run-in with Inspector Reid.

Barrett's eyes flare, and his jaw tightens with the anger that he's hard-pressed to control whenever Reid crops up in conversation or in person. "As long as you keep working for the *Daily World*, you won't be able to stay out of his way. Your investigations will keep pitting you and him against each other. You'll never be safe from him."

"I know." Nobody associated with me, including my father, will ever be safe, either, as long as there's so much bad blood between Reid and me.

"Sometimes I think—" Barrett stops, as though he's caught himself on the verge of saying too much.

"You think what?" I experience an ominous sensation as I imagine the ways in which he could end that sentence.

Barrett shakes his head. "Never mind." He moves toward the door.

I don't want him to leave while we're at odds. "Where are you going?"

"To storm the Bethnal Green Workhouse with an army of constables and arrest those rotters."

My knight in shining armor, out to avenge me! But my thrill of excitement quails before my fear for his safety. "Please be careful."

"*You're* telling *me*?" Barrett laughs with sardonic mirth. "If you're going to that ghost–hunting expedition, I'm going with you."

CHAPTER 16

The next morning, Hugh still hasn't returned. Fitzmorris volunteers to track down people Hugh knows, who might have seen him. While Mick attempts to verify the murder suspects' alibis, I visit other places where my mother and I lived. One house has been demolished; at others, I find strangers who never knew my mother. I save Isleworth for last.

At four thirty in the afternoon, a cab carries me from the train station toward the center of Isleworth. I look out the window and see, through mist and drizzle, the buildings and smokestacks of the Pears soap factory. My mother worked there, and the soap's floral fragrance permeated her clothes, her hair, and our lodgings. I never use Pears soap because a mere whiff catapults me back to that time. Today I hold my breath, but I can't hold it long enough. Inhaling the fragrance, I relive the day I made this journey in June 1874, when I'd finished school and come home for good. I hadn't seen my mother since Christmas, and she hadn't told me about the cancer, so I was shocked by how weak and emaciated she was. I took care of her for the grueling eighteen months until she died.

Fifteen years have passed since I last saw Isleworth, but today it still strikes me as more a small town than a part of London. Situated near the River Thames, the town center covers less than a square mile. Our house is shabbier but still there, in a terrace of undistinguished brick houses near the convent school. I stand outside, gazing at the windows of the second-floor flat. All those days and nights by my mother's bedside, I waited for her to speak one loving word to me. She never did. She could have told me the truth about my father, Lucas, and Ellen Casey's murder, but she kept silent until the end. When she took her last breath, she left me alone to face the consequences of her lies.

Ten minutes pass before I summon the courage to knock on the door. A woman answers. She's shrunken with age, her face as white and puckered as the cap she wears. I'm startled to recognize my former neighbor.

"Mrs. Yates?" I say.

I thought her ancient then; she must be over eighty now. I suddenly remember the Christmas I was sixteen. I'd come home from school, and on the train, a thief had stolen the valise that contained, along with my clothes, the scarf I'd knitted as a present for my mother. Our door was locked when I arrived; she wasn't home. Cold, tired, hungry, and desolate, I sat on the stairs and cried. Mrs. Yates found me and took me into her flat. She gave me tea and a fried-egg sandwich and chatted with me until my mother returned. I forgot her kindness until now.

She squints at me and says, "Who's there?"

"It's Sarah Bain. Do you remember me?"

"What? I'm afraid my eyesight isn't very good, nor my hearing."

When I step closer and repeat my name, Mrs. Yates blinks in amazement. "You and your mum used to live upstairs."

"Yes." I'm so glad to find someone who remembers us.

"I never thought I'd see you again. I'm sorry about your mum."

I'm suddenly as tearful as I was that day she found me sitting on the stairs like a stray dog.

"There, there, dear." Mrs. Yates pats my shoulder. "You'd better come in."

Inside her small, warm, cluttered flat, she serves me tea and biscuits. I recognize the teapot shaped like a hen. I recall that Mrs. Yates was a seamstress, a widow with two sons. I envied the cheerful bustle of their household. Now she tells me that both boys work at the soap factory and are married with children of their own.

"What brings you back, dear?" she says.

"It's about my mother." The lump in my throat chokes off my impulse to confide the terrible story.

"You were missing her, of course."

"Yes." I gratefully accept her sweet, simple explanation. "I thought that if I came here, I might find people who knew her and they could share their memories of her with me."

"Well, I can't say I knew her." Mrs. Yates's manner cools. "She didn't want people around."

Another memory resurfaces. When my mother returned that day, she scolded Mrs. Yates for taking me in without her permission. She dragged me into our flat and slammed the door.

"Was there anyone my mother might have been close to?"

"Well, there was her gentleman friend."

I choke on a sip of tea. "*Gentleman friend*?" After my father left, I never saw my mother look at another man. That she had a suitor is the last thing I expected to learn.

"I saw him when he came calling once," Mrs. Yates says.

In my shock and disbelief, I search for an alternate reason for a man to visit my mother. "He was probably just a salesman."

"A salesman wouldn't have brought her flowers, would he, dear? Or stayed three hours?"

This must have happened while I was away at school. He was another secret she kept from me.

"It's nothing to be ashamed of, dear," Mrs. Yates says, misinterpreting my reaction. "A woman gets lonely on her own. If I'd had a suitor after Mr. Yates died, I wouldn't have said no." She squeezes my hand, feels my wedding ring, and smiles. "Ah, you're married. I'm glad you found a husband."

"What was the gentleman's name?" Now I'm excited; perhaps he has information I need.

"Callahan, I believe he said."

The name is completely unfamiliar. "Do you know where I might find him?"

"I don't want you to think I'm nosy, but one day I saw him on the street. I was curious, so I followed him home."

*   *   *

The Northumberland Arms is a public house on Lower Square Street. I peer in through the window of the white stucco building and see an old man sitting at a table with other customers, who laugh as he tells a story. With his full head of pomaded white hair and the red carnation stuck in the buttonhole of his gray coat, he fits the description given me by the landlady at the lodging house to which Mrs. Yates followed him some eighteen years ago. Mrs. Yates's memory has proven accurate in all but one respect: his surname is Cullen, not Callahan. Fortunately, his house is still existent, and he's still a lodger. John Cullen is well preserved and handsome for a man who must be in his seventies, and I can see why an older woman would have been attracted to him. But what on earth attracted him to my plain, dour mother?

Upon my entering the pub, the chatter and laughter fade as the party at the table behold me, a stranger. "Well, hello, there," John Cullen says. His voice is jovial, his accent common. "Why don't you pull up a chair and join us?"

He seems the kind of man who flirts with anyone female. Then he takes a second look at me, and his jaw sags; his ruddy complexion blanches; his eyes pop. He brings to mind Ebenezer Scrooge seeing Jacob Marley's ghost. I'm as much of a shock to him as his relationship with my mother was to me. To him, I am a ghost— the ghost of a mistress past.

"Say, Johnny, you all right?" the publican says.

Mr. Cullen nods, then says to his friends, "Can you give a fellow a little privacy?"

They move to the bar, casting curious glances at me. I sit beside Mr. Cullen and say, "You know who I am, don't you?"

He gulps ale from his glass, and the color seeps back into his face. "You must be related to Mary Bain."

"I'm her daughter."

His shock turns to suspicion. "Mary didn't have a daughter. Who are you really?"

I'm not surprised that my mother kept secrets from him too. "I was away at school when she lived in Isleworth. I only came home for holidays."

"Well." Mr. Cullen regains a semblance of his jovial, flirtatious manner. "How about a drink for a young lady who's as beautiful as her mother?"

He signals the barmaid. She brings me a glass of ale and lingers until he waves her off. "How is Mary, by the way?"

His charm grates on me like fingernails on a chalkboard. "She died. In 1875."

"Oh. I'm sorry; I didn't know." Mr. Cullen sounds not particularly ashamed of his ignorance or saddened by my mother's passing. "I haven't seen her since a year or two before then. She told me she didn't want to see me anymore."

I can guess why: I'd come home, and it would have been difficult for her to hide Mr. Cullen and me from each other. Liquor could ease me through this awkward encounter, but I don't touch my glass. "How long had you known my mother?"

His eyes avoid mine. "Oh, Mary and I went way back."

"How far back?" I want to know whether they were acquainted at the time of Ellen Casey's murder.

He acts as if he hasn't heard my question. "We'd been out of touch. Then I happened to run into her at the train station." Talking fast, he reminds me of someone frantically shoveling dirt to bury something he doesn't want anyone to notice. He says with a forced laugh, "Never thought I'd see her again. Small world, isn't it?"

"Where did you meet?"

Mr. Cullen seems glad to change the subject. "In Ely. I was a commercial traveler for Pears. I handled the accounts in that region and visited shops and beauty salons to hand out free samples and drum up new customers. Mary's father owned the hotel where I stayed. We met, and she took a fancy to me." He smiles proudly, showing white porcelain false teeth. "I was quite the ladies' man in those days."

That he and my mother both worked for Pears seems a dubious coincidence. I put together what he's just said with what I learned when I visited Ely, her birthplace, last winter. A local gossip told me she'd refused to name the father of her illegitimate child, and folks speculated that it was someone from out of town. I do some mental arithmetic and leap to a stunning conclusion.

"Lucas Zehnpfennig was your son?"

The panic in Mr. Cullen's eyes tells me it's true. Raising his hand to shush me, he looks around to see if his friends have heard what I said.

"You got her with child when she was only fourteen!" I'm too outraged to care that I'm airing his dirty laundry and my mother's. "How old were you at the time?" I calculate a rough estimate. "Thirty?" I regard him with disgust. "You ought to be ashamed of yourself."

"For God's sake, keep your voice down!" Mr. Cullen whispers.

I've blamed my mother for her secrets and lies, for Ellen Casey's murder, my father's predicament, and my own troubled past. But she started out as an innocent child, and the man sitting in front of me is the root of her evils. "You abandoned her to have your bastard and face the consequences by herself!"

"I didn't know she was with child," Mr. Cullen bleats. "And even if I had known, I couldn't have married her. I was already married."

"Of course you were." Contempt joins my disgust. "A married man having fun with a vulnerable young girl."

"A few weeks after I left Ely, Pears changed my territory. I never went back, never heard from Mary. She didn't tell me about the boy until weeks after we met at the train station and started seeing each other again."

My head is spinning; all these revelations are too much. "What did she say about Lucas?"

Mr. Cullen squirms. "She said he was in America. She asked me to give her money, for her and the boy."

My mother had stopped working at the Pears factory before she fell ill. I thought she was living on her savings, but now I see that she had another source of income. Perhaps it wasn't a coincidence that my mother moved to Isleworth, obtained a job at the company for which Mr. Cullen worked, and crossed paths with him again.

"And you paid her because you cared about her and Lucas?" Maybe I've misjudged him. "Because you thought you owed them something?"

He smiles as though he's eaten something rotten and wants me to think it tastes good. "My wife was still alive then. Mary threatened to tell her everything."

My clever, devious mother must have gone looking for him in order to blackmail him. I feel bitterly smug because Mr. Cullen has validated my bad opinion of her; yet I'm appalled because she was even worse than I thought. But something about his story doesn't jibe with the magnitude of his fear of exposure.

"You must have had many affairs, and your wife must have known," I say. His sheepish expression tells me I'm right. "Why was it so important to hide the one with my mother? And why pay her to keep quiet about Lucas? He was a grown man, far away in America. It wasn't as if he was going to show up at your door, demanding that you take him in."

Mr. Cullen mops his perspiring face with his handkerchief. "I don't want to talk anymore. Please go."

Comprehension excites me. "My mother told you about Ellen Casey, didn't she?" The pressure to confide her secret must have built up in her during all those years until it became intolerable.

"Oh, God."

"That's what you couldn't let her tell your wife. What exactly did she say?"

He gazes woefully at me, like a slapped child. "Don't make me tell. Please."

Dread holds down my triumph, like a heavy net thrown over a flock of birds. "Ellen Casey was murdered in 1866. My father, Benjamin Bain, was and still is the prime suspect. You might have read about him in the newspapers. But he's innocent." Desperate for evidence that will exonerate one parent at the expense of the other, I lean closer to Mr. Cullen. "Did my mother tell you what really happened?"

Mr. Cullen recoils.

The thing I hunger for, my father's exoneration, is finally, after all these years, within my reach. I grab Mr. Cullen by his lapels and shake him so hard that the carnation falls out of his button-hole. "If she told you something that would clear my father's name, then you have to tell me!"

The publican calls, "Hey, lady, take your hands off him, or I'll throw you out."

I obey, glad that the publican intervened before my temper overpowered me and I hurt Mr. Cullen and ended up in jail. The odious man is withholding the information that will set my father free and change his and Sally's and my lives forever.

Mr. Cullen smooths his rumpled coat, picks up the bruised car-nation, and puts the flower back in his buttonhole. His eyes glint with spite. "I don't think Mary would have wanted her daughter to know about her, but since she's dead, it won't matter to her. And you seem more concerned about your father than protecting your mother's memory. So I'll tell you: she said she killed that girl. Are you happy now?"

The relief is so massive, I could swoon. My father didn't mur-der Ellen, and I need no longer doubt him. He need no longer live under a false name or sneak around to see Sally and me. We can be an ordinary family, and I can introduce him to Barrett, Mick, and Hugh. I'm already planning a dinner party for him at my house, looking forward to showing him my studio. But there's still the matter of setting things right between him and the law.

"I'll be happy when you tell the police what you just told me," I say.

Mr. Cullen combines a laugh with a gasp. "I'm not telling the police."

"Why not?" I'm dismayed that he's balking at this critical junc-ture. "As you said, my mother is dead; it can't hurt her."

"Because they would want to know why she killed the girl, and the whole story would come out."

"What story?" I know, but I want him to say it.

He clears his throat and looks away from me. "That the boy . . . that he . . . took advantage of the girl. Mary only killed her to protect him. Don't you see?" His gaze pleads with me. "I've been hoping to meet the boy someday, but if I tell the police, he can never come back to England." An odd, shy tenderness inflects his voice. "No matter what he's done, he's my son. My only son."

I nip his fantasy of a reunion in the bud. "I'm sorry, but I have bad news for you," I say. "Lucas died in 1880."

His face falls. "Oh, no."

I remember those weeks after my father's disappearance, when I hoped he would come back, and then my mother's telling me he was dead, and I truly pity Mr. Cullen. Then he draws a deep breath, as if he's shed a burden. No matter how much he wanted to meet Lucas, he's relieved that his illegitimate son the rapist will never disrupt his cozy life. All my sympathy for him vanishes, and I see an advantage for myself.

"So it doesn't matter if the police know what Lucas did," I say. "They can't punish him."

"It matters to me! I don't want my name dragged through the mud."

I'm unsurprised but still outraged by his attitude. "You would let an innocent man be hanged for murder, just to protect your reputation?"

"Find another way to prove he's innocent. Leave me out of it." Mr. Cullen fingers his carnation, trying to mend its crushed petals.

"You are a selfish, vain, despicable monster. *You* ought to be hanged!"

"Aw, I'm not that bad." He flashes his jovial, false-toothed smile. "When someone's in need, I'll give the shirt off my back. Just ask anyone around here."

I'm shaking with anger and my effort to contain it. "You owe me more than your filthy old shirt. You ruined my mother when you saddled her with your bastard. And Lucas grew up to be just like you, with a taste for young girls."

"It must be in the blood." He actually sounds proud, a monster who fathered a monster. "Whatever he did, it's not my fault—I didn't bring him up."

"It's all your fault!" If he'd left my mother alone, Lucas wouldn't have been born, and Ellen Casey wouldn't have been murdered. "I'm going to tell the police what my mother told you."

Mr. Cullen chuckles with sly, condescending humor. "Go ahead. I'll deny I ever knew Mary or met you." He gestures to his friends at the bar, who are openly, avidly watching us, regarding me with hostile gazes. "And they'll back me up."

CHAPTER 17

Two hours later, when I arrive at home, I'm still burning with anger at John Cullen. I wish I'd picked up my heavy ale glass and bashed his face, the consequences be damned.

I find Mick lying on the chaise longue in the parlor, and after I tell him about my clash with Mr. Cullen, I say, "Barrett was right—I shouldn't be so quick to go on investigations by myself. I should have asked him to come with me. He could have taken Mr. Cullen to the police station and made him confess that my mother told him she killed Ellen Casey."

"But you couldn't've known who the guy were," Mick points out. "You couldn't've known he had a personal stake in protectin' Lucas."

"True." I sink onto the sofa, my anger at myself soothed a little. But my premature plans for celebrating my father's freedom have burst like a soap bubble, and I think of him hiding at the Gladstone Arms, afraid that his additional day spent in London will increase his risk of getting arrested. "I'll just have to find some other way to exonerate my father."

"Don't worry; you will," Mick says.

I'm encouraged by his confidence in my abilities and luck, thankful for his companionship. "Any word on Hugh?"

Mick sadly shakes his head. "It's like he dropped off the face o' the earth. Fitzmorris is still out lookin'."

We gaze at each other, sharing a terrible thought: *what if he never comes back?*

The bell on the front door jangles. "Maybe that's him, and he lost his key," Mick says. We run downstairs. Mick unlocks and flings open the door. Outside stands a man wearing a beige mackintosh and black derby, his coat collar turned up and his hat brim shading his eyes so that all I clearly see of his face is his dark moustache and beard.

"I'm sorry; the studio is closed," I say, disappointed because he's not Hugh.

"Sarah Bain?" he says. "Mick O'Reilly?"

"Who's askin'?" Mick says, leery because our notoriety has resulted in strangers showing up at our door, eager for a gawk at us.

"I heard you're looking for Lord Hugh Staunton." His accent is crisp, posh.

My hope resurges. "Have you seen him recently?"

"No." Something in his tone—regret or shame?—tells me that he and Hugh were once lovers. "But I know a place where he might be."

★ ★ ★

Past eleven o'clock at night, Cleveland Street in west London is a dark canyon, filled with fog and smoke, between tall buildings. A workhouse anchors one end of the block down which Mick and I walk; at the other end is a hospital. We stop across the street from a four-story brick building, the only one in the terrace with lights in the windows. I shiver in the cold, uncomfortably aware that I don't belong here, but I couldn't bear to wait at home while Mick went in search of Hugh. Veiled by the fog, we watch solitary men arrive on foot or in carriages. Each casts a furtive glance around the street before he pushes through the gate and knocks on the door. When the door opens, we hear muttered speech, and then he disappears into the building.

"Our turn," Mick says.

We approach the door, and I pull my scarf up higher around my chin. Light shines through a peephole, and an eye scrutinizes us. I stand as tall as I can in the trousers, coat, and bowler hat I've donned for the occasion. It's not the first time I've disguised myself as a man. I've fooled people in the past; I only hope I can this time. The man who answers the door is neat and bespectacled; he looks like an office clerk. He waits for us to speak.

"Abyssinia," Mick says, using the password Hugh's friend gave us.

We're in. The room resembles a public house taproom, with men standing at the bar and sitting at tables. I expected a band, men dressed as women, and couples dancing, but this house of assignation is quiet, the conversation muted. I don't get a good view of anyone, because while the patrons eye me, I avoid their gazes, as if that could keep them from seeing through my disguise.

Hugh isn't among them. I'm hoping he's somewhere else on the premises when a youth clad in the uniform of a telegram delivery boy comes up to me.

"How 'bout a drink?" he says.

I've heard that certain delivery boys conduct business that has nothing to do with telegrams. I'm tongue-tied, far outside my realm of experience. Mick says, "Sorry, he's mine." He takes my arm, steers me back to the doorman, and says, "Can we get a room?"

"Second floor, room three."

Mick and I climb the stairs to a passage in which all the doors are open except one, from which we hear thumps and muffled cries of pain. Mick knocks on the closed door and calls softly, "Hugh?"

There's no answer. I wring my hands, afraid that Hugh has given in to his self-destructive urges and taken up with someone violent. Mick shouts, "Hugh, it's me and Sarah. Are you all right?" He twists the knob, pounds on the locked door. "Open up, or I'm bringin' the coppers!"

The door opens to reveal a stout, bearded, angry man. I can see the dark hair on his chest, because he's naked except for a towel wrapped around his hips. "What the hell?"

Mick and I push past him into the room. It's hot from the fire in the grate, and the air reeks of male body odor. Stretched out on the bed is a slender, pale-skinned man with blond hair, a sheet covering his loins. His arms and legs are spread, his ankles and wrists tied to the bedposts. A horsewhip lies beside him. Red lash marks crisscross his chest.

"Hugh!" I rush to him, then stop in my tracks because he's not Hugh but a younger man, his face soft and pug-nosed.

"What's the fuss?" His accent is Cockney, his manner resentful. "It's just a game."

Now I see his erection poking up under the sheet. Blushing hotly, I turn away, ashamed because I intruded on strangers.

"Sorry. We're lookin' for Hugh Staunton. It's an emergency, and I thought he were in here," Mick says with more aplomb than I can summon. "Either of you seen him?"

The hairy man shakes his head, but the blond says, "Yeah, I did. Can't recall exactly when, though. On the Highgate Archway."

★   ★   ★

Certain bridges in London are notorious for suicides. The Highgate Archway, in the northern part of the city, is one such bridge. Mick and I run along its top span, calling, "Hugh!"

A train thundering along the lower span drowns our voices. The fog is so thick, the night so dark, and the lamps spaced so widely that I can't see more than three feet in any direction. I zigzag from one side of the bridge to another. A horse drawing a carriage gallops toward me, and Mick pulls me clear of its path just in time. The driver curses at me as it passes. Mick and I traverse the entire, deserted bridge, then lean over the railing and look down.

All we see is dark, swirling mist. How far is it to the road below? Forty, fifty, or sixty feet? Did Hugh, in his troubled state of mind, think that if he jumped off the bridge, he would escape his pain and fly into blissful oblivion?

"Hugh!" I cry.

CHAPTER 18

Where the Clerkenwell House of Detention once stood, now only the high brick wall around the perimeter remains. At seven o'clock on this cold, foggy Tuesday night, Barrett, Mick, Sally, and I walk through the unguarded gate. I'm carrying my smaller, portable camera and tripod; Mick has the flashlamp and trunk of supplies. We find ourselves in a vast, open space, where tall piles of rubble look like mountain ranges on the moon. The massive dungeon, with its central octagonal structure crowned by a lookout tower, has been razed. It seems impossible that an edifice that seemed so mighty and permanent, that once contained thousands of prisoners every year, is gone.

Mick says, "When we get home, Hugh will be there."

Last night, after failing to locate Hugh on the bridge or the road below, Mick and I inquired at the local police station, which had received no reports of a jumper. We checked at the nearest hospitals, where no attempted suicides had been admitted, then went home at dawn. Fitzmorris had just returned, in despair because he'd found no trace of Hugh.

"Don't worry, he's fine," Sally says, putting her arm around me.

I pray that if Hugh didn't jump off the bridge, he didn't take his life somewhere else, in some other manner. Our group feels incomplete without Hugh, my usual, stalwart companion on adventures like this. The painful void in my heart grows bigger with every moment he's gone.

"Remind me why we're here," Barrett says to me. "If you don't believe in ghosts, you can't be expecting to find any."

"I do expect to find some of the suspects here," I say. "I'd like a chance to question them again." I'd also like to fully convince myself that ghosts don't exist.

Our conversation lapses. Earlier, Barrett told me that he'd taken a squadron of constables to Bethnal Green Workhouse, but he was unable to find Nat Quayle or the men I'd described who'd attacked Mick and me. They must have figured I would report them and that the police would be coming and made themselves scarce. Now Barrett is stewing, frustrated because he didn't get justice for me, and the tension from our argument hasn't gone away.

"We got company," Mick says.

I become aware of shadowy figures—there must be dozens—walking among the rubble. Barrett says, "I thought this event was just for the Society for Psychical Studies."

"Sally, your article in the newspaper must have brought out the curiosity seekers," I say.

"Yeah, they're lookin' for a little fun before Halloween," Mick says.

Firelight glows from a large, irregularly shaped hole in the ground that looks like an entrance to hell. People descend into it as if they're the souls of the damned. We follow them down an iron staircase to a dank cellar illuminated by lanterns hung on rusty gas pipes on the walls. The gas must have been turned off before the demolition. The scene is as noisy and cheerful as the lobby of a theater on opening night. I see fashionable ladies in fur coats, accompanied by impeccably tailored gentlemen, among the plainer locals. Everyone crowds around the arched entrance to a dim tunnel that's blocked by a man clad in a sleek black overcoat and tall top hat.

"That's Richard Trevelyan," I say to Barrett. "Charles Firth's publisher."

Mr. Trevelyan greets acquaintances and welcomes them into the tunnel. He says to a group of local men, "I'm sorry; this event isn't open to the general public."

"The newspaper didn't say that," one man says. He and his companions push past Mr. Trevelyan. Other people follow suit.

"Good to see you, Mrs. Barrett and Mr. O'Reilly. You can go right in." Mr. Trevelyan flashes his toothy smile at us before he turns his attention to the invading horde. "I say, this is a private event. Stop, please!"

We're swept into the tunnel, a long, wide, straight corridor with brick walls, an arched ceiling, and a worn, uneven paved floor. More lanterns hang from disused gas pipes. Their flames flicker in the cold, damp draft that carries the fetid odor of cesspools. The jail hasn't lost all its power to inspire uneasiness. I shiver, imagining that it's absorbed the evils suffered here for some two hundred years. But the crowds seem to relish the sinister atmosphere. They open the creaky iron grates that barricade the cells, examine the old bunks and washbasins. Other photographers are setting up their cameras. Voices and laughter echo. Unlit tunnels branch off from the main corridor. We come upon a crowd peering into a chamber in which Leonora Firth and four other women sit at a round table, colorful shawls draped over their hats and coats. Smoking incense burners surround a lit candle in the center of the table. A notepad and pencil in front of Mrs. Firth are ready for spirit writing.

"Excuse me, who are you trying to contact?" Sally asks. She's told her landlady that she'll be spending the night with me, and she's happy to escape her curfew, excited to cover the story of the ghost hunt.

"The spirit of a little girl that's been heard sobbing in the tunnels," Mrs. Firth says, pointedly ignoring Mick and me.

Children convicted of crimes were imprisoned at the jail, and I suppose many sickened and died here. I photograph Mrs. Firth and her circle; then I lead Barrett, Mick, and Sally farther down the tunnel. It opens into a large, octagonal room that must be below where the tower once stood. Eight stone pillars in a ring at the center support the ceiling. Bull's-eye lanterns hung on them emanate beams of light that crisscross in midair. A doorway at the far end leads to another dimly lit tunnel. Dr. Lodge in his white coat stands in the center of the room, his arms spread to shield his magnetometer from the crowd.

"Don't touch!" he says. "This is a valuable, delicate scientific instrument."

"Hello!" Anjali, in a gray coat with a black velvet collar and matching black velvet hat, leaves her father's side and runs up to us.

She and Mick smile at each other. The air suddenly seems vibrant, and I don't think it's from the kind of magnetic field that Dr. Lodge's apparatus measures.

Anjali curtseys and daintily extends her hand, palm down, to Mick. "My lord."

Mick bows, takes her hand, and bends his head to kiss it. "My lady."

Anjali giggles with delight, but as Mick's lips touch her skin, her eyes and mouth open wide with sudden terror. She yanks her hand away from him.

"What's the matter?" Mick says, disconcerted.

"You have to go!" Anjali says.

"But I just got here."

She pushes him toward the exit. "Just go. Please!"

"Don't you want me here?" Mick sounds hurt.

"You're in danger."

"Danger, from what?"

"I don't know!"

Dr. Lodge hurries over to his daughter. "Anjali, did you have a vision?"

"Yes, Father, but I've already forgotten what I saw." Her face a picture of distress, Anjali says to Mick, "I just know that if you stay, something terrible will happen to you."

Mick grins, relieved that this isn't a brush-off. "I been through terrible stuff before. I can take care of myself."

"You would do well to heed Anjali's vision," Dr. Lodge says.

"Please!" Her eyes sparkle with tears. "I couldn't bear to see you hurt."

Mick offers her his handkerchief with the masculine condescension of a hero in a romantic novel reassuring the damsel in distress. "Don't worry. I'll be all right."

"She once warned me not to go out, and I didn't listen," Dr. Lodge says. "I was knocked down by a runaway horse. I was lucky to suffer only a broken arm. I could have been killed." He says to Barrett and me, "If you care about your young friend, you should take him away."

"It sounds like you don't want us here," Barrett says.

Dr. Lodge subjects Barrett to his cool, detached scientist's scrutiny. "And you are . . ."

"Detective Sergeant Barrett, Metropolitan Police."

"Oh." Suddenly flustered, Dr. Lodge says, "I just don't want anyone injured. And I don't want this expedition disrupted by trouble of any kind."

I think he's eager to get rid of the police detective and reporters who are investigating the murder case in which he's a suspect. "We'll watch over Mick," I say.

Anjali stands close to Mick. "So will I."

Dr. Lodge frowns. "Anjali, I need your help with my experiment."

Anjali sighs. "Yes, Father." As she reluctantly accompanies him back to the magnetometer, she casts a longing glance at a forlorn Mick.

I wonder if Dr. Lodge is afraid that Mick will take liberties with Anjali or that she'll tell him something that pertains to the murder, something Dr. Lodge wants to keep secret.

Mick and I are photographing the scene, and Sally is interviewing Dr. Lodge about his magnetometer, when angry voices blare from the tunnel. Leonora Firth screams, "Stop them!"

Jean Ritchie, dressed in a long, violet wool cape and a feather-trimmed black hat, marches into the room with another woman who's fair and pretty, with upswept blond hair and a royal-blue hat and coat. They carry megaphones. I'm surprised to see Jean, because if she doesn't believe in ghosts, why come to a ghost-hunting expedition?

Leonora Firth rushes up to Jean. "How dare you show your face here?"

"Oh, I've enough gall to show my face anywhere I like," Jean says with a flippant smile.

Mrs. Firth utters an indignant cry and points to the exit. "Get out!"

"We've as much right to be here as you." The blond woman speaks with an Irish lilt. Now I recognize Diana Kelly minus the luminescent green face paint. "This isn't your private property."

Mrs. Firth grabs Jean by the arm. Diana hits Mrs. Firth with her megaphone and shrieks, "Leave her alone, you crazy bitch!"

The crowd flocks around them to watch. Barrett, the only law officer present, says, "Hey! Break it up!" He wades into the melee and shoves the combatants apart. They glare at him. "Who are you?" he asks Jean.

"I'm the president of the Ladies' Society for Rational Thought." Jean indicates Diana. "This is my second-in-command."

"Ha! The Harridans' Society for Libel and Slander would be more apt," Mrs. Firth says.

"What seems to be the problem?" Barrett says.

"She tried to ruin my husband." Mrs. Firth lunges at Jean. I grab her and restrain her.

"He and his kind have ruined people by cheating them of their life's savings," Diana says.

"The spiritualist movement is too strong for you to destroy with your screeds and lawsuits," Mrs. Firth huffs. "So you took it a step further." She says to Barrett, "She killed my husband. Arrest her!"

Jean regards Mrs. Firth with scorn. "Oh, stop acting the bereaved widow. You had more reason than I to want him dead. Wasn't it humiliating to watch him lavish his attention on everyone except you? Especially when the objects of his attention were female?"

Mrs. Firth gasps and clutches her chest as if she's been shot. "Charles was always a devoted husband to me."

Diana sniffs. "A devoted husband who squandered money on other women who were down on their luck. And how do you suppose they repaid his generosity?"

This is an ugly portrayal of Charles Firth. Am I but one of many women who gained at his wife's expense? Did he intend to extort sexual favors from me, after selling me photography equipment at a discount had put me deep enough in his debt? I don't want to believe it's true.

"I wager you got rid of him so he couldn't land both of you in the poorhouse," Diana says.

Mrs. Firth sputters. "You're just bitter, jealous old maids."

"Better old maids than a fool," Jean retorts.

"Ladies, ladies. This is neither the time nor the place for a squabble." Richard Trevelyan steps into the scene, a noble peacemaker between battle lines. "Miss Ritchie, if you and your friends would please . . ." He extends his arm as if to usher them out.

Jean turns on him. "Oh, you'd like us gone before *your* reason for wanting Charles Firth dead comes to light. You can make extra money now from the sales of his books, with all the publicity surrounding his death."

Mr. Trevelyan grimaces and hunches his shoulders. Dr. Lodge calls to Jean, "Please remove yourselves. You're creating a hostile atmosphere for my experiment."

She laughs. "If ghosts really existed, you wouldn't need a gadget made of scrap iron to detect them. Oh, by the way—didn't you have your own grudge against Charles Firth? I heard he was a member of a faction that wanted to oust you from the presidency of your society."

Dr. Lodge pretends not to hear, but he twists a knob on his magnetometer so hard that it breaks off in his hand.

"Did you get all that, Mrs. Barrett?" Jean says with a sly smile. She beckons Diana and says, "Onward!"

As I marvel that she's handed us three additional motives for three murder suspects, the pair march out of the room and into the tunnel beyond, shouting through their megaphones, "Attention, everyone! Ghosts aren't real! They're a hoax perpetuated on you by charlatans!"

Mrs. Firth sobs, and the women from her séance circle bear her away. More people crowd into the room, and Dr. Lodge says, "This is a disgraceful mob scene. Richard, can't you find a way to barricade the entrance?"

Mr. Trevelyan departs, a man swimming against the flood tide. Reporters accost him, and he stops to give an interview.

Barrett looks around the room. "Where's Mick?"

"I don't see him, or Anjali. They must have sneaked off together." I see the flashlamp and supplies by the magnetometer, where Mick left them. I don't put much stock in Anjali's visions, but I'm alarmed nonetheless. "Sally is gone too."

"We'd better find them," Barrett says.

I leave the camera and tripod with the other equipment so they won't hamper us; I hope they're safe enough. Barrett takes my hand, and as we head toward the tunnel that leads deeper into the prison, he says, "Stay with me. Don't go wandering alone."

I think it wise to obey him this time. Beyond the octagon, the main tunnel is lit, but the cells and chambers are dark. People stray into dimmer branch tunnels, in which the lanterns hang at wider intervals with deep shadows between them. Eerie moans raise goose pimples on my skin.

"It can't be a ghost. It's somebody pretending." But I'm uncertain in spite of myself; the atmosphere breeds superstitious fear.

Barrett frowns at some young toughs joking and shoving one another as they swig from whiskey bottles. "They're from the Somers Town Boys gang. This could turn bad. As soon as we find Mick and Sally, we should go home."

"A splendid idea." I've already gotten enough food for thought from Jean Ritchie.

We venture along a dim, narrow branch tunnel and peer into the darker cells. We find a young couple kissing, but it's not Mick and Anjali. As we push our way through the crowd in another tunnel, Barrett says, "There must be thousands of people down here."

Their numbers seem to be growing by the moment, and I smell liquor on breath that vaporizes in the air. Shrill cries of "Ghosts! Ghosts!" rise above the cacophony of voices.

Half the crowd runs toward the cries, carrying me along; the other half flees in the other direction, taking Barrett. His hand rips loose from mine. I break free of the crowd as it spills into a junction between wider tunnels. Two children clad in tattered white sheets with cut-out holes for their eyes are running about, flapping their arms, and hooting like crazed owls. Spectators scold, laugh, or groan because they were tricked. I retrace my steps, looking for Barrett. He's not where we parted; he must have gone in search of me. I head down the main tunnel, toward the octagon. The crowds have grown even larger, streaming in and out of tunnels. The atmosphere is as raucous as at a carnival, tense with expectancy, as if the main show is about to begin. Amid the roving strangers, some twenty feet distant, I see someone familiar. He's wearing a wool coat instead of a gray smock, and a derby covers most of his blond hair, but I know that puffy-eyed, thick-lipped face. It's Nat Quayle.

Our gazes meet. He's not alone; his companions are the inmate who led Mick and me into the trap at the workhouse and the piggish man who was among our attackers. With their faces partly in shadow, partly illuminated by the flickering lantern flames, they resemble ghouls in a painting by Hieronymus Bosch. They recognize me, and their expressions turn fierce, predatory.

I turn and run. As I weave through the crowds, I hear the men's footsteps pursuing me. What do they mean to do to me? Kill me because I set the police on them? If Quayle wasn't the enemy yesterday, he is now. I shout for help, but people glance at me, then ignore me; they think it's another ghost prank. Some women stand chattering and laughing near the entrance to a tunnel. I hide among them and watch, for a heart-pounding instant, while Quayle and his companions hesitate. Quayle points down the branch tunnel, and the three hurry into it. I race down the main corridor. If I can get to the octagon room, I should be safe; they wouldn't dare attack me under bright lights in the presence of many other people. I pause only to glance into another branch tunnel in search of Barrett, Sally, and Mick. I see a man and woman together, her blond hair faintly shining in the light from a distant lantern. She's turned away from me; all I can discern about the rest of her is the silhouette of her dark dress with its protruding bustle. The man is Richard Trevelyan. He and the woman stand intimately close, talking in loud, angry whispers.

Dr. Lodge said he'd seen a blond woman accost Charles Firth after a Society meeting. Could this be the same woman? Curious to know who she is and what the argument is about, I steal into the tunnel. My shoe crunches on broken glass. Mr. Trevelyan sees me and frowns. As the woman starts to turn toward me, he mutters a warning, seizes her arm, and hurries her away down the tunnel. I follow. Then I see, in the distance beyond them, Nat Quayle and his friends coming toward me. The men quicken their steps, push past Mr. Trevelyan and the woman. I whirl and run. Turning corners, I lose my sense of direction. The crowds are sparser, the tunnels dimmer; I can't find my way back to the octagon. The heavy footsteps behind me sound louder and nearer, quickening with malicious intent. Breathless, I force a burst of speed from my tired legs. On my left side are iron-grated doors to cells; on my right, a solid wall. I've reached the perimeter of the jail. There's nobody else in sight. Ahead is a corner where the wall meets another wall. Just before I reach the junction, one of the inmates bounds past me and cuts off my escape.

I skid to a halt, trapped in the corner. Nat Quayle and the other man catch up with us. As the three surround me like a pack of dogs who've run a deer to ground, I see an opening in the wall near me. It's a tall, narrow slot carved into the stone, the space inside completely dark. Without thinking about what's in there, I hurl myself into the slot.

The men curse as darkness swallows me up. I grope along a passage so narrow that I can touch both sides without fully extending my arms. Rough bricks scrape my fingers, cobwebs graze my face, and a chill, damp draft moans like a madwoman in an asylum. This must be some sort of ventilation tunnel. Quayle and his friends aren't following me. I see, in the far distance, a vertical band of light—an exit. But my relief is short-lived; they might intend to trap me when I come out. Beating them to the exit is my only hope of escape. I fumble blindly while the light at the exit grows larger by tiny increments. The tunnel is divided into sections separated by stone barriers with narrower, higher slots cut in them. I squeeze through the slots, my progress slow and laborious.

The darkness and the enclosed space seem to compress my lungs; I gulp and choke on the draft. None too soon, the band of light at the end is large enough that I can see the stone floor on which I'm stumbling and the brick walls around me. If Quayle and his friends ambush me, so be it; if I stay in here, I'll suffocate.

When I stagger out of the tunnel, the sudden glare of light dazzles my eyes. I blink, look down the corridor, and see perhaps twenty people gathered in the middle, near the wall. They're all gazing down at something on the floor. Nat Quayle and his friends are nowhere in sight, to my fervent relief. One woman presses her hands against her cheeks and screams repeatedly, shrill as a train's whistle. Everyone else seems too stunned to move or speak.

Instinct born of calls to scenes of crimes, accidents, and natural disasters takes over. I hurry to the crowd, elbow my way through it, and see a man crumpled on the floor, his legs bent, his arms flung wide. At first I think he's wearing a red shirt under his black coat, but then I notice the blood puddle spreading from under his body. His top hat lies near his head, his silvery hair gleams, and his bony face is slack. It's Richard Trevelyan. His vacant eyes stare up at the ceiling, and his mouth gapes open, his large, yellowish teeth half submerged in blood like stones around a red pond.

But I just saw him, alive and well, less than half an hour ago. He can't be dead!

Someone is kneeling beside him. My surprise at his death is nothing to my shock when I recognize Mick.

Mick cringes, as though from guns pointed at him. Eyes blank with fright, he holds up his hands, which are red with blood.

CHAPTER 19

"Mick! What happened?" I say.

He rubs his eyes as if to wake himself from a bad dream; blood from his hands smears his face. "I don't know."

Leonora Firth appears beside me, gasps, and moans. "Richard! Oh, no." Her knees buckle, and the women from her séance circle hold her up. "He must have been killed by the same spirit who murdered Charles."

The crowd makes way for Dr. Lodge and Anjali. The girl covers her mouth with her hands as she stares at Mick. Dr. Lodge speaks with a mixture of consternation and excitement. "I did detect a strong magnetic field that indicated a supernatural presence."

His words provoke scornful exclamations from Jean Ritchie and Diana Kelly. "Nonsense," Jean says. "There's the killer, right under your nose." She points at Mick.

As the other spectators murmur in agreement, Anjali utters a cry of protest.

"It weren't me!" Mick says.

I'm horrified, because although I know Mick can't be the killer, I see how this must look to everyone else. To me he looks young and helpless, as much a victim as Richard Trevelyan, but the crowd jeers. Photographers crowd around him with their cameras, and flashes explode. He winces and recoils; the blood on his face and hands gleams red in the bright lights.

"I knew something bad was going to happen," Anjali says mournfully.

I tug at the photographers' arms. "Get away from him!" Mick has never seemed so vulnerable, or so precious to me, and I don't want his picture on the front pages of the newspapers. I shove their cameras and knock one onto the floor.

Its owner swats my cheek. "Bitch!"

"Nab the little rotter before he runs away!" someone shouts.

The stupid idiots have jumped to the conclusion that Mick is guilty, based on nothing but happenstance. A mob rushes toward him, pushing aside the photographers, trampling my feet. I hear Barrett yell my name, and suddenly he and Sally are beside me. We struggle to reach Mick.

He's on the ground, kicking and punching the men who are trying to capture him. "Get yer hands off me!"

A shrill, deafening whistle blares, echoing through the tunnels. The police are coming, and I'm not relieved; their arrival can only make things worse. The heavy tread of booted feet accompanies beams of light that sear my eyes. The crowd scatters like bats at daybreak as police constables invade the scene, shouting, "Break it up!" Mick, Barrett, Sally, and I are stranded with Richard Trevelyan's body in the merciless glare of the lanterns the constables aim at us.

Inspector Reid steps forward from the ranks of the police. "What have we here?"

He's always been the last person I wanted to see, but never more so than now. He halts a few paces from the body and looks down at it, frowning in surprise. His gaze moves to Mick, who jumps to his feet and braces himself. Barrett, Sally, and I step closer to him as Reid notices us. Reid smiles as if he's been given a present.

"Well, well. I've finally got you." Reid seems more delighted to find me than Mick at the scene of what's obviously a crime.

"I didn't kill him," Mick says. "I found him like this."

"Spare me the blarney. You're literally red-handed."

"I tried to stop the bleeding," Mick says, "but he were already dead when I got here."

Reid chuckles. "That's what they all say."

Most of the locals in the crowd have disappeared; they're leery of police who are looking for someone on whom to pin a crime. Most folks still present are the fashionably dressed outsiders. I see them nod, agreeing with Reid.

Barrett points to Mr. Trevelyan's chest. "See the hole in his shirt? He was stabbed. If Mick did it, where's the weapon?"

I look up and down the tunnel and see nothing on the floor. Reid says to a constable, "Search him."

During a brief tussle, the constable pulls picklocks, coins, and a pocketknife from Mick's clothes. He unfolds the knife, looks at the blade, and says, "No blood on it, guv."

Reid seems unfazed. "He must have cleaned it. Or used a different one and hidden it. We'll search later. Mick O'Reilly, you're under arrest for murder."

Spectators cheer; a constable brandishes handcuffs. Mick's chest swells with indignation. "I didn't do it. You got the wrong guy again, you blunderbuss."

His bravado is heartbreaking. Reid's expression darkens with anger at this reference to the time he arrested an innocent man for the Jack the Ripper murders. "Not this time." Gloating satisfaction lights his eyes; he means to pay us all back for our role in the trouble he got into after his mistake.

"You'd better do some investigating before you jump to conclusions again," Barrett says.

"This isn't your case. Back off," Reid says. He and Barrett glare at each other.

"This murder resembles Charles Firth's," I say to Reid. "Two spiritualists murdered, each while hunting for ghosts in underground places. The two cases must be connected."

"The main thing I know they have in common is you and your friends," Reid says.

"The suspects from the first murder are all here tonight," I say. "Richard Trevelyan is still a suspect in that case, even though he's the victim in this one. And then there's Leonora Firth, Dr. Lodge, and Jean Ritchie . . ." I look around and discover they're gone. So are Diana and Anjali. Did they flee to protect themselves from the police? "You should question them."

"Oh, I'll be questioning all the *witnesses*, eventually." Reid's emphasis makes it clear that that's all he thinks the people I mentioned are.

I'm outraged, because I'm sure he means to use any evidence that incriminates Mick and ignore any that doesn't. "A little while ago, I saw Mr. Trevelyan with a woman. They were arguing."

Reid favors me with a pitying shake of his head. "Inventing a suspect to get your friend off the hook. Aren't you smart enough to come up with a better trick?"

"It's not a trick! I think it was Diana Kelly." I haven't seen anyone else with such pale blond hair. "She's a friend of Jean Ritchie."

"I saw them too," Barrett says, stepping forward to put himself between Reid and me. "They went into a tunnel together."

I'm glad to have my statement corroborated but vexed at Barrett for trying to protect me when I don't want protecting; I want to tear Reid's head off. Reid rolls his eyes at Barrett; he thinks my husband is lying for me. He nods to the constable, who seizes Mick and yanks his hands behind his back.

Mick struggles and yells, "Let go of me, you bastards!"

It takes three more constables to hold Mick still. The metal cuffs click around his wrists. The spectators applaud as the constables drag him away, with Reid leading the little parade like a general after a victory on the battlefield. I run after Reid and grab his arm.

"Damn you! He's innocent, and you know it!"

"Unhand me, or I'll arrest you as an accomplice." Reid's sly smile says that arresting me would be icing on the cake.

I pull back my fist to punch Reid. Barrett pulls me away from him, and Sally says, "Sarah, go home. I'll report in to the *Daily World*."

Wild with desperation and fury, I flail in Barrett's grasp. "No! I can't let him do this!"

"Ouch!" Barrett says as I kick his shins. "Sarah, stop. There's nothing you can do now."

As the police march him down the tunnel, Mick calls over his shoulder, "I'll be all right, Sarah." His voice rings with false confidence. "Take care o' yourself."

★ ★ ★

Whitechapel at two in the morning is deserted except for vagrants huddled in doorways and alleys. Rain slices through the fog, glittering in the yellow halos around the streetlamps. Barrett and I arrive at my house without my photography equipment, which we were unable to retrieve before the police cleared everyone out of the tunnels. I doubt I'll ever get it back. The entire Clerkenwell House of Detention is now a crime scene. We're drenched from the walk to the train station; people who left the tunnels ahead of us commandeered the few cabs available. I'm freezing, my hands so numb that I drop the key twice before I can fit it into the lock. We tiptoe upstairs. The house is empty, which can only mean that Hugh is still missing and Fitzmorris is out looking for him. I hoped to share the terrible news with Hugh, hoped we could band together to save Mick. The house is so quiet, so cold.

"Shall I make tea?" Barrett says.

I shake my head. My throat is parched, but in my exhaustion, all I want is to sleep, to have this night end, and to wake up to a brighter day tomorrow.

In my room, Barrett builds a fire in the grate. I'm shivering so hard that my teeth chatter as I peel off my wet clothes. Lacking the strength to wash or put on my nightdress, I crawl into bed naked, curl up, and shiver under the blankets. My face is a frozen mask, my feet lumps of ice. Barrett undresses, climbs in with me, and molds his body against my back, his knees tucked behind mine and his arms around me. I'm thankful he's here; he's all I have left; but he's barely warmer than I am.

"I've friends at Clerkenwell police station," he says. "They'll look after Mick tonight."

It's not the night in the station jail that worries me the most.

"In the morning, I'll go to police court and try to persuade the magistrate to dismiss the murder charge," Barrett adds.

"What if he won't?"

Barrett pauses; his breath stirs my hair. "Mick will be remanded to Newgate to await trial."

I moan in despair. How many defendants who've been found bloodstained at murder scenes have been acquitted?

Barrett hugs me tighter. "We'll catch the real killer before then. We'll exonerate Mick."

Thus far I've failed to exonerate my father, so why should I expect success for Mick? His situation seems hopeless and Hugh's return unlikely. Am I destined to lose everyone I love? I grip Barrett's arm, pull him closer, as if fate will tear him from me too. Gradually the internal heat of our bodies spreads outward, the places where our skin touches grow warm, and I cease shivering. The space under the blankets is a safe, private world for the two of us. I feel Barrett's manhood swell against my back.

"I'm sorry." He sounds ashamed; he pulls away from me. "I know this isn't a good time."

My own body responds with an ache of desire so powerful that my eyes close, my mouth opens, and I almost swoon. It's been such a long time since we've made love, and tonight's experiences intensify my need. The terror when Nat Quayle and his henchmen chased me; the horror of Richard Trevelyan's corpse; the Clerkenwell jail's dark atmosphere of imprisonment, suffering, and mortality—these memories goad me to a blind, instinctive search for something good in life. I turn to Barrett, take him in my hand, and stroke.

"You don't have to," he says, even as he moans and grows harder. He thinks I'm doing it just to please him. "We can wait."

I grab his hands, cup one around my breast and thrust the other between my legs. He caresses me with unusual gentleness, as if I'm so fragile that he's afraid of hurting me. His touch is pleasure that drives me wild with impatience for more. This is our wedding night at last. I move against him, increasing the contact, the friction. Now his lust gives in to mine, and he kisses me. As our tongues and breath melt together, I'm struck by the notion that this is marriage at its most primal level. If we have nothing else in the world, at least there's this physical coming together, a gift from heaven that's soothed humans in times of trouble since time began. I want to make it last, to delay the moment when my troubles reclaim me, but I can't wait.

I push Barrett onto his back and straddle him; I grasp his manhood and slide him into me. We've made love before, but this is something I've wanted to do and thought was too unladylike. My own audacity enflames my need. I ride him as if I'm on a horse. We yell as he holds my hips and bucks under me. All our differences, quarrels, and bad feelings fall away from us. We speed toward the pleasure that, when it comes, is the most incredible we've ever experienced together, and nothing else matters.

CHAPTER 20

In the morning, I cook breakfast for Barrett, the first time as his wife. We sit at the table together, cozily domestic. From the street drift the sounds of wagons rattling and voices calling, of Whitechapel waking up and coming to life. On the surface, this could be an ordinary morning before a day filled with ordinary problems and pleasures. But the sore emptiness lodged in my heart couldn't be permanently banished by last night's passionate lovemaking.

Hugh is still gone, Fitzmorris hasn't returned from hunting for him, and Mick is in jail. Mick and my father are both depending on me to clear their names, and I'm afraid I'll let them down. From the street I hear cries from newsboys, and I can imagine what they're saying: *Murder at the haunted jail! Killer caught red-handed!*

Barrett finishes his burnt toast, runny eggs, and weak coffee. I'm an indifferent cook at best, and this meal wasn't up to even my usual standard. "That was delicious." He squeezes my hand and says, "We can fix this. Everything will be all right."

He leans across the table, and we kiss. A little of last night's rapture comes back to warm me. Comforted, I manage a smile.

Barrett pushes back his chair. "I'm off to Clerkenwell magistrate's court. I'll do my best for Mick. Shall I pick you up at six tonight?"

"For what?" My brain is a mire of apprehension, and among the many things we have to do today, I can't think of one that requires us to meet at an exact time.

"Dinner with my parents," Barrett says.

"Oh, God. I forgot."

Barrett regards me with sympathy; he knows that the last thing I can bear to face is the prospect of more family discord. "You need to eat," he points out.

Neither of us wants to risk offending his mother and adding more troubles to our plate. "All right," I say. "Six o'clock."

★　★　★

The rain has stopped, but Fleet Street is awash in water sweeping garbage, grime, and horse manure into the drains. Moisture saturates the air, and the scene around me—the buildings, the wagons and cabs, and the hurrying pedestrians—is blurred, like an out-of-focus photograph. The droplets that wet my lips taste of bitter, poisonous chemicals. At the entrance to the *Daily World* headquarters, I pause, recalling the countless times I've come here with Hugh and Mick. Inside the building, I walk up the stairs to Sir Gerald's office. I can't bear to take the lift that Hugh and Mick think is so much fun. Their absence is more haunting than any ghost could be.

When I show myself at his open door, Sir Gerald stands up behind his desk and holds out a copy of the *Chronicle* for me to see. The front page has a big photograph of Mick. Kneeling in the tunnel, his bloodstained hands raised, his teeth bared, and his eyes wide in the stark light of the flash, he looks like a vampire interrupted while feeding. A jury that sees this photograph will surely believe Mick is guilty. I want to tear it up, but the newspapers are already all over the city. Instead, I address my new, lesser, but undeniable problem: the *Daily World* has been outdone by its biggest rival.

"I'm sorry I didn't take photographs last night," I say, bracing myself for the reprimand. On top of everything else that's happened, I'm sure to be fired.

"Under the circumstances, I'm not going to hold it against you. And I'm sorry about Mick." Sir Gerald folds the newspaper, says, "This is hogwash," and throws it in the wastebasket. "I know Mick didn't do it. I read the story that Sally gave the copy editor. Mick was at the wrong place at the wrong time, and Inspector Reid took advantage."

He hands me a copy of this morning's *Daily World*. I skim the story, in which Sally defends Mick in the most sympathetic terms, deploring his arrest as "a ridiculous, disgraceful attack by a corrupt police official who shall remain nameless." I'm grateful to Sally for her loyalty, but by taking a potshot at Inspector Reid, she's painted a target on her own back. I'm relieved that Sir Gerald's good opinion of Mick hasn't changed.

"Can you get Mick out of jail and the murder charge dismissed?" I say.

Sir Gerald has friends in high places all over the world. I know he can bend the law to his will, but now he directs his gaze out the window, at the towers and spires of London shrouded in polluted fog. I was foolish to expect such a big favor from a man who has cut my friends and me loose when we've gotten into other scrapes. I suppose I should be thankful I still have my job. Then anger overpowers my despair. After everything we've done for him in the line of duty, and all the secrets we've kept for him, Sir Gerald would stand idle while Mick goes to the gallows?

Before I can voice my thoughts, he turns and says, "When I was in the shipping business, there was a fire on one of my ships. The only survivor was a deckhand. Some fishermen pulled him out of the water. He was burned over his whole body. Before he died, he told them what had happened. A sailor was trapped below deck. He was the captain's son. The captain should have taken the other men into the lifeboats. Instead, he ordered them to help him rescue his son. They all went down with the burning ship."

"That was different," I say. "In this case, a whole ship isn't sinking, and Mick is the only person whose life is at stake."

Reproach darkens Sir Gerald's eyes. "Life isn't only a matter of flesh and blood."

He's telling me that his business is his life, but I already knew. The success of his business depends on his reputation, which he won't jeopardize by pulling strings to free someone the public believes is a murderer.

"I didn't say I won't help Mick," Sir Gerald says. "I'll get a good barrister to defend him at his trial."

He's offering far more aid than I could have expected from him. "Thank you," I say, although I am far from satisfied and still angry.

"I'll be honest with you, though," Sir Gerald says. "Even the best barrister can't always change the minds of a jury that's already decided a man's guilty. The best way to save Mick is for you to find the real killer."

★   ★   ★

In Lonsdale Square, the garden is as deserted and bleak as a cemetery. The fog is heaviest around Leonora Firth's townhouse, as though some magic spell has gathered it like a shroud for the widow in mourning. I want to ask Mrs. Firth if she was involved in Richard Trevelyan's murder, and I won't take any spiritualist nonsense for an answer. Walking up to the door, I smell smoke. It's not from coal in a stove, coming out the chimney. This smoke rises, dense and black, behind the house, above the roof. The house is on fire.

I pound the knocker against the door. "Mrs. Firth!"

There's no answer, no sound from within the house. Running back to the street, I shout at passersby, "Fire! Help!"

Then I hurry around the corner, down the alley behind the townhouses. The smoke billows over the wall that encloses Mrs. Firth's back garden. Coughing, I yank open the gate. Determined to rescue Mrs. Firth, heedless of my own safety, I rush into the garden. There, crackling flames leap from a large metal drum. Mrs. Firth staggers out of the house, her arms laden with clothes. I breathe a sigh of relief to see that she's alive and the house isn't burning.

"What are you doing?" I say.

Mrs. Firth beholds me with vacant eyes; she doesn't seem to recognize me. "Getting rid of these things."

Despite the cold, she's wearing only a dressing gown and bedroom slippers. Her face is red and swollen with tears, her spectacles askew. As she heaves the clothes into the drum, I see a man's shirts and trousers among them. The flames die down for a moment, then flare higher.

"Are those your husband's clothes?" I'm disturbed to see his possessions destroyed so soon after his death. "Why are you burning them?"

Mrs. Firth hurries back into the house, her movements stiff and jerky like a marionette's. She seems to have undergone a mental breakdown since last night. She returns, carrying an armload of papers. Her left foot has lost its slipper, but she doesn't seem to notice. Dropping some papers, she tosses the rest into the fire. A fountain of sparks erupts.

"Look out!" I grab her arm, pull her away from the drum.

She twists free even as the sparks ignite the papers on the ground. I stomp out flames that curl and blacken them. Mrs. Firth mutters unintelligible words and stumbles back to the house.

I follow her. "Is this because of what Jean Ritchie said last night?"

Maybe what she said about Charles Firth was true, and since then Mrs. Firth has faced the fact that her beloved husband ignored her while lavishing kindness and money on other women. Maybe she's taking out her anger on his possessions. If she hears me, she gives no indication. I think the events of last night have tipped her over the edge of madness.

"Did you kill Richard Trevelyan?" I can't picture her stalking him through the tunnels, stabbing him, and running—but less likely people have turned out to be murderers.

Sobbing now, Mrs. Firth steps through the open door. I see, on the floor of a passage, a large heap of things she must have culled from the house. She fills her arms with more papers and clothes. I block her path to the fire.

"Why did you leave the scene when the police came?" I ask.

"Get out of my way." She pushes past me, tramples the singed papers on the ground.

"Where were you before Mick found Mr. Trevelyan's body?"

The roaring flames are so hot, the smoke so suffocating, that I can't go near the drum, but Mrs. Firth stands dangerously close to it. The papers she's throwing in are photographs. She's laughing as well as crying, her movements reckless. A sudden, visceral memory plunges me into the past. I'm ten years old, my mother has just told me that my father is dead, and she's burning his photographs—his life's work, all that's left of him. I fight her, trying to rescue them, but she's too strong, too determined. Now I brave the flames to rescue these photographs. They're Charles Firth's pictures of ghosts in cemeteries, at funerals. As I bend to snatch them, sparks set them on fire. The flames climb up Mrs. Firth's thin satin dressing gown. She screams, reels backward, and staggers as it burns.

I hear whistles shrill and a racket of wheels and hooves in the street. The fire brigade is coming, but I can't wait. I tear off my coat and beat it against Mrs. Firth's legs. She falls on the ground, wailing as the heavy wool puts out the flames. The firemen burst through the gate, lugging a hose, and spray water from a tank and steam engine on the wagon parked in the alley. Soon the fire is extinguished, the garden a sodden mess. The smell of smoke lingers. Spectators gawk from the windows of neighboring houses. I crouch by Mrs. Firth. Her dressing gown has burned to black tatters, and the skin on her legs is red, raw, and blistered. She moans.

"Ma'am, we'll take you to the hospital," says a fireman.

"You should have let me die!" Howling, she lies on her back, banging her head, fists, and heels on the ground.

The firemen turn their puzzled gazes to me. I say, "She's not in her right mind."

As they carry her away on a litter, her howls echo in the smoky air. "I want to die!"

Left alone, I put on my singed coat. Then, compelled by the memory of my childhood, I pick up the single undamaged photograph from among the burnt debris. It's a copy of one I recognize from Charles Firth's studio, of the blond, beautiful female ghost wrapped in a translucent white sheet. I carefully roll it and tuck it in my coat pocket, as if preserving his work could make up for my failure to rescue my father's. Then I see a charred handbill. Enough of the print is legible that I can read the title—*The Ladies' Society for Rational Thought*—and the address below.

CHAPTER 21

Bruton Street is located near the fine shops, restaurants, and hotels of Mayfair, in a terrace that appears to date from the previous century. The elegant, well-maintained houses are built of brick, trimmed with white, and crowned with dormers set in slate mansard roofs. As I walk toward number twelve—the address on the handbill I saw at Mrs. Firth's bonfire—a private carriage draws up outside. Jean Ritchie emerges, wearing her violet cape and feather-trimmed black hat, carrying her megaphone. She sees me and frowns, but she strides up to me without hesitation.

Sir Gerald would like her. She doesn't back away from trouble.

"What are you doing here?" Jean's complexion is pale with fatigue, but her eyes are bright and sharp as ever. "Shouldn't you be trying to exonerate Benjamin Bain?"

I'm blindsided, speechless.

Jean laughs. "Don't look so surprised. I've read about your father in the newspapers."

Regaining my voice, if not my dignity, I say, "That doesn't make him any of your business."

"Point taken," Jean says, "but if *my* father were accused of murder, I would be trying to exonerate him. You don't seem the kind of woman who sits on her hands. I bet there's more to the story of your father than has been published. Am I right?"

She must know I came to talk to her about Richard Trevelyan's murder, and she's taking the offensive. Panic crawls under my skin as my need to exonerate my father clashes with my need to do the same for Mick. The time I spend on one investigation is at the cost of the other, and I mustn't let Jean distract me.

"It looks like you've been out all night," I say. "Where did you go after the spirit-hunting expedition?"

Jean responds with a secretive smile. "Now, that's none of *your* business."

"It is if it has anything to do with the murder of Richard Trevelyan." I raise my voice as pedestrians eye us with curiosity.

"If you want to trumpet to the world about the murder of Richard Trevelyan, I'll trumpet about the murder of Ellen Casey," Jean says in an equally loud voice. She laughs at my frown, then walks up to her door. "Let's go inside where we can spar in comfortable privacy."

In the foyer, a maid greets us and takes our coats. Jean says, "Coffee, please, Marie," and shows me into the drawing room. Unlike the overfurnished, oppressive houses of other rich people, hers is bright, open, and airy, the walls painted a light green. The furniture is of natural, unstained wood, its design simple and rustic. Curtains, carpet, upholstery, and hanging tapestries feature interlocked, abstracted patterns—rose and tulip, iris and bamboo. Stems of dried seedpods in green earthenware vases decorate the plain wooden mantelpiece over the hearth, in which a welcoming fire burns. Vertical stained-glass panels with inset vines and leaves partially divide the drawing room from a library. The total effect is of a fresh breath of nature, with a modern originality that one would expect of Jean.

"This is a beautiful house," I say, not without envy.

"Thank you. It was my grandmother's." Jean gestures to the only old-fashioned item—the lone painting, a portrait of a woman dressed in a style popular some forty years ago. "That's her. She was a leader in the campaign for property rights for women. She also worked for the passage of a bill to make divorces easier to get."

With her long face, bright eyes, and air of vitality, the woman in the portrait bears a distinct resemblance to Jean. I reflect on how much our forebears influence our lives. If my mother had been a social reformer instead of a murderess, what would I be?

Jean seats us by the fire, on clover-and-honeycomb-patterned sofas that face each other across a wooden table strewn with hand-bills and pamphlets. The handbills advertise classes for women in subjects including reading and writing, English language for for-eigners, arithmetic, and business skills. I flip through a pamphlet titled "Female Health" and see shockingly detailed anatomical diagrams of menstruation, sexual congress, pregnancy, and child-birth. Apparently, debunking spiritualism isn't Jean's only interest.

"I use the house as headquarters of the Ladies' Society for Rational Thought," Jean says, as her maid returns with the coffee. She moves the handbills to make room for the tray. "Our classes and meetings are held here. I live upstairs. How did you find me?"

When I tell her, she says, "Poor, deluded Leonora Firth." Pity colors the distaste in her expression. "She's one of the first women I tried to dissuade from believing in ghosts. Needless to say, she wasn't receptive. Why did you call on her?"

"To ask her the same question I came to ask you: did you kill Richard Trevelyan?"

"Leonora Firth is dangerous because she spreads superstition, but do you really think she's a murderess?" Jean's tone scorns the idea.

"Answer the question. Did you?"

"No." Her gaze holds mine, and she doesn't add more denials that would make me think she's lying.

"Then why did you leave the scene when the police came?" I say.

"Do you take milk and sugar?"

I raise my cup of black coffee and narrow my eyes at Jean. She sighs. "I left because there was a chance that they would look for other suspects besides your friend Mick, and I didn't want to get in a finger-pointing contest with Leonora and Dr. Lodge and their colleagues. Since they outnumbered me, I'd have been sure to lose and wind up in jail."

Drinking the hot, fragrant coffee, I wonder if Jean's real reason for leaving was that she herself committed the murder. "Where were you when Mr. Trevelyan died?"

"Diana and I were marching in a tunnel at the other side of the jail, speaking through our megaphones. We were quite conspicuous. Hundreds of people must have noticed us."

That's a good alibi, but not necessarily invincible. "I saw Diana with Richard Trevelyan shortly before he was murdered."

Jean sputters as she sips her coffee. "That's impossible. She and I stayed together the whole time."

I think this woman who's clever enough to stage fake séances is clever enough to play innocent. "How well did Diana know Mr. Trevelyan?"

"She didn't know him at all."

I remember how intimate the two appeared. "Were they lovers?"

"No."

"How well do you know Diana?"

"Well enough to know that she's not involved with anyone. How well do you know your friend Mick? Would you wager your life that he's innocent?"

I ignore her questions rather than jumping to Mick's defense and wasting more time. "I need to talk to Diana. Where can I find her?"

"You really think she killed Richard Trevelyan?" Scornful amusement twists Jean's mouth. "That's ridiculous. She wouldn't hurt a fly."

"Perhaps not a fly, but a man associated with Charles Firth, who sold her fake photographs of her late husband's ghost."

"Are you so sure you saw her?" Jean says. "It wasn't exactly as bright as broad daylight in those tunnels."

"I'm sure." But my identification was far from positive, and Jean has weakened it, which of course she meant to do.

"How's your eyesight? Maybe you saw someone that you mistook for Diana." With a sly smile, Jean hints, "Many women are too vain to wear spectacles."

I can imagine people swearing off spiritualism just to give Jean Ritchie what she wants and shut her up. She's a most vexatious woman. "Where is Diana?"

"She didn't do it," Jean says. "You're just trying to get your friend off the hook by pinning the murder on someone else."

That I can't deny, but I still think it was Diana I saw with Mr. Trevelyan. My patience wearing thin, I say, "Perhaps I should ask your friends Emily and Ruth about Diana."

"Go ahead. They weren't with us last night, and even if they knew where Diana is, they wouldn't inform on her."

I didn't see them, and it seems possible to rule them out as suspects in both murders. "Would you rather answer to the police?"

"I would tell them the same thing I'm going to tell you." Jean puts down her coffee cup, sits up straighter, and announces in a clear, defiant voice, "Diana has left London. I'm not going to reveal where she's gone."

Her secretive smile when I asked her what she'd been doing last night led me to think Jean was with a lover, but now I picture her and Diana packing suitcases, riding in a cab, and hugging good-bye at the train station.

"Did you smuggle Diana out of town?" I demand. "Is that what you did after you left the tunnels?"

"I won't dignify those questions with a reply." A hint of gloating steals into Jean's tone.

I'm suspended between dismay and elation. That my best suspect has decamped is bad news, but it's also evidence that Diana is guilty. Why else would Jean conceal her whereabouts?

"Are you so sure Diana is innocent?" I say, wanting to erode Jean's faith in her friend the way she tried to erode mine in Mick. "Are you as gullible as people who believe in ghosts?"

Jean only smiles at my attempt to rattle her. I stand up, the better to threaten, and say, "I'll tell the police that you're helping her to hide."

Jean stands too, and she shrugs. "Do what you must to protect your friend; I'll do what I must to protect mine."

We glower at each other, heads high, nostrils flared. Our sparring is over, the gauntlet flung down, but Jean has the advantage because this is her house.

"If Diana killed Mr. Trevelyan, you could be arrested as an accomplice," I say.

"I'll take my chances." Jean adds, "If you really want to find out who killed him, perhaps you should look in his own back garden."

On my way out of her house, I barely resist my impulse to sweep the pamphlets off the table and onto the floor.

★　★　★

The neighborhood in which Dr. Lodge and Anjali live has seen better days. Located in Bloomsbury, near University College where Dr. Lodge teaches, Burton Crescent is a Regency-era terrace built on a road that curves around a semicircular garden. The white stucco facades on the ground floors proclaim the grandiosity of the designer and the wealth of the original residents, but now there are many boarding houses with signs advertising rooms to let. Dr. Lodge's house, at the south end, is adjacent to an establishment with a plaque on its gate that reads HOME FOR DESERTED MOTHERS. The house on its other side has meticulously pruned shrubbery in its tiny front garden A maid dressed in a black frock and white apron and cap is polishing the brass hardware on the door. When I climb out of the cab and walk up to the Lodge house, she pauses in her work.

"Lookin' for Dr. Lodge?" She's stout, her face like an unbaked pie—pasty skin, eyes and mouth like slits cut to let out the steam.

"Yes," I say, "and his daughter."

A dirty smile turns her from plain to ugly. "The girl ain't really his daughter, you know." She lowers her voice to a conspiratorial whisper. "Her ma was a pupil at the college. She got knocked up by a Hindoo who was studying there. He went back to India and left her with the little brown brat. She came to live yonder." The maid points at the Home for Deserted Mothers. "She started workin' for Dr. Lodge as his charwoman. One thing led to another— he married her and adopted the brat. It didn't turn out so well for them, though. Her family disowned her, and his disowned him, and then she died of consumption." Gathering up her rag and tin of polish, the maid regards me with the sly satisfaction of a servant who's secretly spit in a guest's teacup. She says, "Good day, mum," and goes inside her employer's house.

I'm shocked because I thought Dr. Lodge's wife was Indian, but it seems she was English, and he's not Anjali's blood father. When he spoke of Anjali's mother, he gave no hint that she was dead. If the maid is telling the truth, Anjali is half an orphan, like me.

I knock on Dr. Lodge's door. The man himself promptly answers. With his bony face drawn from fatigue, he looks more than ever like a medieval saint. "Mrs. Barrett," he says, clearly displeased to see me. "What brings you here?"

For a moment I'm speechless as my opinion of him changes. This stiff, pedantic man married a woman who had an illegitimate child and sacrificed his familial ties. He's raising his half-Indian stepchild as his own, and I think he truly loves Anjali.

"I want to speak to you about last night," I say.

The displeasure on his stern face deepens. "I've nothing to say to the press."

He starts to close the door, and I hesitate for an instant before I use my foot to jam it open. He's a murder suspect, but he and Anjali comprise a pair that's not unlike my own father and me—in danger of being ripped apart by the law.

"I'm not here as a newspaper reporter," I say. "I'm investigating the murder because my friend Mick O'Reilly has been arrested for it. He's innocent, and I'm trying to find out who really killed Richard Trevelyan."

"I don't know, so I can't help you," Dr. Lodge says.

For Anjali's sake, I don't want him to be the killer. I'm reluctant to pressure him, but even as we speak, Mick must be in police court. "Would you rather I publish a newspaper story that says you refused to talk to me and hints that you're hiding something? Other reporters will be after you. So will the police."

His gaze turns icy with hostility. "Publish this in your paper: I didn't kill Richard Trevelyan. It's illogical that I would have, because we were friends. And, from a practical standpoint, he was the publisher of my monographs. Now I'll have to find another publisher, which won't be easy or inexpensive. Are you satisfied?"

"A few more questions. Where were you before Mr. Trevelyan was found dead?"

"With Anjali. You saw us together."

"In the octagon room, yes. But she sneaked out with Mick."

"I was demonstrating the magnetometer. My fellow members of the Society can vouch for me. Furthermore, there were thousands of people in the tunnels. Any of them could have killed Richard, perhaps during a robbery gone wrong."

I can't deny the possibility, but I still think the murder is connected to Charles Firth's. "If Mr. Trevelyan was your friend, then why did you leave when the police showed up? Why not try to help them solve his murder?"

Dr. Lodge's lips thin to a tight, angry line. "Anjali was upset. I took her home."

"I'd like to speak with Anjali."

"That's not possible. She's indisposed."

I wonder if he doesn't want her talking to me because he's afraid of what she might say. "Then perhaps I could speak with her mother." I want to verify the maid's story, if only to satisfy my curiosity.

Pain fills Dr. Lodge's bloodshot eyes. "Anjali's mother is deceased. Good-bye, Mrs. Barrett." He pushes the door hard against my foot.

I step backward so my toes won't be crushed. After the door slams in my face, I pound on it a few times, in vain. Then I trudge down the street, intending to question the neighbors and test Dr. Lodge's alibi for the night of Charles Firth's murder. Maybe he wasn't at home; maybe he left the house while Anjali was asleep and someone saw him. I can't omit him from my investigation just because I would rather not find evidence that he's guilty.

From behind me, a high, girlish voice calls, "Mrs. Barrett, wait!"

CHAPTER 22

A breathless Anjali runs up to me, her open coat flapping like wings over her dark-blue skirt and white blouse.

"Anjali, what are you doing?" I'm glad to see her, but I say, "If you're ill, you shouldn't be outside."

"I'm not ill. I told Father I was because I couldn't bear to go to school."

But she looks peaked, her eyes red and swollen from crying. I choose between my need to question her and my fear for her health. "I'm taking you home."

She walks quickly along Burton Crescent, away from her house. "What's happened to Mick? Father burned the newspapers before I could read them. He wouldn't tell me anything."

I hurry to keep up with her. "Mick was arrested."

"Oh, no!" Anjali turns to me, her gaze filled with despair. "I knew something bad was going to happen to him, and when he wouldn't leave, I should have made him stay by my father and the people from the Society. But I let him talk me into exploring the tunnels. I was so stupid!"

I've often wondered whether I could have prevented Ellen Casey's murder. Perhaps if I'd been home that day, it wouldn't have happened. I feel sorry for Anjali; she can't change the past any more than I can.

"It's not your fault," I say. "When Mick sets his mind on doing something, he's hard to stop." I don't mention that I think it was mere coincidence that Anjali's vision preceded Richard Trevelyan's murder; I don't want to upset her by casting aspersions on her "talent." Nor do I say it's understandable that a girl with a crush on a boy will follow him anywhere. She feels bad enough without my rubbing it in.

"Where is Mick?" she says.

"Probably on his way to Newgate Prison." I doubt that the magistrate dismissed the murder charge, and I don't want to give Anjali false hope.

"Oh, how I wish I could help him!"

"Maybe you can. Tell me where you were and what you were doing between the time you left the octagon room and the time you showed up at the murder scene."

"Mick and I wandered around, and then we started playing tag. I ran, and he chased me. There was a big crowd, and we got separated. I should have stayed with Mick!"

"It's all right," I say, although I too wish they'd stayed together and Anjali could give Mick an alibi. "What happened then?"

"My father caught me. He scolded me for sneaking away. He was angry because I'd made him waste forty-five minutes looking for me when he should have been doing his experiment. On our way back to the big room, we heard screams and followed everybody to see what was wrong. That's when we saw Mick with Mr. Trevelyan's body." She shudders.

I feel a stirring of excitement: Dr. Lodge's alibi has just weakened. According to his own words to his daughter, he'd had forty-five minutes on his own in the tunnels before he found her. That would have been ample time to encounter Mr. Trevelyan and stab him. And then Dr. Lodge could have shown up at the murder scene with Anjali and pretended he was seeing it for the first time. But I'm immediately heartsick, because I've led Anjali to incriminate her father. If the police had questioned me about Ellen Casey's murder, what would I have told them? Did I possess information that I've since forgotten? Could a careless remark from me, a ten-year-old, have sent my father to the gallows before he had time to run away?

Anjali doesn't seem to perceive the import of what she's said. "Mick and I were separated for only a little while. He couldn't have done it."

Now I feel even worse for her, because she's a witness who can cast suspicion on both her father *and* Mick. "When I see Mick, maybe he can tell me something that will help clear his name."

"You're going to see Mick?" Eagerness brightens Anjali's face. "Can I go with you?"

"I don't think so." Newgate is no place for a child.

Anjali chews her lower lip; she nods as if she's made a decision. "Then I'll go by myself." She breaks into a run.

I hurry after her. "Anjali! Come back!" I feel responsible for her, and it's dangerous for a girl to roam the city alone.

On Euston Road, she bolts past cabs and omnibuses, into King's Cross station. I'm a fast runner, but she's faster. Inside the grand, palatial building, she buys a ticket and races down the stairs to the underground before I can catch her. I fumble in my pocket-book for coins, get my ticket, and chase her down to the platform. The train is there, passengers exiting. Anjali jumps aboard. I hurl myself through the door just before the conductor slams it shut. Dropping onto the bench beside Anjali as the train chugs down the track, I glare at her while I catch my breath.

She smiles sheepishly. "I'm sorry, but I really need to see Mick."

I haven't the heart to talk her out of it, and I want to do something to make up for leading her to give evidence against her father. "I'll take you, but I'm bringing you straight home afterward. And you have to promise me you'll never do anything like this again."

"Oh, thank you!" More delighted than chastened, she says, "I promise."

★   ★   ★

Newgate Prison gradually becomes visible through the fog as Anjali and I walk toward it. Details gain clarity, as if on a photographic negative plate in developing solution: first the granite blocks of the high walls, then the bricked-in ornamental windows at the second-story level and the chimneys puffing smoke. When we join the people waiting in a long line outside the visitors' entrance, Anjali whispers, "Have very many people died in there?"

I remember a visit to Dead Man's Walk—the infamous passage between Newgate and the Old Bailey, beneath which hundreds of criminals executed at Newgate lie buried. Not wanting to upset Anjali with grisly tales, I say, "The prison is seven hundred years old. I suppose that many people have died in every building in London that's of similar age."

"I can feel them," Anjali says.

The last thing I want now is more spiritualism. "I thought you only have visions from touching someone or something."

"When a presence is strong enough, I don't need to touch." Anjali casts her gaze up toward the dungeon, where the tops of barred windows show above the outer wall. Faint moans drift down to us. "Mama used to tell Father that I was better than his scientific instruments at detecting ghosts." Anjali smiles, as if cheered by the memory.

I seize the chance to learn the truth about her background. "How long has your mother been gone?"

"Six years. She had consumption." Sadness erases Anjali's smile.

Anjali must have been younger than I was when my father disappeared. "I'm sorry."

"Oh, it's not so bad for me, because I can still feel her as if she's in the next room, and when I touch her things, I can see her. But I know Father misses her terribly. He's lonely with just the two of us."

I feel bad for probing wounds from the past just to verify gossip. "Have you any relatives?"

"Yes, but we never see them. My mother's family disowned her when she had me. And my father's family disowned him when he married my mother." Anjali delivers these sad facts as calmly as if reciting a lesson from school.

There are too many people who would shun the woman because she had an illegitimate, mixed-blood child and the man because he married her. Anjali and her father must have been as isolated as my mother and I were.

Anjali sees my pity and says, "It's all right. We have friends."

I'm glad she's found people who accept her, as I found Hugh, Mick, and Barrett. But if her father were gone, who would take her in and support her? If I discover that he killed Charles Firth and Richard Trevelyan, I must expose him in order to save Mick.

We reach the entrance to the prison, ascend a flight of steps, and walk down a dim passage. Anjali trails her fingers along the wall, then recoils as if it has burned her. "So many people have come this way," she murmurs. "So much unhappiness."

I imagine legions of ghosts attired in costumes from past eras, walking beside us. When we emerge in a courtyard and the inmates yell and wave from barred windows in the buildings that rise around us, I can almost see pale, transparent wraiths among them. Superstition is too contagious. I shake my head to banish the illusion of more ghosts mingling with the folks gathered around the visiting box.

The visiting box is a big iron cage built against one wall. I avoid looking at the execution shed, a little house with wooden half doors like a stable, where convicted criminals are hanged. I hunt for Mick among the caged prisoners, hoping he's not there because he's been released. There are dozens of men, all dressed in gray uniforms. The visitors are mostly women. Now I spy Mick, a solitary figure slouched against the back of the cage. My heart lifts because I'm glad to see him alive, then sickens because his presence means he's been indicted and sent here to await his trial. His uniform is too big for him; he looks smaller, younger. With his expression tense and his eyes shifting as he watches for threats, he seems reverted to the street urchin he was when we first met.

Anjali waves to him, calling, "Mick!"

A grin blooms on his face as he hurries up to us. "Hullo, Sarah. Thanks for comin'." He turns to Anjali, blushes, and says in a gruff, tender voice, "I didn't think I'd see you again."

Anjali smiles and lowers her gaze, suddenly shy. "I was so worried about you, I made Mrs. Barrett bring me."

"Well, I'm glad you did."

I notice a dark-red bruise on Mick's cheek, and his nose is swollen. "What happened to you?"

"The police tried to get me to confess to the murder. They slapped me around a little."

"Oh, how terrible!" Anjali cries.

Fury rises in my throat like hot acid. "Inspector Reid will pay for this." I know Reid isn't only eager to solve the murder case; Mick's injuries are a message from Reid to me, telling me that he'll seize every opportunity to hurt me through my friends.

"Hey, don't go lookin' for trouble with him on my account," Mick says. "It weren't that bad. Is Hugh back yet?"

"No." That he can be concerned about Hugh and me at a time like this! I notice that his fellow prisoners are all older, bigger, and tougher looking than he. "How are you getting along with the other men?"

"Just fine. They ain't gonna mess with a cold-blooded killer." Mick smiles proudly.

Anjali frowns. "They think you did it?"

Mick leans close to the cage bars and whispers, "Don't tell 'em I didn't. If they find out I'm a poor sap who got nicked for somebody else's crime, I'll be everybody's punching bag."

I respect Mick for his ability to adapt to a bad situation, but I hate that he has to pretend he's guilty. "Are you getting enough to eat?"

"Yeah. Food here's disgustin', but Barrett brought me some good stuff. Oh, and Sir Gerald sent over a guy who says he's gonna help me when I go to court."

I'm thankful that Barrett and Sir Gerald are taking care of Mick.

"Do you mean you'll have to stand up before a judge and jury in Old Bailey?" Anjali says, solemn with worry.

"No, he won't," I say with more confidence than I feel. "We'll clear his name before it comes to that."

"Any luck so far?" Mick's feigned nonchalance tells me that he doesn't want to pressure me by showing how much he's depending on me.

I don't want to say in front of Anjali that Dr. Lodge hasn't an alibi. I tell Mick about my talk with Jean Ritchie. "I think Diana Kelly did it. I'll have Barrett mount a search for her."

Mick expels a breath of relief tinged with apprehension. "Hope she turns up." We both remember that Inspector Reid didn't believe me when I said I'd seen Diana with Richard Trevelyan, and it will be difficult to pin the crime on someone who's missing while Reid has his favorite suspect behind bars.

"But I also saw Nat Quayle last night, with two other men from the workhouse." I describe how they chased me. "He had time to kill Richard Trevelyan while I was trapped in that dark tunnel."

"He's a suspect in Charles Firth's murder too," Mick reminds me.

But I can't fathom what Quayle's motive for either crime would be. "We need more evidence. Did you see anyone near Richard Trevelyan's body right before you discovered it?"

Mick frowns in an attempt to recall. "There were people all over."

"Can you describe any?" I say.

Hope shines in Anjali's eyes. "They might have seen the killer."

"Two boys," Mick says. "They were playing ghost, wearing sheets over their heads."

"I saw them too, but we need witnesses we can identify," I say.

"A lady in a red hat. With a guy who was smokin' a pipe. And an old tramp in a patched coat." Frustrated, Mick rubs his head. "I been goin' over and over it, and it's mostly a blur."

"Did you see Jean Ritchie and her friends, or Mrs. Firth?" I can't mention Dr. Lodge due to Anjali's presence.

"No. That I'm sure of."

I turn to Anjali. "Can you describe any people who were around you after you and Mick left the octagon room?"

She responds with an embarrassed smile. "I wasn't paying attention to anyone except . . ." She glances at Mick. "I'm sorry."

I hope she doesn't realize that her father could be the killer, or that if Mick is convicted of the murder, Dr. Lodge will be safe. In my own case, at least my mother is dead and pinning Ellen Casey's murder on her will exonerate my father without hurting her.

Mick glances at me, then Anjali, then me again. I think my failure to mention Dr. Lodge hasn't escaped his notice. His silence tells me how reluctant he is to save his own life at Anjali's father's expense.

"Maybe I can help." Anjali places her palm between the iron bars of the cage. "Mick, if I can touch you, I might have a vision."

I can't deny that her premonition last night proved sadly true. Mick says, "Can't hurt to try," and presses his palm against Anjali's.

The two times I saw her have a vision, it seemed easy and spontaneous, but now she squints as if trying to see in the dark, and her whole body strains with her effort to capture an image from the ether. I feel none of the skepticism or exasperation that Leonora Firth's automatic writing and Dr. Lodge's magnetometer provoked in me. Mick's attention is riveted on Anjali. I sense his hope, his wish to believe in her. My nerves tingle with the intuition that I'm in the presence of something beyond rational understanding and therefore frightening.

Anjali drops her hand. Perspiration shines like crystal beads on her face. Gasping, she says, "I saw the tunnels under the jail. There was someone—a girl or a woman, wearing a white dress. She was crying. I think she's the ghost that people have seen at the jail. I think she knows who the murderer is."

I feel let down, because I think Anjali made up this story—not to deceive us, but out of a sincere desire to help. Perhaps she isn't even aware that she made it up. I also feel foolish because I was ready to believe in her. I try to catch Mick's eye, but he avoids mine.

"The vision ended there." Anjali's shoulders droop.

My skepticism returns, albeit not as firm as before. I can't help wishing Anjali had seen something that would help Mick. His disappointment is written on his face, but he humors her with gentle kindness. "That's a good clue."

I don't voice my critical thoughts about Anjali; I don't want to hurt her feelings. Instead I say, "Thank you for your help."

"I should go back inside the tunnel and find the ghost, and then she can tell me what happened," Anjali says.

"You better not go back," Mick says. "Someone's already been killed there. It's too dangerous."

He's protective of her at his own expense, a sign that their flirtation has developed very quickly into something more. I tell him about Sally's article in the *Daily World* and say hopefully, "Witnesses are bound to come forward."

If they don't, I may need to incriminate Dr. Lodge—no matter what it will do to Anjali and whether Mick and I like it or not.

CHAPTER 23

The bells at St. Botolph's Church toll six o'clock as I hurry out of Whitechapel station. After taking Anjali home and reporting in at the *Daily World* headquarters, I'm about to be late to meet Barrett to go to his parents' house for dinner.

Shouts blare from the alley that runs between my house and the Angel pub. Whistles shrill as police constables barge into the crowd that overflows the alley. Disturbances aren't rare in Whitechapel, but this one so close to home draws my attention, so I jostle my way through the melee. Amid yells and protests, the constables send the crowd scattering onto the high street and emerge with three captives in handcuffs. I recognize the two older men from the neighborhood, a shop clerk and a slaughterhouse worker. I can't tell if I know the third, a mere boy. His nose has bled all over his face and onto the white sheet draped around his shoulders. One of the other captives says to him, "That'll teach you to play ghost and scare everybody to death."

It appears that a Halloween trick has gone wrong. Then I see, in the alley, a man helping a woman to her feet. The man is Barrett; the woman is Sally. I rush to them, calling, "Sally, what happened?"

"Oh, hello, Sarah." Sally picks up her hat from the ground. Her face is streaked with mud, but she smiles brightly. "I heard a rumor that the ghost from St. Peter's was stalking Whitechapel, so I came to report on the story. I got here right when those two men were chasing the ghost."

"She was knocked down by the mob." Barrett's frown encompasses both Sally and me.

"I'm quite all right," Sally assures us. "I have to get back to work." She hurries after the constables and their captives, calling, "Excuse me, I'm a reporter from the *Daily World*."

"You're not the only one who should be more careful," Barrett says.

I'm horrified, and not only because the murder and the publicity have caused the unrest I feared. Sally, following in my footsteps, could have been killed.

Barrett doesn't press the issue; he knows I've gotten the message. "We'd better get over to my parents' house."

"I have to see if Hugh is back."

"He's not, and Fitzmorris isn't home. I checked. Let's go."

My hair is disheveled, wisps escaping from my braided coronet; my clothes smell of smoke from Leonora Firth's bonfire. But if I freshen up, we'll be late to the family dinner. We board an omnibus and take seats on top. With the fog swirling around our heads, obscuring the traffic and pedestrians below us, it's like riding through clouds. I tell Barrett what happened today.

"I'll talk to Mrs. Firth, Jean Ritchie, and Dr. Lodge tomorrow," he says. "Maybe I can get something out of them. And I'll start a search for Diana Kelly."

"Inspector Reid will be furious if he catches you interfering with his investigation."

"There is no investigation. Reid closed the Richard Trevelyan murder case."

I'm dismayed, because I know what that means. "He's sure Mick will be convicted."

"Yes. And he's not considering other suspects because he doesn't want to find out that the killer is someone else."

Such irresponsibility, such corruption, is beyond belief, despite my long history of distrusting policemen—with the exception of Barrett. I never imagined that one would go so far to satisfy a personal grudge. The officers who persecuted my father at least believed him truly guilty. "Was Reid always this bad?"

"He used to have a reputation for leaving no stone unturned during investigations and being a stickler for getting the right man. The Ripper case changed him." Sadness laces Barrett's disapproval.

The Ripper case changed many of the people involved, including me. "That doesn't excuse Reid's behavior."

"You can say that again. By the way, I went back to the Clerkenwell jail. The entrances to the tunnels are barricaded. I couldn't get in."

Meaning, unfortunately, that any clues at the crime scene are inaccessible to us.

"I walked the neighborhood and found lots of people who were down there last night," Barrett says. "Some saw Mick shortly before the murder, but that's not an alibi. And nobody I talked to actually saw the murder or remembers anyone except Mick near the scene."

"When I visited Mick at Newgate, he said he remembered a tramp in a patched coat, and a lady in a red hat with a gentleman smoking a pipe."

"Some of my witnesses saw that couple too," Barrett says. "Some also mentioned tramps. Apparently, a lot of tramps have been taking shelter in the tunnels. The local constables flushed them out before putting up the barricades. I'll try to find the one Mick saw. In the meantime, there's a bit of good news—the murder weapon is still missing."

Tentative hope cheers me. "Even the police can't deny the possibility that someone else killed Richard Trevelyan and took the weapon away."

The omnibus stops. We climb down the stairs and walk hand in hand down Bethnal Green Road. We exchange smiles, remembering last night's lovemaking, and our united strength seems more than enough to cope with whatever the world throws at us. Ahead looms St. Peter's Church. With its windows dark, its foundation immersed in shadows, and the spire on top of the tower hidden by the fog, I could almost believe it's haunted. Under a gas lamp on the corner, two hazy figures stand facing each other.

The shorter one holds out his palm. "That ain't enough. I want five more shillings."

"Forget it," says the taller, heavyset one. "We already shook on the deal."

Their voices are familiar, a confusing surprise. "Porter?" Barrett says, his voice rough with anger at the man who once betrayed him and more recently crashed our wedding breakfast.

Porter turns, his eyes agleam like those of a fox exposed by a hunter's lantern.

"Mr. Coburn?" I say to the other man.

The vagrant who set Mick and me after Nat Quayle looks aghast to recognize me.

"What are you doing here?" Barrett asks Porter.

"Just minding my own business," Porter says with false nonchalance. "Why don't you mind yours?"

I look from Porter to Mr. Coburn. "You know each other?"

"What of it?" Porter says.

Mr. Coburn flutters his hands. "I never seen him before in my life."

Intuition turns my bewilderment into outrage at Porter. "You paid him to give me the tip about Nat Quayle."

"I don't know what you're talking about," Porter says.

"You didn't see Nat Quayle here the night of the murder, did you?" I tell Coburn.

Barrett glares at Porter as comprehension dawns. "Your flunky here sent Sarah and Mick to the workhouse to be attacked!"

Porter shrugs, faking innocence, but he can't suppress his satisfied grin. "I heard they ran into a little trouble there. But don't blame me. *He's* the one who sent you on a wild-goose chase." Porter points at Mr. Coburn.

"Hey!" Stricken with alarm, Mr. Coburn says to Barrett, "It weren't my idea. I just waited for her to come around and then told her what he said to tell her. I didn't see Quayle, but it seemed like a good chance to get back at the bastard for robbing me. I never meant for nobody to get hurt." He backs away, then turns and bolts.

"Did Inspector Reid put you up to this?" Barrett asks Porter.

Resentment distorts Porter's grin. "You always thought I was too stupid to manage anything by myself."

I think he's denying it because he wants credit for Reid's scheme. I'm sure he detests Barrett not only because of past grievances but also out of envy. Barrett has youth, brains, and the rank of detective sergeant—the things Porter wants and lacks.

"Well, fuck you." Porter lumbers away.

Barrett lunges after Porter. I seize him, and he says, "Damn it, Sarah, let go!"

Porter's mocking laughter drifts back to us through the fog. The fight goes out of Barrett, and he shakes his head, deploring his loss of self-control. If I'd let him get hold of Porter, the church would have seen another murder. I tuck my arm through his, and as we continue on our way, I feel him seething with anger.

"At least now we know that Nat Quayle probably didn't murder Charles Firth," I say, trying to put the situation in a happier light. "And if the two crimes are connected, then he didn't murder Richard Trevelyan either."

"Yeah, well, that's one less suspect who never really was a suspect," Barrett says in a surly voice. "Which doesn't help Mick. And from now on, we'll have to watch out for more trouble from Porter. As if we didn't have enough problems already."

Too soon we arrive in Cambridge Heath, the relatively affluent area of Bethnal Green where Barrett's parents live. Their street boasts clean, trim terraces of narrow, two-story brick houses. Welcoming lights shine in the windows, and the savory smell of cooking laces the smoke from the chimneys.

"Where does Jane Lambert live?" The minute the words are out of my mouth, I want to snatch them back.

Barrett stiffens and turns a pleading gaze on me. "Sarah."

I succumb to the jealous impulse that made me raise the issue at a bad time like this. "Which house?"

Barrett sighs and points.

The house looks just like the others. As we pass it, I wonder if Barrett ever made love to Jane there when her parents weren't home. Then the door opens and a female voice calls, "Tommy!"

Barrett freezes. We turn, he reluctantly, I with a mixture of dread and curiosity. A woman hurries toward us, tall and slender, her blond hair coiled in a simple knot. She wears a dark-blue frock and a tentative smile. Her face is attractive but too angular for beauty. I stare in dismay. At the wedding, I was too occupied with other matters to notice Jane, but now I discover that Barrett prefers a certain type of woman. I never asked him about her appearance, but I think he should have told me that she and I look alike. I turn an accusing gaze on him. He hunches his shoulders as if he'd rather be anywhere else in the world.

"Uh, Sarah, this is Jane Lambert," he mumbles. "Jane, you remember Sarah—my wife."

"Yes! We met at the wedding breakfast!" Jane's bright manner doesn't hide the jealousy in her hazel eyes.

"It's nice to see you again." My tone is polite, but my arm tightens possessively around Barrett's.

"I happened to see you walking by, and I thought I'd say hello." Jane gazes at Barrett as if the two of them were alone.

"We're going to my mother's for dinner," Barrett says.

"Is she making her roast lamb?" Jane says. "I remember it from all the wonderful Sunday dinners at your house."

I grit my teeth behind my smile. Barrett says, "Uh, we'd better be going."

Jane smiles at him. "Drop by for a visit next time you're in the neighborhood."

As Barrett and I walk away down the street, I glance over my shoulder. Jane meets my eyes with a hard stare before she hurries into her house.

"She wants you back, *Tommy*," I say.

"Don't be silly," Barrett says. "She knows it was over a long time ago."

I think that not even his marriage is enough to convince Jane to admit defeat. "Are you ever sorry you didn't marry her?"

We've arrived at his parents' house, and Barrett sighs with relief because he can avoid answering my question. "Here we are."

His mother lets us in. The house is filled with a mouthwatering smell of roast lamb. "Welcome home, dears!" The gleam in her eyes when she looks at me says that despite our quarrel, she hasn't given up on her plan to move Barrett and me into the house.

We hang our coats and hats on the rack, and I smooth my messy hair. Mrs. Barrett kisses the air beside my cheek, wrinkles her nose, and says, "Where's the fire?"

"In Islington," I say. "It was set by someone I went to interview about the murder last night."

Barrett grimaces; by mentioning my work, I've started the night off on the wrong note. Mrs. Barrett's face darkens with disapproval before she pastes a smile on it. "I've a surprise for you." She ushers us into the parlor. "Look who's here!"

There, beside Mr. Barrett, stands the Reverend Thornton. It is indeed a surprise, and not just for Barrett and me.

"Good evening, Sarah." Reverend Thornton looks just as disconcerted as I am that Mrs. Barrett has sprung us on each other. "How are you?"

"Fine, and you?" I say politely. The air between us vibrates with tension from our argument at the church. I wonder what my mother-in-law is up to.

"Hullo," Mr. Barrett says, stepping backward, clearly not wanting to get involved in whatever happens next.

Casually, as if unaware of the discomfort she's caused, Mrs. Barrett says, "I invited the Reverend Thornton to join us for dinner."

"How nice," Barrett says. As he greets and shakes hands with the vicar, his glance at me apologizes for his mother and begs me not to make trouble. I look away from him, still sore from our encounter with Jane.

"Why don't we all have some sherry?" Mr. Barrett fills glasses.

"Sit here, dear." Mrs. Barrett seats me on the flowered divan beside the vicar, motions her husband and son to the armchairs, and pulls up a needlepoint-covered bench for herself.

We all drink. I desperately need the strong, sweet sherry to get me through the evening.

"I was sorry to hear about your friend Mick," Reverend Thornton says to me.

I hurry to correct the erroneous impression that the newspapers have created. "Mick didn't kill that man. He's innocent."

"Well, he certainly looked guilty in the newspaper photograph," Mrs. Barrett says. "And I'm not surprised he's been arrested. The minute I met that boy, I knew he was trouble."

Her prejudice infuriates me. "You don't know anything about Mick."

"Sarah," Barrett says in a warning tone.

"I know enough to recognize trouble when I see it," Mrs. Barrett retorts. "You should be more careful about the company you keep—and I don't just mean the street urchin."

I won't let her bait me into an argument about Hugh. "I'm certain the murders at the prison and the church were committed by the same person, and it wasn't Mick. That's why it's important to determine exactly what happened at the church. To get to the truth, exonerate Mick, and catch the real killer."

Mr. Barrett interrupts timidly. "Um, Mother doesn't like shop talk."

I turn to the vicar. "I must speak with Daniel and Lucie. I need to know if they were in the church the night Charles Firth was killed, and if they saw or heard anything."

Reverend Thornton counters with unrelenting obstinacy. "I haven't changed my mind."

"Very well, they can talk to the police. You can't say no to the police." I turn to Barrett, implying that he should question the children.

He frowns because I've put him in the middle of my argument with the vicar, then says, "Mother, something smells delicious. Is anybody as hungry as I am?"

"Dinner's ready," Mrs. Barrett says brightly. "Let's eat."

We go to the dining room, where once again I'm seated beside Reverend Thornton. Mrs. Barrett serves cream of celery soup and leads a conversation about food, the weather, and other innocuous subjects. I contribute little. If she invited me because she wanted to mend fences, she's already defeated her purpose.

We finish the excellent roast lamb with potatoes and carrots, and we've begun the apple tart when she says to the vicar, "I'm so pleased to have Daniel and Lucie in my Sunday school class. They're lovely children."

My instincts tingle alert as I sense that Mrs. Barrett is getting to the point of this dinner.

The Reverend Thornton wipes his mouth with his napkin and flashes a wary glance at me before he answers her. "Thank you. That's very kind of you."

He's obviously afraid I'll repeat my demand to question the children. Barrett and his father shrink in their chairs like soldiers behind the wall of a fort when the enemy starts shooting.

"I think they're adjusting very well to their new life, don't you?" Mrs. Barrett says.

"Er, yes," the vicar says.

"Such a terrible tragedy they've been through." Mrs. Barrett doesn't seem to notice his uneasiness. "Sarah, you haven't heard, have you?"

"Heard what?" I say.

"About Daniel and Lucie's mother. Reverend, perhaps you should tell Sarah the story. We wouldn't want her to get a distorted version from gossip."

Reverend Thornton scowls and drops his fork beside his plate. I perceive that Mrs. Barrett has manipulated him into discussing a sensitive topic. He grips the edge of the table, and I think he's going to storm out of the house before my curiosity is satisfied, but then he leans back in his chair, thwarted by his good manners. He speaks in a gruff, reluctant voice.

"My only daughter, Alice, was a difficult girl, high-spirited and strong willed. She liked popular songs and plays and wanted to be an actress. When she was fifteen, she began slipping out of the house at night to frequent the music halls and theaters and taverns. Many times I went searching for her and found her . . . inebriated." He reddens with shame at being a clergyman whose daughter preferred worldly delights to the religious and moral values he preaches. "I sent her to three different boarding schools, but she ran away from every one. The last time, she eloped with an actor. It was six months before I managed to locate them."

My father had been missing only two weeks before my mother told me he was dead. At least I knew his fate, or thought I did. How terrible it must have been for the Reverend and Mrs. Thornton, the months of not knowing what had become of their daughter.

"They'd joined a ragtag troupe of actors that traveled around England, and they weren't married. The actor already had a wife. It was his wife who told me that he and Alice had gone to Paris. I tracked them to a garret near a seedy theater where they were performing. Such a dissolute life they led!" The vicar's tone conjures up scenes of drunkenness, opium smoking, and revelry with a wild crowd all night, every night. "And—" He rubs his mouth, then says, "She was with child. She refused to come home."

His disapproval seems complicated by other, unreadable emotions. I wonder if he secretly thought it better to have his pregnant, unwed daughter far away in Paris instead of in London to embarrass him in front of his congregation.

"I heard from Alice infrequently, when she wrote asking for money," Reverend Thornton says. "The actor left her when Daniel and Lucie were three. I went to Paris to visit her and the children and bring them home. But she'd taken up with a different man, and once again she refused to leave. She liked living in Paris, outside the bounds of proper society. Eventually, she wrote to say she was ill with tuberculosis and ready to return to England. But alas, I arrived too late to save her. God rest her soul." His voice grows so hoarse that he has to clear his throat several times before he says, "Daniel, Lucie, and I came home without her." He bows his head with regret and grief.

I murmur, "I'm sorry." Condolences seem so inadequate, and I'm horrified to be the audience for such a sordid tale so unwillingly told. Barrett and his father look just as uncomfortable as I feel.

The vicar rises. "Mildred, thank you for a delicious dinner." He doesn't look directly at her or anyone else. "I'm afraid I must be going. Since the murder, I don't like to leave Mrs. Thornton and the children alone after dark. Good night." He bows, then hurries out of the house.

The sound of the front door closing is loud in the silence that engulfs the table. I look at Mrs. Barrett, bewildered as to why she'd forced the vicar to share his family's tragedy with me.

"Isn't it terrible, what can happen when a selfish woman goes her own way without any concern for others? She had her fun, and her family is paying the wages of her sins." Her gaze bores into me.

I stare at her, incredulous. "You put the vicar through that just to give me a lesson?"

"You need a lesson. You dabble in murder investigations, you keep dubious company, and who pays for your bad reputation?" Mrs. Barrett gestures around the table. "*Your* family! Whenever there's a story about you in the newspapers, Dad and I can barely hold our heads up. People stare and talk about us when they think we're not looking. You should stop before you ruin us all." She turns to Barrett. "And you can't tell me you don't mind the trouble she gets you into."

Instead of defending me, he sits silent. His gaze darts between his mother and me, as if we're throwing knives at each other and he's caught in the middle. I stand up and address Mrs. Barrett in a voice that trembles with equal measures of anger and hurt. "If all you care about is keeping up appearances, then I want no part of your family. Now please excuse me—I have to solve two murders and exonerate Mick. He and Hugh are *my* family."

The horror on Barrett's and his parents' faces tell me that my temper has taken me too far. I need to get away before I say something unforgivable, if I haven't already done so. I bolt from the room, grab my coat and hat, and rush out the door and down the cold, dark, foggy street. I walk fast, my feet pounding the pavement. When I stop to catch my breath, my rage dissolves into misery and fear. Did I just destroy my marriage? A new revelation slams me. Marriage isn't only a personal union between a man and a woman; it includes their relatives. It brings not only the right to sleep together without social censure, but a duty to foster harmony within the clan. I never thought of it this way before, perhaps because my parents' marriage was so replete with secrecy, lies, and quarrels. Mrs. Barrett is right about one thing: I had nobody to teach me how to be a good wife. My husband and I have proven ourselves willing to die for each other, but can we live together?

I long to go home, yet I can't run away from my problems with my mother-in-law. Leaving Barrett to face the music alone won't help our marriage. I trudge back toward the house, but the sound of men's voices halts me.

Barrett and his father are standing outside the door, and I catch a fragment of their conversation. "How can they do that?" Barrett demands.

I'm outside the light from the streetlamp nearest the house, and they don't notice me. Mr. Barrett says, "There's no law that says the Metropolitan Police has to give us pensions when we retire."

It never occurred to me to wonder whether retired policemen receive pensions. I gather that Mr. Barrett and his wife live on his.

"But you've been getting your pension for years," Barrett says.

"Word around the station says I won't be for much longer."

Barrett is silent for a moment. "This stinks of Inspector Reid. He's pulling your pension to get at me."

That Reid would deprive an innocent man just to satisfy a grudge against his son! But then it's not just Barrett that Reid wants to get at—it's also me. To punish me for my transgressions, he's arrested Mick for the murder of Richard Trevelyan and closed the case without a thorough investigation. And now he's after the elder Barretts. No matter how little my mother-in-law and I like each other, and no matter how little I count myself as a member of Barrett's family, I am one. And Reid isn't limiting his attacks to Mick and Hugh; he considers my in-laws fair game.

They're paying the wages for my sins.

How much better off his family would be if Barrett had married Jane!

"I hate to ask you, but can you do something?" Mr. Barrett says.

"Oh, I can and I will." Barrett's tone is grim with determination.

I can't let him go after Reid and get himself in trouble. I brought this on the Barretts. It's time for me to correct my deficiencies as a daughter-in-law and contribute something good to the family. It's my responsibility to make things right.

CHAPTER 24

At six o'clock in the morning, I walk down Barnet Grove, one of three streets that form a triangle in Bethnal Green. Steeped in dark fog, the terraced brick houses are relatively new, two stories high, their architecture modern and unembellished. Lights appear in their windows as residents awaken. Their black-painted front doors open directly onto the sidewalk, but trees visible above the rooftops indicate the luxury of a private garden behind the buildings. The only activity is at the south end, where the road is flooded and men are digging up the pavement to fix a broken sewer pipe. Shovels and pickaxes clank against stone. I halt just before I reach the house at the middle of the block.

Last night, I waited outside the Barretts' house until my father-in-law went inside and my husband called, "Sarah? Are you there?"

I backed away down the street as he came looking for me; then I walked toward him and pretended I hadn't overheard his conversation with his father. Putting my pride in my pocket, I said, "I want to apologize to your mother."

She deserves an apology—not for my refusal to be the conventional, obedient daughter-in-law she wants, but because I've endangered her family.

"She's still pretty upset," Barrett said. "Better wait until she calms down. I'll take you home."

I could tell that he was upset, too, and angry at me as well as Inspector Reid. We endured a silent ride on the omnibus. At home, I discovered that Hugh still hadn't returned, neither had

Fitzmorris, and the house felt emptier without Mick. In my bed, Barrett and I lay facing away from each other. He fell asleep while I concocted a solution to the problems I've caused. I can only hope it will undo the damage to our marriage. At four thirty, I rose and dressed, quietly so as not to wake him, then tiptoed downstairs to the parlor. I opened the drawer in the table, took out the pistol, and made sure it was loaded. Then I put on my hat and coat and slipped out of the house.

Now I feel the weight of the gun in my pocketbook. I brought it because walking alone before daybreak is dangerous for a woman. Although I've practiced firing it and I'm a good shot, I've seen the terrible injury a gun can do and want never to see it again. But some impulse makes me open my pocketbook, remove the gun, and study its notched cylinder and the textured pattern on the grip. A night without sleep after the turmoil of the past few days works a dark spell on my mind. I touch the curved trigger and realize that here is a device that could solve my problems.

A strange thrill courses through me. Moving like a sleepwalker, I position myself across the street from the house. I aim the gun at the door and picture Inspector Reid coming out. I smile, tickled by the thought that I could blast him off the face of the earth. My imaginary vision of Reid is so clear that it's as if he's really there, in the flesh. My finger tightens on the trigger. Seeing me with the gun pointed at him, he gapes in terrified shock. With no thought for the consequences, I pull the trigger. The bang of the gunshot drowns in the noise from workers digging up the road. Reid falls and lies still. Blood flowing from the wound in his chest turns the pavement red. I run away, concealed by the fog, triumphant. Reid will trouble me no more.

There's a loud, metallic crash, and the workers shout curses; they must have dropped something. My fantasy evaporates like a dream upon awakening. I see the gun extended in my hand, and the gleeful excitement gives way to horror.

I could have done it. I could have killed Reid.

I stuff the gun into my pocketbook, frantic to hide my guilty intention. An unexpected notion horrifies me: *Was that how my mother felt when she killed Ellen Casey?* Was she so excited, so caught up in the moment, that she didn't care about the consequences? My mind argues that our situations were different. She killed an innocent child; I aimed my gun at an evil man who wasn't really there. But my mother wished death upon someone who'd been an inconvenient, dangerous problem for her, and I almost followed in her footsteps. Now I begin to make sense of the vague notion that's been bothering me about my mother. It's the fear I've been trying not to acknowledge: *Am I the same as her?* There's already blood on my hands, which I thought necessary to shed. But maybe the necessity wasn't my real motivation. What if I reacted on an instinct that she passed down to me? Is her tendency to solve problems with violence the legacy I've inherited?

The sound of a door opening interrupts my awful thoughts, and Inspector Reid comes out of his house. Concealed by the fog and darkness, I stare at him, shaken to the core by what might have happened. Unaware of me, he walks down the street.

A little voice from the house calls, "Daddy, Daddy!"

A boy, seven or eight years old, bursts through the door, runs to Reid, and chatters to him. Reid laughs, bends down to hug him, and says, "Good-bye, Harry. Be good." He sends the child home with an affectionate slap on the bottom.

Suddenly nauseated, I retch and clap my hand over my mouth. I almost did exactly what my mother had done—deprive a child of its father.

Reid sees me, halts in surprise, and frowns. "What are you doing here?"

I stumble across the street toward him. I blurt out the words I've mentally rehearsed on my way here. "May I buy you a drink?"

Reid hesitates, wondering what I'm up to. "Isn't it a little early?"

"Better than too late." If only he knew it really almost was too late for him to have a drink or do anything else.

"How did you know where I live?"

"I once followed you home."

Reid considers, then nods; his curiosity has won out. "I know a place."

We walk side by side a cautious distance apart, like two ruffians who've happened upon each other in a dark alley and are waiting to see who will attack first. At the corner of Columbia Road, we stop at a pub called the Prince of Wales. It boasts a carved stone crown on the roof above the sign, and the decor inside consists of amateur-ish oil paintings of the current and past princes and commemorative mugs, snuffboxes, and biscuit tins. We're alone with the publican. Reid sits at a back table while I fetch glasses of ale. They slosh in my shaky hands. He watches me closely, and after I set them on the table and take my seat opposite him, he switches the glass in front of him for the one by my place, as if he thinks I'm trying to poison him. He raises his glass and waits for me to drink first.

I'm tipping a pint with my enemy, the man I almost shot. When I swallow the ale, for a terrible moment I think it's going to come back up.

Reid drinks, licks foam off his moustache, and fixes me with a narrow-eyed gaze. "Well?"

Setting down my glass, I speak words I never thought I'd say. "I want to apologize for all the trouble I've caused you." It's he who should apologize to me, for offenses that include arresting my friends for crimes they didn't commit and persecuting my father, but I continue. "I'm sorry. Will you please forgive me?"

Reid stares, astonished; then his expression turns sardonic. "Will you forgive me if I take your apology with a big grain of salt?"

"I mean it." At this moment, I do—I'm that desperate to dif-ferentiate myself from my mother, who never apologized for the pain she caused and, as far as I know, never experienced a bit of remorse.

"What else have you got to say?"

"I beg you to drop the charges against Mick. He's innocent. I'm the one you're really after, not him. Please let him go."

Reid smirks; he enjoys seeing me grovel. "Well, it's not my call. The wheels of justice are in motion. His trial is set for November third. A jury will decide whether he walks or hangs."

That's four days away. My heart sinks, but if I'm my mother's daughter, at least I inherited her stiff upper lip. I glower at Reid instead of weeping for Mick.

"When the crime is murder, juries like to see someone pay for it, and Mick has a bull's-eye stamped on his forehead." Reid laughs. "It's just too bad *you* weren't caught with the body."

The gun in my pocketbook is heavy on my lap. I can almost wish I had even more of my mother in me and I'd shot Reid when I had the chance.

"But I'll admit that the case against Mick is circumstantial," Reid says in a confidential tone. "Nobody actually saw him stab Richard Trevelyan. With Sir Gerald's fancy barrister defending him, a jury could let him off."

I look askance at Reid even as I hope he's right. I think he's up to something.

"And I don't want another bungle on my record. So I might be willing to do you a favor, twist a few arms, and get the charge dropped."

A favor from him won't come cheap, but I'm desperate enough to take the bait. "In exchange for what?"

Reid smiles and waggles his finger, making me wait, toying with me. "Here's the deal: I'll get the charge dropped, if you—" He drinks, prolonging the suspense. "If you tell me the truth about what happened during the Ripper investigation."

My heart begins a new, rapid descent when I thought it had already touched bottom. Reid is demanding the one coin I can't give him. The truth about the Ripper wouldn't save Mick; it would only doom him, Hugh, Barrett, and me.

"That's too high a price for Mick's life?" Scorn laces Reid's disappointment. "And you call yourself his friend. Well, you've wasted your time, and mine." He drains his glass, sets it on the table.

I hate to think I've humiliated myself for nothing. I hurry to offer Reid something else he might want. "If you get the charge dropped, I won't tell anyone that you and Mr. Porter set up the attack on Mick and me at the Bethnal Green Workhouse."

Reid beholds me with surprise, then disdain. "It wasn't me. I cut my ties with Porter when he was kicked off the force. If he set you up, he did it on his own."

I can't hide my chagrin. Whether or not Reid is telling the truth, he's not afraid of my accusation, and I can't think of another card to play.

"Here, I'll sweeten the deal." Reid's eyes glint with the recklessness of a gambler who's about to stake his all. "If you tell me what you know about the Ripper, then I'll not only get the charges against Mick dropped, I'll leave you and your friends and your husband alone, for good."

It's more than I could ask—our lives free of trouble from Reid forever—but the price is still fatally high. My perception of him changes. I've seen him as a corrupt man who would do anything to satisfy a grudge, but now I glimpse the honorable police officer Barrett said he was before the Ripper case, who wants to get the right man or know why he can't. Reid thinks the Ripper is still at large, and after six deaths that he takes personally, he's afraid he'll wake up one day to hear that there's been a new murder. He believes I know who the Ripper is, and in order to prevent the next reign of terror, he would sacrifice his revenge against me. He wants justice that badly.

I turn away from him rather than let him see how distressed I am because we're birds of a feather when it comes to justice, because I almost shot him, and because I can't accept his terms. I stand up and walk toward the door, my back straight, wearing my tattered pride like a cloak to dress up my defeat.

He calls after me in a quiet, ominous voice, "You're going to wish you'd taken the deal."

★ ★ ★

I barely make it home before a siege of vomiting begins. When it's over, I crawl into bed fully clothed, shivering and sweating, to recover from my body's physical reaction to the fact that I almost proved myself my mother's daughter. My mind rubs itself raw against the thought of what would have happened had I killed

Inspector Reid. I think Mick, Hugh, Sally, and my father would understand and forgive me if they knew, but Barrett is a different story. He would be duty bound to hunt down Reid's killer. Unable to deny that I had a motive for the murder—and a gun—he would remember that I'd gone out early this morning and suspect me. He would investigate me, and what if he turned up witnesses who'd seen a woman fitting my description near the crime scene or fleeing it after the gunshot? As much as he hates Reid, he couldn't condone the murder of his superior, or cover up for the killer even if she was his wife.

There are sins that not even love can absolve.

Three hours later, I'm still in bed when the doorbell jangles, but I don't move. Whoever is at the door starts pounding on it and forces me to get up. My sickness has passed, but I'm weak and shaky. I totter downstairs and see Barrett, dressed in his police uniform, peering through the window of my studio.

When I let him in, he says, "Why did you leave so early this morning?" He takes a closer look at me. "Sarah, what's wrong?"

I must look awful, my hair falling down and plastered to my gray, haggard face. A trickle of nausea warns me that if I talk about it, I'll be sick again. I should tell Barrett about my conversation with Reid before Reid tells him, but I can only shake my head.

"Oh, God. You're upset about last night," Barrett says. "I'm sorry. That was a mean trick my mother played on you and the Reverend." He takes me in his arms.

I'm so glad he came back to me. After last night, who could blame him if he didn't? I'm rigid with guilt because I'm not correcting his error about the reason for my sad state.

He releases me and says, "Where did you go?"

"I . . . had an errand to run." If he knew what errand, he would be appalled. He wouldn't want me going behind his back to make a deal with Inspector Reid.

"I see." Barrett's tone says, *There you go again, keeping secrets from me.* Then a resigned expression comes over his face, as if he's decided there's no good in piling the old quarrel on top of the new. "Well, I'm glad you're safe."

Even though he failed to take my side against his mother, he's a bigger, better person than I am. I'm glad to be married to him, for however short the duration proves to be.

"But listen," Barrett says, "I've been thinking about Richard Trevelyan's murder, and I'm wondering if we've been going at it wrong."

I'm glad to turn my attention to saving Mick. "How so?"

"What if it's not connected to Charles Firth's murder?"

"*I* think it is." I brace myself for another disagreement.

"Just humor me for a minute," Barrett says. "Suppose Charles Firth hadn't been murdered. What would we do?"

I start to catch his drift. "We would investigate Richard Trevelyan's murder as a unique crime, not the second in a series."

"Yes!" Barrett smiles, excited by his inspiration. "We would look for suspects and clues that are associated with him instead of with Charles Firth."

My hopes resurge. "If we do that, we might be able to solve at least his murder."

"And save Mick," Barrett says.

★　★　★

It's a relief to take action instead of thinking about Inspector Reid. On the train, seated beside Barrett, I'm fervently glad that we're able to work together even when our relationship is rocky. Perhaps our marriage isn't doomed to fail.

"I've news about Diana Kelly," Barrett says. "Remember I thought her name sounded familiar? I checked the police records and found out why. In 1887, she was arrested for stabbing a man. She was a streetwalker in Whitechapel, and he was a customer who got violent with her. It was ruled self-defense, and he wasn't seriously hurt, so she was let off."

I recall Diana hinting that she'd taken desperate measures to support her children after she'd spent her savings on Charles Firth's fake spirit photographs.

"At the station this morning, some of the constables who'd been in the tunnels told me they saw Diana and Jean Ritchie together, shouting through megaphones, just before Richard Trevelyan's body was found." Barrett adds, "I don't think Diana killed him. I think she skipped town because she was afraid her record would make her a suspect."

"That sounds logical," I say, "and she didn't seem to have a strong reason to kill Richard Trevelyan at all, let alone with so many people around and so much risk of getting caught."

I'm upset because it appears we've eliminated a suspect instead of finding evidence to clear Mick. I'm also disturbed by a weird sensation of being uncomfortable in my skin, as if there's something inside it with me, a sharp-edged, foreign, malignant presence. When I turn to the window, I see my mother's face in my reflection.

I gasp.

"What's wrong?" Barrett says.

"Nothing."

But I feel as if the ghost of my mother, dormant until today, has awakened in me. I squirm, trying to rid myself of the sensation. It won't go away. I remind myself that I don't believe in ghosts. But I can't deny that my mother is in my blood, my bones. All these years, her spirit must have been lurking in me, kept alive by my thoughts of her, and my encounter with Reid gave her power over me. If I told Barrett, he would scoff and tell me it's just a fancy. But the fancy has taken hold of me as if with the thorny tendrils of a vine. When the train stops, I leap for the door in an effort to escape. I bump into passengers waiting to board.

"Careful," Barrett says.

The sensation fades when we're walking along Paternoster Row, the busy street in central London that's home to many major publishers. I remember Mrs. Firth saying that if the atmosphere is unsympathetic, spirits won't come, and perhaps the bustle of commerce has quelled my mother's ghost. I breathe easier. We bypass the large bookstores, their crowds of customers, and the heavy traffic, and we turn down Queen's Head Passage, a narrow lane with a thin slice of St. Paul's Cathedral visible at the dead end. Drifting fog gives the illusion that the massive, domed cathedral is moving into the passage, like a wedge driven into a crack. The sign at Trevelyan and Company bears its name in gold letters and a coat of arms—a medieval knight's helmet entwined with ivy.

Barrett tries the door; it's locked. Through the window I see a man moving around inside, and I rap on the glass. He comes over and opens the door. Of average height and stocky build, he has brown hair combed over a bald crown, a bristly moustache, and spectacles. An apron and ink-stained sleeve protectors cover his business suit.

"I'm sorry; we're closed," the man says.

"I'm with the police," Barrett says. "Let us in."

The man's eyes widen behind his spectacles, and he backs away as Barrett and I enter the shop. The shelves are empty, the counter littered with scissors, labels, and rolls of twine. "What do you want?"

Barrett introduces himself and me. "We're investigating the murder of Richard Trevelyan. Who are you?"

"George Newby. I'm his business partner." He exhales a doleful sigh. "Or was."

If I should liken Richard Trevelyan to a thoroughbred racehorse, Mr. Newby would be a workhorse that pulls a cab. "Why are you packing up all the books?" I ask.

"The shop is out of business."

I notice, on the counter, an open mahogany till that contains a small stack of bank notes. "Now that Mr. Trevelyan is dead, you're making off with the goods and money?"

"No." Insulted by my accusation of theft, Mr. Newby says, "They're mine now. That's what our partnership contract says: if one of us dies, the other gets everything."

Barrett regards Mr. Newby with sudden surprise. "Hey, I saw you at the Clerkenwell House of Detention the other night."

"What of it? Yes, I was there. So was half the city."

"Did you kill Richard Trevelyan so you would get everything?" Barrett says.

Mr. Newby puffs out his chest and juts his chin forward. "I did not."

"Can you prove it?" I say.

"I was with friends the whole time. John Dexter and Roger Edmonds, from Longman's—you know, the big publisher. Ask them; they'll tell you."

"I will ask them," Barrett says. We're both disappointed that as soon as we found a new suspect, he produced an alibi.

"It's ridiculous that you would think I killed Richard," Mr. Newby says.

"I suppose because he was a dear friend," I say.

Mr. Newby blinks, then removes his spectacles to wipe teardrops off the lenses. When he puts them back on, they magnify the pain in his eyes. "You would be lucky to have a friend like Richard. It was my dream to start a publishing company, and I couldn't have done it without him. He provided most of the money, and he was good with customers; he sold a lot of books. And he treated me like an equal partner. He was generous that way."

I'm ashamed of viewing Richard Trevelyan as merely a murder suspect and victim. I haven't considered him as a person with friends who are grieving his loss.

"If you think I would kill anybody for this—" Mr. Newby gestures at the boxes of books. "Think again. It's not worth the risk of getting caught and hanged."

"It looks like a good haul to me," Barrett says.

"Ha!" Mr. Newby's expression turns morose. "I'll be lucky if I can sell them for pennies on the pound."

"Didn't you and Mr. Trevelyan publish books of ghost photographs taken by Charles Firth?" I say. "Weren't they best sellers?"

"They won't be for much longer." Mr. Newby pulls a disgusted face. "I warned Richard not to put all our eggs in one basket. I've worked in publishing since I was a fourteen-year-old apprentice at a print shop. We met when we both worked at Longman's. He was an editor; I was in sales. I know that if you want to make money, you have to publish a variety of books, not just ones about spiritualism because they're your favorite kind." Mr. Newby kicks a box that contains volumes of Charles Firth's work. "I told Richard that spirit photographs were a fad that wasn't going to last forever. I also warned him that when you build a business on a fraud, if you get caught, then you're sunk. But he didn't listen."

Mr. Newby sees my dismay and says, "Charles Firth's ghost photographs were fake. Didn't you know?"

"Yes, of course." Despite my skepticism, a part of me wanted them to be genuine, resisted believing that my former patron had stooped so low.

"So you got caught?" Barrett says. "Did somebody figure out that the ghost in their picture wasn't their dear, departed husband or wife?"

"Far from it," Mr. Newby says. "People who believe in ghosts are extremely gullible. Have you ever wondered how those pictures are made?"

I've taken pride in thinking myself not gullible enough to believe in ghosts, but I feel my mother again under my skin, the sharp edges of her personality pricking my vulnerable self. "It could be done with multiple exposures."

Newby points his blunt, ink-stained finger at me and grins. "Well, Charles couldn't always get hold of photographs of the dear departed. Sometimes there weren't any. In those cases, he had to use a model for the ghost. And because he took photographs for so many clients, he used lots of models."

"I suppose he couldn't have used the same model for the ghosts of your granddad and my aunt," Barrett says.

"Right. Charles never told the models what he wanted their pictures for, but using so many models meant a big risk of somebody recognizing himself or herself as the ghost in a photograph and spilling the beans."

"Did somebody?" I say, taken aback because I never considered these practical issues of spirit photography.

"Recognize herself? Yes. Spill the beans?" Mr. Newby says darkly, "It's only a matter of time. Last February, a woman came to the shop. She said, 'Do you know who I am?' Richard and I recognized her at once. She was one of Firth's models. I thought the jig was up, but Richard put on his most charming manner and said, 'I don't believe I've had the pleasure of your acquaintance.'

The woman picked up Charles's latest book, pointed to a photograph inside, and said, 'I'm Eva Piper. That's me.' I said, 'What do you want?' " Mr. Newby chuckles grimly. "As if I hadn't already guessed. She said, 'Give me a hundred pounds, or I'll go to the newspapers. I'll tell them I'm the ghost in these photographs and they're fake.' "

Comprehension is like a bell struck hard inside me, cracking with the force of the impact. "She blackmailed you."

Mr. Newby nods. "Richard said we believed the photographs were genuine, and he pretended to be shocked to learn they weren't. He told her Charles had tricked us and since we were also victims of the fraud, we couldn't be held responsible for it. But she pushed a stack of books onto the floor and said, 'After I talk to the newspapers, these will be worthless. Give me a hundred pounds.' She seemed desperate. Richard told her to ask Charles for money. She said she had, and he'd paid for a while, but then he said he couldn't get his hands on any more cash. I knew that once the story got out, we would be done for. We didn't have a hundred pounds on us, so we persuaded her to take ten then and the rest later. But of course she didn't stop at that. She was bleeding us dry. Richard and I decided it had to stop before we went bankrupt— even if it meant there would be a scandal."

Barrett says, "So you stopped paying?"

"Yes," Mr. Newby says. "The morning of the day he died, Richard told her to publish and be damned. I wasn't there, but I understand she didn't take it well."

Barrett turns to me. "That could have given her a motive for his murder."

I feel a burst of elation. "And Charles Firth's murder. She would have been angry at him as well, because he too stopped paying." Barrett and I smile at each other, delighted to have a new suspect. I ask Mr. Newby, "Can you show us her photograph?"

"My pleasure," Mr. Newby says with bitter satisfaction. "She's probably talking to reporters up and down Fleet Street as we speak. I figured I might as well pack it in before the scandal hit the news. If she killed Richard and Charles, I hope she hangs. If not, do me a favor and arrest her for blackmail." He takes a book from a box, flips through the pages, and hands the open volume to me.

The photograph shows a man, a little girl, and a younger boy, all dressed in black, seated by a fireplace. Above the mantel floats the head of a beautiful blond woman, her hands clasped in prayer under her chin and her eyes lifted to the heavens. Recognition stuns me. I saw an image of this same woman, wrapped in a sheet and posed in a cemetery, in a photograph at Charles Firth's studio and again in the photograph I saved from the fire that Leonora Firth set.

"We need to find out where she was the nights of the murders," Barrett says.

"I can tell you where she was the night Richard died," Mr. Newby says. "She was in the tunnels under the Clerkenwell jail. I saw her arguing with Richard. She must have been trying to wring more money out of him."

"Oh, God." I'm thunderstruck. "I saw them too! But I thought she was Diana Kelly. They're both blond." My mistake sent me barking up the wrong tree. Now I'm amazed to discover that Mr. Newby is the witness Barrett and I need, the one with a clue that could prove to be Mick's salvation. Eva Piper, our new suspect, has to be the blond woman Dr. Lodge saw accosting Charles Firth. In retrospect, our path was littered with omens—her image seen in three different photographs at three separate times—as if our destiny lies with Eva Piper.

CHAPTER 25

"You were right about treating Richard Trevelyan's murder as a separate, unique crime," I say to Barrett as we walk through the crowds along the Whitechapel high street.

Barrett smiles at me. "I'll have to remember this moment." His eyes twinkle with mischief. "You don't often you admit that you were wrong."

I cuff his arm. "Enjoy it. You might not have another chance for a long time." Despite my playful manner, even while I'm enjoying the fresh climate of new hope, I'm troubled. I feel distant from Barrett, as if I'm alone again outside Inspector Reid's house, aiming the gun. I imagine my mother inside me, coiled like an invisible snake with sharp scales. I clutch Barrett's arm, trying to anchor myself to the present, to reality.

"Ouch, you don't need to hold me so tight," he says. "I'm not going anywhere."

The George Yard Buildings, to which Mr. Newby directed us, are located just down the block from my house. Eva Piper and I are virtually neighbors, and although I don't recall ever seeing her, our paths must have crossed before the night of Richard Trevelyan's murder. Barrett and I stand in George Yard, a narrow alley between the Whitechapel high street and Wentworth Street. The alley is a dim tunnel lit by streetlamps at either end. We look up at the pair of four-story brick tenements built some twenty years ago as inexpensive housing for the poor. They're among the most notorious places in London, the scene of Jack the Ripper's first murder.

"Tuesday the seventh of August, 1888," Barrett says.

On that date he was the first police officer at the crime scene. I never saw the scene myself, but I'd known the victim—Martha Tabram. I'd followed the accounts in the newspapers and read quotes from Barrett's testimony at the inquest, unaware that I would solve the crime and that someday Barrett would be my husband.

The exteriors of the buildings look the same as they did during the Ripper's reign of terror, but tenants fled in droves and the glare of publicity revealed the squalid conditions and the abundance of prostitutes. Recently, the flats were renovated and converted to a hostel for students. Barrett and I see fresh-faced young people going in and out of the arched entrance. I hear swatting and bouncing noises from a tennis game in the court outside the settlement house behind the buildings. A wholesome new era of change is under way.

Barrett shows Eva's ghost photograph to a skinny youth lugging a stack of books. "Do you know which flat she has?"

"Number two-oh-five. A snooty bird, won't give a fellow the time of day," he replies.

Beyond the open entrance, a dim passage smells of urine from vagrants who still shelter in the passage at night. I wonder how a beautiful, elegant woman like Eva came to live here. Maybe modeling doesn't pay as well as I thought. The odor joins the scents of onions and fried lard as Barrett and I mount a stone staircase. Martha Tabram was murdered on one of the landings. I picture her lying on her back with her thick legs spread and her skirts hiked up, in a pool of blood from thirty-nine stab wounds. I've heard rumors that her ghost has been seen haunting George Yard. This and other scenes of Ripper murders are certainly haunted by tourists who have a taste for grisly crime. Barrett and I step over a sleeping man who reeks of liquor. At flat 205, I knock on the door.

"Who is it?" a throaty female voice calls from inside.

"Police," Barrett says. "Eva Piper?"

My heartbeat quickens with anticipation; I feel on the brink of catching Richard Trevelyan's killer.

The woman who opens the door is a far cry from the ethereal ghost. Over forty, she's plump, with a large bosom and double chin. Her hair, arranged in a pouf of swirls, is a brassy, unnatural shade of red. She wears a dirty white apron, a green paisley wool dressing gown, and stained green velvet bedroom slippers. She must be one of the original tenants who stayed on after the buildings became a student hostel. The air that issues from the room behind her smells of rose perfume.

"Eva Piper don't live here anymore," she says.

"What's your name?" Barrett says.

The woman chews her rouged, scarlet lips. She eyes Barrett's uniform; her evident fear of the police outweighs her reluctance to tell them anything. "Annie Watts. Miss."

"Miss Watts, do you know the whereabouts of Eva Piper?" Barrett says.

"How should I? I used to live next door, but she kept to herself. Her room was better than mine, so I took it over when she left. Landlord said she skipped out in the middle of the night without payin' the rent."

"When did she skip out?" I say, hoping that Eva Piper's trail isn't too cold.

"Tuesday."

It can't be a coincidence. I say to Barrett, "That's the same night Richard Trevelyan was murdered."

"If she's the killer, it would explain why she left," Barrett says.

Annie Watts's painted eyebrows shoot upward. "Hey, I don't want nothin' to do with no murder." She shuts the door in our faces.

I push it open before she can lock it. "I need to look around the flat." I mustn't ignore the slight possibility that it harbors clues.

"Go away!"

"Let us in, or I'll arrest you," Barrett says.

Uttering a harsh sound of disgust, Annie obeys. The rose perfume is so strong that I can taste its bitter chemicals. The flat consists of a single small room that's cluttered with garments strewn about, laundry hanging from a string, and dirty pans on the stove. On the bed, a large basket contains roses, lilies, and tulips. At first I think they're real, but then I see that the table under the window, lit by the gas lamp, holds wire, scissors, sewing supplies, paint and glue pots, and brilliantly hued cloth and paper.

"You make those?" Barrett asks Annie.

"Yeah. I'm an artificial florist."

The black net stockings and the red petticoat hanging on the clothesline suggest that she, like many other women who sell artificial flowers, has an additional profession of a different sort. She plucks a little bouquet from the table and offers it to Barrett with a coy smile. "A posy for your lady? Only five pence."

Barrett nods, apparently thinking that a sale will make Annie more likely to cooperate. Coins change hands. Annie sprays the bouquet with perfume from an atomizer bottle, adding to the fragrance in the room, then gives the bouquet to me. The petals are coral silk, the centers crafted from yellow beads, the leaves from starched green fabric, and the wire stems wrapped in green silk ribbon. It's a small work of art, a cut above the usual trinkets sold on London streets.

"Thank you," I say. "It's beautiful."

"Coral is for passion," Annie says.

A blush warms my cheeks. Barrett winks at me, then asks Annie, "Is everything in this flat yours?"

"Yeah. That cow Eva Piper didn't leave nothin'." When Barrett and I begin searching the room, Annie says, "Hey, careful with my stuff!"

Barrett finds long blond hairs in the dust under the cupboard—a physical trace of Eva Piper. He lifts the mattress on the bed to look under it, and I look behind the plain wooden headboard. A sheet of white paper is stuck between the board and the wall. Cautioning myself not to hope for too much, I say to Barrett, "I think I've found something."

He helps me move the bed. Annie mutters, "If you break it, I'll have to pay."

The paper falls on the floor. I reach down and pick up THE paper, which is creased, as if was folded into an envelope. At the top is the name JENNY LIND HOSPITAL, POTTERGATE, NORWICH, and an illustration of a building. Below, printed in columns, are fees for BED, BOARD, MEDICINE, PHYSICIAN, and NURSING. Written on the line provided for the patient's name is EVELYN COREY PIPER.

CHAPTER 26

"There's a train to Norwich at seven oh five tonight from Liverpool station," Barrett says, consulting a railway timetable.

He and Fitzmorris and I are at home in the kitchen, eating bacon sandwiches for supper. I would leave my meal and run out the door now, but I have to point out, "That's not enough time to get to the station."

"There's another at nine thirty-seven. It arrives in Norwich at eleven forty."

"Norwich might be a wild-goose chase." I pray to heaven that it isn't. "We would have to stay overnight, and we're not at all certain Eva Piper is there."

Barrett waves the hospital bill.

"Even if she once was a patient at the hospital, she could still be in London now." I'm trying not to set myself up for disappointment. "And she might not be the killer."

"If Norwich is a dead end, we could be back in London by tomorrow, with three more days left to clear Mick," Barrett says.

That's cutting it close, but I'm at my wits' end. "All right. We'll catch the nine thirty-seven train."

I'm upstairs in my room, throwing clothes into a valise, when the doorbell jangles. This time it has to be Hugh. I run downstairs . . . and find Sally in the kitchen. Collapsed in a chair, she dabs a handkerchief against her red, teary eyes. Fitzmorris hovers near her with a cup of tea; Barrett, seated beside her, wears the calm, sober expression he dons at crime scenes. My disappointment at not seeing Hugh turns to alarm.

"Sally, what's wrong?" I say.

"It's Father," Sally wails. "*He's gone!*"

The two words reawaken a panic that has deep, twisted roots inside me. They sprout new growth that crowds the air out of my chest. "What happened?"

"We were supposed to meet for tea. I went to his lodgings, and he wasn't there. I waited and waited, but he never came. I think he's disappeared again!"

"I'm sure there's another explanation." Barrett's tone is steady, reassuring.

I barely hear him over the high-pitched, keening animal cry that fills my mind. It's the sound I uttered when I was ten years old, the night when my father had been gone for a week and I lay in my bed and faced the terrible possibility that he might never come back. Blackness stipples my vision. I'm going to faint.

As I drop into a chair, Sally clutches my hand. Hers is cold, wet with tears. "Oh, Sarah, what are we going to do?"

I force myself to breathe, to stay conscious. I can't fall apart; I'm not a child anymore, and Sally is depending on me. "He must have gone out on an errand and forgotten about your appointment."

Sally looks stung by the idea, but hopeful. "He wouldn't forget me, would he?"

"If he started taking photographs, he could have lost track of the time, like he used to do," I say. "He's probably back at his lodgings by now."

Sally smiles through her tears. "Yes! Let's go and see if he's there." She jumps up from her seat.

I wrestle with conflicting impulses, then make a decision: a few hours' delay probably won't affect my search for Eva Piper or the outcome. "I'll fetch my coat and pocketbook."

"I'm coming with you," Barrett says.

★ ★ ★

I've never been so thankful for Barrett. During the journey by slow night train to Battersea, he lets Sally and me fret about accidents or other terrible fates that might have befallen our father until we've exhausted the subject. Then he tells us he's sure our father is safe and sound and will be upset to see our long faces, so we'd better cheer up. He asks Sally about her job at the *Daily World* and soon has her telling funny stories about people she's interviewed. He in turn relates amusing tales from his police work, such as the time he cornered a robber who tried to escape down a chimney and got stuck. By the time we're walking down the mist-shrouded street toward the Gladstone Arms, we're as gay as the local folks I see heading to the pubs. I think of the vows Barrett and I made at our wedding. He's fulfilling his promise to comfort me. The vows take on a richer meaning than the mere words suggested.

In the dim second-floor passage at the Gladstone Arms, Sally knocks on the door of our father's room. There's no answer. Now I'm afraid he's lying in there unconscious—or dead—perhaps from a stroke. Barrett runs downstairs to the taproom and fetches the publican. Sally and I clasp hands and hold our breath while the publican opens the door to dark silence. He lights the lamp inside the room, revealing the bed neatly made, everything in order, and my father absent.

My panic swells anew, choking me. Sally moans. Barrett says to the publican, "Thanks. You can go."

I look in the cupboard and under the bed and find my father's clothes, trunk, and camera. "His things are still here. He must be coming back."

Sally shakes her head. "You know this is just like the other times. All he took were the clothes on his back. He's left us again!"

I speak forcefully, to convince myself as well as Sally: "No, no. Something else must have happened."

But I wonder if he found the relationship with us too onerous; we're adults, not the simple little girls he remembers. Or maybe he's afraid that our efforts to exonerate him will fail and thinks it will be safer and easier to disappear again and resume his solitary life under a new alias in some obscure locale.

Sally turns to Barrett. "What should we do?"

"Let's go to the taproom and ask if anyone there has seen your father."

"I'll look for clues here." After Barrett and Sally depart, I sit in the chair and inhale deep, shuddering breaths until my heartbeat slows and the panic recedes enough for me to survey the room. His shaving things by the washbasin have a forlorn air, like relics in a seldom-visited museum. I catch a whiff of his clean scent laced with the bitterness of photographic chemicals.

"Where are you?" I say softly.

My voice echoes in the quiet. It's as if he's a ghost that I lack the power to conjure up. I can still feel my mother's malevolent presence under my skin, but my father has never seemed more distant. I go through the motions of searching for clues. His trunk, camera case, and clothes yield nothing. Then I see, on the windowsill, the notebook in which Sally wrote his account of the day Ellen Casey died. She must have left it there, intending to come back later and finish. It seems to give off an unnatural glow, like an enchanted, poisonous apple. I take the notebook to the table, turn the lamp higher, and brace myself. I skip the part of the story I've already read, about how my father discovered Ellen's rape and murder. I skim the next few pages, which describe the terrible bargain he struck with my mother: he would help her and Lucas cover up the murder, then run away and let the police think he'd done it, but only if Lucas went with him. He wanted to protect me from being molested by Lucas as well as protect Lucas and my mother from the law. I knew all this because he'd told me. But I've never heard the next episode of the story.

When Sarah came home from school, I talked to her about her lessons and her friends and pretended nothing was amiss. At supper, I could hardly eat. Mary wouldn't look at me or say a word to me. When Sarah went to bed, I kissed her and told her I loved her. I knew it could be the last time, if things went wrong that night. And soon I would be going away, never to see her again, and I couldn't say good-bye. I almost broke down.

I wipe tears from my eyes. I have no memory of that night; it must have seemed like any other.

Then Mary and I sat in the parlor and waited for Lucas. She kept her face turned away from me, and I could feel how much she hated me. Lucas came back at midnight as we'd planned. He and I went down to the cellar and brought up the trunk in which I'd hidden Ellen's body. Mary clung to Lucas and kissed him and wept. All she cared about was that he was in danger and going away soon. Then he and I carried the trunk down the street. It was a foggy night, and no one was about. We meant to throw Ellen in the river, but she was heavy and it was slow going. We couldn't hire a cab, because if her body was found, the driver might hear about it and remember us. Then we heard voices and police whistles in the distance.

Lucas said, "They must be looking for her. We're going to get caught. We have to get rid of her now."

We went to Greville Street. There'd been a fire recently. Three houses in a terrace had burned. The ruins hadn't been cleared away yet. We sneaked inside what was left of one house, took Ellen from the trunk, and laid her on the floor. I covered her with charred boards. We threw the trunk in a dustbin in an alley. Then Lucas went back to his lodgings, and I went home.

I reread the last paragraph as a cold tide of apprehension laps at me.

Sally and Barrett return. Sally says, "The publican is the only person here who knows Father. The last time he saw him was this morning, walking down the street. He doesn't know where he went." Her voice is heavy with disappointment.

I picture my father vanishing into thin air as he walked away. I stand and hold the notebook open in front of Sally. "You wrote that Father left Ellen in a burned house in Greville Street. Are you sure that's what he said?"

Sally wrinkles her brow, as if puzzled about why I'm asking a question regarding a minor detail from the past. "Yes. I was careful to record every word exactly."

"Why's it important?" Barrett says.

"According to the police report, Ellen Casey's body was found on Gough Street," I say, "at a road construction site."

"It was a long time ago," Sally says. "Maybe Father forgot where he and Lucas left the body."

I want to believe it, but I say, "I don't think he would have forgotten. And his memory of the three burned houses and covering Ellen with charred boards seems very clear and specific."

"What does it matter, where they left the body?" Sally says.

Dread rising in my throat holds my tongue. Barrett reluctantly answers: "That's a discrepancy between your father's story and the official one. It calls the rest of his story into question."

Sally draws back, affronted. "Are you saying he lied?"

"Not necessarily," Barrett says. "But if he got one detail wrong, are the others accurate?"

"Maybe not all of them, but the big, important details, yes." Sally turns to me and sees the wretchedness in my expression. "Sarah . . ." Her expression begs me to quell her own dawning fear.

I can't pretend this mountain is a molehill. "I think Father didn't tell us the truth. Not all of it. Maybe not any of it." Speaking the words hurts, as if I'm gouging out pieces of my heart.

"But Lucas's father told you that your mother confessed to murdering Ellen," Sally says. "That part must be true. Why would he lie?"

"I didn't think Mr. Cullen was lying, but I don't know him well." Although I hate to hurt Sally, honesty compels me to say, "How well do we really know Father?"

Sally stammers, then falls silent. We each knew our father for ten years as children, when we trusted him completely. We've only known him four months as adults, and how much has he changed since he left us? Why should we trust him now, when he betrayed our trust by disappearing then?

"Never mind," Sally says, flapping her hands as if to shoo away stinging wasps. "The important thing is to find him. We should look for him at the hospitals, in case he's been in an accident. Then the train stations and the docks. Maybe he decided to go back to America." She tugs my arm. "Sarah, we need to hurry!"

I experience an unsettling shift, as though the bedrock under my feet has cracked and I'm straddling an abyss as it widens. For twenty-four years I longed for my father. After finding him, I determined to clear his name so that he and Sally and I could be a family. But my doubts gain force. Did he lie about where he dumped Ellen's body? *Is his whole story a lie?* Did he rape and murder her and put the blame on Lucas and my mother? Maybe he was afraid that Sally and I would discover the truth and decided to run away rather than face the music. Now I'm standing on the piece of bedrock that belongs to the present, and I'm moving away from the piece that's anchored to the past, like a ship leaving a harbor. I speak slowly, hesitantly, aware that my words will propel me faster toward an unknown, hazardous destination.

"I can't look for Father."

"Why not?" Sally demands.

"Barrett and I are going to Norwich," I say, and explain about Eva Piper.

She stares at me in disbelief. "Father has disappeared again, and instead of looking for him, you're going a hundred miles to chase a murder suspect?"

I hate to let Sally down, and I'm by no means comfortable with my decision. But Mick is the friend who's stood by me from the day we met, who's saved my life, to whom I'm bound by ties stronger than blood. I'm absolutely certain he deserves my help. I don't know that my father does. I have one hundred percent confidence in Mick's innocence, much less in my father's. If there was ever a moment to cleave to the present and dispense with the past, it's this one.

"We'll catch the first train to Norwich in the morning," I tell Barrett. Wild-goose chase or not, it's more worthwhile than spending precious time on my father.

"No!" Frantic, Sally looks to Barrett for support.

Spreading his hands, Barrett raises his eyebrows at me.

"It's looking more probable that Father murdered Ellen Casey." Voicing my thought feels like the worst kind of treason, but Ellen deserves justice as much as Mick does, and I can't put my loyalty to my father ahead of that truth.

"I don't care about her! All I care about is Father, and I know in my heart that he's innocent." Sally clasps her chest.

"He may have just abandoned us for the second time."

"He didn't. Sarah, please!"

I'm twisting a knife in my own heart. "I'm sorry."

Chapter 27

A hundred miles northeast of London, Norwich seems a city that never quite emerged from the Middle Ages. The cab carries Barrett and me from the train station through cobbled streets lined with ancient, half-timbered buildings. It's as if Eva Piper really is a ghost and we're hunting her in the distant past. Sleet falls on old public houses and churches. Morning mist cloaks a square stone Norman castle that rises above the rooftops. A raw, animal stench billows from a market where people gather around the outdoor stalls and herd sheep and cattle through the streets, just as their ancestors must have done six hundred years ago.

The cab driver lets us off in Pottergate Street, one of many narrow lanes. I recognize the Jenny Lind Hospital, two stories of red brick with three gables, from its picture on the hospital bill. It's newer than the other buildings in the street, and in the reception room, a plaque on the wall states that it opened in 1854 and that the famous Swedish opera singer had performed concerts to raise money for its construction. When Barrett and I join the line at the desk, I notice that most of the people seated in the waiting area are mothers and children. When our turn comes, Barrett says to the nurse behind the desk, "We're looking for Evelyn Corey Piper."

"Second floor, ward two," the nurse says.

We're astounded because we didn't expect to locate Eva so quickly; we can't believe our good fortune.

Upstairs in the ward are two rows of beds, all occupied by children who seem to have serious injuries or ailments. Some have bandaged heads, or legs in casts rigged with ropes and pulleys. Mothers sit at bedsides, and a nurse confers with a physician.

"This can't be the right place," Barrett says.

At the end of each bed hangs a sign bearing the patient's name. We spot a sign that reads EVELYN COREY PIPER. The patient is a boy, seven or eight years old, his blond hair cropped short. Across a dent in his skull at his left temple is a crooked scar outlined with marks from stitches. Smaller scars pock his face. He's eating, or trying to eat, from a bowl of custard on a tray attached to his bed. His fist clutches the spoon; he misses his mouth. There are custard smears on his distorted jaw, his bib, and the bedsheets.

Pitying him, I state the obvious: "This isn't Eva."

The boy glances up at the sound of my voice. His eyes are blue, the left cloudy.

"You were right," Barrett says, his voice laden with the same disappointment that overwhelms me. "This was a wild-goose chase."

I hear a gasp, and we turn to see a woman standing in the aisle between the rows of beds. Tall and slender, she's dressed in a gray coat, and a black net veil on her gray felt hat is folded back to reveal pale blond hair drawn back from a beautiful, familiar face. Her wide blue eyes stare at Barrett and me with alarm.

"It's her!" I say.

Eva drops the china basin she's carrying. It shatters on the floor, splashing water. She turns and flees. Barrett yells, "Stop!"

We chase her out of the ward, along the passage. Barrett collides with a nurse. Eva runs through a door, and I race after her, down a flight of stairs. As she reaches a door at the bottom, I'm five or six steps above her. I launch myself at her with no plan for what's going to happen next. I sail through the air and crash upon Eva. She screams as we thud to the stone floor. Her body cushions my landing, but my right knee hits with a painful impact. Pinned under my weight, she shrieks and flails. I clamber to my feet, hauling her with me. Breathless with triumph and anger, I shove her up against the wall.

"Did you kill Richard Trevelyan?" I shout into her face.

Eva turns away, struggles to break free. "Let me go!"

I hold tight, digging my fingernails into her slender, fragile shoulders. "Answer me!" I think she's guilty and she left Mick to take the blame. I bang her head against the wall while she screams.

"Sarah, stop." Barrett pulls me away from Eva and steps between us.

Eva crumples to her knees, raises her arms to shield herself from me, and wails, "I didn't kill Mr. Trevelyan."

Still panting with fury, I say, "No? Then why did you run from us?"

Barrett pats my arm, urging me to calm down, and says to Eva, "Do you know who we are?"

Peering at us between her spread fingers, Eva nods. "She's Sarah Bain, the photographer from Whitechapel. You're Detective Barrett."

I'm startled because she knows exactly who we are. Then she says, "I've read about you in the newspapers." Her veil, disarranged during our skirmish, slants over her face, and I'm even more startled to realize that I know her from frequent sightings, a veiled, graceful figure ducking into George Yard. Some women wear veils to protect their complexions from the dirty air; perhaps Eva also wears hers to hide her incredible beauty and protect herself from unwanted attention from men. Fate has prevented us from meeting, until now.

"What are you doing here?" Eva drops her hands in a gesture of defeat. "How did you find me?"

"We have questions for you too," Barrett says. "Let's talk someplace more comfortable."

He extends his hand to Eva. She meekly lets him help her stand, and she accompanies us upstairs to an empty sitting room gaily decorated with framed nursery-rhyme illustrations. Barrett seats me on the sofa and Eva in the armchair opposite, then goes in search of tea. Head bowed, Eva dabs her handkerchief at her eyes. As my temper cools, I experience the same sick feeling that came over me after I almost shot Inspector Reid. Once again I've gravitated toward violence to solve a problem. Once again I feel my mother's presence in me, abrading my own self. Her voice echoes in my memory: *We do what we have to do.* She said it when I complained about moving to yet another new neighborhood. Then, I thought she sounded bitter. Now I perceive a touch of satisfaction in her voice, as though she disliked her circumstances but didn't doubt that she'd chosen the right course of action.

I did what I had to do.

It's been my own justification for sins I've committed. Would it have been my excuse if I'd killed Inspector Reid or injured Eva Piper?

Now I see my mother in a different light. She wasn't only a criminal who strangled a little girl to protect her rapist son, as I thought; she was every mother who's ever fought for her child, sacrificing her own virtue. She paid for her crime by never seeing Lucas again and dying horribly from cancer at age forty-eight. But I'm not sure whether I'm finding some good in my mother because I still love her, or whether I need to believe she wasn't all bad because she's in me, and whatever she was, so am I.

Barrett returns with three steaming teacups, a sugar bowl, and a milk jug on a tray. As we all stir our tea, he says to Eva, "Who is Evelyn Corey Piper?"

She cradles her cup in both hands, as if to draw courage as well as warmth from it. "He's my son."

The little boy has her blond hair and blue eyes, but still I'm surprised to learn that she's his mother. I suppose I thought of her as the ghost in her photographs—incorporeal, not capable of something as earthly as childbirth.

"I call him Corey," Eva says. "That's my maiden name. My husband's name was Evelyn. He was a teacher at the Norwich independent day school." Belatedly, I notice that her speech identifies her as a gentlewoman. "He died of pneumonia two years ago."

"I'm sorry." Barrett's compassion is genuine. He's better at interrogating people than I am, kinder and gentler. "What happened to Corey?"

Eva responds to Barrett like a plant unfurling in sunlight. "Last March, we were walking by a factory when the boiler exploded. A piece of metal hit Corey and broke his skull. He had to have an operation to take out the shattered bits. He's getting better, though. He can't walk yet, but he can see out of his good eye, and he can talk a little."

I think of the dent in Corey's head and the custard smeared on his face, and it's hard for me to believe he'll recover completely. Although I can pity Eva, I cling to my belief that she's a murderess. Remembering the hospital bill, I say, "It must be expensive to keep him here."

Eva and Barrett cast wary glances at me, as if they're both afraid I'll pounce on Eva again. "Very expensive," she says. "I had to go to London and look for work. I became a model at dressmakers' shops." Distrust narrows her eyes. "How did you find me?"

I explain briefly, then say, "You also modeled for Charles Firth."

Eva squirms, obviously uncomfortable. "Yes."

"But the money you earned from modeling wasn't enough," I say. "So you blackmailed Charles Firth and Richard Trevelyan."

"Blackmail?" She forces a laugh as red spots flush her pale cheeks. "Whatever gave you that idea?"

"Mr. Newby told us."

She cringes, then takes a deep breath and sits up straight. "So you're married now," she says, glancing at the ring on my hand. "When you have children, you'll understand. As a mother, you do what you have to do."

I blink. It's as if Eva has stolen the phrase from my mind. This ethereal woman is as ruthless on her son's behalf as my mother was on Lucas's.

"Blackmail's a crime," Barrett says, gently reproachful, "even if you did it for a good reason."

"I didn't want to!" Eva cries. "Mr. Firth was a kind man. He asked me about myself, and when he heard about Corey, he raised my wages because he wanted to help me. I took advantage of him." She briefly covers her face with her hands. "I'm so sorry, and so ashamed of myself."

"Did you know what he was using your photographs for?" Barrett says.

"Yes. He told me. I don't believe in ghosts, and at first I didn't like the idea of pretending to be one. But Mr. Firth said that for people who do believe in ghosts, his spirit photographs are a comfort. They feel better when they have pictures of themselves with their departed loved ones. He wanted to help them too."

This is welcome news—that Charles Firth deceived his customers out of the same kindness he showed me. Thanks to Eva, I can believe that his fame and wealth were by-products of his work, not its primary goal, and I can remember him fondly rather than with disgust for his fraud. I feel guilty because I never repaid his generosity, yet Eva has done worse: she repaid him with blackmail.

"Eva Piper, I shall have to arrest you." Barrett's manner is apologetic but firm.

She stares, aghast that this nice man who's been listening to her tale of woe has turned on her. "But what will happen to Corey? He doesn't have anyone but me."

"You should have thought of his future before you blackmailed Richard Trevelyan and Charles Firth and threatened to report their fraud to the newspapers," Barrett says. "You could be sent to a prison workhouse for years. Corey will likely go to an asylum."

"An *asylum*?" The horror in Eva's tone evokes squalid conditions, neglected inmates tied to their beds.

Barrett regards her with pity. "If all you get is time in a workhouse, you're lucky. You're a suspect in the murders of Richard Trevelyan and Charles Firth. If you're tried and convicted, you'll hang. And Corey will lose his mother for good."

I'm admiring his skillful manipulation of Eva at the same time I'm appalled by it.

"No, please!" Eva falls to her knees, raises clasped hands to Barrett.

"I'll tell you what," Barrett says. "You tell me, right now, everything you know about the murders, and I'll overlook the blackmail."

Reminded of my attempt to make a deal with Inspector Reid, I gulp.

"But I don't know anything!" Eva says.

Impatience joins the reproach in Barrett's expression. "Mrs. Piper, we both know you're lying. This is your last chance to tell me the truth."

Eva bursts into tears. "I didn't kill Mr. Trevelyan or Mr. Firth. They were both alive when I left them."

Barrett and I look at each other, stunned by the implication of her words. "Wait," I say. "You weren't just at the scene of Richard Trevelyan's murder, you were also at St. Peter's Church the night Charles Firth was murdered?"

"Oh, God." Realizing that she's in deeper trouble than ever, Eva sobs into her hands.

Barrett gently takes hold of her arms, lifts her, and resettles her in her chair. "You might as well tell us."

Eva nods, drained and meek. I smile with triumph. Barrett looks far from happy, as if he's done what he had to do but hated it.

"Start with Richard Trevelyan," I tell Eva. Much as I want to solve Charles Firth's murder, eyewitness evidence in Mr. Trevelyan's case is more important, as it could save Mick.

Eva sniffles. "I heard about the spirit-hunting expedition from the newspapers. I went because I thought Mr. Trevelyan would be there. Corey's bills were overdue, and the hospital was about to put him out. I found Mr. Trevelyan, and I begged him for money. He said he was as good as ruined already and I could talk to the press if I wanted. And he was going to tell the police I'd blackmailed him and Mr. Firth."

I glimpse another possible motive for Richard Trevelyan's murder. Ruthless enough for blackmail, was she also ruthless enough to kill the man to silence him?

"Then he saw someone watching us and hurried me out of the tunnel," Eva says.

That was me, making my brief appearance in the story she's telling.

"We got separated in the crowd," Eva says. "I searched for him, I wanted to beg him to change his mind, but then people started running and shouting and saying there'd been a murder. I heard someone say it was Mr. Trevelyan. I was afraid that whoever had seen us arguing would report me to the police and I would be blamed."

Unbeknown to Eva, I had reported her, but I'd misidentified her as Diana Kelly.

"I hurried home and packed my things," Eva says. "I took the first train to Norwich."

Just as I thought, she skipped town to avoid a murder charge.

"When you first spotted Mr. Trevelyan, was there anyone with him?" Barrett says.

"There were a lot of people all over."

I'm grudgingly ready to believe that Eva is innocent of at least one murder, but I still hope for more information than she's given us. "What about Leonora Firth or Dr. Everard Lodge? Jean Ritchie or Diana Kelly?" Although Diana wasn't the blond I saw with Mr. Trevelyan, she's still possibly a suspect, and it's more important than ever to place her or one of the others at the crime scene.

"I don't know who they are."

"Did you see Mick O'Reilly?" I say.

Eva responds with a blank look. "Who . . . oh, the red-haired boy who lives with you. No. I didn't know he was there."

Grasping at straws, I say, "Did you see anyone following Mr. Trevelyan or acting suspicious?"

"No." Eva rubs her temples as if her head aches. "I've told you everything."

A sensation of defeat encroaches on me as strongly as it did the evening I hunted Jack the Ripper through the dark, foggy streets of Whitechapel and it seemed I would never catch him, would wander those streets forever.

"Then let's talk about Charles Firth's murder," Barrett says to Eva.

I cling to my hope that the two cases are connected and that solving the first will solve the second and exonerate Mick.

Eva sighs, then proceeds in a weary monotone. "Mr. Firth asked me to model for him at St. Peter's. He said the pictures would look more genuine if I was photographed at the church rather than if he added me in later. So I met him at the church. We went inside and looked around, and he decided to photograph me in the crypt. While he was setting up his cameras, I went across the passage to change clothes." Eva explains, "He'd brought a white gown that would make me look like a ghost. I'd just finished changing when I heard noises above me." Recollected fear animates Eva's tired eyes as she raises them. "Someone else was in the church. Mr. Firth said, 'It's probably the vicar. Keep quiet, so we don't caught.' A little while later, we heard moaning, as if someone was in terrible pain." Eva shivers. "Then growling, slavering noises, like an animal. Mr. Firth said, 'Those are the noises that people have described hearing. Maybe the church really is haunted and I can photograph some real spirits.' He was very excited."

So he'd wanted to believe in the supernatural, wanted to take genuine spirit photographs rather than create hoaxes. I grieve for Charles Firth.

"He said, 'I'm going to have a look. You stay here.' He went upstairs. I didn't think it was a ghost, but I was terrified that what-ever it was would come and attack me. I threw on my regular clothes over the white gown in case I had to run out of the church. Then I waited. Finally, I heard Mr. Firth coming back. He was muttering to himself as if he was angry. I was about to ask him what he'd found when I heard footsteps hurrying after him. Then it sounded like he was arguing with someone. I couldn't under-stand what he was saying or hear the other person. Then he cried out, and there was a thud, as if something heavy had fallen on the floor. I heard the footsteps running away. I hurried to Mr. Firth. He was lying in the chamber by his cameras. There was blood on his shirt. He was breathing hard and fast, and the blood was pour-ing out. Someone had tried to kill him." Eva's face is as starkly white as in her spirit photographs.

I believe Eva, and Barrett nods; he does too.

"I had to get help for Mr. Firth. I ran outside to look for a policeman but couldn't find one. Then I saw a house across the lane, by a big building. I started toward it, but then I heard someone run out of the church behind me. It must have been the killer." Eva hugs herself, glancing fearfully over her shoulder, as she must have done that night. "I hid in the bushes. They ran past me, across the lane." Her mouth twists in an embarrassed smile. "This will sound childish and silly, but I closed my eyes. I guess I was afraid that if I could see them, they could see me. When I opened my eyes, I saw light from the door of the house as they opened it and went inside."

A house across the lane from the church, by a big building. I think back to my wedding day, picture the area, and remember girls playing ring-around-the-rosy outside St. Peter's School and the attached smaller section. I lean back, stunned by the implications of Eva's tale.

"The vicarage," Barrett says, afire with excitement. "The killer is someone from the vicarage!"

CHAPTER 28

Our train to London is delayed because of mechanical problems. While it sits on the track and Barrett falls sleep, I think of how hurt and miserable Sally looked when we left her at her lodgings last night. How I wished I could have told her I'd changed my mind about going to Norwich and promised I would move heaven and earth, immediately, to find our father! When I apologized again, she said, "It's all right. I understand." She was trying her best to see my point of view, and her generosity put me to shame. I remember a time soon after my father went missing. I'd come home from school and begged my mother to help me look for him. It was washday, and she was hanging clothes on the line. She snapped, "Can't you see I'm busy?" I now know that she knew my father was gone for good and hated to keep up the farce of looking for him. To Sally, I must appear as heartlessly cruel as my mother did to me. Sick with guilt, I vow to make it up to Sally. As soon as Mick is free, I'll spend every moment hunting for our father. I'll ask Sir Gerald for a leave of absence from the *Daily World*, and if he says no, I'll resign. But even with that decided, my conscience is far from clear, and I'm afraid that I've lost more than my father.

When Barrett and I finally emerge from Whitechapel station at eight thirty, the smoke in the fog smells of burning wood. The bonfires have started in parks, vacant lots, gardens, and on the riverbank. It's Halloween.

"Are you sure you want to go to the vicarage after we stop at your house to see if Hugh is back?" Barrett says.

"Yes. I can't wait to learn who killed Charles Firth."

It's just too bad that Eva Piper squelched our theory that the same killer also murdered Richard Trevelyan. We can't imagine any connection between Mr. Trevelyan and the vicarage. Mick will have to stay in jail, counting down the days to his trial, unless we can find a way to clear his name.

Along Whitechapel high street, lit candles and plates of food have been placed in doorways to feed visitors from the other side. Adults and children, costumed as animals, fairies, and goblins, go from house to house, singing, "A soul! A soul cake! Please, good missus, a soul cake." They collect small round spice cakes in exchange for their promises to pray for the donors' dead kin. As we approach my house, I see a vagrant lying in the doorway, his face hidden by his bowler hat, his legs curled up under his black coat.

"Sir, you're blocking my door," I say. "Please move."

He jerks upright, pushes back his hat, and the light from the streetlamp falls on his face. He blinks familiar green eyes at me.

"Hugh!" I cry.

"Sarah." He yawns and smiles. "Hullo, Barrett."

A flood of joy almost knocks me to the ground beside Hugh. Gone is the fear that he's dead, that he's never coming back. "Thank God!"

"Nice to see you," Barrett says. The relief in his voice tells me that he too feared the worst. He extends his hand to Hugh, who takes it and pulls himself to his feet.

"I was so worried!" Now that Hugh is safe, my own relief gives way to anger. "Damn you!" I smack his chest.

Hugh laughs. "That's a fine 'welcome home.' "

He takes me in his arms, I'm crying as we embrace. He's solid, really *here*. When he kisses my cheek, his breath is fresh, and he smells clean, of bay rum shaving lotion, not liquor; he isn't drunk or hungover. It's as if summer came early and all is warm, sunny, and bright.

"What are you doing out here?" Barrett says as I step away from Hugh and wipe my eyes.

"I lost my key," Hugh says. "Nobody was home, so I sat down to wait, and I dozed off."

"Where have you been?" I demand.

"Do you mind if we talk inside?" Hugh gives an exaggerated shiver. "I'm freezing."

In the kitchen, he sits at the table, and I watch him covertly as I make tea. He's thinner but neatly groomed, dressed in a white shirt and gray suit that look new. His complexion is rosy, and his eyes have that sparkle that I've not seen since before he lost Tristan. He left a broken man and returned whole and healthy—a miracle. I set steaming cups of tea in front of him and Barrett and say, "Tell me."

Hugh sips tea, warming his hands on the cup. "I went to Switzerland."

"*What?*" Barrett and I say.

Hugh smiles at our amazement. "It's not that far. Only a day's trip by steamship going there and a day coming back."

"Why didn't you tell me you were going?" I say.

"Because you would have tried to talk me out of it," Hugh calmly explains. "I was fed up with writing to Tristan and not getting any reply, so I decided to take action. Action is so much better for the soul than brooding, don't you think?"

"Yes, and . . ." I'm afraid to ask what happened.

"The retreat for ex-priests is in a chalet on a suitably god-forsaken mountain. I went up there and asked for Tristan. The gatekeeper looks like Cerberus minus two of the heads. He said Tristan wasn't receiving visitors. Well, I refused to leave, so finally Tristan came out to the waiting room where I'd installed myself. He said I'd come all that way for nothing, because he didn't want to see me. He told me to go home and never trouble him again."

"Oh, Hugh." My heart aches for his folly. I seethe with anger at the heartless Tristan.

Hugh waves away my sympathy. "It's all right. He said what I needed to hear. It was like lancing a boil—painful but necessary.

Now I can stop my futile pining and moping and get on with my life."

This is what I wanted for him—to face reality and begin to heal—but I hardly dare believe it's true. "Are you sure you're all right?"

Hugh smiles. "Never better. I say, I'm hungry. Is there anything to eat? I sound just like Mick. Where is he?"

"In Newgate Prison." I explain while I toast cheese on bread.

"My God." Hugh shakes his head, sobered by horror. "If I'd been with Mick that night, he wouldn't be on the hook for murder. I shouldn't have left."

"Don't blame yourself," Barrett says. "Nobody could have predicted what would happen."

"Anjali did," I say.

"Who's Anjali?" Hugh says.

"The daughter of Dr. Everard Lodge. He's one of the suspects in Charles Firth's murder." I'm realizing how much Hugh has missed. "Or, I should say, he *was* a suspect."

"Sarah and I just discovered that the murderer is someone at the vicarage," Barrett says, and tells Hugh the gist of Eva Piper's story.

"The august Reverend Thornton, his kindly wife, or his odd grandchildren? Excellent work!" Hugh wolfs down bread and cheese with the appetite he lost when Tristan broke his heart.

"We were about to go over there," I say.

"What are we waiting for?" Hugh tosses his napkin on the table, pushes back his chair, and stands.

"You mean, you want to go with us?" I say, unsure that it's a good idea.

"Definitely. I've been out of the game for too long. The least I can do is help you wrap it up."

His energy seems like a fire made from twigs, liable to burn out fast. "Aren't you tired?"

"Not a bit. My little outdoor nap was quite invigorating." Hurt dims the sparkle in Hugh's eyes. "Don't you want me?"

He's just experienced one rejection; far be it from me to inflict another on him. "Of course I do."

Barrett nods. We're both glad to have Hugh back, and four suspects might be too many for the two of us to handle alone.

Hugh goes to the parlor, dons his coat, then opens the drawer in the table and removes three guns. The sight of them gives me a sickening jolt. This is the first time I've laid eyes on mine since the morning I almost shot Inspector Reid. Hugh checks the guns to make sure they're loaded, then hands Barrett and me our weapons. Mine is cold and heavy in my hand. I shy from thinking about things that happened at the conclusion of our other investigations and what could happen tonight.

Hugh tucks his gun and a box of bullets into his coat pocket, smiles, and says, "Ready?"

★   ★   ★

Just after ten o'clock, Barrett, Hugh, and I walk toward the vicarage. The fog glows orange with the light of bonfires. The night echoes with footsteps and giggles from mischief-makers. Candles burn inside carved gourds on porches; the grotesque faces leer.

"This is almost like old times," Hugh says, his tone cheerful and his steps light.

I don't quash his enthusiasm by reminding him that our last confrontation with a killer was only months ago. My wounded shoulder aches.

"I just wish Mick were with us," Hugh adds.

At the vicarage, my knock on the door echoes through the house, which seems as empty as a tomb awaiting a corpse. After I knock repeatedly for some minutes, the fanlight at the top of the door glows. I recall Eva Piper describing how she saw the killer enter the vicarage. *I didn't get a good look at the person. The fog made everything blurry. I was afraid he would come back out and see me and he would guess that I knew what he'd done. So I went home.* If she'd fetched the police, perhaps Charles Firth's life could have been saved and the person who stabbed him could have been caught that very night. And then my friends and I wouldn't have become involved in the investigation and Mick wouldn't be in jail. It's hard for me not to hate Eva Piper for her cowardice. But of course she did only what she thought she had to do—protect herself rather than risk leaving her sick son motherless and alone in the world.

A woman's timid voice calls, "Who's there?"

"Mrs. Thornton?" I say. The idea that she could be the killer seems preposterous, even though I've met female killers who looked to be equally unlikely culprits. "It's Mr. and Mrs. Thomas Barrett." This is the first time I've announced myself and my husband as a married couple. How odd to do so under such circumstances. "And Lord Hugh Staunton."

The door opens a few inches, affording us a narrow view of Mrs. Thornton in a high-collared white nightdress and brown wool housecoat. Her gray hair hangs in two skinny braids. She looks tired and worried, but she musters the kind, patient smile of a vicar's wife who's accustomed to troubled parishioners coming to her house at odd hours.

"Is something wrong?" she asks.

"We need to talk to you and your husband and grandchildren." Barrett speaks in the calm, authoritative voice he uses while on duty.

Mrs. Thornton's smile fades. "In regards to what?"

"The murder in the church," Barrett says.

Her eyes shift; she steps backward. "They—they aren't here."

Something's not right. I push the door open wider before Mrs. Thornton can close it. She exclaims in dismay as Barrett, Hugh, and I barge into the foyer.

"They're asleep." Her voice is shrill with fright. "Please don't wake them."

"They're asleep, or they're not here?" Barrett says. "Which is it?"

Mrs. Thornton shakes her head. Wringing her hands, rubbing them together, she reminds me of Lady Macbeth.

"Reverend Thornton!" I call. "Daniel! Lucie!"

My ears ring in the quiet as Barrett, Hugh, and I listen for a response. We run up the stairs. Mrs. Thornton follows us, pleading, "Stop. Don't."

On the second floor, we find a room with a rumpled double bed from which Mrs. Thornton must have just risen. A black cassock hangs on a clothes stand, but the vicar is nowhere in sight. Across the hall are two smaller rooms, dolls and stuffed animals in one, model ships and trains in the other. Both beds are unmade, empty. I turn to Mrs. Thornton, who hovers in the hall.

"Where are they?"

She presses her trembling lips together. I can't believe she's harmed them, but their absence and her lack of cooperation quicken my heartbeat into an ominous rhythm.

"Search the house for them," I tell Hugh and Barrett. "The knife too." Then I run downstairs.

Mrs. Thornton staggers after me, crying, "What knife?"

At the bottom of the stairs, I halt and face her. "The knife that someone from your household used to kill Charles Firth. Was it you?"

Her lips part; she stares. "No." The word is a cracked whisper, as much a plea as a denial.

I believe she's innocent. I think she's shocked because she didn't believe her husband or grandchildren could be capable of murder and she wants me to make the terrible possibility go away.

"There was a witness to the murder," I say. "She saw the killer leave the church and come inside this house."

With one hand, Mrs. Thornton clutches the banister for support; the other grips her throat. I point toward the dark rooms on either side of the foyer and say, "Put on the lights."

She strikes matches and lights gas jets, as if she thinks that by obeying me, she'll convince me that this is all a mistake. I hear footsteps above us as Hugh and Mick search the bedrooms and the attic. The parlor is vacant. So is the kitchen, with its chipped sink, old-fashioned stove, battered cupboards, and worn stone floor. Mrs. Thornton wrings her hands while I rummage through drawers until I find the knives.

"Are any missing?" I ask.

Mrs. Thornton shakes her head. Her lips quiver, and her eyes well with tears. I suppose the killer could have stabbed Charles Firth, washed the knife, and replaced it in the drawer with Mrs. Thornton none the wiser. I remember my own horror when I learned that my father was the prime suspect in a murder. Mrs. Thornton is in the same sinking boat that I am—awash with the need to believe, despite incriminating evidence, that a loved one is innocent. I search the pantry, the scullery, a second parlor, a library. They're all uninhabited. Mrs. Thornton trails me to a closed door.

"That's my husband's study. It's where he writes his sermons. He doesn't allow anyone inside." Mrs. Thornton seems to be grasping at shreds of her normal existence.

I fling open the door and light the gas lamps. The room is a mess, at odds with the vicar's dignified, respectable character. Papers are piled high on the desk, books leaning against one another on the shelves and stacked untidily on a carpet littered with dirty teacups and plates, crumbs and mouse droppings. There's a musty, stale, rotten smell. The room would be a good hiding place for anything he doesn't want found. I start with the desk drawers. The upper ones are chock-full of pens and wipers, sealing wax wafers, ink bottles that have leaked, and old letters and stationery.

Mrs. Thornton whimpers, "Don't touch his things. He'll be cross."

From the bottom drawer, from behind some old parish magazines, I lift out a narrow bundle wrapped in a white tea towel. My heart thuds as I unwrap the towel and see dark-brown stains on it. The object inside is a folding knife, the curved blade half concealed in the wooden handle. It looks old, the wood smooth and darkened. Blade and handle are coated with dried blood. This has to be the knife with which Charles Firth was stabbed; I can't see any other explanation for the blood or for the fact of its concealment. Sorrow infuses my satisfaction. The blood is a vestige of my flawed but ultimately kind patron and, indeed, my friend. Loath to touch the murder weapon with my bare hands, I turn it over in the towel. Carved crudely on the handle are the initials D. T.

Douglas Thornton, the vicar.

I don't need the initials to tell me that this knife, hidden in his private study, belongs to him. My gaze falls to the papers on the desk, which are inked with scribbled black handwriting: *Have*

mercy on me, God; in your plentiful compassion, expunge my transgres-
sions. Cleanse away my guilt, and of my sin absolve me.

Barrett and Hugh burst into the room. They stare, incredulous, at the weapon in my hands. Hugh says, "Sarah, you found it?"

I show them the initials. "The vicar is the killer. He's the person Eva Piper saw." I look around for his wife. She's gone. "Where's Mrs. Thornton?"

"Never mind her," Barrett says. "We know where the vicar and the children are."

"In the church," Hugh says. "We saw lights in the windows."

"Keep the knife. It's evidence," Barrett says.

I rewrap the knife in the towel and cram it in my pocketbook as we rush out the front door. Distant voices sing, "Please, good missus, a soul cake." The church's stained-glass windows glow dimly, like watercolor paint smeared in the fog and acrid bonfire smoke. We rush around the corner to the main entrance.

Hugh tries the doorknob. "Damn, it's locked. I wish Mick were here."

I search my pocketbook and dig out the picklocks. Barrett lights a match and holds it near the lock so I can see while I work. Ten matches burn out and my hands are clammy with sweat before the tumblers click into place. Hugh cautiously opens the door, which emits a loud creak that makes us all jump. An instant later, the light in the church goes out.

"They heard us," I whisper. Fear keens through me like an icy gale as I remember other dark places to which we've tracked murderers.

Hugh draws the gun from his pocket and steps through the door. In the vestibule, Barrett finds a box of candles by a holder and coin box. He lights one for each of us. We extend our candles toward the entrance to the sanctuary. Their flames waver in a cold draft that smells of incense and dying flowers. The aisle down which Hugh walked me last week leads to the altar where Barrett and I were joined in holy matrimony by the man who, unbe-known to us, had committed murder the previous night. We stand still, alert. Only the skittering of mice interrupts the sinister quiet.

Then I hear a faint moan. My heart lurches. I clutch at Barrett and Hugh. They turn quizzical glances to me; they didn't hear the noise. I put my finger to my lips.

Several long, tense minutes pass.

The moan comes again, from above us, louder.

We lift our gazes toward the ceiling. At first I think the sound is wind gusting through the church's tower, directly above us. Then I sense in it a human quality that raises cold prickles on my skin. It must be the sound heard by people who claim the church is haunted. Hugh points to the right side of the vestibule. His candle illuminates an open door, beyond which a stairway leads upward. He's through the door, climbing the stairs before I can warn him to be careful. I hurry after him, as usual aware that there's no point in my being safe if he isn't. Barrett curses under his breath as he follows us.

The stairway ascends in a tight spiral within the tower. There's no banister, the steps are slippery stone, and as I mount them, I clutch the walls to keep from falling. I tell myself I'm afraid the vicar, Daniel, or Lucie is luring us into a trap. I don't think a ghost is up there; of course I don't. The confined space increases the anxiety that squeezes my rib cage. Dizzy from going around the spiral, I concentrate on Hugh's legs, a few stairs above me. Barrett's presence behind me provides some comfort. So does the fact that the moans have stopped. At the first landing, light from the street shines dimly through a window. At the second, Hugh, Barrett, and I pause at a closed door. I wheeze, catching my breath, as we draw our guns. I'm praying that we won't need to use them when I hear a moan from the door's other side.

We all jump. Hugh mutters, "Christ!"

This time the moan is unmistakably human. Redolent with pain and suffering, it ends in a throaty, viscous gurgle. I can't help but imagine the ghost of a long-dead cholera victim trapped in the tower, waiting for someone to let it out so that it can wreak unholy havoc upon the world. I stand back as Hugh tries the door.

CHAPTER 29

The door screeches open. Out pours an awful sickroom odor of soiled bedding, bitter medicine, and sweet, fetid decay. Hands full with candles and guns, Barrett, Hugh, and I fling up our arms to cover our noses. Hugh gags, but to me the stench is oddly reassuring—it is of this world, not supernatural. I hold my candle over the threshold.

The room is small, octagonal, with round windows on four sides. Its height lifts my eyes upward to the ceiling's wooden beams, to the hollow cone that forms the tower's spire. At the center of the room is a bed with wooden rails on its sides. In the bed, covered by piled quilts, lies a woman with long, matted brown hair that straggles out of her knitted pink woolen nightcap. As Barrett, Hugh, and I move toward her, I breathe shallowly, but the stench of her infiltrates my nostrils, my mouth. Her emaciated face is a patchwork of gauze pads and sticking plaster, the visible skin mottled red and gray. She wriggles to pull her hands from beneath the heavy quilts. Her skeletal wrists are tied with cords to the bed railings. She feebly turns from side to side. Hollow eyes, so obscured by yellowish film that I can't discern their color, shine in the candlelight.

Not a ghostly victim of some terrible illness, but a live one.

Hugh speaks in a tone of utter disbelief. "The vicar is not only a murderer, but he's holding this woman prisoner in the church?"

Barrett rubs his head, as perplexed as I am. "It looks that way."

"But why?" I can't imagine for what purpose Reverend Thornton would do such a thing. I can't tell if the woman can see us; maybe she's blind. Her mouth opens. Most of her teeth are missing. Her gums and chapped lips are coated with thick, greenish mucus. She moans and shudders, her suffering terrible to behold. She gurgles on the mucus and drools it onto her pillow and quilts, which are already stiff and reeking with it. Her filmy eyes roll.

"This changes things," Barrett says.

I nod. Reverend Thornton is a murderer and apparently a kidnapper; he and his grandchildren are still at large; and Mick is still facing trial for a crime he didn't commit. But . . . "We can't walk away from this poor sick woman and go about our business."

"That would be cold," Hugh says.

Justice for her is as important as justice for Charles Firth.

"Ma'am, you're safe now," Barrett says to her.

"We'll take you to London Hospital so you'll be cared for," Hugh says. "I'll pop over there and fetch an ambulance." He hurries down the stairs.

"What's your name?" I ask the woman.

She grunts, and I can't tell whether she heard me, whether she's trying to speak or uttering sounds of distress. Barrett pockets his gun, and I replace mine in my pocketbook. We stand our candles in an empty glass on the bedside table, which is cluttered with medicine bottles, measuring cups and spoons, boxes of bandages, a pitcher, and a washbasin. Reverend Thornton must be doctoring his prisoner. While Barrett attempts to untie the cords that bind her wrists to the bed, I discover other cords tied to the rails and covered by the quilts: her ankles are bound too. The knots are tight, strong.

"It would be faster to cut them," Barrett says. "Is there a knife, or scissors?"

Seeing none on the table, I reach in my pocket, bring out the wrapped knife, and unwind the stained towel. "But it's evidence in Charles Firth's murder. If we cut the cords, the blood will rub off the blade. There might not be enough proof that the vicar is guilty."

"You don't need proof that I'm guilty."

Startled, Barrett and I turn to the door. There stands a man in an old brown tweed coat with patched elbows, his face unshaven. It takes me a moment to recognize the vicar. Stripped of his clerical trappings, he looks a different person, a stranger.

"That's my fishing knife. It belonged to my father." A sad smile curves his mouth. "You can arrest me, Detective Barrett. I'm turning myself in."

Barrett and I are speechless with astonishment. We can't believe it's as easy as this. For a moment I can't think of anything to do but rewrap the knife and put it in my pocketbook for safekeeping.

"I killed Charles Firth." Reverend Thornton's voice is hoarse, his face creased with pain, as though his shame is a razor blade in his throat. "It was unconscionable of me to try to get away with it. I'm sorry for the trouble to which I put you. Now I'm ready to accept the punishment for my crime, and my sin."

I blurt the foremost of my many questions. "Why did you kill him?" Anger boils up in me. "What did he ever do to you?"

Barrett shakes his head, motions me to wait, then points at the woman in the bed. "Reverend Thornton, who is this?"

The vicar expels a breath replete with sorrow. "She's my daughter, Alice."

I'm confused. "Daniel and Lucie's mother? I thought she was deceased."

"No." The vicar gently tucks Alice's skeletal hands under the quilt. "But it won't be long now."

I comprehend that the woman's restless motions are death throes. Barrett opens his mouth, hesitates, and closes it as if he can't decide which question to ask next. Then he says, "Why are you keeping her here? She should be in a hospital."

"I couldn't take her to a hospital."

"Why not at the vicarage? It would be more comfortable than here."

Reverend Thornton caresses Alice's mottled forehead. "For the same reason I couldn't take her to the hospital—I couldn't let anyone see her or know what ails her. It would bring disgrace upon not only her but our entire family."

"What's so disgraceful about tuberculosis?" Barrett asks. It's a horrible disease, often fatal, but common and not kept under wraps.

"She doesn't have tuberculosis." Reverend Thornton bows his head over his daughter and lowers his voice. "It's syphilis."

Syphilis, the disease that is contracted via carnal relations and causes skin lesions, blindness, paralysis, and insanity, among other ills, in its advanced stages. The disease that polite society talks about in whispers, that brands the afflicted as pariahs—and, if the afflicted is female, a whore. Alice must have caught syphilis from one of her lovers in Paris. Now the situation begins to make a twisted sense.

"When you brought her back to England, you hid her in the church," I say to Reverend Thornton. "That's why you keep the church locked, not because of thieves. That's why you didn't want me poking around—you were afraid I would find her. And the children know she's here. They tried to scare me away."

"Yes. I couldn't let you talk to them because they might let the secret slip."

Barrett's face shows dawning, appalled enlightenment. "So she's the ghost. Do you carry her around the church at night? Did your curate catch you?"

The vicar nods. "I give her laudanum to make her sleep and ease the pain. But when she wasn't as sick, sometimes she would wake up and go wandering. Once or twice she managed to get outdoors. She thought she was lost in Paris, trying to find her way home."

It was Alice whom Nat Quayle saw in the graveyard. I remember Anjali describing her vision of a woman wearing white. Had she seen Alice Thornton in the crypt?

"Now she's in danger of falling out of bed and hurting herself." The vicar touches the cords. "I've had no choice but to restrain her."

"What happened that night?" I'm satisfied with his explanation of the prisoner in the tower, less so with his confession, which sounded too pat.

"I came to check on Alice," the vicar says.

Andrew Coburn didn't mention seeing him; if the vagrant was outside the church that night, he could have been asleep, or too drunk to notice or recall anything.

"I take care of her," the vicar explains. "The children can't, and Mrs. Thornton doesn't know she's here."

I thought myself incapable of being surprised by anything else he said, but I was wrong. "The children know she's alive, but you've kept your wife in the dark?"

"The children know because Alice came home with us on the boat from France. But I couldn't tell Mrs. Thornton. She's a highly virtuous woman, and if she learned that Alice is afflicted with a disease born of sin, she would be devastated. It seemed better to let her think Alice was safe with God." Misery shrouds the vicar's face as he contemplates Alice. She gasps for breath as her body's restless movements grow feebler. "She will be soon enough."

And I thought my family's scenario—a murder, a living relative presumed dead, and a conspiracy to hide the truth—was too extraordinary to encounter more than once in a lifetime.

"Alice had soiled herself," the vicar says. "I undressed her, and while I was washing her, she started moaning. Mr. Firth must have heard. He came and found us."

I picture Alice naked on the bed, the vicar with his hands on her, and Mr. Firth's shock.

The vicar speaks slowly, with long pauses between sentences spoken in a voice that grows hoarser by the moment. "He said, 'Who is she? Who are you, and what have you done to her?' I was alarmed to see a stranger when I'd thought no one else was in the church. I was horrified because he'd seen Alice and me, and I knew how it must have looked. I said, 'I'm the vicar of this church. Who are you, and how did you get in?' He introduced himself and said the curate had given him the key so that he could take spirit photographs. He pointed to Alice and said, 'So *she's* the ghost.' "

How disappointed Mr. Firth must have been to discover the sad truth about the supernatural phenomena at the church.

"Then he pushed me away from Alice. He covered her with her quilt and started untying the cords around her wrists. I said, 'What are you doing?' He said, 'I'm rescuing her.' I said, 'This isn't what it appears to be.' He said, 'That's what all criminals say when they're caught. You're a man of God, and you're keeping this woman drugged and tied up for your own filthy pleasure. I won't let you get away with it.' "

Barrett presses his fingers against his temples, as if trying to stimulate his brain into comprehending the incomprehensible. "Why didn't you tell him that she's your sick daughter and you were taking care of her?"

"I thought that if he made it public, there would be a scandal, and everyone would know about Alice. Including Mrs. Thornton."

"Is that when you killed him?" I'm grieved to realize that Charles Firth died not because of his fraudulent spirit photographs or because he'd made enemies, but because he'd followed his characteristic impulse to help someone in need.

"No. I grabbed him." The vicar pauses, longer this time. "We fought. We fell onto Alice, and she began to scream. She didn't understand what was happening, and she was terrified."

I remember the slimy substance Dr. Phillips found on Charles Firth's clothes at the morgue—not ectoplasm but Alice's drool, its scent redolent of chemicals from her medicines. It must have gotten on them during the fight.

The vicar clears his throat, and his gaze turns inward, as if he's watching the events unfold in his memory. "Then he stood back and said, 'I'm going to fetch the police. They'll see that she gets home safely, and they'll put you in jail so you can't hurt other women.' He hurried down to the crypt. I went after him, to the chamber where he'd left his cameras. He started packing up his things to take with him. I begged him not to tell the police. He said he was damned if he would cover up for me." The vicar's voice shrinks to a raspy whisper; he seems to be losing it. He clears his throat twice more before he says, "That's when I stabbed him." Drawing a deep breath, he rolls his shoulders, as if confessing has relieved him of a heavy weight.

I picture Eva hiding and listening while the final, fatal confrontation took place. I can't believe this is the same man who officiated at my wedding, who epitomized the sanctity of the church. He looks like a downtrodden, careworn laborer I might see on the streets of Whitechapel. I wonder if the chaos in his study is a manifestation of a mental breakdown caused by the stress of bringing his ill daughter home from Paris, sneaking her into the church, and caring for her while keeping her presence a secret from everyone but the children.

"Then I went back to the tower. I put clean clothes on Alice, gave her more laudanum, and tucked her in for the night." Reverend Thornton's raspy speech alternates with pauses and throat clearing. "I went home, hid the knife, and went to bed. By that time, the whole thing seemed like a bad dream. I half convinced myself that it hadn't happened. But when I woke up in the morning, I knew that it was all too real. I had killed a man. I realized that my only hope of protecting myself and my family was to deny any knowledge of the murder."

I think back to the wedding and remember my happiness when Barrett kissed me. All the while, the Reverend Thornton stood by with darkness in his heart, aware that the body of the man he'd stabbed to death lay in the crypt below us.

"How could you?" Barrett demands. "Kill somebody, and then marry Sarah and me the next day as though butter wouldn't melt in your mouth?" He beholds the vicar with a mixture of disbelief, confusion, and anger. "I respected you. I trusted you. I thought you were an honorable man, an example to follow. *How could you?*"

Reverend Thornton flinches as if Barrett's words are stones hurled at him. "I'm sorry I've disappointed you." He turns to me. "I'm sorry I dishonored your nuptials."

Amid my own bewilderment and indignation, I see him as if he's a stranger. My memory of his kindness to me darkens like the edges of a page torn from a diary and dipped in acid. His old, threadbare coat hangs on a man who seems just as devoid of a soul, of morality, as a wooden statue.

"We're not the only ones you owe an apology to," Barrett says. "There's my mother and my father and everyone else in the parish. And don't forget Charles Firth's widow."

"I know." The vicar looks humbled and contrite, but his voice regains strength as he says, "That's why I'm prepared to accept my punishment. I've only one thing to ask of you before you arrest me: please don't tell anyone about Alice."

Surprise raises Barrett's eyebrows. Disapproval draws them into a frown. "What am I supposed to do? Just leave her like this?"

"It won't be for long."

"Who will take care of her in the meantime? And what will happen afterward?" Barrett's question alludes to the major problem of a corpse in the tower.

A sigh of resignation deflates the vicar's chest. "I shall have to tell Mrs. Thornton. She'll make arrangements."

I suppose that foisting the burden onto the wife he's kept ignorant is the least of his sins. Barrett says, "How do you expect to keep Alice's passing a secret? There will have to be a death certificate and a burial."

"I hope there will be enough time between my arrest and her passing that the public won't connect the two events. Mrs. Thornton will have to explain many things about Alice, but nobody needs to know that she had anything to do with my killing Charles Firth."

I'm so angry at the vicar that I hate to grant him any favors, but I remember how my mother and I were shunned by neighbors who thought my father had murdered Ellen Casey. I pity Alice Thornton, her children, and her mother, all innocent bystanders to his crime. I look to Barrett, expecting him to agree with me that the vicar should have his wish.

Barrett paces the floor. "I don't think it's possible to leave Alice out of the picture. She's your motive for killing Charles Firth. Without her, what are you going to say at your trial? That you killed him for no reason? The jury might not believe you." He halts, faces the vicar, and shakes his head. "You're guilty, you confessed, but you might be acquitted."

"That's a good point," I say. Heaven forbid that Charles Firth's murderer goes free because important facts were withheld from the jury. Barrett and I can't risk such a subversion of justice.

"Please." Reverend Thornton's voice is back to normal, urgent with desperation. "I'm begging you, for my family's sake."

Barrett turns from side to side, like a man trying to see a way out from between a rock and a hard place. "Because of everything you've done for my family, I wish I could do what you ask. But I can't."

"We'll have to testify at your trial," I remind the vicar. "What are we supposed to say?"

"You can say I told you that I thought Mr. Firth was a burglar and I stabbed him in self-defense."

"I won't lie to help you cover up your dirty secrets," I say. Heaven knows I've plenty of my own, but I draw the line at keeping those of my friend's killer.

"You're asking us to lie in court, under oath." Offense flares in Barrett's eyes. "Forget it. Lord Hugh has gone to fetch an ambulance for Alice. It will take her to the hospital. I'm taking you to the police station."

The vicar bows his head in sad, resigned dignity. "So be it."

I'm thanking God that at least one crime is solved, and without violence, when a shrill voice cries, "No!"

CHAPTER 30

Lucie Thornton stands in the doorway. She wears a blue wool coat over a long white flannel nightdress, and on her feet are the little red rubber boots I saw at the vicarage. In the frame of her dark, tangled hair, her face is contorted with terror. She must have sneaked up the stairs and overheard the whole, awful scene.

"Lucie, go back to the house." The vicar's tone is sharp with alarm.

Ignoring him, Lucie glares at Barrett and me and stomps her foot. "You can't take Mama and Grandfather away." Her babyish voice quivers.

I think of the day the police interrogated, threatened, and beat my father while I listened. There's no saving Lucie's grandfather, but I have to get her out of here so she doesn't see the ugliness of what happens next and dwell on it for the rest of her life. I hold out my hand to her. "Lucie, come with me."

"Daniel, stop them!" Lucie cries.

From the dark stairwell behind her, Daniel steps into the room. His coat sleeves and his blue-and-white-striped pajama trousers are too short; he's outgrown them. With his tousled blond hair, he looks like a child who's just gotten out of bed, but his soft face has hardened into new, grim angles. He's carrying an ax. My heart sinks. The violence I thought we'd avoided is now all too possible.

"Go away," Daniel says to Barrett and me. His voice cracks. "Leave us alone."

"Daniel, put the ax down." Barrett speaks with deliberate calm.

Daniel raises the ax in both hands, and his strange smile plays across his face. Our guns are useless; Barrett and I can't shoot a child. To cut short a life that's barely begun, to destroy his innocent hopes and dreams, to bereave those who love him—the very thought is impossible.

"I've been protecting my mother ever since I got big enough," Daniel says. "Once she brought a man home, and he started beating her. I hit him with a chair. I broke it over his head. Then there was the man she owed money to. He made her sell herself to other men to pay it back. I followed him across a bridge, and I pushed him off. He fell in the river. He couldn't swim." Daniel utters a hearty masculine laugh that slides up to a giggle. "I watched him drown."

He's shockingly not so innocent after all. Lucie smiles up at Daniel, her eyes shining with hero worship. I feel a complicated mixture of revulsion and pity. The twins have seen too much, and Daniel took matters into his own hands at too young an age. He must be half mad.

The vicar beholds his grandchildren with a horror that says he didn't know all the sordid details of Alice's life and that the things Daniel has done are a complete surprise to him. "Daniel." He holds out his hand. "Give me the ax."

Daniel tilts his head at his grandfather. "Why are you going to let the policeman arrest you?" His childish bewilderment contrasts with the bulky muscles of his body, the big hands holding the ax. "You didn't do anything wrong." Either Daniel didn't overhear the vicar's confession or he didn't understand it. Again I wonder if his mind is slow.

"That's enough, Daniel. Go home, and take Lucie with you." Reverend Thornton moves toward the children, waving his arms, shooing them to the door.

Daniel stands firm. "You only tried to help after the man was dead."

Lucie pipes up, "You shouldn't have to go to jail, Grandfather."

The candlelight wavers, as if from a sudden change in the atmosphere, while I begin to suspect that there's more to the story than has been revealed. Barrett asks the vicar, "What are they talking about?"

The vicar shouts at the children, "Go!"

Barrett steps between them and the door. "I want to hear what they have to say. Daniel, were you in the church that night?"

"Yes." Relief colors Daniel's strange smile. He brings to mind a pupil who's been waving his hand in class and the teacher has finally called on him. "Lucie and I both were."

It's just as I speculated previously: the children were at the scene of the murder, and Reverend Thornton didn't want them to talk to me and reveal what they know.

The vicar groans. "Daniel, for God's sake, be quiet."

"Grandfather, I'm only trying to help you." Daniel says to Barrett, "Lucie woke me. She was upset because she'd dreamed that a ghost had killed Mother. That's why we went to the church—to see if Mother was all right. When we got here, she was asleep. We climbed in bed with her and lay there together."

The image of the children snuggled against their dying mother fills me with sorrow. If there's anything worse than a father suddenly gone missing and presumed dead, it's this gradual, secretive, nightmarish demise.

"Mother started moaning and moving around," Daniel says. "I got the bottle of laudanum. Lucie held her mouth open, and I poured some in."

Alice's moans, and the growling, slavering noises she made when she swallowed the laudanum, are the sounds Eva Piper described.

"That's when the man came here," Lucie says.

"Don't listen to them," the vicar pleads. "You know that children make things up."

Lucie pouts. "We're not making it up."

"He asked us who we were. After I told him, he asked who she was." Daniel points at Alice. Her head rolls from side to side as her body convulses. "He asked why she was hidden in the church."

My heart contracts with dread as I absorb the fact that it was the children, not the vicar, whom Charles Firth confronted.

Suddenly I remember the dinner with Barrett's family and the vicar's hoarseness when he talked about his daughter's death. He was lying—just as he lied when he confessed to murdering Charles Firth and his voice went hoarse.

"I told him she's our mother and she's sick and nobody is supposed to know," Lucie says.

"He said he was sorry, but he couldn't let her stay here like this," Daniel says. "He tried to untie her, but the knots were too tight."

That was how he got her drool on his clothes, not during a fight with the vicar.

"So he said he was going to tell the police, and they would help him take her to a hospital," Daniel says.

"We followed him to the crypt," Lucie says.

An eerie sensation accompanies my new recollection of Anjali Lodge's vision: *A girl or woman wearing a white dress. She was crying. I think she's the ghost that people have seen at the jail. I think she knows who the murderer is.* Anjali was true in her vision and false only in her interpretation. It was Lucie Thornton she saw.

"I begged him not to tell," Daniel says, "but he said she needed help and he wasn't going to change his mind."

That was the argument Eva overheard. Reverend Thornton turns his back on his grandchildren, as if he's despaired of silencing them, of forestalling the consequences.

"So I took out my knife." Daniel holds the ax in his left hand while, with his right, he pantomimes reaching in his pocket and bringing forth the weapon.

I picture the initials, D. T., carved on the handle. Not just the vicar's but Daniel's too, on the family relic passed down from grandfather to grandson.

"And I stabbed him." Daniel makes a thrusting motion with the imaginary knife.

The "ghost" in the last photograph Charles Firth took was Daniel, not the Reverend Thornton. I see my shock reflected in Barrett's eyes. Daniel is the culprit of the crime to which his grandfather has confessed, and it was Daniel and Lucie whom Eva Piper glimpsed entering the vicarage. Still, I find myself making excuses for the boy. He's too young to understand fully that impulsive actions can have permanent consequences and murder isn't a game in which the defeated opponent comes back to life when it's over. I understand why, after Reverend Thornton learned we'd found the knife, he was so eager to take the blame for the crime: he'd been protecting Daniel, who is an innocent despite his guilt.

"It wasn't my fault." Daniel's tone changes from matter-of-fact to petulant. "He wasn't supposed to be in the church. He didn't have the right to take our mother away."

"If he hadn't come, Daniel wouldn't have needed to stab him," Lucie says. "He deserved it." She nods her head once, emphatically, as if to say, *so there.*

Daniel's strange smile returns. "I always protect my mother." He moves closer to her bedside. "I always will. Even if it means I'll go to *H-E-L-L.*" He raises the ax.

Even as excitement stirs my blood and my muscles tense for a fight, I say, "What did you do then, Daniel?" I have to keep him talking and stave off violence.

"Lucie and I went home. We woke up Grandfather and told him what had happened. He taught us that it's best to be honest." Daniel sounds like a child reciting a Sunday school lesson. "Grandfather, shouldn't you be honest now? And tell these people that it was me, not you, who stabbed that man?"

Reverend Thornton turns to show us a face ravaged by grief. "I told the children to go to bed. Then I went to the church. I found Charles Firth dead in the crypt, with the knife sticking out of his chest." His voice is hushed but clear; he's telling the truth now. "There was nothing I could do for him except pray for his soul."

I picture Charles Firth lying surrounded by his cameras, the self-timer in his hand, while the vicar muttered useless, ritualistic words.

"Then I pulled out the knife. I locked the church, went home, and hid the knife in my study. I meant to get rid of it later, but I was afraid of being seen. I told the children that if they were asked about the murder, they should say they'd been asleep all night and didn't know anything." His mournful gaze encompasses Barrett and me. "When you have children, you'll understand—for their sake, you do whatever you must." His words are an eerie reprise of Eva Piper's.

Barrett has fallen silent, his expression woeful as he beholds the clay feet of the man he placed on a pedestal of virtue. "Reverend, you obstructed a police investigation. You lied, and you instructed the children to lie. That's perjury." For lack of other words, he's resorted to the language of his profession. "You made yourself an accomplice after the fact of the crime."

The vicar stands his ground as if bravely facing a firing squad. "That's not all I did. I believe you're also looking for the person who committed the murder at the Clerkenwell House of Detention. Well, you've found him."

This is how it must feel during an earthquake, when the ground that was once solid and stable begins to move and the most remarkable thing isn't the motion itself but the fact that there's no stability anywhere near. I say, "You're confessing that you killed Richard Trevelyan?"

"I am."

I had given up on my theory that the two crimes were connected. When the vicar confessed to the first, I reluctantly accepted that solving it didn't solve the second or exonerate Mick. Now, new hope springs from the shambles of disappointment.

"You've already confessed to one murder you didn't commit," Barrett reminds the vicar. "Why should I believe you this time?"

"Because this time I'm telling the truth."

I take a closer look at the vicar. The old coat makes him appear less like a leader in the church than one of its lower-class, impoverished members.

The coat.

I point at it as another quake upsets my precarious balance and my knees buckle. "Reverend Thornton, did you wear that coat to the spirit-hunting expedition?"

He looks down at it, touching the worn, patched tweed. "Yes. I thought that if I wore my usual garments, I might be recognized."

I exclaim to Barrett, "He's the tramp that the witnesses saw!" I'm thrilled to be vindicated, to see a chance of saving Mick.

With a skepticism born of hearing many dubious tales during his police career, Barrett challenges the vicar. "Did you even know Richard Trevelyan? What reason could you have for wanting him dead?"

"I didn't know him. I'd never laid eyes on him until that night."

"Then why . . ."

"I wanted to direct your attention away from the church. I was afraid that if you kept snooping around, you would find Alice. I was also afraid that you would force Daniel and Lucie to tell you what really happened with Charles Firth. But if there were another, similar crime somewhere else, his murder would appear to be one in a series, and my family would be left in peace. When I read about the spirit-hunting expedition, it seemed like the perfect opportunity."

His voice isn't hoarse; he's not lying. Barrett's response says he hasn't failed to notice. "You plotted to kill a total stranger, in cold blood." Barrett is visibly appalled, distraught. "Just to throw us off course."

It seems worse than killing, in the heat of the moment, a trespasser who'd stumbled onto his family's dirty secret.

"I was desperate." The vicar glances at the children, who huddle together, whispering anxiously. But he doesn't seem desperate now. The elation in his eyes is like that of a gambler who thinks he has a winning hand. "I went under the old jail and hung around the crowds, watching and listening." I picture him in his old coat, anonymous in the throng. "I saw Richard Trevelyan giving an interview to some reporters."

I saw him too, and I'm shocked to realize that his murderer was close by me.

"He seemed to be someone important in the spiritualist community," the vicar says.

"And you thought he would be a perfect victim." I wish I knew what he's thinking now.

"Because if another spiritualist were murdered," Barrett says, "it would seem that the culprit was the same one in Charles Firth's case—either a ghost he'd conjured up or a human with a grudge against spiritualists. You found the right person in the right place, and you got your wish. Good for you."

The vicar flinches, nettled by Barrett's sarcasm. "I didn't mean to kill Mr. Trevelyan. I only meant to frighten him and cut him just enough that it would be taken seriously, then run away. I followed him around, and when he wandered into a tunnel that was vacant, I saw my chance."

I picture the tramp pursuing Mr. Trevelyan through the tunnels, away from the crowds, while Nat Quayle chased me.

"I drew my knife, and I was a few feet behind him when I tripped on a stone. He turned around and saw me."

I envision the fear and horror on Richard Trevelyan's face, his gaze riveted on the knife the vicar held, as he realized he was about to become the victim of an attack.

"The next thing I knew, he'd grabbed my arm, and we were fighting. During the struggle, the knife went into him." Beneath the vicar's guilt, I perceive cunning. As I try to figure out what he's up to, he appeals to Barrett. "His death was an accident."

Contempt twists Barrett's mouth. "An accident *you* caused. You're as guilty of his murder as if you'd intended it from the start."

Daniel knits his brow as he struggles to make sense of what he's heard. "But it couldn't have been you, Grandfather. The knife was in your study. I know. I checked every night."

"I used a different knife," the vicar says. "It's in the river now. Before I came home, I threw it off the Waterloo Bridge."

That explains why no weapon was found at the scene. I'm furious at the havoc that the vicar's misbegotten scheme to protect his grandson has wrought. "You covered up for Daniel, and then you covered up for yourself and let Mick get arrested!"

"I'm sorry about Mick. I never meant for him to come to harm." Reverend Thornton's manner is contrite but brisk, as if he wants to shunt this issue out of the way. Lucie and Daniel whisper frantically to each other. "I'll explain to the magistrate that I'm guilty and Mick is innocent."

Mick exonerated and released was all I'd wanted, but right now it's not enough. I want to throttle this man whom my mother-in-law used in her effort to reform my bad behavior.

Barrett demands of the vicar, "Why are you telling me all this now? You were never a suspect in Richard Trevelyan's murder. You could have kept quiet and gotten away with it."

"Because I want a favor from you in exchange for my confession." The vicar turns brazen, reckless, the gambler showing his cards. "Let me take the blame for both murders. Let Daniel go free."

My anger is a hot pressure that threatens to explode me into pieces. "Of all the nerve!" That one killer should use his crime as a bargaining chip to save another is beyond untenable.

The vicar ignores me; he looks to Barrett, whose opinion is the one that counts.

Barrett meets his gaze with a cold stare. "That's too big a favor."

"Why?" The vicar seems disconcerted that his self-sacrifice might be for naught. "You'll solve both murders. You'll deliver a criminal to justice."

"Is that what you think I want? To close the cases at the expense of the truth?" Barrett shakes his head.

"I'll be hanged for one murder. Why not two?" In a tone that hints at his desperation, the vicar says, "If Daniel is charged with murder, he'll be tried as if he were an adult. If he's convicted, he'll be . . ." He stops himself before the boy can hear him say *executed*.

"Daniel's confessed to another murder in addition to Charles Firth's," Barrett says, his manner hard and unforgiving.

"Daniel is too young to know what he's doing! He's made mistakes."

I can hardly believe the vicar is trivializing Daniel's crimes, as if the boy had cheated on a test at school.

"He didn't learn from his first mistake," Barrett points out. "You're asking me to let him go free to make more mistakes that could cost more people their lives."

Reverend Thornton offers clasped hands to Barrett. "Please. Give Daniel a chance. He can be reformed."

But I think Daniel lacks a basic sense of right and wrong, and I doubt there's a way to correct his deficiency.

"You want me to bend the law for your grandson, yet you were willing to let Mick, who's not much older than Daniel, be hanged for the murder you committed." Barrett says contemptuously, "Well, I won't." He's honor bound to serve justice, a vocation as sacred to him as religious vows ever were to the vicar. "Reverend Douglas Thornton, you're under arrest for the murder of Richard Trevelyan." He seizes the vicar's wrist, locks one handcuff around it, and then beckons to Daniel. He's come unequipped to arrest two people, and he'll have to handcuff Daniel and the vicar together.

"Daniel, stop him!" Lucie cries.

The boy blinks, frowns, and raises the ax at Barrett. My heart thumps. Before anyone can speak, there's a loud, retching, choking sound from Alice. Her eyes bulge; her mouth opens wide as she gasps for breath. Daniel drops the ax as he and Lucie rush to her side. Mucus oozes from her lips and rattles in her throat. The vicar, with the handcuffs dangling from his wrist, flings back the quilt that covers Alice. She wears a white flannel nightdress, and he opens its collar and bodice to give her air. She's so emaciated that I can see the rapid flutter of her heart under her gray, translucent skin. A convulsion seizes her body, shakes the bed. The children grab her skeletal hands and cry out with fear. She inhales a wheeze that strains her wasted muscles; she stiffens, as if struck by lightning; then she goes limp. Her face relaxes, her eyelids droop, and her head lolls. She's not breathing, and the flutter of her heartbeat has stopped. Everyone stands motionless in the sudden, awful silence.

Reverend Thornton's face is a mask of sorrow. "She's gone."

CHAPTER 31

The children burst into agonized sobs. I've seen death too many times before, but I would have to be made of stone for this one not to move me. Alice's death is a poignant end to a troubled life and horrendous suffering. She died in the company of the people who love her, and the children's grief is so heart-wrenching, so pure.

"Holy Lord, almighty and eternal God, into your hands we commend your servant Alice," the vicar intones. "Forgive *her* sins and embrace her in your mercy, so that death may be for her the portal to everlasting life in your glorious presence."

After my mother told me that my father was dead, she forbade me to cry or to speak about him. There was no funeral, nothing to mark his passing except the flight from the only home I'd ever known to lodgings in a strange part of town. The memory brings a lump to my throat. Barrett wipes his eyes.

Reverend Thornton tenderly kisses Alice's mottled brow. "May you rest in peace. May the eternal light of our Lord Jesus Christ shine upon you."

"Amen," Barrett and I say quietly.

Daniel and Lucie fall to their knees beside the bed, still clutching Alice's hands. The sound of their sobs fills the tower. The vicar turns to Barrett and me, his expression a mixture of grief and surrender. He puts his hand on Daniel's shoulder and says, "It's over. We're going with Detective Barrett."

He gently raises the weeping boy to his feet and pries his fingers off Alice's lifeless ones. Daniel shuffles as his grandfather leads him to the door, meek and obedient now that his mother is beyond the need for his protection. His face is a red, swollen, tearful mess, his man's body like a suit of clothes that's too big. I feel so sorry for him that I wish Barrett could spare him.

"I ask only one thing of you," the vicar says to Barrett. "Please look after my granddaughter and my wife."

"I will," Barrett says, serious because he understands how direly his decision will affect the remaining members of the Thornton family. But he doesn't back down; Alice's death doesn't change the fact that he knows his decision is the right one. "Sarah, could you take Lucie home and stay with her and Mrs. Thornton until I come back?"

"Of course." I dread telling Mrs. Thornton what's happened.

Lucie lets go of her mother's hand, her huge, dark eyes streaming tears and ablaze with anger.

"I won't let you take him!" She darts forward and picks up the ax.

"Look out!" I cry as Lucie swings at Barrett.

Barrett dodges. The ax is almost as long as Lucie is tall, and so heavy that its momentum sends her reeling. She crashes into Daniel. He stumbles against the vicar, and they both fall down.

"Lucie, stop!" the vicar says as he struggles to his feet.

Young, confused, and grief-stricken as Lucie is, she knows she's about to lose her brother, her protector—all that's left of her immediate family. She swings the ax again, staggering under its weight. Barrett lunges and grabs the wooden handle. Lucie screams and tries to jerk the ax away from him. Reverend Thornton shouts, "Don't hurt her!"

He runs to them and wrestles with Barrett while I grab Lucie from behind. Lucie is a shrieking, writhing, kicking frenzy. In the midst of the melee, something clatters to the floor. It's Barrett's gun, fallen out of his pocket. It slides over to Daniel, who's sitting on the floor as if he lacks the will to stand. Daniel picks up the gun. He seems puzzled, unsure of what it is.

"Daniel, shoot them!" Lucie cries.

Mindlessly obedient, blinking away tears, Daniel aims the gun at Barrett and me and pulls the trigger. A loud bang reverberates. Sulfurous smoke hazes the air. Barrett and the vicar yell. Lucie breaks free of us, and my heart thunders with panic as I look around to see where the bullet went.

The vicar drops to his left knee beside Alice's bed and clutches his right calf. Blood reddens his fingers. Barrett and I stare, horrified that he's been wounded yet relieved that no one was killed. Daniel cringes as if he knows he's done something bad and expects to be scolded. He tosses the gun away from him. Barrett picks it up, replaces it in his pocket so that it can't shoot anyone else, and he and I rush to the vicar's aid.

Lucie, carrying the ax, rushes to Daniel and cries, "We have to go."

Daniel remains on the floor, his thick legs spread in front of him, his face scrunched up like that of a baby on the verge of bawling. Barrett pushes up the vicar's trouser leg. The blood trickles from a raw, circular wound on the fleshy part of his calf. As Barrett touches the wound, the vicar grimaces in pain.

"I can feel the bullet under the skin. I don't think it hit an artery, but I'm not sure," Barrett says.

I'm as fearful about the prognosis as I would be if I'd been shot. In one important way, Reverend Thornton's life is worth more than mine. He's the only one who can exonerate Mick. From among the items on the table, Barrett snatches up a cotton pad and a length of gauze, and he applies a makeshift bandage and tourniquet to the vicar's leg.

"Daniel, don't give up," Lucie pleads, tugging his arm. "I need you!"

The boy's eyes glimmer, as if Lucie's need has restored his wits. He lets her pull him to his feet, drag him out the door.

I say to Barrett, "We mustn't let them get away." I doubt they'll go home to the vicarage, and I don't know what I'm more afraid of—that they'll be hurt while at large in the city, or that they'll hurt someone else.

"Stay with the Reverend." Barrett stares into my eyes for a moment, begging me to do as he says, for once in my life. Then he runs after Daniel and Lucie.

If there's any time to honor my vow to obey my husband, it's now. The vicar limps toward the door, and I step in front of him, my arms outspread. "Oh, no, you don't." I can't have him in the middle of whatever happens when Barrett catches the children. I need him alive.

"Let me go to Daniel and Lucie," Reverend Thornton says. "I can convince them to surrender."

"Really? A minute ago you didn't have much influence over them." It occurs to me that if he finds the children before Barrett does, they all might escape together, and without them, how can I prove who killed Charles Firth or Richard Trevelyan? The knife is circumstantial evidence, and their confessions will be mere hearsay—probably not enough to convince Inspector Reid and exonerate Mick.

"Get out of my way." The vicar raises his hand to strike me.

Although he's taller and heavier than me, he's wounded, and I think I could win a fight with him. But I'm afraid that my temper would overpower me. Then I see the handcuff around the vicar's wrist and, dangling from a short chain, the other cuff that Barrett didn't have time to put on Daniel. I grab the open cuff, yank the vicar over to Alice's bed, and lock the cuff around the wooden rail. Then I race down the stairs, with my pocketbook that contains the knife and my gun, as he shouts, "Come back!"

Outside the church, the temperature has dropped, and moisture from the fog condenses into cold drizzle that dilutes the bonfire smoke. The world beyond ten feet distant from me is murky yellow where streetlamps glow, shades of black and gray everywhere else. As I pause at the door to listen for Barrett and the children, the bushes rustle. A dark shape oozes forth, and I shriek as I jump.

"All this noise, a fellow can't get a decent sleep," says a slurred, familiar voice. It's Andrew Coburn.

"Did you see two children come out?" I ask him.

"Yeah. They went that way." He points down the street.

As I head in the direction indicated, the dark figure of a man looms before me. I yelp, scared half to death a second time.

"Sarah?" It's Hugh. "I've brought the ambulance. Was that a gunshot I heard? What's going on?"

Now I notice the lit lamp on the ambulance wagon parked in the street, the hazy forms of the horse and driver. "Barrett. The children." I blurt a garbled explanation.

"Don't worry; we'll find them. Then we'll go back for the Reverend," Hugh says. "Mick will be out of jail before this night is over."

Amid the hoots and cackles from Halloween revelers comes the loud, brittle tinkle of glass shattering.

"It came from over there." I point toward St. Peter's School, invisible in the fog. A hunch compels me to say, "I think Lucie and Daniel went in there."

We run through the schoolyard, past the shadowy forms of swings, slides, and teeter-totters. The three-story Gothic building materializes, dark except for a lamp burning above the arched main entrance. The door is open and the windowpane in it is broken. The blackness within the building exudes a silence thicker than the fog.

"How clever are those children?" Hugh whispers.

He's asking if this could be a trap they've set. I think of Lucie and Daniel pretending to be ghosts in the church. "Clever enough."

Somehow I'm certain the children are in there—and so is Barrett. The ring on my finger feels warm, as if with some mystical energy flowing from him to me. I draw my gun from my pocketbook. Despite all the wisdom that warns me against venturing into dark places where danger lurks, I tiptoe through the door. After I've disobeyed Barrett, I'm determined to honor at least one of my wedding vows—to protect my husband. I'll shoot anyone who's a threat to him, even a child.

Hugh is right with me, his gun in his hand. In the foyer, broken glass crunches under our feet. We steal into a long, wide passage. The smell of chalk dust, lye soap, and the sweet, musty, young-animal scent of children takes me back to my school days. Across the stone floor lie faint stripes of light from classroom doors. A whimper comes from the darkness at the far end, blood-chilling yet familiar.

It's Lucie. Is she playing ghost again, to lure us?

The whimper breaks into sobs. We move cautiously forward. Halfway down the empty passage, Hugh points to the classroom on our left. As we peer across the threshold, the sobbing that emanates from within stops. Dim light shines through the windows. Rows of small chairs at low tables face the teacher's desk. As we step into the room, there's no sound, no motion.

"Lucie?" I call in a low voice that I hope doesn't sound threatening. "Come out."

A large object hits me hard across my thighs. I exclaim. Suddenly the air is full of flying, crashing missiles. Hugh yells as they bombard him. Lucie is throwing chairs at us. Hugh falls, cursing. As I move to help him, my leg tangles in a chair and I fall flat on my face. Giggles accompany a pattering of footsteps as Lucie runs out the door.

"I lost my gun," Hugh says. "Go after her while I find it. I'll catch up."

Fortunately, I've managed to hang on to my gun. I hurry out to the passage, hear giggling, and see Lucie standing at the end. As I run toward her, she turns and darts through a door. I follow her into a stairwell that's so dark, only the first two steps are visible. Lucie's quick footsteps ascend. I cling to the banister, grope my way up through the black, echoing shaft. A door above me slams. Reaching it, I try the knob. The door doesn't budge; it's locked.

"Lucie!" I bang on the door, receive no answer.

Instead of trying to pick the lock in the dark, I grope back down the stairs and hurry along the passage to find another way to the upper floors. I look into the classroom where I left Hugh, but he's gone. Why didn't he follow me? Apprehension seeps through my veins. Did he spot Daniel? Is he alone with the boy?

Some twenty paces distant, in the darkness between two classroom doors, stands a figure clad in a long, shapeless robe. With its head blending into its shoulders, its face invisible, it embodies the word *ghost*. My heart gives a violent lurch; my eyes pop and my mouth opens. I instinctively raise my gun, taking aim even as I think ghosts must be impervious to bullets.

The figure moves toward me, into brighter light, and now I discern its long braids and a haggard, familiar face. "Mrs. Thornton." Relief washes over me, so powerful that I could faint. "You gave me a scare."

"My husband. My grandchildren. Where are they?" Her voice quavers as if she's suddenly ancient and senile.

"I'm sorry; I haven't time to explain—"

Lucie steps out from behind Mrs. Thornton. I see the cricket bat in her hand the moment before she swings it at me. I duck, and the flat wooden bat whistles over my head. She and Daniel are playing a game of divide-and-conquer, separating Hugh and me, the better to finish us off. *What have they done to Barrett?* Lucie whacks my shoulder. The force and the pain of the impact knock me to the floor. I grab her ankle with my left hand. She squeals and kicks, but I bring her down. Before she can hit me again, I punch her with my right fist. The gun I'm holding lends unexpected weight to the blow. My knuckles crack against her skull. She goes limp. I untangle myself from her, my heart pounding.

Mrs. Thornton falls to her knees beside her granddaughter. "Lucie!" As I clamber to my feet, she looks up at me and cries, "What have you done?"

Hitting Lucie was an instinctive act of self-defense. My relief that I've put at least one of the children out of action turns to horror as Lucie remains motionless. Her grandmother shakes her and calls her name; she doesn't respond.

If my mother really did kill Ellen Casey, is this how it was for her? Not a deliberate, cold-blooded decision to strangle the girl but an unthinking impulse like mine, an accident?

It doesn't matter. Nor does it matter that Ellen was an innocent victim who'd done nothing to hurt my mother whereas Lucie attacked me. Ellen is dead, regardless of my mother's motive. So is Lucie Thornton, regardless of mine.

Mrs. Thornton cradles Lucie's body in her arms and wails. My mind tries to deny what my eyes see. Maybe there's still a chance of saving Lucie. The ambulance is outside; I could take her to the hospital. But Barrett and Hugh are somewhere in this building with Daniel, who is just as capable of violence as Lucie, ten times stronger, and probably insane. And now I see, with awful, nauseating clarity, that I'm even more like my mother than I feared. Leaving Mrs. Thornton weeping over Lucie, I run down the passage. Protecting Lucas was more important to my mother than the child she'd just killed. Saving my husband and my best friend are more important to me.

I find another staircase, grope my way up. In the second-floor passage, meager light spills from a doorway. I hear grunts and ragged breaths, as if from a wounded animal. Is Barrett lying in there, hurt and helpless? I rush into the room. Large, with tall windows set in medieval stone arches, it's furnished as a gymnasium. Leather mats are piled in a corner; bins contain rubber balls; cricket bats hang on one wall, archery targets on another. On the scuffed wooden floor, Barrett and Daniel circle each other. They're like boxers in a ring, except that Daniel is armed with the ax. Their faces shine with sweat in the light from a gas lamp by the door. They're breathing hard, as if they've fought and retreated multiple times.

"Sarah." Barrett glances at me before he returns his attention to Daniel. His gun is nowhere in sight—he doesn't want to kill Daniel, even in self-defense, even though the boy is a murderer. "Stay back."

Daniel is the one making the grunting noises—incoherent expressions of rage, fear, misery, and aggression.

"Watch out for Lucie," Barrett says. "She's around somewhere."

Sick with guilt, I can't tell him why Lucie is no longer a threat to us.

Daniel begins hacking at Barrett as if he's chopping down a tree. He staggers; he's panting; his aim is wild. Barrett stumbles as he dodges. They're both exhausted, and their fight is bound to end soon, with the first one to make a serious mistake the loser. I can't let it be Barrett. But if I shoot Daniel after I've just killed his sister, I will be doubly a child murderer, twice as bad as my mother.

Daniel and Barrett retreat, gasping. As they circle each other, Barrett says, "Aren't you tired, Daniel? Stop, and I'll take you home so you can rest." He sounds sincere; he's talked many criminals into surrendering; but Daniel only moves toward him, as if to attack again.

"Are you hungry?" Barrett says. "How about some hot chocolate?"

If Daniel surrenders, he's not going home, and there won't be any hot chocolate in prison. Either the boy knows it and isn't tempted by the false promises, or he doesn't hear what Barrett is saying. Now Barrett rushes him and grabs the ax handle. They yank, stagger, and whirl as they fight for possession of the weapon.

Daniel screams, his face crazed with panic. He kicks Barrett, who falters. Daniel slams him against the wall. On my wedding day, "forsaking all others" seemed an abstract, ritual pledge, but now the fierce instinct to defend my husband rises in me. Barrett pushes back hard; he lets go of the ax and sends Daniel stumbling across the room. I feel the dreaded swelling, roiling, abrasive sensation as my mother's ghost stirs within me. Against my will, I sidle around the room, pointing the gun at Daniel, angling for a good shot.

"Sarah, no!" Barrett shouts. I can see that he doesn't want a child's death on his conscience or mine. He, like most everyone else, would rather turn Daniel over to the executioner. "Let me handle this."

I aim at Daniel's legs, thinking I can wound him just enough to stop him. He's moving erratically, my hands are shaking, and I quash the idea because my shot could go wild and kill him—or hit Barrett. But my mother expands inside me, egging me on. My thoughts are a churn of conflicting impulses, my body the battleground in a war for possession of my soul. The temptation to shoot Inspector Reid was nothing compared to this. I hunger to fire one shot after another at the boy who's menacing my husband, to hear the bangs, see the pain and shock on Daniel's face as he drops, feel the trigger click after the bullets are all spent. My love for Barrett demands it. My mother's grim voice whispers in my mind: *You do what you have to do.*

My hatred of my mother undermines the power she's exerting upon me from beyond the grave. I think of Barrett kissing me at the altar. If I shoot Daniel after Barrett told me not to, will that be the one disobedience he can't forgive, the one wedding vow I shouldn't have broken?

I'll be lucky if he can live with me after learning that I killed Lucie. If I kill Daniel too, I won't be able to live with myself.

For a moment, the world falls silent, and Barrett, Daniel, and I seem to pause in our tracks as if time has stopped. I feel something shift inside me, oddly akin to the time I climbed into an overcrowded omnibus, a man nudged me hard, and I fell onto the street. It's me pushing against the ghost of my mother.

She falls away from me. I lower the gun.

Daniel roars and charges at Barrett. As Barrett peddles backward, he skids on the slippery floor. His feet fly up from under him, and he crashes onto his back. Daniel raises the ax over his head, as if to split a log of firewood. I cry out and hurl myself at Daniel's back as he brings the ax down. Barrett yells. Daniel and I thud to the floor together. The breath puffs out of me, my vision shudders, and everything blurs. He lies under me, heaving and mewling, too weak or dazed to fight anymore. I scream Barrett's name.

Barrett is crouched, unhurt, near the spot where Daniel almost cleaved him. My relief fades when I see that he's bent over Hugh, who's lying on his back on the floor, mouth open, wheezing. Blood spreads on the floor under Hugh. The ax is embedded in the right sleeve of his coat, between his shoulder and elbow.

"He came out of nowhere," Barrett says, gasping. "He took the cut for me."

I hobble on my knees to Hugh, shouting, "Hugh! Oh, no." I sit and lift his head onto my lap so he needn't lie on the dirty floor. I cradle him as sobs wrack me.

Hugh gazes up at me, his breaths shallow and labored; he smiles. His face, white and waxen, glows as if he's the statue of a saint surrounded by candles lit by the faithful. He whispers, "Sarah. Don't cry," then grimaces in agony. "This is for the best." Love and rapture shine through the pain that fills his eyes. "I did something useful with my miserable life. Now I can die in peace."

CHAPTER 32

At nine o'clock in the morning, I pace the floor in the waiting room in London Hospital. Seated visitors eye me nervously, as my clothes are still covered with Hugh's blood. I've been here for seven hours, since the doctors rushed Hugh to the operating theater. I left only long enough to send notes via messenger to let Fitzmorris, Sally, and Sir Gerald know what's happened. I've heard no news of Hugh, and I'm terrified that he won't survive.

If only I hadn't misinterpreted his bright, cheerful manner! I thought he was getting over his heartbreak, but he was anticipating the end of his suffering. He went to the vicarage with me not just to help solve the murder, but because he wanted a confrontation with a killer, an opportunity to die an honorable death rather than commit suicide. How I wish I could have stopped him before he put himself between Barrett and Daniel!

But I can't wish it were Barrett gravely injured instead of Hugh. I can only pray that Hugh survives and my husband's life wasn't saved at the cost of my best friend's.

A nurse approaches me and says, "There's no news about Lord Hugh, but the little girl is awake, and the physician says she's going to be all right."

My relief is incomplete but massive. Last night, while Barrett and I carried Hugh out of the school to the waiting ambulance, I remembered Lucie Thornton. I went back for her, even though mere minutes could have meant the difference between life and death for Hugh whereas nothing could be done for her. Barrett and I rushed them both to the hospital, where the physician discovered that she was unconscious, not dead. I crumpled to my knees and thanked God. But Lucie's survival doesn't expunge the fact that I struck her and could have killed her. That I helped save her doesn't make me any less like my mother. But even while my guilt eats away at me, I wish I'd shot Daniel before Hugh jumped into the fray. I thought I was winning the battle with my mother, proving I'm a better person than she was.

But she stood by Lucas, and my inaction led to Hugh's terrible sacrifice.

I try to find something good that has resulted from solving the murders. We obtained justice for Charles Firth, but that won't bring him back. I think of his widow, lying in some other hospital with her self-inflicted burns. Mrs. Firth will probably be disappointed to learn that her husband was killed by a mentally disturbed boy rather than a vengeful ghost. The knowledge might shake her cherished faith in the supernatural, her only comfort in her time of mourning. I remember the photography equipment I lost in the tunnels under the Clerkenwell jail. As soon as I can, I'll visit Mrs. Firth and offer to purchase new equipment from her husband's store, at full price. At least the sale might help her financially.

Barrett enters the room with Mick. Here, to my relief, is the one good thing to come of last night. Overjoyed, I run to Mick, throw my arms around him, and hug him tight.

"Watch out; I stink like the jail." Mick's smiling face looks drawn, thinner, and older; for the first time, I notice reddish whiskers on his jaws. "Is Hugh gonna be all right?"

"I don't know."

Barrett fills me in on what happened after he left Hugh and me at the hospital and went back to the church. "I brought the vicar here. They took the bullet out of his leg, patched him up, and put him to bed in the ward. He wrote out his confession and signed it. He'll be transferred to Newgate eventually. I left a constable guarding him while I took care of business at the station. The murder charge against Mick has been dropped."

That's one burden lifted off my shoulders, but another remains. "And Daniel?"

"He was curled up on the floor in that room where we left him. When I spoke to him, he didn't seem to hear. I had to send him to Bedlam."

The insane asylum is such a terrible place that I feel sorry for Daniel in spite of everything. "What will happen to him and Lucie?"

"When Lucie is well enough to leave the hospital, she'll live at a children's home. Mrs. Thornton is in no shape to look after her. She took it hard enough when I told her that Daniel and the vicar are both guilty of murder. When I told her about Alice, she didn't believe me until I showed her the body. It was too much for her. She had a stroke, and she's here in the hospital too. As for what happens next . . ."

Barrett pauses, troubled, before he says, "The vicar said in his confession that he killed both Charles Firth and Richard Trevelyan. You and I will have to testify at his trial. The verdict will depend on who the jury believes—him or us. It looks as if Daniel won't be fit to testify."

The trial is a bridge to cross another day. In light of everything that happened last night, I'm thankful the outcome wasn't worse. Barrett and I know the truth about Charles Firth's murder, the vicar will hang for Richard Trevelyan's, and perhaps insanity is punishment enough for Daniel. Heaven forbid that he's ever set loose on the world.

The nurse returns and says, "Lord Hugh is out of surgery. You can see him now."

Barrett, Mick, and I exclaim with relief. She escorts us to a private room, where Hugh lies in bed. He's covered with blankets up to his chin, his eyes closed and his face so drained of blood that his lips are colorless. A white-coated doctor is taking his pulse. Mick frowns, blinks, and holds his hat over his chest, as if he's at a funeral. I think of my wedding day and remember my words to Hugh before he walked me down the aisle: *If I fall, will you hold me up?* He's fallen, and it's beyond my power to hold him up. I cover my mouth; if I speak, I'll start crying and not be able to stop.

"Lord Hugh is on morphine," the doctor says. "He'll be unconscious for a while."

"What's the prognosis?" Barrett says.

"It's too early to tell. If he recovers, he may lose his arm."

After the doctor is gone, a visitor tiptoes into the room. It's my mother-in-law. Barrett says, "Ma? What are you doing here?"

She's more plainly dressed, more subdued than I've ever seen her. "Your father's friends on the police force heard about what happened last night and told us. I came to see how Lord Hugh is doing." She looks at Hugh. Nobody speaks; his condition is obviously dire. "I also wanted to talk to Sarah." She flashes me a quick, sidelong glance, as if afraid to look directly at me. "In private?"

I wonder what she's up to; Barrett seems on the verge of saying this is a bad time; but Mick says to me, "Go on. We'll hold the fort."

I follow Mrs. Barrett to a waiting room that's drabber than the one at Jenny Lind Hospital. We sit down. Mrs. Barrett fidgets with her hands, then blurts, "I'm sorry for the things I said about Lord Hugh."

I can't summon the ill will to retort, "You should be." Her manner is so genuinely contrite, devoid of her usual hostility toward me.

"He saved my boy's life." Her voice trembles; her eyes well. "I'll do whatever I can to make it up to him."

Our love for Barrett is the one major thing we have in common. Her new appreciation for Hugh goes a long way toward softening my attitude toward my mother-in-law.

"But that's not all I wanted to say." She draws a deep breath, musters her courage. "I'm sorry for how I've treated you, Sarah. I want Thomas to be happy, and I had my mind set on the kind of wife I thought would be right for him."

An image of Jane Lambert flashes through my mind.

"But that night you came to dinner, after you ran out of the house, I had to accept that his idea of 'right' is different from mine," Mrs. Barrett continues. "He told me in no uncertain terms that he loves you, he's happy with you, and I should learn to love you too—or I'll be seeing a lot less of him."

I'm surprised and gratified to learn that Barrett stood up for me after all.

"I promise to be kinder to you and mind my own business." Mrs. Barrett takes my hand; I involuntarily flinch at her touch. "Will you forgive me, Sarah? Can we start over?"

A leopard doesn't change its spots, at least not overnight. I don't quite trust her, and I can't forget how bad she's made me feel. But a chance for a rapprochement with my mother-in-law is another thing Hugh gave me in addition to my husband's life. I can't reject a gift he bought me at such a price. With that in mind, I smile at her and squeeze her hand.

"Yes, Mildred," I say.

When I go back to Hugh's room, Mick says, "Look who's here."

"Hello, Mrs. Barrett." Anjali is standing with Mick at Hugh's bedside, her usual vivacity quieted by the circumstances. "I came as soon as I heard that Mick was out of jail and your friend was in the hospital. I made Father bring me. He's waiting downstairs."

When I ask her how she heard, I expect her to say she had a vision, but she says, "It was in the newspaper."

The night editor at the *Daily World* must have read my note to Sir Gerald and stopped the presses so that my version of the events at St. Peter's could be published in the morning edition.

"Anjali, why don't you try to see if Hugh is going to be all right," Mick says.

My skepticism rebels at the idea, and Barrett frowns, but we don't object. Anjali lays her hand gently on Hugh's forehead. He doesn't move; the slow rhythm of his shallow breathing doesn't change. She gazes into the distance, her expression serious but calm.

"Well?" Mick says eagerly.

"I saw him running and laughing in the sunshine," Anjali says.

The words evoke a vivid image of Hugh alive, happy, and exuberant. I can hardly bear seeing him lying pale and motionless in his hospital bed.

Mick smiles. "It's good, then."

"I think so." Anjali smiles too.

Remembering her vision of Lucie Thornton, I'm not unwilling to accept that she really had this new vision, but one could interpret it in various ways. It could be of Hugh in the past, or in heaven after he's died of his injury. Anjali may lack mystical talent but instead have a special ability to empathize with people and understand what they need. I mentally shut the door on those possibilities. If there was ever a time to believe in the supernatural, it's now.

EPILOGUE

Clerkenwell police court is a drab, windowless box with stained plaster walls. The occupants are trapped inside a maze of partitions built of dark, grimy wood—the magistrate in his bench between shelves of law books; the clerk at a desk below him; reporters in a pew. I sit among the spectators, between Barrett and Sally, on a bench behind the wooden barrier that separates us from the court proceedings. The room is chilly, the air pungent with the smell of wool coats wet from the rain. Gas hisses from light fixtures on the ceiling. Chatter from the audience quiets as a constable leads my father into the room.

My father's white hair is mussed, his clothes wrinkled, his eyes puffy and dark-shadowed after a sleepless night in jail. He plods, hampered by the shackles on his wrists and ankles. I'm sick at heart, my mouth dry and bitter as if I've eaten ashes. It's the moment I've been dreading ever since my reunion with my father, the moment he's been dreading for twenty-four years. His gaze finds Sally and me and he turns away, ashamed to have us see him in such disgrace. He bows his head as the constable puts him in the dock—a platform enclosed by black iron rails, in front of the barrier. He slumps, facing the magistrate, his back to us. Sally's face is tight with misery as she stares at him. I clasp her gloved hand. She firmly withdraws it and won't look at me.

It's three o'clock in the afternoon, an hour after Sally interrupted my vigil in Hugh's hospital room to tell me she'd found our father. She said she'd gone back to the Gladstone Arms, and a customer had seen the police arrest him in the street the day he went missing. She hasn't spoken to me since she broke the news. There's nothing I could have done to change the course of events, but Sally hasn't forgiven me for deserting her and doubting his innocence. The withdrawal of her affection is more hurtful than if she'd slapped me.

"State your name," the black-robed magistrate says to my father.

"Benjamin Bain." His voice is a dull monotone, devoid of hope.

"You are charged with the rape and murder of Ellen Casey, which occurred on the twenty-second of April, 1866."

Barrett holds my hand. Constables stationed around the room look at him as though he's strayed from their flock to join the ranks of the criminal classes. He gazes back at them, his head high and his expression defying their pity and scorn. I think that for him, this will be the ultimate test of our marriage. His father-in-law on the hook for murder will do his police career no good.

"I will now hear the evidence," the magistrate says.

Inspector Reid strides into the room. Of course he was behind the arrest. That day we drank together at the pub, he must have known where my father was, must have been looking forward to this day. How he must have enjoyed his secret and my ignorance! My hatred for him has never been more bitter or more furious. My muscles tense with the urge to lunge at him. I may have exorcised the ghost of my mother, but I'm still her daughter.

Seated in the witness box, Reid gives his name and rank. "Benjamin Bain was the last person to see Ellen Casey alive. He's admitted that she was in his house, modeling for photographs, the day before her body was discovered. The investigating officers identified him as the primary suspect. The fact that he's been on the run for twenty-four years is strong evidence of his guilt. I revived the investigation and hunted him down."

His voice is calm, matter-of-fact. He doesn't look at me, but I can feel his attention on me like the hot, focused, bright beam of a police lantern. I don't need to be psychic to read his thoughts: *If I can't get you, I'll settle for your father.*

"You may speak in your own defense," the magistrate tells my father.

Sally covers her mouth with her trembling hand. Her face is pale, grayish. Our father mumbles, "I didn't do it."

His voice is weak and sheepish instead of ardent with conviction. Barrett grips my arm to warn me that defending my father and making a scene will get me in trouble, not get my father out of it. I don't move; my tongue is numb. The faith behind my quest to exonerate my father has worn thin, and his poor showing only adds fuel to my doubts.

"You are hereby remanded to Newgate Prison to await your trial." The magistrate bangs his gavel.

As the constable leads him out of the dock, my father gives Sally and me a last glance that brims with love and despair. My love for him, steadfast during all the years he was gone, collides with my doubts. I'm the ground in a battle between my childhood self, who wanted nothing more than her father to return, and the older, skeptical, distrustful woman I have become.

Sally runs out of the courtroom. Barrett and I hurry after her. We catch up with her in the rainy street, where she bends over and vomits into the gutter, retching and sobbing.

I try to comfort her. "We'll prove he's innocent. Everything will be all right." My own voice echoes with the same insincerity that put a lie to my father's plea of innocence. I feel someone watching me, and I turn to see Inspector Reid at the courthouse entrance.

His face wears a strange, sad smile, as if his victory is sweet but he regrets that our feud is over. He says, "I told you that you would wish you'd taken the deal I offered. I'll see you at your father's trial."